YOU BEFORE ANYONE ELSE

Also by Julie Cross and Mark Perini

Halfway Perfect

YOU BEFORE ANYONE ELSE

JULIE CROSS & MARK PERINI

sourcebooks
fire

Published by Sourcebooks Fire, an imprint of Sourcebooks, Inc.

P.O. Box 4410, Naperville, Illinois 60567-4410

(630) 961-3900

Fax: (630) 961-2168

www.sourcebooks.com

Library of Congress Cataloging-in-Publication data is on file with the publisher.

Printed and bound in the United States of America.

WOZ 10 9 8 7 6 5 4 3 2 1

To all the dreamers dreaming.

CHAPTER 1

Eddie

"Name?"

"Eddie Wells." I stop myself from adding "sir" to the end—a habit that's been beaten into me since learning to talk. Regular guys don't bother with those formalities.

The guy in front of me holds out a hand, and before I can react and shake it, I realize I'm supposed to hand him something.

I don't have one of those book things yet. All I have is a color printout of a few Polaroids that I just took at the modeling agency. The girl who I explained this to is all the way across the room, holding the clipboard with my size card.

Six people are now staring at me. My palms dampen, but I avoid wiping them on my jeans. I could tell him that I'm not sure how this is all supposed to happen, stumble over my words and look like a desperate idiot, but I doubt that'll win me any jobs.

I lift an eyebrow. "So…are we taking some pictures? I haven't done this before, but my agent said we were taking pictures."

He stares hard at me, raising an eyebrow to match mine. Everyone else is still, watching. Finally, the girl with the clipboard jumps into action. She and the guy who seems to be in charge lean their heads together, looking over my size card and whispering loud enough for me to catch most of it.

I hear the girl mention Shay Silver, the agent whose office I left less than thirty minutes ago. Last week, right outside a store in Soho, I had just put in an application to work there, and Shay had stopped me and promised ten times the income doing this modeling thing. I hadn't believed her, but after looking into it, skepticism turned to hope. And my decision was made—leaving home, defying my parents, lying to nearly everyone, and pretty much giving up my friends, social life, and well...my life as I know it. *Knew it.* All to stand in front of these people while they whisper about me.

"Eddie Wells," the guy in charge says. "Good call shortening your name. The real thing is a bit of a mouthful."

I roll my eyes. "No kidding."

Laughter fills the room, and I have to work hard not to do the deer-in-headlights thing. Or tug at my shirt collar. Shay Silver had spent a good forty-five minutes going on about the types of jobs I could book, the clients who would like my look, whatever the hell that might be. I understood exactly two things from that conversation—directions to the casting and her advice to appear confident.

"You don't have to know what you're doing to look like you belong, Eddie."

I've never felt more out of place in my entire life, but the goal is only to *look* like I belong.

Within seconds, the guy in charge is directing me to stand in a line while a photographer takes pictures. I do what I'm told, keeping my face and shoulders relaxed like I don't care if they like me or not. It's an attitude I've never really tried out before, and I'm surprised how freeing it is. To be someone else.

"What do you like to do for fun, Eddie?" the photographer asks me.

Fun. I think I remember that word. Barely. But what does Eddie Wells like to do for fun? "Whatever I can get away with—parties, concerts, skydiving. I'll try anything once."

"The hair is great," someone says, not even bothering to whisper.

My hair is dark, curly, out of control, and always too long for my mother's approval. She has my father's personal assistant send me monthly haircut reminders, most of which I ignore.

"Really goes with the image."

There they go with that image talk again.

"Eighteen—legal and on the loose," another guy says.

This time, I refrain from rolling my eyes. I'm probably supposed to agree with that one.

The talking about me while I'm standing right here goes on for a few minutes until the girl with the clipboard leads me out of the room and back into the lobby.

There's a guy who Shay introduced me to at the agency waiting in the chairs. Dima. He's older than me by a few years. Either Russian or Hungarian. He grins when he sees me. "How'd it go, man? You survive?"

The girl is still around, so I shrug and say, "Who knows?"

"I hear ya," he says. "You looking for something fun to do

3

tonight? I'm having a party. We could use a few more pretty faces, if you know what I mean."

Just the word *party* turns my stomach. But Eddie Wells likes parties. "Uh, yeah, maybe I'll stop by."

He gives me the address along with a fist bump, and then it's his turn to be subjected to the people inside the room.

"Eddie? Got a question for you," the girl behind the desk says. "You didn't list an address on your form."

"Right. The agency is still trying to hook me up with a place, so...yeah."

This could be a problem. I glance at the door Dima disappeared behind, and then I turn and give the girl his address. Who says I'm not good under pressure?

She quickly jots it down without question. "So, Eddie Wells... Are you available tomorrow?"

I try not to smile and instead shrug. "Don't know. You'll have to check with my agent."

On the inside, I let out the biggest sigh of relief.

CHAPTER 2

Finley

"What do you like to do for fun"—he looks down at my card and then adds—"Finley?"

I take my spot in the center of the room, quickly fluffing my hair and tossing it over one shoulder. "Well, I have a morning yoga ritual, and I've just mastered the scorpion forearm stand pose. And knitting. I'm getting pretty good at hats. I usually spend the weekend having movie marathons with my roommates—right now, we're all super into Toby Rhinehart. Anything he's in, we watch a dozen times."

The Toby Rhinehart stuff is a bit of a stretch. I do like his movies, but I also heard that Alexander Wang just hired him. I don't know what this casting is for, but if it is for Wang, I figured being a fan of the headliner couldn't hurt my chances.

The guy gives me a tight-lipped smile and continues asking me the basics, while others around the room make comments that any decent person would have made an effort to at least whisper.

"Too sweet."

"The blond-haired, blue-eyed, girl-next-door look is hard to make edgy."

"Especially with Grandma's knitting needles in the picture."

I force myself to smile and answer questions, ignoring the conversation and laughter happening to my right. I'm dismissed literally thirty seconds later, but I wait until I'm outside under the mid-June heat before releasing my frustrations.

That was pointless. And also like the hundredth time I've been labeled too sweet or not edgy enough. My agent really needs to stop sending me on these suicide missions.

Or maybe it's me.

I check my phone for the third time since leaving the building. I slow down my pace, not ready to get on the subway and lose cell reception. No text from Jason. My stomach sinks, and then I hate myself all over again for caring. Why do I keep calling and texting him? It's unhealthy. I know it's unhealthy, because my abrasive and downright rude roommate, Summer, has told me this many times. This morning, for example, she said, "Get the fuck over him, Finley. The whole 'let's be friends with our high school sweetheart after breaking up' doesn't actually mean you will be. How long has it been?"

It's been a year. I'm pathetic. But he's home for the summer from college, and home is less than an hour commute from New York City. It changes things. Maybe.

I use every ounce of self-control I have to scroll away from Jason's name on my phone and pick a new person to call. "Hey, Dad."

"Hey, Fin," he says.

The sound of water splashing and my little brothers' raised voices come in loud and clear in the background. "So, apparently I'm too cute and not edgy enough for today's client."

"Again?" he asks. "Did you get those tattoos I recommended?"

I laugh, feeling ten percent better already. "No tattoos. I think I'm ready to tell my agent to give up on booking these more mature jobs for me."

"Fin, you gotta be willing to move a little outside of your comfort zone."

"You're my dad," I argue. "You're supposed to hate the idea of me being rebellious."

"It's acting, honey. Doesn't change who you are. And maybe instead of staying in your apartment on a Friday night knitting and watching movies, you should go out, do a little research. Some method acting."

I hear a loud shout of *cannonball!* followed by more splashing. "Dad, do you think it's a good idea for the boys to be in the pool without Grandma or me around?"

My head is now clouded with visions of Connor or Braden sinking under in the deep end, arms flailing, while Dad tries to maneuver his wheelchair to the side of the pool and get him out. And then the neighbor finding all three of them at the bottom of the five-foot end hours later.

"They're great swimmers, Fin. Relax."

"They're five. Nobody is a great swimmer at five." I have the sudden urge to turn around and catch a train to Connecticut for the weekend. New York City still overwhelms me. And knowing most of my high school friends are back home makes me itch even more for something familiar.

"I've taught them rescue skills," Dad jokes. "Boys? What's the number to nine-one-one?"

I hear them both laugh and shout, "Duh? Nine-one-one."

God, I miss them. I go a few weeks without seeing them, and they've both practically become different people—new words, new skills, new everything. And I'm missing it by living my life in New York. At least, that's what I'm supposed to be doing. Really, I'm doing it for my dad. Maybe if I stretch out of my comfort zone a bit, he'll stop worrying about me so much. "All right. You've pissed me off, and now I'm ready to go perform wild acts of rebellion. So thanks for that."

"Parenting at its best. Have fun, Fin. Talk to you later."

Now all I have to do is think of something unruly that I might actually enjoy.

I rack my brain for ideas all the way back to my apartment, and after a quick and somewhat uncomfortable conversation with my youngest roommate, Elana, and her mother—who is French and speaks literally no English—I find Summer in her room. I close the door behind me, just in case Elana's mom has picked up any English since this morning. That woman is fiercely overprotective. Last fall, Elana came to the United States on her own and became an instant star. But some pretty bad stuff happened to her, and her parents put the brakes on and took her back to France for a while. Now, she's here again for some summer work. With her mother. They've only been here a week, but already, Summer has put in many complaints to the agency. Good news is we both got discounts out of it. Which is why I tolerate French Mama with little complaint, while Summer does just the opposite. Unlike me, she doesn't need the money.

"She won't stop cooking fish! I opened all the windows, and I still can't get the smell out!" Summer says the second I shut the door. She's sprawled out on her bed, a bottle of bright-red nail polish in one hand and the brush in the other. "Fish covered in shit that's probably a million calories. If I wanted to live with someone's mother, I would have stayed at home."

Home for Summer is a posh apartment in midtown with her distant and very successful mother, who happens to be a creative director for *Vogue*. And who is way too busy for her daughter.

"What kind of wild Friday night activity do you think I could successfully pull off?" I ask, leaning my back against the door.

Summer looks up. I've intrigued her. Usually, she doesn't bother with eye contact. "Still getting the Mary Sunshine label?"

"Something like that," I admit. I'm not one to get competitive about jobs, but Summer gets all the best high fashion gigs. She's leaps and bounds ahead of me. And don't even get me started on Elana. I mean, God, she's only fifteen.

"Burn your knitting needles."

"Come on, I'm serious," I plead.

She rolls her eyes. "Okay, Miss Irish Catholic Goody Two-shoes. You're not a virgin, are you?"

I fold my arms across my chest, glaring at her. She knows I had a boyfriend for all four years of high school.

"Good." She smiles. Summer likes getting to people. It's one of many defense mechanisms. Yes, I've been to therapy. I learned the lingo. "That opens the options a little. What about drugs? You tried any?"

"No, but—"

"I'm not suggesting you become a meth addict, though that has worked for some before, but I mean, like, coke or molly, something that gets you in touch with a new side of yourself." She waves at me to shut up when I try to protest again. "It's empowering. You'll feel like a whole new person after. Or maybe a little adventure in sexual exploration. Something purely about pleasure, as in your pleasure, not his."

Already, I'm envisioning ripping some faceless hottie's clothes off and taking advantage of that lock on my bedroom door.

"Dima's having a party," she says, either reading my agreement to this plan from my face or not caring either way. "Come with me. I'm sure there'll be plenty of trouble for you to get into." Summer opens a drawer beside her bed and tosses a handful of condoms my way. They fall to the floor, scattering. "Take some of these, just in case. Never go to a party without condoms. That's what my mom always tells me."

I look them over, not wanting to commit to anything besides simply attending this party upstairs. "Think I need that many?"

"Better to have and not need."

My mom used to say that all the time. Somehow, I doubt she would have been proud of my application of the saying in this context.

CHAPTER 3

Finley

"What are you so afraid of?" Summer asks.

I take a sip of the beer Dima brought me a few minutes ago. "Oh, I don't know, addiction, overdose, puking on some innocent victim's shoes, random drug testing by the agency…"

Summer laughs. "Drug testing on models? Yeah, that'll be the day."

Okay, so maybe I just don't want to do it. Even if I should be in my so-called experimental phase.

I wouldn't exactly label myself a rule follower, but I guess I'm just cautious. I haven't always been this way. Not that I've done drugs, but before high school, I was all about ballet. Let's just say I had a rep for being the sassy troublemaker. My mom being my ballet teacher may have had something to do with my behavior. My fingers immediately move to the cross dangling from my neck—I've only removed it a couple times over the last four years. Somehow, it's always warmer than my hands.

I debate texting my dad to ask him if he's done coke or molly. He'd probably tell me. But I wouldn't want to freak him out. Seems like a conversation better reserved for a weekend visit instead of late on a Friday night when I could be too far gone to help, for all he knows.

I glance around the room and finally spot someone I know: my friend Alex and his girlfriend Eve. Alex and I did a big Calvin Klein shoot last year, and Eve was the photographer's assistant. Actually, Eve used to be a model too, another preteen/teen phenom like Elana, who headlined that CK shoot along with Alex. My part had been fairly small, and still, that was my biggest job ever.

"Have you met Alex?"

Summer shrugs, grabs two more shots of vodka, and hands me one. "Like I would remember."

I down the shot quickly and prepare to talk to Alex and Eve. Maybe they've done drugs and can advise me. But my buzzing phone distracts me. I pull it out of my purse and glance at the new text.

JASON: Yeah, it's so weird to be home again. But I missed it.

My stomach flip-flops. He replied to my text. Hours later, but still…this could mean—

"Oh lord, you're pathetic." Summer is leaned toward me, reading over my shoulder. "That's probably enough for you to live off of for another six months or so, right?"

I glare at her and shove the phone back into my purse.

"No comeback? Wonder why…" She pretends to be in deep thought. "He said he missed *it*. Not you. Cut the fucking cord already. It's not healthy."

If only it were that easy. When you're in a relationship with someone for four years, you get so comfortable with that person. It's daunting to start all over again.

I make my way across the room to see Alex and Eve, who are leaning against the back of the couch, more absorbed in each other than anything else.

"I heard Elana's back from France?" Alex asks me, keeping his voice low.

"Yep, her and her mom. I think her mom is driving her crazy, but that's to be expected. French Mama is driving me crazy too."

They both laugh at the mention of French Mama, but I can't take credit for that title. Summer made it up.

"I can't believe her parents let her come back to New York," Eve says.

Alex smiles at her. "You're just upset that they're here and not in France where we can hit them up for lodging."

My gaze travels back and forth between the two of them. "You guys are going to France? Are you going for Fashion Week?"

Eve shakes her head. "Nope. I did the Prada shoot, and I'm done for good. Got tuition for next year covered."

Even though Eve had supposedly quit modeling a few years ago, she pulled a one-last-job stunt last spring to cover her tuition at Columbia. She's a photography student with a lot of experience under her belt.

"We're doing the cheap travel, backpacking in Europe but without actual backpacks thing," Alex explains.

Across the room, another beer pong player is being requested. This could possibly be the most adventurous thing I'm willing to do here. I turn to Alex and Eve again. "Well, good luck in Europe. I'm gonna go play beer pong."

"Hey." I grab Dima's shirt sleeve. "You need another player?"

He looks me over, deliberating. "Sure. Be the new guy's partner."

"The new guy?" I glance around. What does that even mean? New to the party, like he just walked in? I've been here fifteen minutes.

"He's new to the agency," Dima says. "First casting, and he books some big job."

"So we hate him then, right?" I joke. I turn around to head toward the game table and run right into a guy about my age with wild, dark curly hair and designer jeans.

"This guy," Dima says to me and then turns to the new guy. "Got you a partner. Finley. She lives in the agency apartment downstairs."

They exchange a look that says I've been mentioned before. I'm not liking that too much, but usually, I don't come to these parties. Instead, I bang on the door at two in the morning to tell them to stop thumping around like elephants. Maybe I got a bad rep.

While we wait for Dima to find a partner, I snatch two beers from a nearby cooler and offer one up to New Guy. "So, Dima said you're new, but he didn't say where you're from."

"Uh...the Midwest."

"The Midwest." Okay. Someone doesn't want to get personal. "Like Wisconsin or like Chicago?"

"Chicago...well, not in Chicago, but around it, you know?" he says.

"Right." I pop open my can and take a drink. "What's your name? I'm sorry, I don't think Dima said..."

"Eddie." He lifts his gaze again. "Eddie Wells. And you're Finley Belton, the girl who lives downstairs."

Summer breezes past me but stops when she spots me holding the beer pong ball. "Beer pong? Oh, you wild animal...grrrr." She holds up her tiger paws and growls at me.

I give her the finger and then turn back to Eddie. "I'm *one* of the girls who live downstairs."

"One is too bitchy, one is too underage, and one is nice," he recites, most likely quoting Dima.

This is exactly what I'm trying to escape tonight. "Dima called me the baby bear?" I'm secretly hoping he catches my reference to Goldilocks.

"No," Eddie says. "He called you Finley Belton, but I added the nice part, because you brought me a beer. And it is just right, not to mention you're talking to me instead of staring and whispering to other people about me."

Points for his fairy tale knowledge, and I'm sure the whispering is the result of whatever big job he's landed. Too many models at this party.

Eve tries to be Dima's partner, but he refuses and tells Alex to play with him. Eve opens her mouth to protest, but Dima holds up a hand. "Don't even. I know your type. You'll engineer some fancy trick shots. No Ivy League players showing me up. I got a rep to protect."

"Fine," Eve snaps. "I'll just stand here and look pretty. And I'm definitely rooting for Fin and..." She gestures toward the new guy.

"Eddie," I fill in for her. "Eddie from Chicago."

"Eddie from Chicago," Eve repeats. "Good luck."

Summer returns and stands beside Eve, both leaning against the back of the love seat.

"Fin makes a great partner," Summer says to Eddie. "She knits. Lots of finger dexterity."

I shoot her a glare and will my face not to heat up. So not cool.

CHAPTER 4

Eddie

"Finger dexterity, huh?" I say to Finley.

Dima might not have used the word *nice* when he gave me the quick 411 on the models downstairs, but he had labeled Finley as too sweet. But without proof, I'm undecided.

She looks at me, a big smile on her face. "Yep. That's a thing."

It's a thing. All right then. I nod toward the table. "You take the first shot."

"Just so you know—" Finley rolls the ball between her fingers.

"Don't worry, I don't have any expectations." This is true. Tonight is a big test for me. I've been away from the party scene for months. I need to prove to myself I can be this, be here, without getting out of control. Because if I can't, I have a lot further to go than I realized.

"I was going to say," Finley says, prepping for her shot, "that I'm extremely competitive. Meaning, if you screw up"—she tosses the ball and sinks it, easy—"I might kick you off the team. But don't take it personally."

A cheer erupts from the two girls beside us—the animal-noise girl and the Ivy League girl. Dima downs the cup of beer, and Finley leans closer to me. Her hair brushes over my arm. "So what's your technique? Do you have any trick shots?"

"Yeah, well…" I start to say and then, "No."

She laughs. "At least you're honest."

Depends what you ask me. "I'll drink first. Will that help?"

Dima's partner—Alex, I think—makes his shot. I hesitate for a second and then down the beer. Damn, these cups are way too full.

Finley gives me a pat on the back. "Well done. Maybe that can be your job?"

I hold the ball in my hand, and I'm nervous all of a sudden. It's just a stupid-ass drinking game, but I can't get my father's voice out of my head. *You play something, you sure as hell better win.*

"I recommend the arch technique," Finley says. "Nice and easy, big arch."

I look at her and smile. She's completely serious. Somehow, this takes the pressure off me. Like if she's worried, I don't have to be. "The arch." I nod. "Nice and easy."

"You got this, Eddie," Finley says.

And for a second, the world is at my fingertips. Then I realize no, I don't got this. The ball taps the inside of a cup and then hits Dima right in the crotch.

I scratch my head and avoid looking at Finley. I need to get out of my own damn head. "Sorry."

"It's okay. Next time."

Luckily, Dima misses his shot. Finley goes for the bounce shot this time and sinks it again, earning her a cheering section of four or five people now. Alex picks up that cup to drink, then passes the second to Dima.

The Ivy League girl points a finger at Dima. "Do not get him drunk. We have an 8:00 a.m. flight."

Like Finley, Alex makes his second shot. I offer to drink the beer, but Dima stops me. "She has to drink. That's the rule."

"You just want her impaired," Ivy League girls says. "If you aren't considering weight or metabolic rate, it's hardly fair to make everyone drink the same amount."

Dima spreads his arms out wide. "And this is why I don't allow Ivy League players. None of that shit in this game. Keep it simple. Otherwise, I'll get a fucking headache."

"He's right." Finley picks up the cup, staring it down even longer than I had. "Rules are rules."

She chugs the beer like a champ and tosses the empty cup aside. When it's my turn again, I focus more on my shot, less on all the noise in my head. Maybe all this newfound inner peace will kick in. Right. About. Now.

"Yes!" Finley shouts. She spins to face me. "That was beautiful. Perfect arch."

I'm about to thank her, but the animal-noise girl distracts me. She's making some kind of gesture that I'm pretty sure would be in the crude category, but it's hard to tell. "Uh, what is she…?"

Finley turns around, and her cheeks and the tips of her ears turn bright red. "Summer. Stop."

Summer. The bitchy one.

"Tourette's," Finley says to me. "She doesn't like to talk about it."

And Finley Belton. The sweet one.

She jumps into a deep explanation of why my last shot was so great, and her words start to blur together in this hypnotic way that relaxes me, makes me forget about anything outside of Finley and her jeans, hugging her ass perfectly. And the tank top straps that keep shifting, exposing more bare skin.

"What do I like to do for fun?" Finley says, tossing the ball in the air and catching it again. I shake my head. I missed something. "This is what I should have said."

"What? Parties?" I ask.

"That stupid casting guy," she says, rolling her eyes. "What do you like to do for fun?" She mimics his voice perfectly. We must have had the same casting today. "I should have said I'm a beer pong champion."

"And you play poker and scratch your balls a lot," I suggest.

She nods. I think the beer is working its magic. "Yes. That. Probably ride a Harley too."

"So what did you tell them?" I ask.

"The truth. Unfortunately."

I smile again. "Cute."

"So they said." She tosses the ball at the wall beside us. It bounces off and lands squarely in the cup sitting in front of Alex. "Cute sucks."

Yeah, agree to disagree.

CHAPTER 5

Finley

Eddie and I have one cup left. And it's my turn. Problem is that Alex and Dima have only two cups left, which means I've drank a lot of beer. And my partner is really cute. (Is it fair to call him cute? I hated on cute a little while ago.) So he's distracting. Like right now. Eddie's hands land on my shoulders, and he massages them, boxing ring–style.

"You ready for this?" he asks. "Still seeing singles? Just one cup down there, right?"

I squint and focus on the other end of the table. "Yep, one red Solo cup."

He's about to let go of me, and I'm not ready for that yet. I reach up and grab his T-shirt, tugging him closer. "I have to tell you something."

"What?" he asks, all serious.

"I'm not really good at beer pong." I stare down at the cup and aim. "This is all just a ploy to seduce you."

"Really?" Eddie asks, and I have to look up at him from over my shoulder. He's got nice eyes. And a nice chin. Even upside down. "You haven't missed any shots..."

I ignore Eddie's logic and continue on my path. "I heard people saying you're the next big star, so I figured I'd get to you first. I'm good like that. Always thinking about my next big move."

"Blondie," Dima says. "Get a move on it."

Finally, I let go of Eddie's shirt. But I can feel him close behind me. Before I release the ball, he leans down and whispers, "I have to tell you something."

"What?"

"I'm not really good at beer pong," Eddie says. "This is all a ploy to seduce you."

I laugh. "Clearly."

The ball leaves my hand, bounces once on the table, and then plops right into the last cup of beer. I pick up the cup with the ball in it and hand it to Dima. "That's the game, and that's what you get for calling me the nice one."

He shoots a glare at Eddie and then grins at me. "It's all relative. I mean, compared to you-know-who..." He gives a nod in Summer's direction. She got bored with our game and is chatting up some guy in the kitchen.

Eve says a quick good-bye to me and Eddie and then drags Alex out of the apartment. He doesn't look drunk. Much.

I wave my hand over my face, fanning it. All the people packed in a small apartment have made it stifling in here. I head for the back door, and Eddie follows right behind.

"Where are you going?" he asks, worried.

Cute.

"Just getting some air." I snatch a water bottle from the kitchen counter. "It's hot in here."

"I'll go with you," Eddie offers. "In case there are balance problems."

I give him this look like he's crazy. "I just won beer pong. My balance is amazing."

Dima's balcony is identical to mine except without plastic furniture. I lean over the railing and look. This must make Eddie nervous, because he rushes over and casually rests a hand on my back.

"I live right there..." I point a finger south. When he doesn't lean over to look, I turn to face him. "I'm fine, I swear. You're free to go have some party fun. Do some 'shrooms, get laid, get a haircut."

He laughs. "Get a haircut? At midnight?"

I shrug. "Or a tattoo."

"I don't really know anyone in there." He glances at the sliding glass door and then up at the sky.

"Aw, poor new guy." I pat his cheek and then leave my hand there for a few seconds. His skin is soft. "No friends. Everyone's jealous of your big job. What do you do for fun, Eddie?"

Whatever he says is obviously the answer, because somehow he got a big job today, and I didn't. I bet that's more hearsay than truth.

"Well..." He slides an inch closer to me. "Sometimes, I like to knit hats for little orphaned dogs. And subway rats."

I tilt my head, studying him. "Yeah...sorry. You're not right for the part. Too sweet."

Because Eddie Wells is not even close to my type, I can just enjoy him and not worry about screwing anything up.

"Is that what he told you?" Eddie asks. "The casting guy?"

I touch a finger to his lips. "Can't say. It'll ruin the illusion. I won't be as interesting."

He leans into my finger. "Doubtful."

I can feel my pulse against his lips. I don't know where this is going, but it isn't the kind of moment that stops. For a minute, we stay just like that. Neither of us says anything. But Eddie's got this look like he's far inside his head. I thought it would be me deliberating this, thinking. Thinking way too much.

I push away from the railing and take a few steps toward the door. "It's probably time for me to go back downstairs. Want to walk with me? All the stairs, balance issues..."

This isn't exactly a talent of mine, asking guys back to my apartment. I've only done it, like, never. So maybe I'm wrong about Eddie's hesitations. Maybe he's being polite. And when I leave, he does follow me. Even grabs a backpack near the door.

I try not to look at Summer when we exit Dima's apartment. I stay a couple steps in front of Eddie on the walk to my front door.

I could just ask him to come inside and hang out.

But maybe we'll get in my room, and I won't even want to do more than kiss him. Is that allowed? I don't know the rules.

Because the beer is still talking for me, I blurt out those exact words.

"What rules?" Eddie asks. His forehead wrinkles. He cups the back of his neck with his hand, his shirt lifting, revealing a strip of his abs.

I almost chicken out. But then I keep thinking about this feeling and how it might not be here tomorrow and how much I like it. How much I want to follow the path in this mysterious tunnel and see where it leads.

"Rules," I repeat. "Like if I ask you to hang out in my apartment and you say yes and then—"

He nods, catching on. "Right. Those rules."

Yeah, you know them, Eddie. Probably much better than I do.

But that doesn't sound too bad, a guy who knows what he's doing. My heart is slamming against my chest now. That was a lot of bold in one sentence. But my unskilled beer pong partner maybe isn't so impressed with my bold streak. "My 'nice' label scared you off, huh?"

"No." He shakes his head. "It's not that." He rakes a hand through his hair.

Now I'm just plain curious. Not like I haven't caught him looking at me several times tonight. Not like he hasn't found excuses to touch me. So what then? "Oh, you have a girlfriend?"

"No," he says with just the right amount of time between my question and his answer—not too quick, not too much thought.

"Okay, what then?" I hope that doesn't sound pushy. I'm honestly curious.

Eddie doesn't say anything. Just moves closer, lifts a hand, and picks up the cross on my chest.

"Oh, that," I say, trying to calm my heart with his fingers right near it. "I also have a poster of Jesus above my bed. Wanna see it?"

Eddie laughs, the tension finally breaking. "Yeah, okay. What the hell?"

I grin. Finally. He gets it. What the hell? That's the attitude.

I open the front door and pull him through the apartment as quickly and quietly as possible. The second we're in the privacy of my own room, Eddie's hands are in my hair, and he lowers his lips to mine. It's like we'd both been wanting to do this for hours. I can't get close enough, can't get his shirt over his head quick enough.

It's fast and fun and light. Light as air. Though that could be the beer.

CHAPTER 6

Eddie

Other than the bad taste in my mouth, I don't have any signs of a hangover. Which means I got it right this time. Alcohol only. No drugs. And I drank just enough to have fun but not so much that I screwed up my entire life. Maybe you can't screw up your life twice? Maybe it just goes from not-screwed to screwed?

Finley's bed is soft and girlie smelling, but I'm sure it beats Dima's couch, especially with a party going on all around. Not exactly sleep-friendly.

I roll on my side and check out Finley. She's lying on her back, still sound asleep—snoring—her blond hair a tangled mess all over the pillows. Guess we got a little wild last night. A grin spreads across my face. This whole adventure was not something I'd planned on. I'd even say it was something that freaked me out a little—sex with a stranger. Right when we started stripping each other's clothes off, the doubts crept in. I hadn't done this in months. Not since Caroline. And that turned out to be a nightmare times ten.

Finley must have sensed my hesitation, because she opened

a drawer next to her bed and pulled out a pack of pills, waving it in front of my face. Then she grabbed a handful of condoms and set them on the nightstand. "Birth control. Condoms. We're good, okay?"

The logic and attraction clearly won over any doubts.

Finley stirs, waking up slowly. I push some of the hair off her face. "Hey…"

Her eyes dart around then widen when they rest on me. She shoots upright and shoves me out of the bed. "What the hell are you doing here?"

Uh-oh. Not good. "You invited me, remember?"

She releases a groan and then jumps out of bed, flashing me a little skin before she can get a robe on. "I invited you last night. Not this morning!"

Oh good. She remembers inviting me. I open my mouth to reply, but I'm interrupted by my jeans hitting me right in the face.

"I'm gonna be late, and you're still here." She's flying around the room, pulling items from the closet and tossing them onto the bed. She sees me still standing by the bed, holding my pants, and freaks out. "Put your clothes on! Seriously. You were supposed to leave after—"

Her mouth hangs open midsentence, her eyes roaming up and down my body, like she's remembering that we had sex. She laughs, shaking her head. "Of course. It figures I'd screw this up."

The clock beside the bed catches my attention. Oh shit. I booked a job. This morning. And I left home yesterday with no new home to go to. "Hey, do you think I could use your bathroom, maybe take a quick shower?"

Her eyes grow even wider. "Are you kidding me?"

"So that's a no?" I slide my pants on and glance around for the rest of my stuff.

Finley swoops down, scoops up my clothes and backpack, then shoves them at me. She unlocks the bedroom door, opens it, and pushes me outside, slamming it behind her. I stand in the living room, my shoes, shirt, and bag in my arms still.

"No!" A voice says. I look around and spot a dark-skinned, middle-aged woman in the kitchen. She glares at me and stalks in my direction, waving a spatula. "No, no, no!"

I spin around and head for the door. The crazy woman starts swearing at me in French, moving closer and waving that spatula like she plans to beat me with it. I dive for the hallway and walk barefoot up one floor before I stop to catch my breath and put my shoes and shirt on. I knock, quietly at first, on Dima's door, then louder after he and his roommates don't answer. A door opens next to Dima's apartment, and an old guy pokes his head out and glares at me.

All right. Guess I'm not showering this morning. I'll have to find a public bathroom to at least clean up a little.

I walk outside and get hit with warm June air despite the early hour. Starbucks is around the corner. After assessing the cash situation in my wallet, I decide to limit myself to only a small regular coffee. I sit down at a table to plug in my phone, and I'm welcomed with several text messages. The first is from Lana, my dad's assistant.

LANA: Your father wants to set up dinners for you with a few of his friends. Let me know what your schedule looks like once you're settled in.

The second one is from RJ, one of the only friends of mine I still talk to who hasn't ditched me, whose family hasn't been ruined by my father's actions. But lying to loyal, helpful people makes communication with said people a bitch. Well, the guilt is a bitch anyway.

RJ: Dude, how the hell is Princeton? U so don't deserve to be there but hope ur having a blast. Maybe I'll take a train out there sometime soon.

I almost can't read the next text after RJ's, but I haven't been able to talk to her in weeks, so I'm compelled to see her words at the very least.

CAROLINE: Heard you left yesterday. You made the right choice, E.

I stop reading after Caroline's text, ignoring the three my older sister, Ruby, sent. I rub my temples and try to take in slow deep breaths, pulling my thoughts back to last night. To the calm focused energy I had while my hands wandered over Finley's body. I think this is going to be my happy place.

For most of my life, girls have either made me anxious, guilty, nervous, or some combination of those three things.

Not that I didn't enjoy any of those experiences, but the enjoy-
ment came in tiny doses while the rest of my feelings consisted
of the previously mentioned anxiety, guilt, or nerves. But last
night, with Finley, it hadn't been like that at all. I worried it
would be—and did it anyway. Something about her made me
feel important, purposeful. She liked everything I did and told
me, straight up. I've never had a girl do that before.

I mean, it would have been nice to get a more positive
reaction from her this morning, but then again, this was
obviously something new for her. I don't hate that part. It was
a lot of new for me too. Like this modeling job I'm heading to
now. Jesus, how the hell did I end up here?

CHAPTER 7

Finley

I can't believe I'm late. How could I not set the alarm? I'm never late. My agent, Kara, is going to kill me. And it's Marc Jacobs. Granted it's a lookbook, but still, I haven't had a job in weeks.

My first drunken one-night stand, and then I'm late to my comeback job. If that's not rebellion, I don't know what is. Summer and Dad will be proud. In fact, I think I may have heard a whistle of encouragement from Summer when she walked past my bedroom door last night.

My head is pounding. I need some water or coffee or both. I pay the cabbie and rush out the door while working on unknotting the tangled mop at the top of my head until I reach the studio.

As soon as I'm at the door to the studio, Alan, a man with salt-and-pepper hair, introduces himself as the producer. I rattle off an apology. I'm never late, so excuses aren't at the ready.

"I'm sor—"

"One more minute and I would have called your agent." He turns his back on me and walks off.

"Thanks—"

"Not another word," he says over his shoulder. "Talent's here! Get her in hair. Hope you got coffee, Eliza. You're gonna need it."

I run my hands through my hair, wishing I'd had time to take a shower. Wait…Eliza is here. I know Eliza.

I make my way to the hair station and spot Eliza right away. He's quite a character. Exactly the type you don't want to combine with a hangover.

"Oh my God, honey! Look what the cat dragged in."

Blood rushes to my cheeks. "Sorry I'm late…and sorry my hair is…well, like this."

Despite the "look what the cat dragged in" comment and the wrinkled nose, I get a kind reply. "I'll have my manservant start you up, and you'll be in tiptop shape in no time."

"He's your assistant, not your manservant. Be nice," I tell him, attempting to be cool and relaxed like an edgier model would probably be after arriving late.

Eliza's assistant gives me a smile. "He's just mad at me because I'm younger than him."

"They're breeding assistants snarkier and snarkier with every passing day. So where were you last night? Avenue, 1 Oak, or Marquee? Why didn't you invite little old me? Not cool enough?"

I'm saved from answering when Alan comes over and talks to Eliza in hushed tones, gesturing to his watch. Eventually, he scurries away to set.

"Someone's got their britches in a tizzy. Okay, manservant, we need to get her done ten minutes ago, so double-time, chop, chop. Hair needs to stand up like a candle. And get makeup in here too. Tell her breakfast is over."

Now my curiosity is kicking in. "What's the concept?"

"Didn't you see the set, darling?"

I shake my head. When would I have had time to look around?

"It's a birthday cake, and you're going to be the decadent gothic ornament."

I suppress a sigh. I'd been hoping for something outside of the sweet label—which would rule out posing on top of frosting and cake—though I don't know why I thought it would actually happen, considering how my castings have gone lately. But Marc Jacobs is all about being ahead of the trends, so I thought maybe…

Doesn't matter right now. I need to focus and be glad I have a job today.

I walk over to the anxiety-ridden stylist's station. Emmy has five different dresses steamed and ready to go. I'm not so disappointed in the concept that I can't take a second to swoon over the bold graphics mixed with the gothic nineteen twenties styling. It's a beautiful collection. And it's Marc Jacobs. Not exactly shabby.

I dress quickly, being careful not to mess up the big fancy bow in my hair and all the confetti. Alonzo, the Italian photographer, seems to have no issue with the late start of everything. Still, I apologize.

"It's no problem, bella. I get to enjoy my espresso and make sure the light is perfect for you, so you look like an angel."

Would he still call me that if he knew about my night?

I blush again, taking my place on top of the huge white cake, using the prop stylist's hand to get up there. No doubt it was good for me to go out and be spontaneous, but this morning-after stuff is embarrassing.

The prop stylist gives me the lowdown on the set and where I can step and where I can't.

"Just be careful of the gumdrops—they're hollow. You could get your leg stuck, and the undercarriage is all plywood."

I avoid thinking about legs getting stuck and switch up my pose. But my mind is racing with thoughts of hangovers and last night's hookup. The hookup who failed to exit the apartment prior to the morning like he should have. I'm pretty sure I flunked one-night stand 101.

I don't make it five minutes without the photographer calling out for Emmy.

"We need her to look more…what do you Americans say? Bad to the bone? Maybe she needs a necklace or a bag?" He turns to me. "And Finley, could you give me more anger, more aggressive facial expressions?"

Here we go again. Too sweet.

"Too angry," Alonso says, reacting to my mood shift. "Maybe you tone it down a little, give me something in between?"

Feeling my blood slowly boil, I take a deep breath and let the loathed words slide right over me.

"How close are we with that necklace and bag?"

The stylist runs over with a whole mess of pocketbooks and necklace choices, her assistant in tow carting even more options. She whizzes through six different bags and necklaces before settling on the one that will magically turn me into the rebel everyone needs me to be.

As I move from pose to pose, my confidence finally rises. I watch Alonzo for a reaction. For verification.

"Better, Finley," he says after a few minutes.

A wave of relief washes over me. Finally. Something is going right. Or better, at least.

"Okay, let's get Finley changed," Alonzo shouts after a good forty minutes of shooting in outfit number one. "And can I get a shot list? I'm only the photographer, for fuck's sake."

The producer runs over with his sheet, and I overhear him say, "Second model just arrived. Eliza has Eddie in makeup. He'll be ready in two."

The photographer and producer continue their fervent conversation, but I don't hear any of it. Not after the name Eddie was dropped.

Of course. This is so freakin' typical.

CHAPTER 8

Eddie

"Whoa! Be careful with that, dude." I lean back as far as I can in the chair, blinking rapidly while the makeup brush keeps coming at me. This is worse than the dentist. Not to mention my sixties British rock and roll outfit. How do they expect guys to wear pants this tight? You can see the outline of my junk. My mom will have an instant heart attack if she sees this. She won't, right?

The makeup guy sighs for, like, the tenth time and shakes his head. "This isn't a painful process, darling."

Yes, it totally is. "Sorry," I mumble. My gaze drifts sideways, and I catch a glimpse of a blond with her hair standing straight up in the air. Even through the dress, the shape of her body is familiar. Suddenly, she snaps around, a glare already planted on her face.

Finley.

She stomps toward me, glancing around to see if anyone's watching. "What the hell are you doing here?"

"Wearing makeup, apparently." She really did seem sweet last night.

JULIE CROSS AND MARK PERINI

"Right. You're wearing makeup. At the same Marc Jacobs shoot as me." She shakes her head. "A whole apartment full of guys, and this is the one I hook up with."

A mixture of hurt and amusement hits me at once, and I'm not sure which one to give more attention too. Why does it even matter? Last night wasn't about today. It was about last night. As it should be. I needed that.

Finley's glare dissolves, and her expression shifts to reflect guilt. "I didn't mean—"

"It's fine." I shove a pointy pencil out of my face, pissing off the makeup guy even more. "You're allowed to feel overwhelmed." I flash a grin. "I can have that effect on women."

She rolls her eyes but looks calmer than a minute ago. "Sorry, it's not really about you. I just tend to fail at anything impulsive."

Finally, Eliza says, "I've had enough, manservant. If you need something from me, I'll be on the couch." He storms away. For good, I hope.

I turn to Finley. "Trust me, you did not fail at the important stuff."

"Yeah?" Her cheeks turn a brighter shade of pink, but she nods, looking pleased, and turns around. "It *was* pretty fun."

I watch her walk away behind a curtain. Her dress falls to the floor, exposing her bare shoulders. I shift in my chair and command myself to look away, but I can't. The makeup assistant turns his gaze and follows mine, then looks back at me, cocking an eyebrow. I shift my attention forward and shrug. "What?"

"Nothing."

Emmy walks over with some steampunk accessories for me to wear and leads me down the hallway to the other set.

"We had to rent two studios for this job. Marc decided he wanted to go with the grungy London alley–style lookbook and not the birthday cake set. It's probably a bit cooler for your book." I finally figure out what the hell she's talking about when we pass a huge, life-size debutante cake.

"So Finley was on top of that?" I nod toward the set.

"Yeah, she was a cake adornment. Precious concept, isn't it?"

I can just imagine Finley up on that cake, fuming about hooking up with a guy who ended up at her job the morning after. I shouldn't laugh, but I have to.

When we finally arrive on set, everyone introduces themselves in one rapid procession.

I run through all the names a few times in my head. It's impolite to not address someone by their full name after they've given it. Alonzo, Roberto, Emmy, Alan, Eliza—who's clearly still not happy about our makeup session before—and Eliza's assistant, who still remains nameless.

"Okay, you can take your place on set," Alonzo says.

I make my way between a "God Save the Queen" poster with a yellow mustache and a turned-over red garbage pail.

"Here is your story," Alonzo says. "You are a rich school-boy, cutting class to go smoke and drink with his friends." I stand there unchanged. I didn't know I'd be playing a character from "Smokin' in the Boy's Room." "I know it sounds like a lot of emotions to get into one picture, but just see what you can do with it." Without warning, Alonzo starts snapping pictures like a fiend. "Okay, change up your pose. Let's see what you got."

I still haven't moved. I mean, what the hell am I supposed to be doing? It's not like I have a drink in my hand or a cigarette. My stomach is in knots all of a sudden. I give what probably looks like an aloof expression and cross my arms.

Alonzo shakes his head. "No, no, no. I don't want it to feel posed. It should feel lifestyle cool."

So pose without looking posed. Sounds easy. Plus, I'm in the middle of a cheap replica of an alley in Hackney. This is really not helping.

I see Finley off to the side, watching. When Alonzo pauses to adjust the lights, she steps closer and whispers, "Don't think about the camera. Imagine you're back at the party last night, hanging out."

Returning to the party leads to thinking about the walk up to Finley's room and everything that happened after.

"Perfect, bello!" Alonzo calls, startling me. "Keep that expression. Just change your pose."

Finley gives me a smile from her spot in the corner. The sweet Finley returns.

CHAPTER 9

Finley

"What are they shooting over there?" Eddie's leaning a little too close to me while we both sneak a peek at the studio beside ours.

I spot a familiar face standing near the stylist.

"Prada," I say, working hard to keep the jealousy out of my voice. "It's for the fall-winter line."

"Isn't that—"

"My roommate, Summer," I finish for Eddie.

Unlike my giant birthday cake set, Summer's spotlight is under an elegant, makeshift dance studio with a white grand piano in the center. The dress she's wearing is absolutely gorgeous. It's short, light purple, and it flares out like a tutu. Her hair is piled in a bun on top of her head. At five eleven, Summer easily has a couple inches on me. My five eight status is something all my agents have tried to hide or divert attention from. And now I see why. Those three inches look like a foot under the lights with the dress and the set.

My stomach sinks. A wild, edgy side might not be enough to get me here.

Summer looks up and spots me. I give her a little wave. But

then, after wrapping up my last shots and saying good-bye to the crew, I take a stab at being a good sport and walk over there to say hi. Behind me, Eddie gets called back to set, and some of the day's anxiety lifts off me, knowing he'll go his way after this and I can go mine. Not that he isn't nice to look at. Not that I didn't love his hands on me last night. But the beauty of all of that lies in the moment. Not the future. At least, I think it does.

"This is kind of amazing," I say when I reach Summer.

She's standing behind a chair, leaning into it, her face filled with anxiety. "Yeah, how about I go stand on top of your birthday cake and you can try balancing in these?"

Summer's height drops a few inches, and she sticks out a foot, revealing a pointe shoe dyed purple to match her dress. Okay, so I'm not going crazy. She really did look taller all of a sudden. "You shouldn't stand in those if you don't know how."

"Try telling him that," she snaps, nodding toward the photographer less than twenty feet away.

I squat down to examine the shoes more closely. The ribbons are incorrectly sewn, as are the elastics. And they aren't broken in at all. I tap her right foot. "Drop your heels."

She lowers to the floor, but when I push her feet out into wide second position, her toes curl over. "Those shoes are too small for you."

Summer shifts to one foot and shakes out the other, like her circulation is cut off. "Figures. My feet are too big for Prada. All the dieting in the world won't fix that."

My mom had a saying, one I'd heard too many times to count: *your shoes are your instrument*. I watched her stand in front of countless ecstatic eleven-year-old girls and recite that piece of wisdom before their first pointe class. She would have had a heart attack watching anyone's feet being shoved into a shoe that's so obviously the wrong size.

"Why do you need to stand in these? Can't they just drape you across the piano and show off your matching feet or something?"

"The ballet shoe heels," Summer explains and then gestures at four girls in wardrobe right now. They're all wearing identical dresses to Summer's except different colors—one orange, one pink, a nude, and another in light blue. The heels they're wearing are a boot style that travel almost to the knee, and the front mimics a pointe shoe, giving the leg a longer, slimmer look. And emphasizing that "beauty is pain" message high fashion folks love to spread.

I look back down at Summer's feet. Now it makes sense. She's going to stand up and show the comparison between pointe shoes and the ballet heels. Even without turning my head, I hear the distinct sound of one of the girls stumbling in those heels.

There's a lot of commotion on set with all the assistants testing lights and shifting props, trying to get everything perfect.

"Sit," I order.

She bites her lip like she's nervous, which is not very Summer-like behavior, but eventually, she plops down, her knees shaking. I peel the shoes off and start the process of warming them up, first flexing the shank, allowing for easier bending. I bring both shoes closer to my face and inhale the familiar scent. I'm immediately transported to an empty, dust-covered studio in Connecticut. One that's waiting to be brought back to life.

I shake those thoughts from my head and quickly kick off my

flip-flops and slide my feet into the purple pointe shoes. They're a little big, but I shut down my mother's voice, lecturing me about the importance of a proper fit. I stand and then rise up to half relevé, pushing my arches forward with the hope of giving the shoes a wider range of motion.

Summer stays on the floor, rubbing her toes. "How do you get your feet to go sideways like that?"

I rest a hand on the chair Summer had been holding with a death grip moments ago and push all the way onto my toes. And just like that, I'm inches taller. The rush of adrenaline makes it easy to ignore the pain in my feet from lack of practice and zero padding in the toes.

Summer's mouth falls open. "Forget the sideways feet. How do you do that?"

"Practice." Hours and hours of practice. A wardrobe of leotards and tights and very little else. Bloody toes and sore muscles. The inability to walk across wood floors in socks without doing at least one pirouette. I'm not sure if my body can move that way anymore, but it's all still in my head. And my heart.

"Okay, but how do I fake it in a matter of minutes?" Summer asks, bringing me back to the reason I put on the shoes in the first place.

I release the chair and drop my heels, then press back up on pointe a few times in a row. "I'm hoping to make these bend a little easier for you. Let me see your toe point?"

She stares blankly at me.

"Point your feet."

Summer's toes curl over. She's slightly flat-footed but supporting herself decently. Probably helps that she wears heels all the time. Prada is lucky her ankles aren't weak, because she could have broken a bone just by attempting to stand in pointe shoes. Obviously, the creative talent behind this concept knows nothing about ballet.

"Summer, we're ready for you!" the photographer's assistant calls.

I do one quick pirouette and then lower to my normal height and quickly remove a shoe. By now, the photographer has taken notice of me and is striding this way.

He points to the remaining purple shoe on my right foot, then the one in my left hand. "What is this?"

For a second, the anxiety returns to Summer's face, and then she pulls it together, arms folded over her chest, diva expression plastered on. *Now* she looks like the daughter of *Vogue*'s top creative director.

"What is this?" Summer repeats, giving me a nod. "A professional. That's what. Did you think I'd be able to master an art form that takes years of practice in an hour? You want me in this shoot, and you want this concept, then I'm gonna get it fucking right. And hopefully without a broken bone."

His face changes from suspicious to sympathetic, maybe even a little nervous. "Of course, sweetheart, whatever you need."

My jaw drops open. Wow. So this is what it's like to make it big. Maybe if I tell off a few photographers, I can get the diva label and start booking some big jobs? That definitely wasn't sweet and innocent, that's for sure.

"Finley?" Summer says, lifting her eyebrows, passing on a silent message to me. "What's your professional opinion regarding these shoes and my ability to stand in them for the shoot?"

"Um…well…" I look at the shoe in my hand and then quickly remove the other one. "They're a bit small for her. If she had the correct size, it might make it easier to—"

"We have plenty more." The photographer lifts a cloth from a nearby table, revealing more than a dozen boxes of pointe shoes.

I hesitate, my gaze drifting between the shoes and the two of them. What am I doing?

"The right size, Finley…" Summer prompts.

"Oh, yeah." I kneel on the floor and sift through the boxes, pulling out a size that I know will at least be better. I spot a package of toe pads as well and grab one of those. "Try these."

The photographer stands there watching. His hovering makes me nervous, so I busy myself searching for a pair close to my size. I locate a box on the very bottom of the stack and remove them. These shoes are nude colored instead of purple.

"These feel better," Summer says after getting both shoes on. "Especially with the padding in the toe."

I tell her to take them off again and go through the same process of bending them with my hands. Then I put on the nude-colored pair and show her how to break them in by doing pliés and half relevés. When I push up all the way onto my toes, the photographer claps and says, "Brilliant!"

For a moment, I'm five years old again, looking into the studio mirror, attempting to mimic the brown-haired woman beside me, dancing on top of her toes. Back then, it had looked like magic to me.

Relax your shoulders, Fin. Real ballerinas have loooong necks, like a giraffe.

Goose bumps pop up all over my arms, the voice in my head surrounding me like a cool breeze.

"Do you need her legs to be straight?" I ask, forcing myself back to the present.

"Yes, straight long legs," he says.

Summer's flat feet will make standing straight very difficult. "What if she's facing backward, leaning against the piano?"

His face wrinkles, and he scratches the back of his head. With a sigh, I walk over to the set and place my hands on the slick surface of the piano, going up on my toes. Both he and Summer follow. He doesn't say anything, but I can hear him thinking, trying to rearrange the concept. I grab Summer and put her in my place. Leaning against the piano, she manages to get all the way on her toes, but her face wrinkles in pain.

"Is it supposed to hurt this much?" she whispers to me.

"Another reason to have the back of your head to the camera. You can glance over your shoulder and get some face in the shot," I say.

"Maybe," the photographer finally says, then grabs one girl at a time and arranges them in different poses around Summer, all of their calves long and flexing in response to the heels and pointe shoes.

The assistant is beside him now, both of them speaking in a mix of French and English. I catch a few words from the assistant when he says, "I still like her standing on top of the piano better, but this works too."

Standing on pointe on the piano? Jesus. She would have broken more than an ankle. But then again, what's more edgy than a broken neck from a modeling shoot, right?

I back away from the set, allowing the lighting people to make the proper changes, but I don't get all the way out before I bump into someone. I spin around, and I'm pressed up against Eddie.

Like last night. Except with clothes on this time.

He drops a hand onto my shoulder to steady me. "So, Finley Belton…you're harboring a secret talent?"

My face heats, and I can't look him in the eye. That whole "we had sex" thing really makes small talk difficult. I bend down and remove the nude-colored pointe shoes. "Yeah, apparently, I'm a professional consultant for Summer. Looking forward to sending her the bill for my expert services."

He's back in his normal clothes again, the curly hair returned to its semi-unruly state, and by the looks of it, he's gone through great effort to wipe his face clean of all makeup. In fact, his skin looks red from scrubbing so hard.

"You're all done for the day?" Lame. Like I said, small talk is weird. Maybe any talking after last night is weird? I'm in brand-new territory, so I have no idea what this is supposed to be like.

"Yep, thank God," Eddie says, shaking his head. "That was torturous. I don't know how you do this all the time."

"Well, it pays the bills." I hold up the shoes, looking for an excuse to end this conversation. "I better return these."

"I'll go with you. We can walk out together."

Great.

I have to walk past the Prada set to get my flip-flops and bag. Summer catches my eye and mouths, "thank you."

Coming from a spoiled diva model, that's quite the kind gesture. And even though today sucked, it was nice to be good at something. To feel like I belonged, even if my consultant position was made up on the spot.

I try to return the nude-colored pointe shoes to the stylist, but she waves a hand and says, "Keep them. We were told they can't be reused."

It's hard to tell if she's unhappy that I "ruined" an extra pair of shoes or not, but whatever. I tuck the shoes into my bag and head for the elevator, feeling the heat of Eddie beside me.

He reaches for the down button and then leans against the wall, facing me. "Tell me about ballerina Finley. I'm only familiar with model Finley."

I sigh again and contemplate banging my head against the wall. This is so not how you do a one-night stand. Besides, how familiar could he even be with model Finley? We just met last night.

CHAPTER 10

Eddie

"What's there to tell? I used to do ballet." Finley taps her toe and stares down the elevator doors, willing them to open.

Normally, evasive answers would be a cue for me to back off, but for some reason, the more walls she drops between us, the more I want to figure out how to knock them down again. They were down last night almost from the moment we were introduced.

And the ballet thing? The girl has obviously worn many pairs of pointe shoes in her past, and yeah, I'm surprised to find this out. And people don't surprise me very often.

Except Caroline. She gets the queen of surprise title after the last several months.

My stomach twists into knots, remembering her text from this morning. *You're doing the right thing, E.*

I don't know if I'm doing the right thing. I just know that I'm not doing what Caroline thinks I'm doing. Lying to my parents is one thing, but lying to her…

The elevator doors open with a loud squeal, and I realize Finley's staring at me, waiting for me to move. "After you."

Her forehead wrinkles as she steps inside the elevator. The doors close, but I block her from pushing a button and lean closer, resting a hand on either side of her, my fingers curling around the railing. I'm instantly taken back to last night, the heat filling the small space between us. Yes. This is what I need. My happy place.

"Look," I say, enjoying her instant reaction to me invading her personal space—wide eyes, mouth falling open, and her pulse... I can feel it speed up when my chest brushes hers. "I know you're all, 'I failed at the impersonal one-night stand,' but really, there's only one rule, and I don't think either of us broke it."

Her eyebrows lift. "What's that?"

I inhale, and even with the large quantity of hair gel on both of us, I still get a trace of her familiar scent, one that involves fruit and sex. My own heart picks up. "The only rule is to have fun. And I definitely enjoyed myself. What about you?" *Have fun and avoid a scandal.*

Her eyes lock with mine, cheeks reddening. Her fingers crawl up my T-shirt, wrapping around the material covering my heart and pulling me so close our noses touch. "I had fun, Eddie."

My lips brush against hers, both of our eyes fluttering shut. *God, yes.*

A jolt and loud squeak followed by a stream of sunlight breaks the spell, and we jump apart just as the doors open, revealing the stylist from the Prada shoot.

"Okaaay..." she says, embarrassed. "I'll wait for the other elevator."

The doors shut again, but Finley keeps her distance, except for the weight of her gaze as she studies me, deciding something. Her hand freezes over the L button. "My mom was a dancer. She taught me."

Okay, let's pretend like we weren't just about to get it on in an elevator.

My eyebrows shoot up. "A dancer? Like a professional?"

"Yes." She presses her index finger into the button, slowly lifting it up, causing the elevator to jolt into motion. "With the New York City Ballet. And my parents used to own a dance studio."

"Used to?" I ask. "Your dad is a dancer too?"

"It didn't work out." She shrugs and then adds, "My dad is a high school music and drama teacher. Definitely not a dancer."

Finley exits the elevator when we reach the lobby but doesn't hurry out the door as quickly as I anticipated she might.

An awkward silence falls between us, and I realize this is probably the part where I'm supposed to reveal something personal. But that could lead to a tangled mess of lies. Well, a new tangled mess, because I'm already in one—being Eddie Wells from Chicago and all that. And yet, I don't want to walk away right now. The second I'm alone, I'll retreat back inside my head again. Worrying. Thinking months ahead instead of right now.

"So...which way are you headed?" I point toward the door and then remove my phone from my pocket, flipping through emails as an excuse to avoid eye contact with Finley. I feel like I might be wearing my secrets for her to see.

She points north. "Back to my apartment."

The first email in my inbox is from someone at Shay Silver's office with the subject *Found you an apartment!*

I scan the email and see nothing about cost or location, just mentions of bunk beds and roommate numbers totaling in the double digits. Surely it can't be that pricey if we're packed in like sardines.

I tuck my phone away and follow her, my shoulder brushing up against hers. "My agent found me a place to stay."

"That's good." She glances at me then back at the sidewalk. "I'm sure it's hard being so far from home and not having a definite place to stay."

Far from home? Oh right. I'm from Chicago. "Yeah, I haven't showered since yesterday."

Finley's cheeks flame up again. "Sorry about that. I was a total spaz this morning. But you're right. Impulsive fun is still impulsive fun, even if I screw up by giving my autobiography the day after."

"Your autobiography is very interesting."

She rolls her eyes again. "Right."

"Correction—I'm very interested. How's that?" What the hell am I saying? I'm very interested…it sounds like I'm agreeing to a courtship or something. This whole being Eddie Wells game is causing a serious identity crisis. I'm reverting to the eighteen hundreds. Pretty soon, our fathers will be trading horses.

Finley stops in the middle of the sidewalk, turning to face me, her arms folded over her chest. "What game are we playing right now? I'm pretty disjointed by all of it."

You and me both.

I let out a breath and try to be as real as possible. "I just wanted to pick your brain about some stuff. Since you're the experienced professional and all. How much do you think this apartment is gonna cost me?"

She stares for several seconds and then continues walking and nods for me to follow. "How many people? Where is it located? And how many rooms?"

I show her the email I'd just read.

"Hard to estimate exactly without a location. But it's probably around twelve hundred a month," she says.

My stomach sinks. That cuts into my potential savings in a big way. "Wow, that's heavy. What do you think we'll get from Marc Jacobs?"

"Around two grand. But then the agency gets their twenty percent cut. " She takes in my concerned look and adds, "It takes some time to build up a steady income. Don't worry about being ahead for these first few months. You'll get there. They obviously love you if you've booked Marc Jacobs on the first casting. Though you might want to reconsider being a royal pain in the ass to the makeup people."

I've only booked two other jobs thus far. I mean, I've just been at it a day, and I do have another casting this afternoon, but still...there are no guarantees. My plan for the summer is to pile as much money as possible into my bank account and then get the hell out of New York City. I'm not here to slowly build a modeling career.

"How long have you been at this?" I ask.

"Since I was sixteen," she says. "I was only supposed to be working for a year after graduation, until I saved up enough for college, but I barely have a year of tuition, so that plan is on the back burner."

There's something hiding between those words, and for a moment, the intrigue of figuring it out distracts me from my current housing and money issues. But I think she's already revealed more than she's comfortable with, so I'm not going to push.

I quickly type a reply to the agency:

Sounds good. What's the address?

I stare at the screen for several seconds after hitting Send, even though it's not likely I can go there now.

"Hey," I say, touching Finley's shoulder. "Any chance you know a place I could take a shower, shave, use a bathroom that doesn't require latex gloves?"

She gives me a sheepish grin. "Wish I could help you out, but my roommate's mom already flipped out this morning. She needs at least twenty-four hours to calm down."

The crazy, swearing French woman. "Yeah, I don't want to face that again."

"Wait!" Finley digs through her purse, coming up with a bright-pink card. "Got this last time I was at the agency. They've got a pile of them on the receptionist's desk. It's a punch card for the gym I belong to. Great showers. Free shampoo and hair products."

I take the card from her. It's good for ten free visits. "Thanks, this will help me out until—"

"You move into your new place," Finley finishes.

"Yeah, right. My new place." I attempt to look interested in the card. "So why is a rock-climbing and fitness center giving away punch cards at a modeling agency?"

She laughs and pats my stomach. "Can't have the models getting beer bellies, right? We gotta stay in shape. Also doesn't hurt to have a few models at your establishment, so they say."

Yeah, I could see that. I mean, if I were a coach potato, I'd probably change my ways for the chance to look at Finley every day.

I flip over the card and look at the address. "You know what? I might head over there now. Want to join me? I'll loan you a punch."

"I don't have workout clothes with me." She smiles. "Also, I have a yearly membership. I just grabbed one of those in case my brothers wanted to come with me sometime."

My stomach twists, my brain conjuring an image of two beefy guys cornering me in an alley, asking me exactly what I did with their sister. "Right. That's smart. Bring reinforcement to the gym. All those hormonal guys on steroids eyeing you in spandex..."

Finley laughs. "Uh...they're five. Almost six."

Huh. Definitely not in-line with my mental picture of them. "So more the wall-climbing age than the picking-up-girls-in-spandex age?"

"Yep, wall-climbing, furniture-climbing, parachuting off very tall objects, shooting liquid out of their noses—the usual little boy stuff." Finley pauses at a street corner and points to the subway station across the street. "You'll want to take..."

I tune out her lengthy detailed directions and instead enjoy the view that comes with her arm-raising and her shirt creeping up, exposing her lower back. She catches me staring and drops her arm, giving my shoulder a shove. "You're gonna get lost if you don't pay attention."

See, that's what I love about her, none of that *don't look at me, I'm slightly imperfect* shit.

"That was worth the misdirection." I hold up my phone. "Google Maps will get me there. Don't worry."

Another awkward silence falls between us, like neither of us knows if this is the last time we'll see each other, and I can't decide if I want it to be. I don't. I think. But considering the fact that I'm one big ball of lies and have no plans to stick around this state, let alone the city, beyond the end of the summer, it's better if it is our last time together.

"Sure you can't come with me?" I ask again. "Show the out-of-towner around town?"

Finley shakes her head.

"You just want to rush home and put those pointe shoes on again, don't you?" I reach for her hand and tug her closer. "Thanks for letting me stay over last night. Even if you didn't actually invite me to stay."

"You're welcome." She lifts her free hand and touches it to my mouth. "Don't do anything to ruin this."

"Like what?"

"Like giving me your number." She releases me and steps back, a look of satisfaction on her face. "Think about it. You're going your way, and I'm going mine, and we don't have each other's numbers, might never see each other again. I'm getting some of the one-night stand stuff right."

Her excitement is too cute for me to want to ruin it by reminding her that I know where she lives. And we're with the same agency. "You're a complete mystery. Fifty years from now, you'll still be the hot blond that I spent the most amazing night of my life with."

"You are so full of it." She looks pleased though as she turns around to head in the opposite direction. "Bye, Eddie Wells," she calls over her shoulder.

I watch her walk until she's too small to identify, and then I cross the street and head for the subway station. It would have been nice to get her number. Lying to Caroline makes it difficult to talk to her anymore—too much guilt and anxiety. Besides, I'm not legally allowed to contact her. And my friends from school? Let's just say we've drifted apart the past few months. Maybe everyone but RJ. Except RJ plays for Team Caroline.

So yeah, Finley could help fill a hole in my life, but I can't be selfish anymore. I need to stick to my plan and let her stick to her plan.

My phone buzzes in my hand. I glance at the reply from the agency, and I'm glad I didn't get this sooner. It would have ruined Finley's plans, knowing my summer apartment is in the same building as her place. Maybe we won't run into each other?

CHAPTER 11

Finley

Six in the morning, and I'm wide awake, making an egg-white omelet. Even after a Toby Rhinehart movie marathon with Elana kept me up late last night (okay, so maybe I am a fan of his). I figured the break in my usual morning yoga ritual yesterday had my body screaming for an early morning intervention. But it wasn't yoga I craved. Those brand-new, ready-to-be-danced-in pointe shoes sat on my dresser, calling to me all night long. *Break me in, Finley. Bet your fouettés suck.*

I slide the omelet onto a plate and leave it sitting on the counter. I'm too excited to eat. It's hard to even remember now how I could let ballet fade out of my life. Of course, I had my reasons. Pretty good ones, I think. But that adrenaline rush I got yesterday, simply pushing up on pointe...tough to top that feeling.

After lacing up the pointe shoes—they fit even better than yesterday—I move the couch back a few feet and roll up the rug on the living room floor. I face the TV and stand in fourth position, preparing for a pirouette, my pajama pants nearly hiding the ballet shoes. But it's too quiet in here. The second I hear the clump of my pointe shoes hitting the floor, I'll be distracted worrying about

Summer waking up, though she sleeps like the dead. And Elana and her mom left this morning before six for a shoot in Pennsylvania.

I grab my iPod and strap it to my waist, then pop in my headphones, blasting the music. I warm up my feet like I'd done with Summer at the Prada shoot, and then, taking a deep breath, I attempt a simple, single pirouette on pointe.

The turn isn't terrible, but not great either. The rush of adrenaline is, however, amazing. I practice turn after turn, quickly moving from singles to doubles. But when I attempt to add a fouetté after a double pirouette, I accidentally kick the TV and fall into the vertical blinds covering the sliding glass door that leads to the balcony. I'm about to move the couch back a few more feet, when I spot a pair of hairy legs through the glass door.

I let out a yelp that would have had French Mama running out here, spatula in hand—where the hell is she when I need her?—but instead, I'm left with the option of either waking Summer or moving the blinds a bit more to see if those legs are connected to anything. Oh God, they'd better be connected to something.

My hands tremble. I scramble to detach my phone from my waist, punch in 911, and let my finger hover over the call button. I reach up and check the lock on the door—it's up and secure—before slowly peeling back the blinds. I squeeze my eyes shut for a second and then open them, making sure to focus on the hairy pair of legs stretched out on a plastic patio chair Summer uses for her daily fifteen minutes of vitamin D (this is all her fault!). My gaze travels at snail pace, taking in the tan cargo shorts and hemline of a black T-shirt.

Come on, Fin, just do it.

I shift my focus higher and catch the steady rise and fall of a chest. My breath comes out in one long gust. Thank God. Not a dead body.

I'm on my feet quickly, much less freaked, although if I'm being logical, a dead body poses little threat to me, while a live body...

I shake the thought away and peel back the blinds enough to see the rest of Hairy Leg Guy. My eyes land on the familiar face, the wild curly black hair.

Eddie Wells.

What the hell is he doing—sound asleep—on a plastic chair on my balcony at six thirty in the morning?

I sink back on my heels, studying him. Maybe this is my fault for pointing out my balcony the other night. I unlock the door and slide it open just enough for me to slip outside. Then I creep as quietly as possible onto the balcony. He lifts a hand to his face and rolls onto his side. I freeze in place, watching, but he doesn't wake, despite the sun landing right across his face.

For nearly two minutes, I stand there eyeing his backpack, unable to make a move. He was so careful to haul that thing everywhere he went the other night. Even in the heat of our clothing removal session, he stepped away for a moment to tuck it in the corner of my bedroom. And checked to make sure both zippers were secured. Twice.

So yeah, I'm dying to get a look inside while he's out cold. I force away the guilt. Privacy hardly applies when someone is trespassing, right?

Kneeling on the ground, I unzip his backpack. It's quieter to remove one item at a time than to rifle through it. A minute later, lined up on the concrete balcony, are the following items: deodorant, toothbrush, electric razor, expensive designer shorts, designer T-shirt, cologne (which I take a moment to sniff)…

No comb. Figures.

What is he, some kind of nomad? I thought he had an apartment worked out. Or maybe the airline lost his luggage and he's only got his carry-on.

My fingers land on what feels like a leather billfold. I remove it and look it over. It's Prada, probably costs three or four hundred dollars. I sit down on the ground and open it up. My gaze lands first on the driver's license tucked behind the clear plastic cover. If it weren't for the mess of dark curly hair in the photo, I would have thought Eddie was a pickpocket. Not only because it's a New York State license and Eddie claimed to be from Chicago, but also because the name across the top is Edward James Wellington IV. Not Eddie Wells.

But seriously, Eddie is a fourth? There are four of him? As my dad would say per our PG household rules, holy shiitake!

Not only did Eddie lie about his name and state of residence, his address is right here in the city, not far away from this apartment. And yet he's sleeping on my balcony in a hard plastic chair after complaining yesterday about the cost of agency apartments.

My brain is working on overdrive while I lean against the sliding door. He lied. Pretty much about everything. He made me think, yesterday after the shoot, that he's struggling financially, that he really needed money. If he lives at this address, and not as the butler or butler's kid, then Eddie—or Edward Wellington IV—has probably never worried about money a day in his life. What if this is some story our agency concocted? Make him look like he came from nothing, a human interest story. If the agency hadn't pulled some similar shit last year, with my roommate Elana, I should add, I don't think my mind would even go in that direction.

My thoughts drift back to Eddie pausing outside my door, not sure if he wanted to come in. But outside of his name and hometown, which he barely talked about, it had felt real. At least to me.

I glance at him again. Still sound asleep, he scratches at a red bump on his neck. A mosquito bite, most likely. And probably one of many. With a heavy sigh, I return the items I pulled from his wallet moments ago and begin tucking everything back into his bag. Whatever event or reason caused Eddie to lie about his name and history and live out of his backpack isn't something simple. This has complicated and messed up written all over it. The question is, do I want to get involved or steer clear? And how can I steer clear of this guy if he keeps showing up at my jobs and on my balcony?

And I still can't decide if I'm pissed off at him or not. I mean, I should be, right?

CHAPTER 12

Eddie

"Eddie?"

A soft hand shakes me, creating a nice distraction from the intense itching going on all over my body. When I realize it's Finley Belton, the very person who I'd hoped wouldn't spot me out here this morning, I bolt upright.

She steps back, assessing me. I can't read anything from her expression.

"Oh, hey..." I glance around like an idiot, squinting at the sun. "I was just—"

"Sleeping on my balcony?" she prompts, one eyebrow lifted.

"The guys in my place needed a little alone time last night." I point a finger at the floor above us. "I was gonna crash at Dima's and then..." I pinch the bridge of my nose, remembering the awkward minutes I spent in Dima's apartment before sneaking outside on the balcony and climbing down the fire escape.

Finley and I both notice her lack of bra at the exact same time. Her cheeks turn a nice shade of pink, and she folds her arms across her chest. I avert my gaze upward.

"Then what?" Finley asks in a tone that clearly indicates my answer will determine how pissed off or weirded out she is from finding me out here.

"Then I didn't really care for their choice of evening activities."

"Like what? Was it boy-on-boy related, because I heard that Dima likes to play games where—"

That would have been awkward but different, much different. "More like the tossing drugs onto a table for everyone to share kind of game."

The exact thing I'd been so afraid of the previous night. The scene had been too familiar. But luckily, I had my head on straight enough to get the hell out of there.

"Oh." The smile fades. "Right."

"Right."

"Not really your scene, huh?" she presses, her voice a little softer, less judgmental.

"No, not really." I lean over and reach for my bag, then stand and toss it onto my shoulder. "Sorry for crashing here without asking. Won't happen again."

Finley blocks my path to the fire escape. "I looked in your wallet," she blurts out.

My stomach knots. I know where this is headed. Guess I had that coming, considering where I left my wallet. I take a deep breath. "Look, it's not as bad as it seems. I just—"

"Needed a rags-to-riches story for PR purposes?" she suggests, the judgment returning.

"No, nothing like that." In fact, I don't want any story. Seriously. I want the opposite of a PR story. Is that a thing?

"You just didn't want anyone to know where you're from?"

She leans against the metal railing surrounding the balcony, and I'm surprised by the lack of judgment on her face. "Yeah," I admit, because that's technically true. Maybe there are other truths I can give Finley without telling her everything. I can't risk telling her everything. I can't even risk letting myself think everything. "My parents think I'm at Princeton right now. For the summer program."

Finley's eyebrows shoot up. "You're going to Princeton?"

"Obviously not." I don't mean to snap at her, but it's a sore subject. Four generations of Wellingtons have attended Princeton. It may sound ridiculous to other people, but the Princeton weight has been pressing down on me my entire life.

"All right," Finley says, her voice softening. "So you got into Princeton, but you're not going. What *are* your plans? To make your own money and let yourself get cut off by your parents?"

Man, that really sounds cliché. But still, I nod. "Basically."

"So is anything you've told me thus far actually true?"

I think for a minute, swallow back nerves. "I really am bad at beer pong."

For several long seconds, we stare at each other. "No knitting hats for orphaned dogs?" Finley says finally.

I shake my head and wait.

Another long pause, and then she opens the door and gestures for me to come inside. "No one's here except Summer, and she's sound asleep."

My gaze drifts downward, and I notice her feet for the first time. "Nice shoes. Did you sleep in those?"

She rolls her eyes. "No."

The ballet shoes are quickly removed and tossed onto the couch.

I scratch at a patch of bug bites on the side of my neck while taking in the new living room arrangement. "Huh. I don't remember the couch being there the other day."

"People are always moving stuff around." Finley waves a hand and walks over to the fridge, opening it and staring inside without a specific purpose.

"I wonder why anyone would want the couch practically smashed against the wall and then all that room in middle. All that empty floor space." I spin slowly like I'm really thinking this through.

"Fine," she snaps. "I was practicing. You caught me. Laugh all you want."

I'm not laughing. It's cute and a little sexy that she was dancing—braless—around the living room in pointe shoes. I bend over to examine the very tasty-looking omelet resting on the counter that divides the kitchen and living room.

Finley snatches the plate right out from under my nose and dumps the omelet into the garbage. "You can't eat that."

I didn't expect her to turn over her breakfast to me. That would be rude. Even though I'm completely famished. She goes back to the fridge and begins tossing items onto the counter. "It's been sitting out. I'll make you a fresh one."

Now I feel bad. "You don't have to—"

"Sit," she orders, pointing at a chair pulled up to the counter. "You slept on my balcony without permission, so now I'm forcing you to eat my cooking."

"Talk about hardships." I sit as commanded and watch Finley move around the kitchen in pajama pants. "The view is really nice here."

She glances over her shoulder and sees that I'm looking at her backside, not the balcony. She cracks an egg into a bowl one-handed. "No more of that. We're done with that."

I grin. "Are you convincing me or yourself? I couldn't tell."

"I'm serious, Eddie." She sets the bowl down and crosses her arms. "I need to succeed at the one-night stand, which means you and I are just having a friendly, coworker-type chat. Got it?"

I hold my hands up in surrender. "Got it."

She gives a satisfied nod and spins around again. I lean on one elbow and continue enjoying the view. In a little while, I'll have to go back to my hellhole apartment with way too many dudes in it, so this is nice. Accidentally getting caught.

My cell, with its one percent battery remaining, buzzes. I glance quickly at the newest calendar event: *Manhattan Trust, meeting with lawyer, one hour.* My stomach flips at the reminder, and I must look nervous or something, because Finley stops what she's doing.

"What?" she asks.

The knot in my stomach double-ties itself. But I shake my head and force a grin. "Nothing. Just a thing I have to go to in a little while."

"A thing?" Finley asks. "That explains so much."

She's just set a freshly made omelet in front of me, so I busy myself shoving a big bite into my mouth. The cheese is so hot, it burns my tongue. "This is really good."

I've distracted her with compliments, and we discuss anything but my "thing" while I finish eating and then convince Finley to let me wash all the dishes—it's the least I can do.

A little while later, I glance at the microwave, checking the time, and immediately snatch my bag up and toss it over my shoulder. "I better head downstairs and get a shower before my...meeting."

"Yeah, sure," Finley says while shoving a clean bowl up into a tall cabinet. "Wait..." She stops and turns to face me. "Downstairs? Does that mean your agency apartment is..."

Uh...yeah. I give her a grim smile. "I didn't mention that earlier? I could have sworn that I did."

"Nope." She shakes her head slowly. "Perfect. Just perfect."

"We might not run into each other much," I offer. I don't know what else to say. She offers up a halfhearted nod and good-bye when my hand ends up on the doorknob seconds later. I guess that's to be expected.

But would it be that terrible if we did hang out?

CHAPTER 13

Finley

"Would it be that awful if we did hang out?" I ask Summer. "I mean, like, every once in a while, not all the time. He seemed like he needed a friend."

It's probably lonely lying to everyone you know.

"Only you could turn a one-night stand into a charity event." Summer snatches the bag of mini rice cakes from my hand and closes them. "I said you could have one, not one hundred."

"Don't worry," Elana says to me from her spot at the end of Summer's bed. "My mom will be back from the store any minute, and I'm sure she's got something planned for dinner."

I groan internally, and Summer groans out loud. "How many sticks of butter do you think she'll use tonight?" Summer snaps. "Three? Maybe four?"

"Probably olive oil too," Elana adds. "Last night, she wouldn't let me leave the table until I cleaned my plate. She said that's what American children do."

It's amazing how quickly Elana's accent is fading. I mean, I've heard that happens, especially with younger people, but by the end of the summer, no one will even know she's from France.

"Enough calorie talk," Summer says. "Finley needs an intervention. We gotta talk her out of adopting the freeloader guy from the party."

"No, we need to go back to our *Vampire Diaries* episode," I try. "Toby Rhinehart guest-starred this week."

"Toby Rhinehart is an overrated, overpaid, photoshopped pretty boy with way too many fucking kids," Summer rattles off.

"Don't even..." I fake gasp, wishing for this debate instead of the Eddie intervention. I shouldn't have brought him up.

"Eddie," Elana inserts. *No help at all. Thanks.* "His name is Eddie."

Summer waves a hand to stop her. "Don't give him a name. For Finley, that's like the starving kids in those commercials begging to be sponsored for pennies a day."

Okay, so I left out the part about Eddie being Edward James Wellington IV when I filled my roommates in on the balcony incident. Eddie seemed so committed to his new identity that I kind of feel committed to it as well. Which is really weird. He's the one taking advantage of me—well, of my balcony and my omelet-making skills.

"I caught him. He's not sleeping on your vitamin D chair anymore. It's a big building. I probably won't see him ever again," I say, using my most convincing tone.

Summer rolls her eyes. "That's what everyone says after they feed a stray cat."

"He's lucky my mom didn't catch him," Elana adds.

The three of us sit in silence for several moments. No one can disagree with that. French Mama is scary.

"How was the sex?" Summer blurts out.

"Why?" My face heats up. I glance at Elana, whose dark eyes are wide with interest. "Maybe now isn't the time—"

"Give me a break. Jesus, the girl is hardly innocent." She gives Elana a one-second glance.

Elana's expression stiffens, but she says nothing. Smart girl. She's figured out Summer's need to get that big reaction out of people.

Summer stands and brushes the crumbs off her designer lounge-wear. Yep, she and Eddie have nothing in common. She turns her attention from Elana to me. "I wasn't asking for a play-by-play, just a one-word answer."

My cheeks warm even more. "Good."

"Good?" she repeats. This seems to stump her. The front door opens, and Summer perks up. "I'm gonna stop her before any fish is cooked. What the hell is wrong with chicken?"

Elana and I are left alone in Summer's room. I look Elana over carefully. She's had a rough year—one deserving of its own story—and Summer dug up that dirt, tossed it right on the floor in front of us. That can't be easy for Elana. "Hey...you okay?"

She picks at a loose thread on the comforter. "Yeah, it's just weird. Being back here. Especially with Alex and Eve..."

A big part of Elana's drama last year involved a fake relationship with Alex that landed them a big CK gig. I did that Calvin Klein shoot too, and Eve was the photographer's assistant. When all that drama went down, Alex and Eve got worried about Elana and decided to get French Mama involved—Elana had been in America under the supervision of our modeling agency. Which basically means no supervision. Something Alex and Eve deemed problematic, to put it politely. So basically, it's their fault Elana is being tortured by her mother.

"They're in Europe right now," I point out. "For a couple weeks, I think."

Elana nods. "I know."

Elana's mom calls her into the kitchen. She jumps up immediately. After she's gone, I return to my room and stare at my phone for several seconds before pulling up Jason's number on my phone. I haven't spent the last ten months thinking about my ex who dumped me before going to college, I swear I haven't. But scrolling through Facebook and Instagram the past couple weeks, knowing my high school friends are all home for the summer, it makes me wish for that life again. Movie dates with my nice boyfriend, weekend trips to the mall with friends, hanging out in my backyard pool with kids from school, with my dad and brothers. I miss the safe familiarity of it.

I stare at Jason's number in my phone. On impulse, I hit call. My heart picks up speed. Not out of love exactly, but more like from the guilt that comes with failing to stay away. I'm about to hang up and text him a "sorry, I butt-dialed you" excuse, but he answers on the first ring.

"Hey, Fin, I was just gonna call you."

I sink back against my headboard. All the new unfamiliar that came with my hookup with Eddie is erased by this voice that I know so well. It wraps around me like a favorite sweatshirt.

"Really? What for?"

"Your brothers' birthday party next weekend. I got invited," he says. "What were you calling about?"

I clear my throat. "Oh…um, the party. Of course. Gotta make sure we have enough goodie bags."

God, I'm lame.

"Well, I'm willing to sacrifice mine for the greater good if needed."

"I figured. Hero complex and all that." I take a breath, trying to be the cool New York City girl most of my friends assume I've become. "So…does that mean you're coming?"

He's my fucking neighbor. Of course he's coming.

"Uh-huh. I'll stop by for a little—"

Summer pops her head in my room, a big grin plastered on her face. "We're having chicken tonight!"

I gesture to the phone so she'll shut up, but that only gets her riled up more. "So, I'll see you next weekend then, Jason?"

"Jason? Oh no. No way." Summer bounds toward me and snatches the phone from my hand before I can stop her. "Hi, Jason. It's Summer."

She moves quickly toward the door. I dive at her, grabbing her around the waist. We both end up tangled together, half in my room, half in the hallway.

"Finley's going through a program," Summer says to Jason. "She's not supposed to have contact with people from her past for a while."

"Give me the fucking phone," I hiss at her. I reach for it but end up banging my elbow on the doorframe.

"And she's way too busy having good sex with models to have time for you."

Oh my God, I'm gonna kill her.

Summer hangs up on Jason but flips over on her stomach,

still scrolling through my phone. "You need to delete him from your contacts."

"Give me the damn phone!" I get my fingers on it this time, but her grip is too tight. In a moment of desperation, my other hand stretches toward my desk, feeling around for a pair of scissors. I hook my index finger through the handle and then hold them above Summer's head.

"Think Prada would mind if you showed up tomorrow with a bald patch?"

Summer looks over her shoulder at me, wide-eyed. "You bitch."

"Phone?" I hold out my hand, and she drops it into my palm. I'm about to let her up when both of us notice Elana and her mom standing in the hallway, staring at us.

Elana's mom shakes her head and says something in French. Elana looks us over as if to say *and I'm the one who needs supervision?*

I push off the floor and get to my feet again. Summer does the same. She straightens her clothes, puts every hair back in place. "Someday, you'll appreciate everything I've done for you."

I glare at her. "Next time, I'm leaving you alone to break an ankle in pointe shoes!"

"Next time, I'm calling animal control," Summer taunts from down the hallway.

Still pissed and experiencing a mega adrenaline rush, mostly panic-related, I slam my bedroom door right in Summer and Elana's faces. I stare at Jason's name still up on my phone. What the hell do I say to him now? I can't think of anything, so instead, I message Eve on Facebook so I can vent. I hit send before I remember that she's probably enjoying crepes in France right now.

ME: I think I've figured out which girl Summer was in
high school.
EVE: You mean Regina George?

I laugh despite the anger still floating above my head like a
dark cloud.

ME: Exactly. Want to help me bury her alive? Or drop
her off in Jersey. That's probably just as bad. U can have
her room.
EVE: Actually...Alex and I are thinking about getting an
apartment together.
ME: That's serious.
EVE: I know, right?

I can't help being a gossip addict. I switch to messaging Alex.

ME: An apartment together? What's next? Marriage
proposal?
ALEX: Not until tomorrow. Duh. Who proposes on a
Monday?
EVE: He's not proposing. Don't listen to him. It's a
convenience thing, that's all.

Those two are way too cute.

EVE: How was the rest of the party? We made our
flight, luckily.

I leave Alex hanging and answer Eve.

> **ME:** Well…things went in an interesting direction after u left.
> **EVE:** Details. Please.
> **ME:** Go have some European fun. I'll fill u in when u get back.
> **EVE:** Come on! I'm dying here. Plus we're on a train for the next hour.

I hesitate before finally deciding to launch into a detailed explanation of the Eddie Wells story. We go back and forth for a good thirty minutes.

> **EVE:** U want friend advice or therapy jargon?
> **ME:** IDK. Neither. Both. LOL.
> **EVE:** OK let's go with in between. Now is the time to be selfish. If u aren't benefiting from these interactions with Eddie, it's not worth continuing.
> **ME:** So don't offer to feed and house him? And what about Jason?
> **EVE:** LOL. Kind of. As much as this pains me to say, Summer is probably right about Jason. But u never know. He did say he was about to call u…I can't even begin to figure out his motives there. If any at all.

Guess I'll have to wait for next weekend and see for myself. And see him again, which hasn't happened for almost a year. After

Summer pretty much told him I was in rehab and a sex addict, it should be a fun catching-up session.

My thoughts quickly drift from Jason to Eddie. It's good that I have Eve to talk to about him, because my friends back home, several of whom I'll see this weekend, would probably freak out about Eddie lying, saying he's from Chicago. That part doesn't bother me much, if I'm being honest. Maybe my months living in the city have changed me somewhat. New York is full of people hiding where they're from, who they were before they got here. And it's not like I didn't deliver my own evasive answers to Eddie. I didn't really tell him about my mom, not the most important part. I didn't really tell him about the studio or why I haven't danced in years. Or that the one thing I want more than anything is to reopen my parents' studio, that I'm saving up to do just that, despite knowing my dad will be completely against it. So really, Eddie's lie about his hometown seems minimal compared to what I skillfully left out of our conversations thus far.

Eve told me once that Alex used to joke, back when we were all working on that CK shoot together, about there being an invisible fortress around me. I've never really thought of myself like that, a secret keeper. I figured that was more about me still being hung up on Jason and not ready to date again, but maybe it's more than that?

Maybe I'm just afraid to really want something—out loud, in the open—because what if I can't have it? What if it doesn't work out?

The weight pressing on my chest is so heavy, I only sit on my thoughts a few moments longer, and then I snatch my gym bag from the floor and toss it over my shoulder. In a last-minute decision, I snatch the pointe shoes from my dresser and throw them into the bag. Maybe one of the fitness rooms will be empty, and I can sneak in some dancing.

The hall is already filled with delicious scents of butter and garlic. My stomach rumbles in response. I'm about to bolt out the door, but Elana's mom rushes over from the kitchen. She spits out a bunch of really fast French, then rests both hands on my arms.

Elana looks up from the schoolwork her mom is probably making her do at the kitchen table. She sighs before saying, "She says you should have something to eat before you go out."

"It's fine. I'm going to the gym—"

French Mama interrupts with more words I can't understand, but her tone combined with that concerned maternal tone tells me enough. Without warning, a lump forms in my throat, and warmth spreads from my neck up to my cheeks.

"She says you're too thin, and you need more protein," Elana rattles off, her tone the opposite of her mother's.

I exhale and look away from the concerned face in front of me and glance Elana's way. "Tell her thanks and to save some leftovers for me. I'll eat after the gym."

Elana repeats this, and French Mama finally releases me, looking satisfied with this compromise. I rush out the door before anything changes.

Outside in the fresh air, I try to forget French Mama's motherly tone, her face, but my thoughts drift to my own mother. To me racing out the front door to meet my friends at the park and my mom stopping me, telling me to come in and eat my dinner. Often, when I'd resist, she'd simply toss the food into a container and tell me to eat while I walk. Or sometimes at the studio, between classes, I'd go to my dance bag to change shoes and find a container of fruit or a granola bar that I hadn't put in there. My mom had.

And I used to wonder when she thought about these things. What point in the day did she think, *Finley's going to need a snack about five o'clock, between modern dance and tap?* Having taken care of my brothers for years now, I get having those thoughts now, but to think about someone thinking about *me* like that...it comes with mixed emotions.

CHAPTER 14

Eddie

When I walk through the doors of my new building, hours after the meeting with the bank lawyer, my mind is still there. At that polished table. In that office too big and too clean to belong to anyone normal. I've been walking around most of the afternoon, thinking. Part of me is panicking, saying *what the hell have I done?* If my father found out...

But the other part of me is relieved. Go ahead, tell him everything. Let's get this disowning me thing over with.

And I can't stop thinking about the look on Robert Lowman's face when he spoke to me in that lawyer way where someone pretends to know more than they do so they can find out how much you know.

"I don't think you're aware of the terms your grandmother set on the trust," he said, tapping his fingers against that polished table in a perfect rhythm.

"I'm aware of all the terms," I told him. *"That's why I'm here. I'm going to need access to those funds in the next few months."*

Mr. Lowman's fingers stilled, and he sat up straighter in his leather chair. Before saying anything else, he shot a glance at his associates

at the other end of the table. "And you think you'll meet these...
uh...terms"—he stopped to clear his throat—"in the near future?"

Without hesitation, looking him square in the face, I said, "Yes."

His eyebrows shot up. "How soon?"

My own gaze drifted toward the extra people in the room taking
notes. They were probably confused as hell. Good. "September."

"Well, that is soon." More throat clearing and the inability to look
me in the eye. "And your parents?"

I shook my head. "Not involved. And I'd like to keep it that way.
After this development in September, I won't receive any financial
support from them."

Truth is, I'm not technically using any of their support right now.
Even the cell phone they pay for is only being used for communication with my parents and sister. I got a new phone a few weeks ago
so that I could contact Caroline without them knowing.

"I see." He sighed and looked at me again. He was over the
shock at this point and ready to get down to business. "All we need
is tangible proof that the terms have been met, then you'll sign on
the dotted line and be granted full access to the trust within a few
months. Though I do recommend an interest-only withdrawal policy,
perhaps working with a financial advisor—"

"That's it?" I interrupted, shocked myself by how simple this
might be.

"Yes, sir." He twirled his pen for a moment, and I knew he was
about to ask me how I found out details my parents weren't even
privy to. "You were how old when your grandmother passed away?"

"Fourteen," I said, even though I knew he was good enough at
math to figure it out himself.

"And you don't think it's possible you misunderstood anything? Maybe we aren't talking about the same terms? I'm sworn to keep that confidential, but if you just shared your thoughts...?"

"Nope, no doubts," I said. And it was true. My grandmother was one of the few people in my family who I actually got along with. We shared in our dislike for my father—her own son. She told me the terms of this trust, and I'd told her she was nuts, keeping that much money from her own son and daughter-in-law. It was never me Robert Lowman was sworn to secrecy from. "You're sure there's no way for my parents to find out about this money before it's turned over to me? No way for them to gain access to it?"

"No, sir," he said with a nod. "Not possible."

I stood up, and he shook my hand. "You can't discuss this meeting with my parents, right?"

After everything that went down last winter and all the shit with Caroline, my parents would definitely be suspicious of me meeting with any lawyer.

He dragged out his answer, leaving a two-second pause that felt like two hours. "Correct. I'm legally bound to keep this conversation between us. And any future conversations."

Hours later, and it's still sinking in. It feels so official now. Which is why I can't focus on much else today, including the crowd outside the apartment door.

I give a weak "hey, how's it going" to Joey, the coke addict I'm now sharing a bunk bed with (talk about friends in high places). He's standing outside the apartment door, chatting up two girls who live somewhere on this floor. He lowers his voice after seeing me, and I'm sure he's promising to hook them up with some of his stuff. I shake my head and start to put the key in the door but stop when I hear a familiar voice behind me.

"Oh no, you don't," Summer says. She appears to be dragging Finley away by her shirtsleeve. Summer glares at me. "You may be hot and good in bed, but you're just a stray animal."

Joey and the two girls stop talking and listen in with interest. I, too, am quite interested to hear how Summer plans to compare me to a stray cat. I lean against the door, my arms folded over my chest.

Finley covers her face with one hand, clearly embarrassed. Did she say I was good in bed? I mean, how else would Summer know this—

"Stay away from my balcony," Summer demands. Then, before I get a chance to answer, she turns to Finley. "See this guy? Not healthy. Now, let's go find you a man with a fancy wallet."

I crack a smile. Finley Belton must be good at keeping secrets. Because I definitely have a fancy wallet. And she definitely rifled through it this morning. This only makes me want her more. Unfortunately.

"Bad date?" Joey asks when they're completely out of earshot.

"One-night stand," I say for Finley's benefit. I know how much that label means to her.

Inside the apartment, the couch is littered with takeout containers, and the sink is piled with week-old dirty dishes. I glance at the half-opened door to the bedroom I've been assigned to and then turn quickly after seeing that one of the bottom bunks is occupied. With three sets of feet. All tangled together, all contributing to some X-rated noises. I glance around again and decide it's probably a good idea to continue my long walk. Everything I currently own is already on my back, thank God.

Jesus, maybe I am a stray?

Summer is probably right to keep Finley away from me. It's complicated. *I'm* complicated.

If I were Finley, I'd stay far away from me too.

CHAPTER 15

Finley

Friday afternoon, I'm wheeling my duffel out of my apartment when I nearly plow into Eddie. He's walking down the hall, his backpack slung over one shoulder.

I haven't really talked to him since the morning I found him asleep on the balcony, but we've bumped into each other a few times. Summer's warning about my "animal-rescuing habit," plus Eve's advice to make sure that I'm benefiting from this—whatever this thing is that he and I are doing—had me reeling back a few steps, giving myself some space to assess the Eddie situation.

"Hey," I say.

He turns to glance over his shoulder as if just noticing me. "Oh…hey, Fin." His gaze drifts to my bag. "Going somewhere?"

"Yeah." I untuck the hair from behind my ears, attempting to cover my now-heated cheeks. Why am I blushing? "My little brothers' birthday party is tomorrow. At my house. In Connecticut…"

Eddie shifts his eyes from my bag to my face, and for a moment, we just stand there, neither of us knowing what to say. Eddie opens his mouth, but the door to the stairwell flies open, and five or six of the guys from his apartment come sprinting down the hall. Both of us dive out of the way, and Eddie ends up pressed up against me. After they pass, he clears his throat and steps back.

"Are they going out?" I ask. That might make for a quiet night in the apartment for him.

He stares at the door they all disappeared behind. "No, they're strung out. Apparently, it's extended to the apartment beside yours."

"And that requires hallway relay races?"

I expect Eddie to crack a joke or tell me something that makes sense. Instead, his expression darkens, but he shrugs and says, "Beats me. I'm not asking questions."

Above our heads, it sounds like a herd of elephants are running through the hallway. Then the stairwell door flies open again, and the group of guys is even larger this time. One dude with slicked-back hair and red eyes stops in front of Eddie and gives him a light smack on the cheek. "Come on, rebel boy, join the party! It's gonna be forty-eight hours of loaded fun."

"Loaded fun," Eddie repeats dryly. "Nice."

After they've gone again, I glance at Eddie. He looks completely overwhelmed. "Maybe a good weekend for a visit home?"

"Yeah, maybe." He diverts his eyes from mine. It doesn't take a genius to figure out that he's not going home, despite the fact that home for him is only a few blocks away.

"They might have trouble staying loaded for forty-eight hours without these…" Eddie reaches into his sweatshirt pocket and holds up a clear plastic bag full of colorful pills.

I lean in to get a closer look. My heart picks up at the mere sight of the drugs. I glance both ways down the hall, checking to make sure we're alone. "Where did you get those?"

"Just plucked them off Mr. Grease Head."

"Just now? While I was standing right here?" I lift an eyebrow after he nods. "So it's not only breaking and entering for you. You're a pickpocket too?"

Eddie smiles for the first time today. "Piano player, actually. But you know what they say…"

I snatch the bag from his hand. "These need to go away."

He follows me into my apartment—luckily, we're alone—and watches, saying nothing when I dump the pills into the toilet and flush them away. "You don't think I'm polluting the water supply, do you?"

"If you are, you're not the only one." Eddie heads for the apartment door, holding it open for me. While I'm locking up again, the guys come running through the hall for a third lap, this time with a few girls in tow and several bottles of liquor sloshing as they sprint past us.

"Seriously," I snap. "Are they actually trying to accomplish something? Record-breaking consumption while running through apartment halls?"

"No idea." Eddie shakes his head and glances at the stairwell. He looks miserable. "Well…have a good weekend."

I exhale. Yep, have a good weekend, Finley. A good weekend rounding up old friends who are probably too busy to hang out. A good weekend not trying to get your ex back like a pathetic, lovesick girl, and definitely not making attempts to rescue guys who were supposed to be one-night stands.

Even though Summer has made valid and very vocal points regarding my lesser habits, I'm rooted to my spot in the hallway, watching Eddie head over to the stairwell, the weight of whatever he's facing right now heavy and present in each step. I release a sigh loud enough to make him turn around. Then while I'm grumbling, calling myself all kinds of names inside my head, I do probably the best thing possible to prevent the success of my life improvement plan.

I nod in the direction of the elevator. "Come on. You're going home with me."

CHAPTER 16

Eddie

I don't know what I expected to see when I walked up to Finley's Connecticut home, but the lived-in, warm, and slightly cluttered ranch home in front of me is beyond anything I could have conjured. My curiosity had spiked even more on the train ride here after I noticed Finley starting to look nervous.

A man with Finley's blond hair rolls toward us across the driveway in a wheelchair. Finley watches me watching him, maybe to see if I have a reaction to him being in a wheelchair, but I'm too worried about other things. I slow my walk, not sure what he'll say about me being here with his daughter. I brace myself for a glare or a pointed look, but his smile is warm and nonthreatening.

Finley leans down to hug him, and then when she straightens up again, she turns to me. "Dad, Eddie…Eddie, my dad."

I stick a hand out. "Nice to meet you, Mr. Belton."

He looks me over, one brow lifted, before reaching out to shake my hand. "Call me Sam." Then he turns to Finley. "I see you took my advice. Where did you find this one?"

Finley blushes. "Friends, Dad. We're friends."

She shoots me a look like *please don't mention that night at the party.* Seriously? I don't have a death wish. He might be in a wheelchair, but his upper body is built. He could definitely fire a shotgun or swing a bat just fine.

"Eddie's with One Model Management and lives in my building. But his apartment is a bit *hectic* this weekend. He needed a place to stay."

I cough back a laugh. Hectic is one way to put it. I clear my throat. "Hope that's okay, sir?"

Finley's dad rolls his eyes. "Jesus. Mr. Belton is bad enough. Definitely don't call me sir. Ever."

"Sorry, sir—" I stop and shake my head. Finley and her dad both laugh. "Sorry."

I trail behind Sam and his wheelchair when he heads inside. The second the door opens, two towheaded, identical little boys race out.

Finley scoops up the first one and kisses his cheek. The kid wrinkles his nose and swipes at his cheek. "I swear you guys get bigger every time I see you."

She sets the kid down, and we all head into the foyer. Finley introduces me to Connor and Braden, which is a bit pointless, because I'll never be able to tell them apart. I make a mental note of Braden's red shirt today compared to his brother's white T-shirt. Finley carries Connor inside, his little arms tight around her neck. I shift from one foot to the other, slightly uncomfortable. I don't have a single memory of my sister Ruby ever hugging me. Or my parents, for that matter.

Braden tugs Finley into what looks like a family room, or

it might be their living room. He's talking her ear off, going a mile a minute, but I drown out the words, my gaze sweeping the room. The walls are covered with family photos, not the stiff portrait studio type that we have in a couple places at my home, but more like candid shots of family vacations and what might be the backyard pool, or pictures with Finley and her brothers in pajamas around a Christmas tree. Another wall is covered with artwork, the kind made out of construction paper with blobs of paint that resemble handprints.

Large foam puzzle pieces connect together on the floor to form a mat in the corner of the room where bins of toys and LEGOs sit around it. A chalkboard hangs at eye level for the boys with each of their names written on it, plus "Fin" and "Dad." Tallied numbers are beside each of the boys' names.

I spin slowly in a circle, the voices around me melting into the background as I take in the room. I can't imagine having toys and construction paper in any of the rooms in my home. One of my favorite nannies, when I was around Connor and Braden's age, kept toys in plastic containers under her bed for me and would pull them out and let me play on the kitchen floor while she made dinner. Until Ruby told my mom, and I got a new nanny a week later.

The crushing fear and anxiety of needing to make a new home comes down on me again, and for a few seconds, I can't breathe.

A tiny hand closes in mine, and I jolt back to life. Braden, the red shirt twin, tugs at my hand. "Wanna help with the *Star Wars* ship?"

I can feel Sam watching from my right side. Did I look weird standing here staring at the walls just now? I look down at Braden again. "Uh…sure."

I sit on the red, yellow, and blue foam puzzle-piece floor with both boys. Braden does all the talking, while Connor remains silent. From the chatterbox twin, I learn that Grandma gave them the *Star Wars* LEGO set for their birthday and that Grandma lives in the house next door. Also that the boys' real birthday was two days ago.

"Fin sent us a giant box of coloring books and Hot Wheels," Braden says, using his arms to model the size of the large box.

Despite all the information sharing, I'm still sitting on a couple big questions regarding this family. But I shove those aside for now. Slowly, I slide a hand toward the LEGO pile in front of me. I haven't spent any time around little kids, and I'm quickly realizing how alien they seem to me.

"A big box of Hot Wheels, huh?" I say to Connor, trying to get him involved in the talking.

Connor nods, his head down and gaze focused on the LEGOs.

"He doesn't talk lots," Braden tells me. "Cameron calls him deaf all the time, but deaf means you don't listen—"

"Hear," Finley and her dad both say together. Sam adds, "Deaf means you can't hear."

"Right. That's what I said. Hear." Braden dumps a box of LEGOs onto the foam floor, mixing them with the new *Star Wars* set. "Cameron says Connor is deaf, but he's not."

Connor shakes his head, agreeing with his brother.

"And Miss Leonard made Cameron sit out recess today and yesterday 'cause of it."

"Sounds like Cameron is stupid." I snap a few sections of the ship together and then look up when I feel two pairs of eyes on me. Both boys have sat up straighter, eyes wide, like I've suddenly grown another head.

Braden finally turns around and picks up a piece of chalk from the board. "How do you spell Eddie?"

I spell it slowly for him while he prints my name on the board, the *d*'s facing the wrong direction. Then beside my name, he adds a tally mark.

"Oh...I got a point?" I don't know what great thing I did to score on their chalkboard, but whatever, I'll take it. "Thanks."

Behind me, Finley laughs. "That's the bad word board. Whoever has the most points at the end of the day helps with the dishes or has to clean the bathroom."

I scan my memory of the last couple minutes, digging for any swearwords that may have slipped, but come up empty. Finley leans down, her breath hitting my neck, causing goose bumps to form, then she whispers in my ear, "Stupid."

Stupid? That's a bad word? "That's a bad word?"

Finley and her brothers all nod. I'm about to apologize when Sam interrupts, and he and Finley start making plans for dinner. After they disappear into the kitchen, I'm left with the alien kids and the LEGOs.

We work together building the ship while Braden continues filling me in on the details of his life. The more minutes pass, the less awkward it feels. But then my phone vibrates in my pocket. The second I glance at the number, my stomach plummets. I excuse myself before stepping out onto the back patio.

CHAPTER 17

Finley

Dad and I head out back, each of us carrying a plate of burgers to grill. The second we step onto the patio, Eddie's voice rings loud and clear from around the side of the house.

"I'm sorry I missed the appointment...of course I'm still planning on signing—things are crazy with my Princeton classes right now. It's not easy to get back to New York."

I open the grill, allowing it to clank loudly to dilute Eddie's voice. Dad follows my lead, lighting the grill and making more noise than necessary.

"...I'd rather you didn't tell her that I haven't signed yet..."

"So," Dad says, obviously wanting to let Eddie have his privacy. "Jason is back."

I groan internally, remembering Summer's embarrassing hijacked call to Jason last week. "Yeah, I know."

"Yes, sir," Eddie says to the person on the phone. "Tuesday night. Princeton alumni center. Got it."

"Anything happening with that?" Dad asks, working hard to ignore Eddie.

"Not sure." I slide the first burger onto the grill and let the sadness and confusion roll over me. What am I not sure about? Jason or me? I don't think we're a factor any more.

Before I have to decide, Eddie comes around the house and onto the patio. He's startled to see us here but hides it well. The color has drained from his face, and his eyes no longer hint at amusement but instead are full of panic.

"What's wrong?" I ask immediately.

He scratches the back of his head, his gaze drifting from me to the pool in the backyard. "Oh…nothing. I'm good. Just had to take a phone call…" Dad and I both hang there, waiting for more, but Eddie forces a grin and points at the pool. "Wow, nice. How deep is it?"

Dad and Eddie begin a lengthy discussion on the inground pool structure while I cook dinner. On the train here, I got super nervous thinking about everything Eddie doesn't know regarding my family. I'm surprised he hasn't asked me more, but maybe this is one of those "treat others as you want to be treated" situations. He's not asking much, because he doesn't want me to ask about his family. Or phone calls that leave him panicked.

Later, after dinner, Eddie and I get roped into hanging decorations in the backyard for the party tomorrow. All *Star Wars*–themed, of course. Eddie seems oddly comfortable, and I'm back to wondering what he hasn't had a chance to sign because he's been so busy with "classes" and who this "her" is. *Forget it, Finley. It's none of your business.* He's just hanging out for the weekend. Nothing more.

"Where do you want the Jedi banner?"

I shake my head and refocus before glancing around the patio, which is now lit by light-saber torches. "Um, I think maybe

here"—I point to the edge of the patio roof that faces the pool—
"but it might be too high to reach without getting out the ladder."

"We can do it." Before I realize what's happening, Eddie hoists
me up onto his shoulder and grabs a roll of tape along with the
banner. His fingers spread deliberately across my stomach, and my
heart picks up speed in response. But when my dad rolls into the
family room, glancing outside, Eddie shifts his hand to a more
polite location on my hip. "I've never had a birthday party with
decorations like this."

"Like what?" I ask, reaching for the post to secure one corner of
the banner. "*Star Wars*–themed? Me either."

Eddie laughs and tightens his grip on me before walking across
the patio to hang the other side. "I mean kid-themed. I can't
even remember a birthday party of mine with kids other than my
older sister."

"Never?" I tape the other corner up, and then Eddie backs up
so we can check out the Jedi sign that reads "Happy 6th Birthday,
Braden and Connor."

"Nope," he confirms. "But I don't remember all my
parties, I guess."

I know very little, but I'm already disturbed by the coldness
of his home. Then Summer's accusations come back, and I work
hard to lump Eddie into the wounded animal category. But when
he sets me down on the ground again, the heat of his body hitting
mine, all I can think about is him gripping me tight after I led
him up to my bedroom the night of the party, his voice quiet and
confident in my ear, telling me to relax, telling me I'm beautiful
and perfect and yeah…

I take a giant step back from him and say as firmly as possible. "We're just—I mean, you're here as my friend. Got it?"

"Got it." The amusement returns to his face. He leans in to add, "Naked friends."

I point a finger at him in warning. "Once. And only once."

"Right. Of course. Gotta be true to the one-night stand club." Eddie lifts an eyebrow, his grin too big and confident.

My dad chooses that moment to open the sliding glass doors and say, "So...I'm assuming you don't need me to get sheets and blankets for the pullout couch?"

I snap around to face Dad, my cheeks probably bright red. "Why not?"

He shrugs. "Just figured Eddie might be staying in your room."

"Dad!" Jesus Christ, why can't he be a normal father and pull out a shotgun at the sight of a boy near me?

He holds up his hands in surrender. "Sorry. Just trying to be cool, you know?"

"Well, stop," I snap. "And yes, sheets. Blankets. Pullout couch. All of that."

After Dad is gone, I glance back at Eddie, expecting more of his teasing, but he looks almost as embarrassed as I am. Maybe even a little anxious. He scratches his head again. "You don't think he heard the naked friend comment, do you?"

I laugh, the humiliation already dimming. "No, he didn't hear you. And even if he did, it wouldn't be a big deal. Unfortunately, he *is* one of those cool dads. Maybe not cool, but realistic. I am eighteen. Not fifteen. And I live on my own now."

An awkward silence falls between us—the problem with

one-night stands, I'm quickly learning—and we both put a bit more distance between us and continue the decorating. When we finally go back inside, my dad and the boys are in bed. I hang back, not wanting to stand close to Eddie now that there's a bed in the family room. Eddie doesn't go near the couch bed either. He strolls past the photos on the wall, stopping at one hanging above the mantel.

"Is this your mom?" Eddie asks. I nod, waiting, knowing what's coming next. Eddie adds, "She doesn't look like you at all."

"Yeah, I know. My mom used to joke all the time that my dad must have been running around on her, since none of her kids look like her." I slide closer to him, assessing the photo of the dark-haired woman. It's been a while since I've really looked at these photos and remembered my mom like this. I'm still staring at the picture, my thoughts elsewhere, when Eddie says, "Was it a car accident?"

I wouldn't say that it's difficult for me talk about it. I've made peace with it, I keep my mom close to me, and I believe in heaven. But whenever I have to explain to someone who doesn't know anything about my family, someone like Eddie who've I've kept things cool and casual with, it's not easy.

Heat rushes to my face. I glance sideways at Eddie for a second and see that he's moved on to one of our last family photos, one where my dad is standing to his full height of six feet two and my brothers are little rubber-necked infants.

I open my mouth to answer Eddie's question but then decide to nod instead. I don't want to hear any emotion in my voice. I don't want to move backward.

"Were you—" Eddie starts.

"No. I was at the studio." I take a breath, surprised by how steady it is. Surprised that saying these details out loud hasn't transported me back to that day. "Connor and Braden were in the car." Worry creases his face, so I add, "They were fine. Barely a scratch."

Eddie turns to face me, his gaze so heavy and intense that I pull in a breath and hold it. "You have her eyes."

I hang on to his gaze, my feet shuffling closer until heat fills the space between us and completely envelops me. My head clouds with a million thoughts—*Who are you, Eddie Wells? What is your story? Why does it seem like you have so much to tell? And why is your mouth so easy to stare at? And why do I want to kiss you so badly?* I can hardly remember kissing him the first time, or maybe I'm refusing to let myself remember, but this only means it would be like the first time again.

My fingers brush lightly on the front of his T-shirt at the same time as his hand drifts over a loose strand of my hair. My eyelids begin to flutter and close, my heart thudding a million beats a minute.

Behind me, a door opens, and I jolt back to reality. Eddie releases a nervous laugh, and I shake my head and back away. "Friends. Just friends."

Both of us pull ourselves back together. Eddie seems to be done with his Belton family inquisition, so I move on to more technical hostess duties.

For a couple minutes, while I'm handing Eddie a towel, pointing out the bathroom, and showing him the path that needs to stay clear for my dad's wheelchair, it does feel friendly. Just friendly. But when I finally close my bedroom door and I'm lying in my bed, my heart's still racing, and my cheeks are still warm.

I bury my face in a pillow and groan loud enough to release some of my frustrations but not enough to alert anyone else.

Summer is right. I'm drawn to the guys who need rescuing. This has to stop. Now.

CHAPTER 18

Finley

I had anticipated one or likely two little boys keeping me from sleeping in this morning, so I'm not too bothered by music waking me up. I roll over in bed, glancing at the clock: 7:10 a.m. Definitely not too early for Connor and Braden to be up. Especially on the day of their birthday party—something that has become a neighborhood affair around here.

I toss back the covers and venture out to the living room to see the twins seated on either side of Eddie on the piano bench. I lean against the doorframe and watch Eddie's fingers fly over the keys—he wasn't kidding when he said he was a piano player. The music book opened in front of him is one of my dad's favorites— *Broadway Belter's Songbook*. He's helped tons of actors land musical roles with these songs over the years, even some who were less than stellar singers.

Conner and Braden are, in fact, belting out the lyrics to "Maybe This Time" while Eddie plays along. Eddie's wearing a bewildered look, but he smiles when he glances over his shoulder and spots me. He lightens his touch on the keys and asks, "Is this too loud? Your dad is still sleeping, right?"

"He'll wake up to his favorite song," I say with a shrug, not wanting to explain that my dad has probably been up for at least two hours. It takes him that long just to use the bathroom and get showered and dressed in the morning, but I know he wouldn't want me to explain that to Eddie.

Eddie returns to playing at full volume while my brothers continue to sing. The longer I stand there, the more animated all three of them become—even Connor, who often uses music as his excuse to speak—and the more I'm laughing.

"Why do they know this song?" Eddie shouts to me.

Dad wheels in and answers, "Because it's in their blood."

I roll my eyes. "Because they've been force-fed show tunes since birth and aren't allowed to listen to the radio."

"It pays the bills, right?" Dad flashes me a grin and then moves closer to Eddie. "You sing too?"

"As little as possible," Eddie says, and my dad laughs.

Dad flips pages in the *Broadway Belter's Songbook* and thus begins a testosterone-fueled show tune jam session. I watch for several minutes, surprised by how at ease Eddie now seems in front of a piano compared to around my dad last night. After a way too loud rendition of "Everything's Coming Up Roses," I retreat to the kitchen to make breakfast. The songs continue on and off for a couple hours until my grandma comes over from next door to get the party food ready and the boys are too wired to stay inside any longer.

"Don't go in the pool until I get out there!" I shout at Braden when he nearly plows me over while I'm carrying their *Star Wars* cake.

Eddie brushes up behind me. "You know, if you give directions using a negative, they only hear 'go in the pool.'"

I stop my life-saving quest to turn and look at Eddie. "Who are you, Dr. Phil?"

"Everyone knows that rule." He flashes me one of his cheeky grins and opens the sliding glass door so I can put the cake outside.

I'm about to tell him exactly what I think of his little rule when my foot catches on the step, and the cake slides from my arms.

My heart jumps up to my throat, but a pair of familiar hands reach out and steady both me and the box. My gaze travels up until it lands on my preppy, polo shirt–wearing ex. My stomach knots, and I'm stuck staring at him and working through too many non-Summer-approved lines in my head until I finally settle on, "Hey…"

CHAPTER 19

Eddie

The preppy crew-cut guy smiles at Finley in that I've-seen-you-naked way, and my eyebrows shoot up.

"That could have been very bad," Finley finally says.

Preppy dude grins. "Where do you want this?"

"Oh…" She looks around like she hasn't planned it all out already—she recited all the table purposes to me last night when we set up. "Uh, over here, I think."

She leads him across the yard to the designated cake table, and I turn to Sam. He leaves me hanging for several seconds, enjoying the power. "Since you and my daughter are just friends, I guess it's not a secret."

"What's not a secret?"

He nods toward the dude in the pink polo. "That's Jason. Finley's high school boyfriend. He lives next door."

"I thought Grandma lived next door?"

Sam points to the house on the right. "Other next door."

"Huh." I step closer to the pool and tug my shirt off. I already promised the quiet twin I'd swim with them. "Convenient."

"Yeah, until they break up and Fin spends nearly a year

hoping it'll work out again." Sam sighs. "I think he might be dating someone and hasn't broken the news to her."

I squint in the sunlight and glance out at Finley, who does in fact resemble a girl wanting the attention of this particular guy. A mix of jealousy and sympathy washes over me. "How long did they date?" I ask Sam.

"Four years."

Four years? Jesus. Wait, I don't have any right to be jealous…right? *Just friends. Definitely not naked friends.*

"Eddie!" Braden shouts. "Do a cannonball!"

I prepare to run and jump in the pool, but Finley breaks eye contact with pretty boy and lifts a hand to stop me. "Be careful where you jump. It's not a wide pool."

I point a finger at her. "Nice job. You used my technique, didn't you?"

While I'm in the pool with the boys, people start showing up. Lots of people. Some are kids, some are high school friends of Finley's, and many are entire families. I can't help looking around and guessing who knew Finley's family when it was still whole, still complete with a mom and a dad who could walk. Maybe everyone knew them back then. Maybe I'm the only one here who had to put the pieces together himself by looking at family photos on the wall. And despite our casual relationship, part of me wants to know more, like what happened when Fin found out about the accident, who was driving, how bad were Sam's injuries? Obviously, he was left in a wheelchair, but he gets around so well and has such a great attitude. But I can tell Finley is past all this; she's had years to digest and accept. It's not fair for me to come in here and drill her for details, just because I'm a little curious. I had a hard enough time asking her the few questions I have asked.

Soon, the pool is packed, and I'm making my way out, grabbing the towel Finley gave me last night. The scent of grilled hot dogs and baked beans is heavy in the air as Sam and Grandma spread food out onto every empty table. I'm about to dry off, grab a plate, and head for the biggest food table. But then a blond in a bright-pink bikini strolls right past me. And not just any blond but the girl I spent the night with less than two weeks ago. My heart picks up speed. I'm so caught off guard by this barely clothed Finley—when did she change?—that I don't notice the tall brunette in platforms heading toward Jason until Sam bumps me from behind and nods in their direction. Worry drifts over his face.

We can't hear what's being said across the yard, but we don't need to hear. Jason introduces the brunette to Fin, whose smile is about as believable as sardine-flavored ice cream at McDonald's. I don't exactly have a solid plan, but I drop my plate onto the table and head across the yard as backup. That mix of jealousy and sympathy returns, only this time, the sympathy is dominant. My hand slides into Finley's, and I give it a squeeze. She snaps around to look at me.

"Hey." I lean in like I'm kissing her cheek and whisper, "Need some help?"

She swallows, her eyes already glossy, but gives me a small nod.

I stick a hand out to Jason. "Eddie Wells."

JULIE CROSS AND MARK PERINI

"Jason…" he says, his gaze darting between me and Fin. He gives the brunette a quick look too. "And this is Zoe. We, uh, go to school together. In Texas."

He brought a girl back from Texas? Definitely a bad sign.

Zoe introduces herself, the southern accent thick and syrupy. I release Finley's hand and slide my fingers across her bare back. She jumps when my hand reaches her hip but covers her surprise by pretending to swat a fly on her stomach.

I lean down—so there are some selfish motives to this rescue mission—and plant a kiss on her bare shoulder. "Your dad is looking for you. Something about needing more ketchup."

"Right." Finley nods, her cheeks bright pink. "Ketchup. I should go take care of that."

Jason's forehead wrinkles. He's still looking at me. "Oh…are you guys—"

"Yes," Finley and I both say together, then she turns around to leave, calling, "Nice meeting you, Chloe."

I follow her inside through the laundry room. "Her name is Zoe, not Chloe."

"I know that." Finley shuts the laundry room door and leans against it, her chest rising and falling rapidly.

I hang back and give her a moment to process, watching her eyes turn glossy all over again. "Fun party, huh?"

She squeezes her eyes shut, and when a couple tears leak out, she swipes them away quickly. "God, I'm an idiot."

"Hey…" I rest my hands on her shoulders. "Don't cry, okay?" I half expect her to fall apart even more—this has happened to me on several occasions when I've said those words to girls at school—but she nods.

"You're right. I need to be okay." She shakes her head. "Or at least give the appearance of okay."

She pushes the door open again and pulls me by the hand outside, lacing our fingers together. I open my mouth to question the deliberate touching—you know, 'cause we aren't naked friends anymore—but Finley turns to me and says, "Good thing I brought a hot model as my date for the party, right?"

I stop, holding both of us in place. "Wait, I'm not—I mean—"

"Not what? A model? Yes, you are. We did Marc Jacobs together." Finley lifts an eyebrow, challenging me. "What else are you, Eddie Wells? A college student? A guy who sleeps on people's balconies?"

"That was only one time," I point out. But her question sinks in further than I expect it to. She's right. I'm not at Princeton for the summer intensive, and I don't want to be there in the fall. I sure as hell don't want to be a model for very long. I don't even really want to be one right now. I hadn't even planned on telling anyone about it, that's for damn sure. I've been so focused on the immediate, on fixing the shit storm I created months ago and not becoming my father that I haven't really let myself figure out what I do want to become.

"Relax," Fin says, breaking me out of my own head. "I'm not going to say anything you don't want me to."

I force a grin and let my gaze wander slowly over her. "Good thing I brought a hot model as my date..."

"Cute." Finley rolls her eyes, but she smiles, which is much better than the tears in the laundry room. "Obviously, we know so much about each other."

Jason is watching us from across the backyard. I lean close to Finley and whisper, "I know plenty about you. I know you have a mole right here"—I brush my thumb over her hip and slip it under the material of her swimsuit—"and that you're ticklish here…" I slide my fingers down her spine to the lowest part of her back. Her eyes meet mine, and she holds my gaze, distracted from our previous conversation.

I'm about to share a few more details I acquired from our one night together, but two little kids with squirt guns run between us. She narrows her eyes at me, pointing an accusatory finger. "No more of that Mr. Smooth Guy stuff."

I snort back a laugh. Mr. Smooth Guy? That is so not me. But I guess Finley wouldn't know that. She only knows Eddie Wells, model, mysterious guy with secret reasons for escaping the hold of his wealthy family.

Okay, so I sound like a douche. Great.

CHAPTER 20

Finley

"You okay?"

I drop the wet towel I'd been folding, startled by my dad's appearance behind me. "Yeah, why?"

Dad's gaze follows mine as he looks through the sliding glass doors out at the back patio and pool.

My face flushes, and I make a bad attempt at covering the fact that I was just staring at Eddie. More specifically, Eddie pulling himself out of the pool, preparing to take another turn in the cannon-ball contest he's entered with my brothers, despite it being dark out now and the last guest having left an hour ago. I opted out of leaving with some of my friends, going out with them. They looked a little too eager to rehash the Jason-has-a-new-love thing and way too curious about Eddie for me to survive lying through that type of inquisition. And it would be lying. Because we're not really a thing.

"Do it again!" Braden shouts while treading water in the deep end.

"Jason," Dad prompts. "And his plus one. How are you taking it?"

The hurt and confusion from earlier today returns. "Right. That."

"Let me ask you this." Dad's wearing one of his rare serious expressions. "What did you expect to happen today when you saw Jason again?"

I sink down into the family room chair and sigh. "I don't know. I just thought maybe…"

"Maybe he'd be here for you?" he finishes when I can't.

I shake my head, still not sure. "Not exactly. Just that it would be okay if he was here for me. But he wasn't. He's not."

"Because it's over?"

I nod and force myself to say those words out loud. "Because it's over."

Dad pats my knee, his familiar silly grin returning. "Well done, honey. Tomorrow, we'll move on to phase two."

"Phase two?" I wait for him to answer, but Connor and Braden open the sliding door, both dripping wet.

"Fin, we have to do our thing." Braden tugs at my hand.

Connor has a big blanket in his arms. I can barely see his face behind it. "Yeah, our thing…remember?"

It takes me a few seconds to recall last summer when the boys turned five. We'd laid in the grass after their party, staring at the stars while I made up stories about moms who went to live as princesses in the sky while they watched over their family. It wasn't easy for me to talk about my mom like that—she is very real to me and very fantastical to my brothers—but I could tell it was important to them. So I told them it could be a birthday tradition, as in once a year. I never thought they'd remember.

Eddie appears by the door, dripping wet, a towel around his waist. "Is it time for the thing? I heard it's time."

I crack a smile. Guess it's time for the thing.

··◆··

Connor is passed out, curled up against my side, and Braden is snoring with his head down by my feet and his feet kicking my stomach lightly.

Beside Braden, Eddie tucks an arm behind his head and yawns. "No offense, but I think the 'princess turned accountant keeping count of all the unauthorized stars' story was a bit of a snooze. For them, of course. I was enthralled by it."

I reach across my brother's feet and smack Eddie lightly in the chest. "Yeah, it was the story that put them to sleep. Not the fact that it's three hours past bedtime and they swam for most of the day."

"Okay, maybe that contributed."

I return to lying back and staring up at the sky, enjoying the calm rhythm of four different breaths mingling together, the warmth of Connor and Braden's bodies serving as a blanket, and the softness of the actual blanket beneath us. I follow a path of stars, connecting one bright-white dot to another until I'm practically in a trance.

"Your necklace," Eddie says, and my fingers immediately land on the cross against my chest. "Is that—I mean, do you—are you like…"

"Religious?" I suggested. "A little. My family is Catholic. I believe in God. Heaven and hell. I believe things happen for a reason often involving a higher power. But it's not something I think about often." Mostly just when I think about my mom and where she is now.

Eddie nods like this makes sense to him. "I have a friend who's Catholic. It's like that for her too."

I want to ask more, ask about this mysterious female friend of Eddie's and exactly what he means by it "being like that for her too," but then I decide the comfortable silence we've been in is more appealing right now. And for a few minutes, that's exactly where we end up.

"Jason asked me how we met," Eddie says.

The cool night air along with the scent of grass and sound of tree frogs returns. I turn my head away from the sky and look at Eddie. "What did you tell him?"

His way-too-intense blue eyes meet mine. "I told him we met at a party."

"The truth." I turn back to the sky, surprised at how simple that answer became. "I'm not usually this pathetic—"

"I don't think you're pathetic," Eddie says, his voice low and filled with depth that I'm certain now is keeping me coming back for more.

"It's just been confusing for me. Last summer, things were okay with us, but then he got more and more distant and…" I clear my throat, determined to be cool about this. "Anyway, I haven't seen him since we broke up."

Eddie starts humming an unfamiliar tune and then eventually adds lyrics that are ridiculous and all about "The Boy Next Door." I laugh so hard, my entire body is shaking. "Of course. You're hot, you play the piano, *and* you can sing. No wonder my dad has such a crush on you."

"Just your dad?" Eddie wiggles his eyebrows. "Who was that girl staring at me while I climbed out of the pool?"

"My insane twin who often makes poor dating choices." The grin falls from his face, and he closes his eyes. Guilt washes over me. "Not that you're a bad choice—"

"I'm definitely a bad choice." Eddie rolls over and looks up at the sky. I stay silent, waiting for him to explain, but instead, he changes the subject. "Earlier, when you said that thing about me being a model and basically nothing else—"

"I didn't mean it like that," I argue.

"No, you were right. I spent so much time trying to fix—trying to not be something, that now, I don't know what I want to do. Is that weird?" He looks at me again, like my answer is super important to him. "Typical rich kid whining about Dad's plans for him, right?"

"I don't think that at all." I shake my head. "I was supposed to spend the year figuring out my life plan, but now it's summer again, and I haven't applied to any colleges. I'm getting some jobs but not a ton. And what I really want to do is—"

I stop myself before admitting the truth. But Eddie hangs on this, propping up on one elbow. "What?"

For a second, I want to tell him the truth, but I hold it in and instead say, "Find a nice boring boyfriend with stability who won't need me to save him from himself."

Eddie lifts an eyebrow. "Boring, huh? That's your type?"

The dozen or so times he found an excuse to touch me this afternoon come rolling back. Even with little boy feet and two tiny bodies between us, I feel like his hands are everywhere all at once. "Yep, that's my type. Boring and predictable and every synonym for those two words."

"That's understandable." Eddie slides closer and leans over me.

My heart picks up speed, my body betraying our just-friends clause. "Good, because I would hate for you to get the wrong idea. I mean, your show tune knowledge and cannonball skills alone are enough to…"

Eddie picks up a lock of my hair. Slowly, he slides it between his fingers. "You're not my type either. Too pretty. Too nice. Too smart. Too perfect. I'd hate to go after someone I could actually fall for…"

I'm sure he can hear my heart; it's so loud. Each beat feels like a million seconds happen between it, and the world around us moves in slow motion. My gaze shifts from Eddie's hand in my hair to his face as it moves closer and closer—

Dad clears his throat, and Eddie jumps, scooting so far from me, he's hanging off the blanket now. "Just came out here to see if my kids were ready for bed."

Eddie hops up to his feet to help but can't seem to make eye contact with Dad. "I got this."

Dad and I both watch him scoop Connor up off the blanket so carefully he barely stirs. There's a moment where Eddie looks down at my dad, and I can sense what he's thinking, that he can't carry his own kid to bed and how bad that must suck, but luckily, he keeps the sympathetic looks to himself and asks, "You want one?"

Dad reaches out to take Connor. "Sure."

Eddie repeats the careful picking up with Braden, then he strides across the yard and is inside before Dad has had a chance to figure out how to wheel himself and keep Connor, who is slumped against him, asleep. He nods in Eddie's direction and then glances at me. "So what's his story?"

I sit up. "What do you mean?"

"He's neither here nor there." Dad shifts Connor so he's securely on his lap and then rolls forward a few feet. "He lied about being away at college to someone. He ignores calls and stresses every time he gets one."

"How do you know that?" I eye him suspiciously. It's not like my dad to judge or make assumptions about people.

Dad shrugs. "I've kept an eye on him."

Before I can chastise him for spying on Eddie, he rolls toward the house and up the ramp leading inside. I lay back again, staring at the sky, but this time, I'm shifting around pieces of a puzzle called Eddie Wells, trying to find a shape or picture to them.

A couple minutes later, a warm body stretches out beside me. "Braden woke up when I put him in his bed. Apparently, it was Connor's bed."

"He likes to sleep near the window," I say, still distracted by Dad's questions.

We return to lying on the blanket, but the absence of two six-year-olds makes this a very different activity. After a few minutes, Eddie speaks again. "Your dad is worried about me, isn't he? He heard me lie about Princeton?"

I shrug and fake disinterest. "It's none of his business. Or mine."

"Yeah, okay." Eddie releases a breath and turns to face me but instead rolls onto his back again. "It's just that…I'm trying to—I need to do something, and it's something I told people I wouldn't do—"

"What people?"

"My family," Eddie admits. "And some really good friends. One really good friend who needs me right now, and I'm not there."

I don't know why he's telling me all this now. It doesn't help answer any of my questions about him. Plus, it's too vague to offer advice.

"You don't have to say anything," Eddie adds after I'm silent for way too long. "I just want you to know that I'm not running away from shit. I'm kind of doing the opposite. Only, I don't know…" He sinks back again, deep in thought.

I scoot closer and lean over him. "None of that sounds either boring or predictable. Which means my instincts about you were right."

I reach out a hand to smooth his hair again, but he catches it in his and brings it to his lips. Heat spreads from my wrist up my arm. His eyes lock with mine. "Finley?"

"Yeah." I breathe out the word, too afraid of hearing excitement in my voice.

"It's okay if you like me." Eddie slides a hand up my arm, over my shoulder, until it rests on the back of my neck. "It doesn't have to change everything. It doesn't make you weak. Or whatever else Summer called you."

"It doesn't?" I whisper.

Slowly, Eddie shakes his head. "No, it doesn't. Even if I'm a mess and completely wrong for you. And even if you're super sweet and not up for what I'm dealing with…I still might like you anyway."

"Yeah?" I lean in closer just as Eddie releases my hand and touches my cheek instead. Instead of answering, both of his hands shift to my face, and he brings me closer until my lips touch his.

For a second, I try to recall our first kiss, the night we met, after I'd dragged him up to my room, but I come up empty. Other moments from that night are vivid, but this one is fuzzy. But right now is so crystal clear and moving in slow motion that I know I won't forget anything.

And the world becomes this kiss, and this kiss becomes two kisses and then three. Soon, I'm lying beneath Eddie, his hand in my hair, his mouth against my neck. He shifts from being over me to beside me, and then the same fingers I watched flying over the piano keys this morning move slowly, torturously, beneath my dress. I close my eyes and do nothing but feel. Everything. All of it.

"I'm not...we can't..." Eddie mumbles, his breath as quick and jagged as mine. "Not with your dad right there."

As if in answer to that, the outside lights flicker off. Eddie jolts up, glancing around. I close my eyes again and laugh before hooking my fingers around his neck and bringing him closer. "Relax. He's not going to come out here."

"Yeah, but he knows we're here." Nerves leak into Eddie's voice.

I smooth a hand over the back of his hair and open my eyes. "And normally that would keep him from turning the lights out. He's giving us privacy." The stiffness that's taken over his body doesn't let up, so I pull myself up enough for our lips to touch. "Just kiss me, okay?"

So he does. Long and slow and perfect.

But eventually, Eddie pulls away, his forehead resting against mine, both of us breathing hard. "This is the last thing I need right now."

I slide my hand up his back. "Me too."

"But if I didn't have to—" Eddie stops and shuts his eyes. "If things were different…you would be exactly right. For me."

I try to shove away the questions that rise from that statement, the longing I'm feeling, wanting it to be true.

Oh God, I do like him.

"Hey…" Warm fingers touch my face. "You okay? Want to stop?"

I look up at him. His dark eyes are now full of concern. "I can't remember… Do you remember—that night after the party—do you remember kissing me?"

"Yeah." Eddie exhales, looking relieved. "You were standing by your nightstand, holding the drawer open, rambling about condoms and brand names and the product reviews you read on Amazon—"

I squeeze my eyes shut. "Damn. I did do that, didn't I?"

"You did." He smiles. "And then I kissed you, because I was so taken by our compatibility. I, too, have an addiction to reading product reviews."

I flop onto my back and groan. "Why are you so adorable?"

His forehead wrinkles. "Is that a good or bad thing?"

"It's terrible," I lie.

He stretches out beside me. "How about I tell you every single thing about me until you're so repulsed and turned off, we can easily part ways?"

Even while saying this, he's doing more adorable things, like gently pulling me toward him until my head is on his shoulder and my palm over his heart.

Yeah, this sucks. Completely.

CHAPTER 21

Eddie

I open the door to Finley's dad's car, step outside, and lift my sunglasses to get a better look at the old building in front of me. It's a Victorian-style place, brown with pink trim. A rotted wooden sign sits tilted in front: *Belton Academy of Dance, Music, and Acting.* "Is this—" I start.

"My parents' studio," Finley finishes. "Well, it was anyway."

She strides toward the door, and I follow much farther behind. We're supposed to be picking up steaks to grill for dinner tonight. Finley glances over her shoulder and stops when she sees me lagging behind her. "Come on, I want to show you the inside."

There's a "for sale" sign out front, and that has me moving even slower. The last thing I need right now is breaking and entering charges.

Finley reads my mind. "The real estate agent is my dad's best friend. He gave me the combination."

I relax a bit and watch her expertly open the lock box and retrieve the key. "You come here often?"

She just shrugs and holds the door open for me. Through

the doors is a narrow hallway leading to a lobby. A staircase—clearly no wheelchair access in this old building—in the lobby leads to the basement, where the two dance studios sit. The larger room has an upright piano, not as nice as the one at Fin's house, but still decent. Mirrors cover two entire walls, and ballet barres fill the other two. I sit down on the piano bench. I'm still not sure what we're doing here. "Let me guess, you stuffed those pointe shoes from the Prada shoot in your purse?"

She blushes and shakes her head. "Nope." But then she pulls out a worn pair from the bag on her shoulder. "These fit me much better."

I laugh—I can't help it. "So we're here to practice."

While she puts her shoes on, I entertain myself playing around on the piano. Mechanically, my mind chooses a classical piece, and for a moment, I'm transported back five years to some stuffy, rich old people party my parents forced me to attend. My mother then forced me to play the piano for all her rich friends. *Something Beethoven or Bach*, she'd said as if she knew anything about music. Someone had mentioned having a friend at the Juilliard School to my dad, and he'd marched right over and put a stop to me playing, which had been fine by me.

I shake off the memory and switch to playing something lively, less classical and more blues feel. But I quickly become distracted by Finley warming up.

"Doesn't that hurt?" I ask when she stands on the very top of her toes.

"Yeah," she admits. "But mostly because my feet aren't as tough as they used to be. I've got to get them worked out more." She drops back down and turns to face me. "What was that song you were just playing?"

I shrug. "I don't know. I think it's part of something I heard once and a little improv."

"Improv?" She lifts an eyebrow. "Like you just made it up?"

"Sort of. I mean, it's jazz, so that's part of the style." I don't know why, but this discussion embarrasses me. Maybe because it's too much fun for me to play like that to have it critiqued and turned into something, well, not fun.

"Please don't tell my dad about your jazz ability. He'll dig up his saxophone and turn the living room into a lounge, full of cigar smoke," Fin says, and I laugh. She sifts through her bag before setting sheet music in front of me. "Can you play this?"

"*Don Quixote.*" I've actually seen this ballet. Fell asleep in act three, if I remember correctly.

I play through the music a couple times and then when I begin the third time, I look up, and she's dancing, expertly moving through choreography that really connects with the music. My fingers fumble, distracted by her, and I have to refocus. I get stuck halfway through, unable to turn the page quickly enough, and Finley stops to catch her breath.

"I'm out of shape," she says, though she really doesn't look that winded.

I angle myself on the bench to face her. "Why aren't you dancing instead of modeling?"

She hesitates before answering, her gaze focused on her feet. "I stopped ballet several years ago, when the studio closed."

I gesture at her ballet shoes. "Obviously, you haven't."

"I hadn't danced, not in pointe shoes anyway," she admits, "until last week at that photo shoot with Summer." Finley shakes her head. "But I don't want to dance professionally. I used to when I was younger, but now I want to teach. Here. I want to reopen this dance studio. For my mom."

Silence falls between us; obviously, this is a bigger deal than I realized. I don't know what it's like for her, losing her mom. I mean, I kind of hate my parents, so it would be different for me.

My gaze drifts from Fin to the sheet music. "Again?"

She nods, and I'm relieved to have something to do. I stumble a lot less with the music this time, but my head's a mess, knowing she's shared this big secret with me, she's trusted me with a part of her that's far from basic casual information. I want to run, and at the same time, I want to take advantage of being alone with this beautiful girl who is possibly the nicest person I've ever met. When Finley makes her way closer to me, close enough to reach, I hook an arm around her waist, pulling until she's sitting on my lap.

Her face heats, but she smiles at me. "I was wondering how long it would take you to realize that we're alone."

I lean down to press my lips against her neck. "You really are trying to ditch the good girl image, aren't you?"

She stiffens in my arms, alarmed by this reminder. I want to tell her that she's got me all wrong. I'm not the smooth guy with all the right lines she's imagined, but part of me likes the confidence that comes with this misrepresentation.

"On second thought..." Finley presses a hand to my chest

and pushes up to her feet again. She's out of my reach in two seconds flat. "I like you better playing piano."

I glance at the piano keys in front of me and sigh. "You're probably the only one."

CHAPTER 22

Finley

"You didn't even look at this!" I hold the pool catalog up for my dad to see. "Even Grandma thinks we need an alarm. Our cover isn't secure at all."

"I'll look at it later." Dad plops the last of the dinner dishes into the sink and grins at me. "Let's talk about your friend, Eddie. Has the title shifted to something different?"

My cheeks burn, so I drop my gaze to the catalog and flip the pages quickly. "I don't know."

"Right. 'Cause friends usually make out in their backyard for an entire hour."

I launch the pool accessory book across the kitchen but miss hitting him with it. Then I glance out the window to see if Eddie's still outside with the boys. His shirtless silhouette pops into view, along with two smaller ones on either side of him. "It's complicated, okay?"

He holds his hands up in surrender. "Fine. I'll leave you alone."

I give a satisfied nod. "Thank you."

"It's just—" Dad stops abruptly when I toss him a look that says *What now?* He lowers his voice and continues. "Listen, it's not something I'd normally get involved in. It's just that I saw him looking up a phone number online this morning. Robert Lowman Esq., trust fund specialist."

"Jesus, Dad. Seriously?" I attempt to hide the curiosity from my voice, but I doubt he's fooled.

He wheels closer to me and drops his voice even more. "I just want to make sure you're safe—you're still my baby girl. He could be in trouble, Fin. He could be into gambling or drugs?"

Well, I already know that Eddie's in a hurry to make money based on his recent and seemingly secret modeling career. I replay the anxious look he had worn when he mentioned sticking around his apartment this weekend with his drug party roommates. Somehow, I doubt drugs are the cause of Eddie's secretive behavior. But gambling? I guess it's possible. Maybe he's trying to hide his debt from his family by working it off.

"I know that he's got some secrets, but I don't think it's anything dangerous or illegal." Of course, I have some reservations. I'm just trying to put it all together in my head. Or to not put it together. Let it go. That could be the best option. But why would he need to contact a trust fund specialist?

"Don't trust funds usually kick in at twenty-one?" I ask. "Eddie's only eighteen."

"I think they can be set up any way you want." Dad shrugs. "And both gambling and drug circles aren't unheard of with kids from boarding schools like Eddie's. He's a legacy. They have all kinds of secret societies, and it's just expected that they join and do whatever the group is doing."

It all sounds so dramatic. I sneak another peek out the window at Eddie, watching him run a hand through his messy, wet hair. His swim trunks dip dangerously low, and he tugs them up the second he notices. Connor and Braden shout to Eddie, persuading him to do another dive. Instead of following orders, he makes a big show of leaning against a chair, pretending to be too busy picking his nose. Both my brothers collapse into giggles on the pool deck.

He doesn't seem like a trust fund legacy guy who lives for secret societies, drugs, and gambling. But what the hell do I know?

"I'm not trying to totally freak you out," Dad tells me, despite all the hypotheticals he's brought up. "But I'm usually a pro at reading kids Eddie's age. They're never as mysterious to me as they think they are."

"Except him," I point out, earning a careful nod from Dad. "You're probably right. He's got a bookie who's about to add him to a hit list, and now we're involved. We probably shouldn't leave him alone with the boys."

Dad lets me leave the kitchen and head outside without another word. I don't know what to believe. Maybe that's the point. Maybe the risk is not caring either way. Sometimes, people deserve a chance to be taken at face value. Without the past or future hanging over them.

"Fin, make Eddie show us another back dive!" Braden demands when he sees me. "I wanna learn!"

Eddie straightens up, looking concerned. "Remember, you promised me you wouldn't try it without me here?"

"Yeah, yeah," Braden concedes. "Cracked heads. Bloody guts everywhere."

Yet another mental image to keep me up at night.

"Hey, guys," I say more to Eddie than my brothers. "We have to get going soon. Eddie can't do back dives for you all night."

A chorus of disappointed noooos ensues, but Eddie does one more back dive and then heads inside to change. Shortly after, we're sitting on the train back to Penn Station.

The quiet, the lack of constant activity we've had all weekend, is unnerving.

Eddie's leaned against the window, looking like he might fall asleep any second but also like he's trying hard not to. The backpack resting at his feet has a big wet spot on the side where he most likely shoved his swimsuit. I'm about to reach in and pull it out, hang it on the empty seat in front of us to dry, but then I hear Summer's voice again, calling me a mama bear and telling me I can't help falling for guys who…what? Need help keeping their clothes dry? Would I not know what to do with a guy who had it all figured out? Someone who knew how to keep his clean laundry clean or how to sleep outside without getting bug bites? I'd like to think that's not true, that I would be fine with someone who didn't need my help all the time, but what if it is true? This has psychological disorder written all over it.

Instead of focusing on my issues, I impulsively decide to bug Eddie about his. I tap him on the knee and wait for him to look at me before blurting out, "Do you have a gambling problem?" Probably a bit too loud for the silent train.

"Huh?" His forehead wrinkles, and he sits up straight again. "What?"

A woman across the aisle glances at us and then looks away.

Embarrassed, I lower my voice. "A gambling problem," I repeat. It sounds even more silly the second time.

"Gambling, like betting on shit? Like playing blackjack in Atlantic City?" Eddie scratches his head. "I'm not sure what you mean."

"Any of that," I say, knowing already that it's not true. "Did you lose a bunch of money and you owe it to someone?"

"No." He seems to contemplate this for a beat, then says, "Besides, don't you have to be twenty-one to get into casinos?"

"Yeah, I think so." I sink back into my chair, wishing I hadn't brought it up. "Forget I mentioned it."

"No problem." He goes back to leaning against the window, but I can feel his eyes on me. "It's complicated, isn't it?"

"What?" I ask, even though I know exactly what he means.

Eddie hooks a finger around my pinkie. "This. You and me."

Something about the openness of his expression—like I could say anything, and he wouldn't stop holding my finger with his—causes all the feelings I've been stuffing away this weekend to resurface. "It's more than complicated. It's irrational."

"Completely," Eddie agrees, and he turns to face forward, appearing to be deep in thought. "But it's not complicated if it's just this. You know? Like this weekend. Like bumping into each other at a party. Like...I don't know, just this."

I get what he's saying, and it's both disheartening and a relief. What he told me the other night, about it being okay for me to like him, is true. And there's no rule that says that we both have to rearrange our lives because we had a fun weekend together. Because I showed him my secret place and told him things I'm afraid to tell my own father. It felt good to talk about it. It felt good to kiss Eddie the other night, under the stars with no intent of thinking too far ahead. It felt good and empowering to take Eddie up to my room that night we met at the party. In truth, none of this has been bad. I could make it that way if I wanted.

Or I could just let him keep holding my hand and enjoy the remaining forty-five minutes of this train ride.

My long silence, my body relaxing against the seat again, provided enough of a response for Eddie. He sinks farther into his own seat, gives my hand a squeeze, and says, "We're good?"

I manage a small smile. "Yeah, we're good."

The tension that had sat in the air between us is gone, and the rest of the trip flies. Both of us spend the time checking our schedules and spilling about what jobs we're doing this week. When we finally walk back into our apartment building, I try to think of something important to say.

I'm about to put my key in the door when Eddie drops his hands to my hips, slides me over, and turns me around. My heart gives two quick beats in response, and all I can think about is Eddie's mouth getting closer and closer to mine. I reach up and take his face in my hands, pulling until our lips finally collide. His fingers skim my sides, my hips, my legs, then slip under the back of my shirt.

After I don't know how long, I pull away from him, my eyes still closed. "Why are you so good at this?"

Eddie laughs and touches his forehead to mine. "So maybe we'll bump into each other again? Sometime soon?"

Those are the words I'd been digging for and couldn't form.

"Yeah, maybe," I say, still out of breath.

He kisses me again, quick but lingering, reluctant to release me. And then I watch him walk down the hall, and for the first time, I think, *What if we never bump into each other again? Are either of us going to decide to walk over to the other person's door? On purpose? With a purpose?* All we've done so far is decide not to run into each other, and it's happened anyway.

What if I want it to happen? Will that ruin everything?

CHAPTER 23

Eddie

Two weeks ago, when Finley kissed me in front of her apartment door after I spent the weekend with her family, I'd thought, *How long until this happens again?* And ever since, I've been counting everything.

The number of stairs between her floor and mine: 82
The number of jobs I've done without her: 9
The number of times I've "bumped" into her: 7
The number of times that was accidental: 1

So of course, when my phone rings, and her name is on the screen, my heart jumps up to my throat, and I immediately think, *Number of times she's called me prior to right now: 0.*

I've just walked into "the apartment"—I refuse to attach "my" to this hellhole—after a long day of shooting for Alexander Wang. I glance around, relieved it's empty, before answering the call.

"Eddie?" a voice asks. Not Finley. A kid. "Hi, Eddie!"

"Hey, who is this?" I ask, even though I have a pretty good idea.

"Braden." His voice is muffled like he's moving around too much to keep the phone in the right place or he's got it upside down. "What are you doing?"

"I'm—well, I'm—" Checking around my apartment for roommates who may have OD'd. Thinking a little too much about your sister. "Just hanging out. What are you doing?"

And speaking of your sister...

"Want to come to our swim meet?" Braden blurts out. "I'm doing a relay, and Connor is too, and we get ribbons even if we lose."

I work hard to avoid saying *huh?* or *what?* "A swim meet? Right now?"

"No, tomorrow," Braden clarifies, like I should know this already. I hear Connor saying something in the background. "Right now, we're watching the policeman in the window—"

"Braden, where's Fin?"

"Connor, look! The taxi guy is yelling at the policeman. Eddie, can he go to jail for that?"

"I don't know..." I spin in a circle until my gaze fixes on the window. Outside, I can clearly see a uniformed officer. I move closer, craning my neck to the side, and sure enough, there's a cab driver with practically his entire upper body hanging out the window, fist waving in the air. His front tire is up on the curb, pressed against a fire hydrant. "Are you guys in Finley's apartment?" Are they alone?

"Duh," Braden says. "We're on her phone."

Obviously, we're getting nowhere with this phone call. "Hey, Braden...I'm gonna knock on the door in a minute. Ask who it is, and then, if it's me, open the door, okay?"

"'Kay," he says and adds, "Wait, you mean one minute like sixty seconds or one minute like when Dad is watching grown-up shows and we're not allowed in the den and he says one minute but then it's dark out—"

"Count to thirty, okay?" I head out the door and down the hall, taking the stairs two at time. I'm a little out of breath when I knock on the door.

"Who is it?" I hear Braden ask both through the door and the phone.

"Eddie."

After lots of rattling, the door finally opens, and sure enough, two little blond boys are standing in Finley's living room. It's weird to see them here, outside of their playroom or backyard pool.

"Did someone open the door—" The bathroom door flies open, and Finley steps out, gripping a towel tight around her, her hair dripping wet. She sees me and lets out a yelp, then clutches her chest, probably after recognizing me. "What the he—heck?" She narrows her eyes at her brothers. "Did you guys open the door? I told you never to do that."

Braden points a finger at me. "Eddie told us to."

I hold up my phone. "They called me. I thought they were alone."

"I was in the shower." Finley stalks over to Braden and snatches her phone from him. "For, like, two minutes. Obviously, that was too long."

While Finley gets dressed, leaving her bedroom door open a crack, she explains that her dad is sick and her grandparents brought the boys here to have lunch with her and go to the zoo, and she wanted to keep them overnight, but she's just got a call about a very last-minute casting.

"Want me to hang out here with them?" I ask.

Finley reopens her bedroom door, wearing a white sundress that makes her skin look tan and the freckles on her shoulders stand out. She's frantically pulling a brush through her wet hair. "I can just bring them along. I'm sure they can sit somewhere and wait."

"I'm done with work for the day," I tell her. "I don't mind hanging out with them."

She hesitates, looking me over like I'm a stranger at an interview. "But there's a possibility I might have to stay longer and do a fitting if they like me, and I don't know when that would be done."

"All the more reason to *not* take the kids with you," I point out.

"Yeah, okay," she says slowly, then looks me over again. "Are you sure? They haven't had dinner, and this place can feel really small after an hour or so—"

To prove her point, Connor stands on the coffee table and launches himself toward the couch. "Cannonball!"

I catch him midjump, before he completely misses the furniture, and toss him over my shoulder. "I'm sure. Now go finish getting ready. We're fine."

I'm not sure if we're fine or not, but it feels right, helping Finley out for a change. But she does have a point about this apartment being small in comparison to the house her brothers live in with two different living rooms, a big backyard, and lots of room to run.

I grab every breakable item in sight and put it up as high as possible while the blow-dryer runs in Finley's bedroom. Ten minutes later, she joins us again. Her hair is dry and flowing down her shoulders, and her lips are shiny with lip gloss. She crosses the living room in a few long strides and turns on the TV, flipping through the channels until a cartoon appears.

"They'll watch this show for hours," she says. "That should keep them busy."

Both boys sink into the couch and stare, mesmerized, at the cartoon.

Finley stands in front of me, scrolling through her phone, looking worried all over again. "You've got my number, right? I'll text you my dad's number too and my grandparents'..."

I give her a good once-over. "You look nice."

"Nice?" She wrinkles her nose. "Maybe I should change?"

"No," I protest. "You look perfect."

She does.

"Perfect like perfectly sweet?" Finley asks. "Or perfect like wild and sinfully perfect?"

"Both," I say right away. Definitely both.

Her face flushes, but she seems pleased with my answer. She turns to her brothers, who barely acknowledge her now that the TV is on. "Be good, okay? And try not to...you know, move or anything."

She heads for the door but stops to ask me again if I've got my phone on and charged. Finally, she leaves, probably late for her casting. After I lock the door behind her, I pick up the remote and shut the TV off. I recently read an article about kids' TV programs causing hyperactivity. It seemed like a valid enough argument, so I figure it's not worth the risk.

"Hey..." Connor and Braden both say, returning to planet earth at the elimination of the overstimulating TV show.

"What happened?" Braden asks.

I hold my hands up like I have no idea. "Probably too many people are watching TV in the building. I think it turns off so all the TVs don't explode."

They look disappointed but accept my answer. We go on an apartment-wide hunt for games of any kind. Which means I walk around shutting the door to Summer's designer-filled bedroom and Elana and crazy French Mama's tidy room with two neatly made twin beds pushed against opposite walls. The boys tear through Finley's room. I quickly figure out that knitting needles are way too close to weapons, makeup can be mistaken for finger paints, Finley has made a hobby out of writing business plans and researching mortgage loans, and she collects college applications but leaves them all mostly blank.

While saving a stack of papers from a glass of water that got knocked over, I also discover that she has eighteen grand stuffed into a savings account. I dry the wet carpet with a towel and try to erase that last bit of information from my memory. Is she really going to do what she said she would? Reopen her parents' studio?

I put her room back in order and herd the boys out of there.

I'm almost ready for the TV to have a miraculous recovery when I spot a five-thousand-piece NYC skyline puzzle on top of the refrigerator.

"That's too many pieces," Braden argues. "We can't do it."

"Yeah, probably not." I pretend to examine the box closely. "It says ages eight and up. You guys are only six, right? You're not old enough to do this puzzle."

Braden folds his arms over his chest and stares me down. "We can too! We're against eight-year-olds at the meet tomorrow."

Connor nods along with his brother and then tugs on my shorts, trying to get me to hand over the box.

"You guys sure you wanna try it? It's really hard…"

That seems to clinch the deal. We get to work sorting pieces by color at the kitchen table, and then I let them spread out different sections of the puzzle on the kitchen floor. Seeing the pieces spread all over the tile floor gives me another idea. One of my nannies used to tape parchment paper to the floor and let me draw pictures. I dig through drawers until I find a roll of paper and some masking tape. Soon, we've got sheets of parchment for each section of the puzzle and the boys are using crayons they brought to sketch the outline of each building before searching for the pieces.

We're all so busy working, none of us notices the sun setting until it's nearly dark in the apartment. I go around flipping lights and check my phone for yet another text from Finley. She's sent me twenty already. One message to tell me that she is staying later for the fitting, and nineteen other messages to give me additional directions and ask how the boys are doing.

ME: So I shouldn't offer them some of that tequila under the sink with dinner?
FINLEY: Not funny.
ME: Braden wants to know if he can have the box of sugar cubes from the pantry. Also, how do they take their coffee?

I'm elbow deep into making what was supposed to be grilled cheese sandwiches until I discovered the lack of cheese in the fridge and has turned into grilled PB&J when the front door opens and Summer walks in, several shopping bags dangling from her hands.

She takes in the kitchen mess, puzzle pieces everywhere, kids drawing on the floor, and a look of disgust takes over her features. "That's it. First the French Mama invasion, and now we're apparently offering preschool. I'm moving."

She stomps off to her room and slams the door. The boys look at me, and I just shrug and go back to cooking.

I cut the crusts off the sandwiches at Connor's request. I figure he doesn't ask for much, so the crust thing must be pretty important to him. I watch them carefully while they examine the sandwich and practically dare each other to take a bite. They turn out to be a hit, because they're devoured in minutes. "Which one are we in?" Braden asks, pointing to the puzzle box with the skyline picture.

I carry all the dishes to the sink and load them into the dishwasher. "I don't think it's in the picture."

He's still looking at the photo, trying to find this building, so I dry my hands and point to the very bottom of the puzzle.

"This is mostly the Central Park skyline. If the picture kept going south"—I trace my finger several inches below where the photo ends—"then we would be somewhere around here."

Both boys lean in closer. Braden touches his finger to a building on the Upper West Side. "Who lives here?"

"A guy who owns a really big bank," I say. "He has his own helicopter."

"Cool," Braden says, then Connor points to another building, signaling for Braden to ask, "Who lives here?"

"Madonna. Do you know who that is?" The boys shake their heads, and I keep going with the geography-pop-culture lesson. "Steven Spielberg lives there…he makes movies."

I hesitate before touching another not-so-tall Upper West Side building. "And my family lives here."

"Wow." Braden studies the photo and then asks, "What does your family make?"

I stare at the home I haven't been to for weeks. "Money."

They both shrug as if to say *boring*.

Yeah, exactly.

CHAPTER 24

Finley

It's after ten when I finally get back to my apartment. I half expect to find the boys sitting on the couch, still watching TV, but the living room is vacant. The kitchen is littered with sections of a puzzle I've never put together before and evidence of something having been cooked…well, prepared, anyway, based on the crumbs on the countertop and some dishes in the sink.

The door to my bedroom is half-opened, the light still on. The boys are sound asleep on my bed—Connor curled in a ball and Braden spread out like a starfish. Eddie is also asleep, leaned against the headboard, his neck turned in an uncomfortable position, a copy of *People* magazine spread across his lap. I still can't figure out how I started this day having hardly talked to or seen Eddie in two weeks and now he's here, sleeping in my apartment. With my little brothers. But then again, I guess that's sort of been our thing all along. Barely more than strangers, and then suddenly, we're in each other's personal space, diving in swimming pools with family members.

Except I haven't really been in Eddie's space at all. He's only been in mine.

He stirs, his head flopping from one side to the other, and then mumbles something under his breath. I freeze in my spot, listening. "No, it's fine… I'm fine… I didn't take too much."

I move closer, debating waking him up. Sweat trickles from his forehead down the side of his face. His breathing shifts to a more uneven rhythm. In his sleep, he lifts a hand to his shirt collar, tugging at it. "I can't…I just…I don't know. I don't know."

I glance from Connor to Braden—they're still out cold—then back to Eddie. He's shaking his head, protesting something. Suddenly, without warning, he jolts upright, tilting the bed. I dive forward, placing a hand on Connor's side, making sure the movement doesn't knock him off the bed. Eddie slides to the end of the bed, and I immediately shift Connor into a safer spot near the middle.

At the end of the bed, with his feet now resting on the carpet, maybe preparing to stand, Eddie appears to be gasping for air. I kneel in front of him, trying to figure out if he's awake or asleep. "We shouldn't have—we can't… I can't…" he mumbles.

I grip both his shoulders and give them a gentle shake. "Eddie…hey…you're okay."

He scrubs a hand over his face and then looks at me. I wait, watching him slowly come back to life and figure out where he is. He closes his eyes for a moment, and then they're wide open again. He glances over one shoulder, checking out the bed, and then pats Connor's ankle. His breathing is still ragged, like he's on the verge of hyperventilating. I shake him again, getting him to face me. "Relax, okay?"

"Yeah, sure." He nods, looking half-confused, half-embarrassed. "Sorry. I should go."

I keep studying him—I'm still not a hundred percent sure he's awake—while he attempts to stand, loses his balances, and grips the dresser. He pats along the wall all the way to the door and heads out into the hallway. I grab the blanket from the end of the bed, toss it over the boys, then flip the lights off before following Eddie.

He stops again on the way to the front door, when he reaches the couch. Spots appear on the back of his T-shirt from sweat. I jump in front of him, holding a hand to his chest. "Maybe you should sit for a few minutes?"

Eddie shakes his head but sinks down on the couch anyway. His face drops into his hands like it's too heavy to hold up. "It's so weird… I feel like—like I'm—"

"Sick?" I suggest. I perch myself on the edge of the coffee table, not wanting to give him room to exit.

"Strung out. High." Eddie lifts his head and looks at me. "I feel like I'm high."

"Maybe you have a fever." I rest a hand to his forehead. It's cold and clammy but not warm.

"Feel this." Eddie grabs my hand and places it over his heart. It's racing. He pulls in another ragged breath. "It's like I can't catch my breath."

He's sounding more coherent now, and already, some color is returning to his cheeks. I don't know how to reason with him except to do just that, reason. "You didn't take anything to make you high, right?" He shakes his head—thank God—and I lean in to get a good look at his eyes. "You're not strung out or whatever. Try to breathe more slowly."

I leave my hand over his heart, waiting for the rhythm to slow.

CHAPTER 25

Eddie

The here and now is slowly returning with each much more controlled breath I take in. And shit. Why did that feel so real?

Finley's palm stays pressed to my chest, and the more my heart slows back to normal, the more my limbs resemble Jell-O. I lift an arm to wipe sweat from my forehead. It's a pointless endeavor, considering my entire shirt is soaked.

This is exactly how I woke up that morning. Heart racing, sweat-covered, dizzy, disoriented. A girl leaning over me, asking if I was all right. I look at Finley, and all I can see on her face is concern. But the second she decides I'm okay, she's gonna want answers. She's gonna want to know for sure that I didn't take care of her little brothers while under the influence. She might want to know why I'm familiar with the feeling in the first place. For a moment, I debate not telling her anything. She's kind and accepting. But then I remember her dad—also kind and accepting but more skeptical when it came to me being around his daughter.

I lift Finley's hand from my chest and return it to her lap. "I'm not high," I assure her.

"Yeah, I know," she says, but there's a hint of worry in her voice.

"Last year...last winter..." I blow out a breath. "I partied a little too hard. It went really bad."

"Define 'really bad.'"

No way can I define all of it, but she deserves some information about this guy she's invited into her life. "A bunch of kids—friends of mine—got caught. It was a big deal. Lots of influential families involved."

"So lots of rich kids?" Finley asks. "Is that why you changed your name? If I Google Eddie Wellington IV, am I gonna find a drug bust story about you?"

She's way more calm than I expected, but I have a feeling this is the *before* reaction, not the *after*. "If you Google me, you won't find anything about it. My father made sure of that." I laugh, but there's no humor in it. "He threw some of my friends and their families under the bus just to get my name out of anything. I'm not so popular among my old crowd anymore."

"But you were there?" Finley prompts. "And high?"

I stare up at the ceiling, unable to look at her. "Yep."

Not just high but out of control. Reckless. Not much different from the idiots I'm now forced to live with. Karma, I think.

"And now you're not running away from things while running away from Princeton and your family," Finley rattles off.

I'd forgotten that I said that to her before. That tidbit of information makes it more difficult to explain the stuff tonight without all the pieces. "I mean, I'm being real about me and who I am. I don't fit in with my family. Before all that shit went down, I felt like that too. I've always felt like that. I secretly hated my life, but I couldn't admit it. Most of my friends party because they can. They can get away with it. They have enough connections to keep them in all the right schools—it's a power trip. But for me, it was always about getting out of my own head."

"I bet you're not the only one from your crowd screwed up by their family," Finley points out. She hesitates before asking, "So you're an addict? A recovering addict?"

"No." I sit up quickly, getting a look at her face. She's still pretty calm. Careful. "I mean, I don't think so. I just made some poor choices." Understatement of the century.

"I'm not judging. Just wanted to know." She crosses one leg over the other, causing her white dress to slide higher up her thigh. "You were drinking the night we—"

"Hooked up," I finish for her after her face flushes. I can't believe she's still blushing about that. "Yeah."

She flashes me a smile. "It would be weird if you were breaking sobriety or something."

There's a small ounce of truth in that. I pick at a thread on my jeans. "Actually, that night was the first time I did anything that resembled partying since...but it was a good thing. The last thing I want is to go from one extreme to the other. It felt normal. Controlled."

She lifts an eyebrow at the word *controlled*, and I'm wondering if she's replaying the same mental images as I am—clothes being flung around her bedroom, hands roaming all over each other, mouths roaming all over each other...

I laugh and shake my head. "Okay, maybe it was a little wild. But good wild."

"Definitely good."

We stare at each other for a moment, heat building in the space between us. "Thanks for listening."

"You're welcome," she whispers.

I lean in an inch closer. "I'm sorry if I freaked you out."

"It's fine," she says in a way that also says *stop talking and kiss me.*

My mouth hovers a millimeter from hers when the dead bolt turns on the front door. We jump apart, and seconds later, Elana and French Mama are walking through the door. One of them flips on the main light, illuminating the whole apartment. I grip the arm of the couch, bracing myself for more French swearwords and possibly a spatula, but French Mama just glares.

Finley turns bright red, of course, and stands up quickly. "Well, thanks for watching my brothers, Eddie. I really appreciate it."

Elana turns to her mom and translates this, then she points to Finley's room, where her brothers are clearly visible from the light that's just been turned on. French Mama studies the boys from doorway and then speaks in French to Elana.

I try not to laugh after hearing what she says, but I can't help it. Finley gives me a questioning look, so I whisper what I heard to her. "She said this is what happens when you talk to boys."

"You speak French?" Finley asks, keeping her voice low. "And what happens? Twins?"

"Apparently." I listen for another moment and hear Elana

explain that Connor and Braden are Finley's younger brothers. They both gush about how cute they are and how they're too skinny and need to be fattened up. "She thinks they're cute."

"You speak French." Finley shakes her head. "Of course you do."

I stand up and head for the door. I've been lucky so far, avoided the spatula, but I don't want to get overconfident. Finley follows me, and we both stand there for a second, not knowing what to say.

"So..." I glance at the boys asleep in the bedroom again and then back at Fin. "I kind of told Connor and Braden I'd go to their swim meet tomorrow. If that's okay with you? And your dad?"

"You're coming to my brothers' swim meet," Finley repeats. "In Connecticut."

"If that's okay?" I say again.

She looks like she's not sure what to think, but eventually, she nods. "I'm sure they'll love it if you come."

"And you?" I rest my fingers on her waist and gently tug until she's right in front of me. "You won't mind if I'm there?"

"No, I won't mind." There are a million words inside her words, like *I hate that I want you there, I hate that we're supposed to be done with this, whatever this is.* But none of those words escape her lips.

I'm about to kiss her. For real this time. But Elana's mom bangs a pot against the stove a little too loudly to be accidental. Finley drops her forehead to my shoulder and laughs. "You should go. Before it gets ugly."

No one needs to tell me twice. I'm out the door and down the hall in no time. But I can't bring myself to go back to the apartment yet. It's too early. Especially after what I relived tonight. I need to walk. Think. Move. One foot in front of the other.

I need to see Caroline. Maybe it's time to come clean with her too.

After I'm outside in the warm summer night air, I shoot her a text.

> **ME:** Where r u?
> **CAROLINE:** Jail (a.k.a. my bedroom).
> **ME:** Can I sneak in?
> **CAROLINE:** No, too risky.

Disappointment washes over me. I try to relieve it by walking past all the buildings I named off for Connor and Braden tonight. When I walk past the side of my building, a small part of me wants to go home. Hang out in my room and blast music, ignoring the rest of the house. It's possible no one is home.

Instead of going in, I sit inside the deli across the street, staring up at a bedroom that is currently holding a girl prisoner.

> **ME:** U can wave at me if you want...
> **CAROLINE:** What?? Why aren't u at Princeton??
> **ME:** Relax. I'm just home for the weekend.

I sigh and push away from my table, then toss my untouched sandwich into the garbage.

Yeah, so much for coming clean.

CHAPTER 26

Finley

"So…" I nudge Eddie in the side with my elbow while spreading a thick coat of sunblock across my nose. "What's this about too many TVs on in the building causing an explosion?"

"Where'd you hear that?" Eddie snatches the bottle of sunblock from me and squirts a good amount into his palm. "Think we'll be able to see the race from all the way over here?" He points to an open spot near lane eight. "What about there? The video will turn out better."

My dad is still getting over his cold, so I ordered him to stay home this afternoon. Which means it's up to me and Eddie to play the part of sports parents. He seems to be taking this way more seriously than I am.

I follow him while he makes his way to the open spot. "Back to the exploding TVs…"

"Right." He keeps his eyes on the starting blocks instead of looking at me. "Just figured I'd keep them busy without the TV, so they don't, you know, become hyperactive or whatever."

I work hard not to smile. It's like the second I'd walked out the door yesterday, he Googled child care and then followed whatever recipe he found online. "You're the youngest, right?"

Eddie glances at me. "Why?"

"No reason." I pass him a bottle of water from the cooler on his shoulder and then take one for myself. "Just that I can tell you haven't had any opportunity to take care of kids before."

Eddie, who has just brought the water to his lips, nearly chokes on his first gulp. He coughs a few times before speaking. "Uh…well, my older sister is just as clueless about kids. She never would have been asked to take care of me." He flashes me a sheepish grin. "Too many nannies doing everything."

I roll my eyes. "Where is your sister?"

"She's at Brown." He turns his attention back to the pool, where a girls' backstroke race has just begun. "She takes classes year-round."

"Like you," I can't help saying, because he is, according to his family, currently at Princeton summer school. This earns me a nonthreatening glare from Eddie. "But what is she like? And Brown…I mean, it's not Princeton. How did she get away with that?"

"Ruby actually earned her college admission," Eddie says, dry and without emotion. "She got into Princeton and about a dozen other schools on her own. And she was allowed to go to college wherever the hell she wanted, because she doesn't have, as you put it, a number after her name."

"You mean because she's a girl?" I work to keep the shock out of my voice. It's all so archaic.

Eddie nods and stares out at the pool in front of us. "If my dad actually paid attention, he'd realize she's the son he always wanted."

The conversation halts temporarily, because a large group of parents have jumped up from their seats to cheer. One middle-aged guy appears to be following his daughter while she swims her four lengths of backstroke. He's whistling with his fingers in his mouth. "Pick it up! You're way behind!"

He's too busy yelling at his kid to notice that he's about to run into us. Eddie grabs the back of my tank top and yanks me back a couple feet to avoid getting plowed over.

"So she's not nice, I take it?" I ask, getting back to Eddie's sister.

"Ruby?" he asks, still distracted by the sideline dad. "I wouldn't use the word nice to describe her, but she's not a screwup. She doesn't get in trouble. Ever. She always does the right thing. But she's not obedient. She's outspoken and liberal, which is infuriating to both my parents."

"Huh," I say. "She sounds pretty cool."

Eddie just shrugs as if to say he wouldn't know. I get it. They aren't close. Maybe they're just too different. Maybe their house is too cold and unforgiving to cultivate any kind of relationships.

"What race are we waiting for again?"

"The eight-and-under fifty-meter freestyle relay." I pull the schedule out of my pocket and unfold it. "After this backstroke race, then the girls' relay, then the boys."

Yelling Dad heads back our way, jogging to keep up with his daughter, who's now on the last lap.

"I might trip that dude if he doesn't watch where he's going," Eddie says. Then he elbows me like I'd done to him several minutes ago. "So...I saw your business plan."

I snap around to face him, keeping my voice low. "How? When?"

"After the TV turned off, there was some running around,

digging for stuff to do. I caught a glimpse of some of your paper-work when I saved it from a glass of water." He doesn't look even a little bit ashamed of his snooping. "You're really doing it, then? The studio, rebuilding it?"

I kick at a piece of gravel on the pool deck with my toe. "I want to, but there's a lot to figure out. I've gotten somewhere the past couple weeks though."

"Somewhere?" Eddie prompts.

Even though I'm trying to be annoyed, I can feel a smile working its way onto my face.

"Well, I definitely have enough saved up for start-up costs, according to an assessment I got last week. So really, all I need is a solid business plan—I'm working on that now—and some evidence of potential students, staff. That kind of stuff."

"That's awesome," Eddie says. "Since this Princeton thing isn't working out, I might need another job. So if you're looking for a piano player…"

"I know where to find you," I say, smiling. But then I can't help thinking, will I know where to find him? Like, in six months? His presence always seems so temporary, like he's a guy on his way to somewhere else.

"There they are." Eddie points a finger at my brothers.

They're hopping around in their little knee-length Speedos with the other two boys in the relay. We worm closer so that I can get it on video. The first little boy steps up on the starting block and holds his position. "God, it's so high up. Why did it not look that high when everyone else was going? Do you think they'll hit their heads on the bottom of the pool?"

Eddie takes the phone from my hand and holds it steady before hitting record. I'd been shaking it up and down. "They dove off the blocks in practice, I'm sure," he points out.

These kids all look so tiny compared to the teen girls who just finished swimming backstroke. The tone sounds, and the first set of swimmers are off the block and into the water—most belly flop. Connor steps up on to the block as soon as the first boy is in the water. A red-haired kid gets in line next, followed by Braden.

"Braden is the anchor," Eddie says. "He must be the fastest."

I decide not to mention that it's not likely, with a hundred and fifty kids on the team, the coach has any times recorded yet, and he probably can't tell anyone apart, especially identical twins. But then I'm distracted by the fact that Eddie did just that.

I hold my breath when it's Connor's turn to dive in. He manages to surface without a cracked head. "Hey," I say to Eddie. "You can tell them apart."

Eddie glances at me but holds the camera perfectly in place. "Oh, you know, lucky guess."

Like all the kids on the team, my brothers are wearing identical green-and-blue-checkered swimsuits. And they're far away, where there isn't the Braden-is-talkative-and-Connor-isn't identifier to fall back on. I set the thought aside and cheer for my brother, who is holding his own on this two-lap quest. They aren't winning, but they're somewhere in the middle.

The next kid, unfortunately, is a bit slower, and the relay team falls behind. The whole time he's swimming, Braden is standing on the block, jumping up and down, cheering for the kid to go faster and desperate to get in there and help. I nearly walk over there just to get him to stand still so he doesn't fall off, but luckily, one of the timekeepers beat me to it.

By the time Braden dives in, he's got a lot to make up.

But he totally does it. He's way faster than any of the boys out there. The rest of his team is so excited at the other end of the pool, even Connor is yelling for him.

But the flip turn he's been so excited to do—none of the other kids in his relay have it down yet—goes wrong somehow, and he ends too far away to push off the wall. He drops his feet and stands in the shallow end, so he can touch the wall.

The judge at the end of Braden's lane raises an arm. Braden doesn't see any of this. He takes off swimming, gaining more ground and pulling close to the lead. Eddie glances at me, but neither of us say anything out loud, not wanting it to end up on the video.

Braden is the first to touch the wall. His team practically clobbers him, they're so excited. None of them realize what happened at the end of the pool, not even Braden. When the boys in the lane beside them are all handed blue ribbons, Braden and his team look around, trying to figure it out. I head in that direction and feel Eddie following behind me. By the time we get to the starting blocks, the red-haired kid is crying, Connor looks close to tears, and another kid with copper skin and dark hair is throwing a fit. The boys are all holding green participation ribbons limply, like offensive vegetables.

Braden is saying over and over again to his eighteen-year-old coach, "I touched the wall, I know I touched the wall! I promise I did!"

I'm about to scoop him up and get out of the way when the

tantrum-throwing kid's dad blocks my path and turns right to Braden. "You can't put your feet on the bottom of the pool! You made your whole team lose."

"Dude, back off," Eddie says to the guy before I have a chance to get closer.

Connor finds me and hooks himself to my side, soaking my shorts with pool water.

"He doesn't even know why they were disqualified," the angry dad argues to anyone nearby listening.

Eddie looks like he might throw a punch, and yeah, I wouldn't mind seeing that, but no…

"He's six!" I say, lifting a hand to cover Connor's ear. I look over at poor Braden. His lower lip is trembling now.

The man turns to the wide-eyed, freaked-out teenager hired to coach my brothers. "Why are you putting six-year-olds in the relays if they don't understand how it works! I'm not paying for my kid to get stuck with younger kids who keep screwing up —"

Eddie presses a hand to the guy's chest and lowers his voice. "Back the hell off. Go somewhere else and have this conversation like a fu—like an adult."

The guy clenches his jaw like he's struggling to hold in another outburst. Eddie seems to consider this progress, because he drops his hand and backs up a few steps. He steers Braden by the shoulders away from the crowded starting blocks, just as the head coach is approaching to deal with Angry Dad.

I pick up Connor, because he's crying now, and I know he doesn't want anyone to see. He buries his face in my shirt and grips my neck so hard, he's practically choking me.

"I touched the wall," Braden keeps saying to Eddie, his voice more and more wobbly from tears.

"I know you did, buddy," Eddie says. "I saw you. You were really fast."

"The fastest," Connor says with his face still in my shirt.

We walk a few feet away from the drama, and then I look over at Eddie, assessing him. He's still tense, ready to pounce on something. Or someone. I set my free hand on his arm. "Hey, thanks."

He exhales and nods but doesn't say anything. His gaze follows Braden, who walks to the nearest garbage bin and tosses his green participation ribbon.

"Can we go?" Braden pleads.

I tell him yes right away, despite the fact that neither boys have their shoes or shirts. Connor mentions he left his goggles by the starting blocks, and I just tell him we'll get new goggles. All I want to do is put them in the car and get away from this mess. I end up buckling them in and then pulling up to the front and running back in for their stuff. I avoid eye contact with anyone, and I'm in and out in less than a minute.

Eddie is tucking the cooler into the trunk when I get back to the car. He slams it a little too hard and then looks guilty when he notices me watching. "Sorry."

I lean against the trunk beside him. "You okay?"

"I can't believe that asshole," he says. "What the hell is his problem?"

I shake my head. "His kid got beat by a six-year-old. He didn't like that very much."

"That's no excuse. You can think that shit, but you can't just walk up to someone else's kid and say it." He looks at me, waiting for me to disagree. I don't. "Now those boys are gonna be upset over this for who knows how long. They looked ruined—"

"They aren't ruined, I promise." I'm working hard not to smile, while Eddie is clearly still frustrated. I rest my hands on his arms, which is enough to distract him. His gaze travels to my fingers. "I'll make you a little bet…"

One eyebrow shoots up. "A bet, huh?"

"I bet you that both Connor and Braden will be back to their old selves within an hour."

He shakes his head. "You're kidding? That was traumatic." He waits for me to change my answer and then says, "Okay, what are we betting?"

I flash him my most innocent smile. "Whoever is wrong has to do some skinny-dipping in the backyard pool tonight."

CHAPTER 27

Eddie

Finley hops into the car all casual, like she didn't just drop the image of naked swimming into the space between us. If she's trying to distract me, mission accomplished. My thoughts are completely forced away from punching asshole dads and stealing blue ribbons for Connor and Braden. I climb into the passenger seat and wait for her to tell me she's joking. She's busy asking the boys what music they want to listen to.

"So what now?" I prompt, wondering exactly how we're going to spend this recovery hour. I glance back at the kids. Connor is still teary eyed, and Braden is still fighting off tears. I don't see them bouncing back from this in sixty minutes. No way.

"Lunch?" Finley asks, looking at the boys through the rearview mirror.

Braden wipes his face with his towel. "Can we get Dairy Queen?"

I turn forward again, tossing a sideways glance in Finley's direction. She keeps her expression neutral, but it's there in her tone when she answers her brother: *I told you so.* "Sure."

"Don't worry, Eddie," she leans in to whisper. "I won't take any pictures of you."

··◆··

Forty-seven minutes later, Braden and Connor race up and down the play structure at Dairy Queen, aiming the plastic squirt guns that came with the kids' meals at each other, laughing and shouting.

I turn back around in my seat to face Finley. "I don't think it's a fair bet when you let them get ice cream before their meal. How am I supposed to compete with that?"

She flips her blond hair over one shoulder and shrugs. "The Blizzards would have melted. And look at that line." She points to the inside counter. "It's a mile long. I didn't want to have to go back and wait again."

"Why?" I challenge. "Because it would have taken longer than sixty minutes?"

She picks up a cold french fry and tosses it at me. "Did you want them to be ruined over that race?"

I narrow my eyes at her. "Of course not." I'm relieved they've bounced back. I'm just shocked that they have.

"Kids are resilient," Finley says. "Much more than adults. You should have seen me and my dad on the boys' first day of kindergarten. It's like we were trying to convince Connor he was too shy and timid to go because we weren't ready."

I look at the playground again, watching the kids run around. "Do you ever feel stuck? Like you're not allowed to be selfish and just worry about you?"

She laughs. "Did my dad put you up to this?"

"No, why?" I face her again.

"That's kind of his thing when it comes to giving me life advice." She busies herself sorting burger wrappers and ketchup packets into piles. "He's afraid if I take too much responsibility for the boys now, then I'll regret giving up my glory days later or whatever."

The cheeseburger and fries churn in my stomach. "Is that just about Connor and Braden? Or the studio too?"

"The studio too," she concedes. "My parents didn't become anything like their parents, so my dad thinks something went wrong if that's what I want to do. But honestly, I'm most comfortable like this. Here. I'm happy at home."

Her gaze flicks to my mine for a moment, and then her face flushes. I wait for her to clarify that she meant here with her brothers and not me, and when she doesn't, I make another point. "You're comfortable when you're dancing too. Not just comfortable. You look, I don't know...*right*."

She doesn't say anything for a long second, and then she practically whispers, "Yeah?"

I nod. "Yeah."

My fingers land on hers from across the table, and I'm just about to grip onto them when Braden's squirt gun aims at me, water hitting the side of my neck. I turn to him and lift my hands in surrender. "Hey! I'm unarmed."

"Sorry," Braden says. He's already in search of a new target. He calls over his shoulder when he's several feet away, "Can you come to our next swim meet, Eddie?"

Finley glances at her cell phone. "Fifty-nine minutes."

Damn.

I lean on one elbow, staring at her. "You look really excited about this win." She blushes again. Ha. "So I'm just supposed to swim naked. Alone. While you watch. Something about this feels off."

"No...I just—I thought—" she stammers, her face growing more and more red.

"I'm messing with you." I reach for her hand again and make sure she's looking at me. "I'm probably looking forward to paying my debt more than you are. In fact, I'm ditching the"—I glance at the calendar on my cell, reading the title of the party I agreed to go to tonight—"new fragrance launch for Alexander Wang tonight just so I can hang out here. Alone. In your pool. Possibly not alone..."

I don't know what kind of reaction I'd expected from that confession, but when Finley jerks her hand back, her mouth falling open, I'm not sure what the hell I've done.

"You got an invite to Alexander Wang's fragrance launch! How?" She lifts her hands, seeming both exasperated and impressed. I think.

"I don't know—"

"Oh my God!" she squeals. "You know who's going to be there?"

I shake my head, and then Finley proceeds to rattle off the name of a bunch of celebrities who could be in attendance and some rapper who is apparently rumored to be the secret musical guest.

People around are starting to stare at us.

"Okay, so it's a big deal?" I ask, keeping my voice low, hoping Fin will follow my lead.

She gives me this *Are you kidding me?* look. "You have to go! Seriously. Where is it?"

Hmm, let me think about that for a minute: go to a stuffy party where I don't know anyone and don't care to, or stay at Finley's house tonight with the potential for naked swimming. Kind of a no-brainer.

Regardless, I decide to humor her and pull up the email invite on my phone for her to see all the details.

"The Boom Boom Room!"

I reach across the table and put a hand over Finley's mouth. "Shh..."

"You have to go," she repeats, handing my phone back. "I bet Summer didn't even get an invite. How did you?"

Okay, so call me an idiot. I didn't know this party was such a big deal. Or maybe I've been forced into attending stuffy parties way too many times in my life to be impressed by this one. "I met that one dude, the movie star guy in the cologne ad—"

"Toby Rhinehart!" Finley says and looks at me like I've gone nuts. "How did you meet him?"

"He was at the shoot the other day for Alexander Wang—" I get interrupted several more times to explain how I got a job with Alexander Wang, something Finley would kill for, apparently, if only she could ditch that "too sweet" label.

"This is what happens when you leave it up to fate for us to run into each other again. I missed all the good stuff," she says.

"Two weeks, and you're suddenly adding Alexander Wang to your résumé."

My forehead wrinkles. "I don't have a résumé. Not for modeling anyway."

"Whatever." She waves a hand. "So you met Hollywood's biggest young male actor, and he just decided to invite you to the fragrance launch that he's headlining...yeah, 'cause that happens to everyone."

I shrug. "I didn't even know him. I was trying to watch the World Cup game on my phone, and it was pissing off the makeup people. They were about to poke my eyes out with eyeliner pencils, I think. Until what's-his-name showed up and got really excited that I was watching the game. Guess his phone crapped out on him and lost reception during the second half."

"So you bonded over soccer."

"Sort of." I pile the garbage onto a tray and stand up so I can toss it. "The line is shorter now. You want a Blizzard?"

"Sit." Finley grabs my hand and pulls me back down. "What next? He invited you to the party after you guys watched the game?"

I work hard to remember the details. Seriously, it was ten minutes of my life that seemed more ordinary in comparison to other recent events—like that photo shoot with horses last week. "Um, actually, he asked if I wanted to go get drinks and watch the next game somewhere."

"Did you?" she presses.

I shake my head. "I had just got to the shoot. I didn't leave for, like, five more hours."

I hadn't been in a "hang out and make friends" mood anyway. I was watching soccer to distract myself from thinking about all my recent screwups or Finley. Probably both.

"He said he'd be back in town today for the party, and I said maybe I'd come—I didn't want to be rude. And then he took my number, and someone from the agency sent me the invite."

Finley leans on one arm, seemingly deep in thought. "I bet it was one of those 'I appreciate you treating me like a normal person' situations, you know?"

"Why wouldn't I treat him like a normal person?" I give her a good once-over. "This fangirl Finley is definitely a new side of you."

I get a glare in response to that, and she snatches up the tray right from underneath me and stalks away to toss our garbage. On the way back, she checks on her brothers and gives them a ten-minute warning. She sits across from me again, the glare now gone. "Okay, I'm done with the inquisition now. Back to normal."

"Good." I glance at the line inside. I really do want a Blizzard. "How do you feel about Heath Bar?"

"Chocolate ice cream?"

"Sure." I grin and then head inside. Finley reaches for her phone the second I'm out of sight, which has me grinning even bigger. She's probably texting all her model contacts to see if they got invited.

When I return with a Blizzard way too big for us to finish, she sets her phone down and looks up. "I was right. Summer didn't get invited. She's pissed."

I crack a smile and hand her a plastic spoon. "That's a positive, right?"

"They're giving out Wang's newest handbag as a goodie bag." Finley digs her spoon in and takes a big bite.

"I prefer your *Star Wars* goodie bags," I say with my mouth full of ice cream. "Especially the Fun Dip. You just don't get many opportunities to enjoy Fun Dip after age ten or so."

"Those handbags are worth at least a thousand dollars," Finley says. "And I'm sure they're full of stuff worth at least that much. Makeup, skin care products—"

"You know how much I love makeup. This party is sounding more and more like my thing." I flash her a smile, which she returns easily, like this is one of many more hangouts to come. Could it be possible? At least for the summer?

At least until everything about my life changes?

"That must be your appeal." Finley turns the spoon upside down in her mouth, drawing my attention there. "You've got that attitude like 'I don't give a shit about titles and labels, I'm going to the party if it sounds fun.'"

"Fun like Fun Dip," I add. Then I say something I may possibly regret, especially given what we had planned for tonight already. "We could go? To the party."

"We?" The spoon freezes in her hand. "This sounds like a date. Thought we weren't doing that."

Yeah, I think I need a refresher course in defining a date, because I'm pretty lost right now as to where the lines fall. "It doesn't have to be a date." The second the words are out, I realize I should have said, *Do you want it to be a date?*

Finley opens her mouth to reply, and then seems to change course. "I didn't get invited, remember?"

My phone is still resting on the table. I punch in a quick text to what's-his-name.

> **ME:** Hey, how's it going, man? Might stop by the thing tonight.

Finley leans in to read my text and scrunches her nose when I type "the thing." Whatever. Fragrance launch is way too many letters. "I can't believe you have his cell number."

> **TOBY RHINEHART:** Cool! Did you see that Brazil game?
> **ME:** Yeah. I nearly kicked the TV over. Those refs…wtf?
> **TOBY RHINEHART:** Right? Jesus Christ, who finds these guys?

Finley is watching this exchange, a bewildered look on her face.

> **ME:** Seriously. Mind if I bring a date tonight?
> **TOBY RHINEHART:** Not a problem. Just give me a name and I'll add it to the list.

The second she reads that reply, Finley tries to take my phone from me to stop me from typing in her name. But I don't get why. She's the one who is super into this party.

> **ME:** Finley Belton.
> **TOBY RHINEHART:** Done. See ya tonight.

"Oh my God," Finley says, returning to fangirl Finley. "Now you have to go."

"Now you have to go," I point out.

"Why? So I can turn back into a self-indulgent fangirl?" She shakes her head. "I'm not in love with that side of me."

"That Wang shoot paid a shit-ton more than the other jobs I've done," I say. "Seems like it's worth going if you can, you know, network a little."

"Network?" Her forehead scrunches like it's a foreign word. Which is pretty cute. I might be clueless about modeling stuff, but I've done my share of working the party crowd. Usually old women with fund-raisers to restore old things or old men with a number following their name.

"I bet Wang's people invite all his competitors to these parties. I think that's a standard. Maybe you can introduce yourself, be like, 'Hey, I put on clothes every day, and I'm really good at it. Why don't you pay me to do it for you?'"

Finley laughs, nearly choking on her ice cream. "Thanks, that's exactly what I'll say."

Connor climbs into the seat beside me, and I hand him another spoon in case he wants to join the ice cream party. "Connor, don't you think your sister should introduce herself to people she wants to work for?"

He nods, and Braden barges in on my other side. "Shake with your right hand."

I lift an eyebrow. "That's good advice."

"I can't go." Finley shakes her head. "Besides, I don't have anything acceptable to wear."

"Ask Summer. She's got a closet full of high-end stuff." I look at the kids. "Right, guys?"

Braden waves a hand in front his nose. "Her room is stinky."

Finley's eyes widen. "Please tell me you didn't mess around in Summer's room."

"Too much perfume," I tell her. We were only in there long enough for me to shut the door. "So we're going then."

"This is completely pointless." She drops her face into her hands and groans. "You're forgetting that Alexander Wang and all his competitors have already labeled me too sweet, spends too much time with grandma's knitting needles."

I slide the ice cream in front of her and lean forward, lowering my voice. "It's not pointless. People's memories are short. And don't forget about the handbag. And as far as not being edgy enough, you'll be with me. I'm all edges. Like five of them. Before the end of the night, everyone will be calling you wild rebel Finley."

She suppresses a laugh. "I can't believe anyone thinks you're cool."

My thoughts exactly.

And wait…does this mean our bet is off?

CHAPTER 28

Finley

This morning, I was at a swim meet, swatting flies and piling greasy sunblock onto my face. Now, I'm at this way too fancy party, way too nervous to talk to anyone, and wearing a way too tight dress. (Summer is a whole size smaller than me.) Eddie, on the other hand, is completely unaffected. He also looks much more comfortable wearing a close-fitting black blazer with slim, pinstriped slacks. A waiter passes us with a tray of champagne glasses. Eddie snatches one and then looks at me. I shake my head. "This has to be the fanciest place to throw a party in the entire city."

He eyes the glass, apparently decides he doesn't want it, and sets it down on a nearby table. "The Guggenheim has a really nice event room."

I lift an eyebrow. "Oh yeah? Mr. NYC Party Expert. You should start a blog."

Two actors from *CSI: NY* breeze past us, a small crew trailing behind them. I squeeze Eddie's arm and whisper, "Oh my God, that's—"

"The cop with the dead father and the scientist guy who only goes out at night," Eddie finishes. "We should go say hi."

I grip his arm tighter, holding him in place. I shake my head. Eddie shrugs and stops a waiter with a tray of some kind of shrimp. He asks the guy all about the food and then offers me one. I shake my head again.

"Do you want anything else to drink?" Eddie asks me after the waiter has left us.

His behavior has been suspiciously date-like tonight. I almost call him out on it, but I'm too tongue-tied.

"I think we stayed long enough, don't you?"

"Seriously?" Eddie looks me over and then laughs. "All the work it took to get here, and you want to leave after fifteen minutes? I don't even think the host is here yet."

"Alexander Wang?" I glance around the big, beautiful, intimidating room. "Not like I was planning on talking to him."

Eddie couldn't care less how long we stay. He's trying for my benefit. This was a bad idea from the start. Networking won't change the fact that I'm not anywhere near cool enough for these people and their jobs. Eddie nudges me in the shoulder and nods toward a girl clear on the other side of the room. Summer. "So she did score an invite?"

"Her mom," I explain, gesturing to the very put-together woman beside her. "She never would have loaned me this dress if I got to go and she didn't."

Summer surprises me by giving me a tiny wave. I figured she'd avoid any contact with me, considering how low on the model chain I am. She's super uptight when it comes to any networking-type events. Like she even needs to network. Everyone knows her already. A guy I recognize from a big billboard in Brooklyn walks past us; his name's Sean or Steven. He's currently linking arms with a woman who is high up in the Gucci world. The guy waves to Eddie, but he just stares at him in return, his body tense. Finally, he gives a small nod.

"What?" I ask.

Eddie watches the guy's retreating form and then looks back at me. "I had to check that dude for a pulse the other day. He'd been passed out on my floor for a good twelve hours."

Jesus. I don't envy his living situation one bit. "Okay, now I'm definitely ready to go."

"Follow me," Eddie says, taking my hand and steering us through the party people.

I'm expecting him to move toward the exit, but instead, we end up on the outside of the room. It's lined with floor-to-ceiling windows, showing off an amazing panoramic view of lower Manhattan and the Hudson. Eddie turns me by the shoulders until I'm facing the windows. I lean against a small counter made to hold drinks and look outward at the river.

"Not bad, huh?" Eddie says.

His hands land on my shoulders. He slides his fingertips down my arms and then steps closer to me until his front brushes my back.

I try to resist relaxing into him—touching has been minimal for us since our almost-kiss last night—but fail miserably. I lean my head back against his shoulder and close my eyes for a second. "I could be watching you cannonball into the pool naked right now."

"True."

Warm lips graze my shoulder and then drift to the crook of

my neck. I close my eyes again and sigh. We are definitely entering date territory. "How are you so calm right now? Is it all your
upscale party experience?"

"You're right. I've done stuff like this a lot. Too much. Though
never with cool celebrities. Usually people well known only to avid
readers of the *Wall Street Journal* and *Forbes*. With those parties, the
goal was not to have any personality."

"And here?" I ask.

"Here, the goal is to have fun and maybe even be the most fun
person. I have trouble with that now. Having fun." He slides his
hands down my arms again and laces our fingers together. "But I
think I'm getting somewhere right now."

"Where?" I laugh. "First base?"

He moves my hair off to one side, allowing him to touch his
mouth to more of my bare skin. "Second base if I'm lucky."

"In this dress? Not a chance you'll manage getting a fingertip
underneath it."

In response to that, Eddie slips a finger under the shoulder
strap and slides it over a couple inches. His lips head right for the
newly exposed skin. Heat builds all over me, and I'm suddenly
appreciative of my short, lightweight dress compared to Eddie's
long sleeves.

I close my eyes again, and the sights and sounds of the party
vanish. "What if I like this too much to wait for the next time it
accidentally happens?"

The words are out of my mouth before I can stop them.

"You mean the party?" Eddie asks. "I knew you'd warm up to it."

"Not the party." I slide my hand into his famously unruly

hair and gaze out at the lit-up sky. "I mean you. Being in my personal space."

"I love your personal space," Eddie says.

The room pops into view again. "Maybe you're not doing enough to turn me off. I mean, do you have to be so nice and able to tell my brothers apart?"

The more I work to not compare Eddie to Jason, the more I do just that. It's not really fair to give Eddie points just because he's good with my little brothers. But it's not like I can help what makes me into him.

And I am. Into him.

"I didn't mean to," Eddie says. "I even told myself last night, 'don't look them directly in the eyes, or you might risk learning their names.'"

I laugh again. The butterflies are flapping in my stomach—I can't seem to make them go away when Eddie is around. "Maybe we're having a summer fling. That's a thing, right?"

"Sure." Eddie plants several more kisses on my neck and shoulder, and soon, I'm dizzy from them. "Is that your way of saying that I don't have to 'accidentally' run into you? I can ask you out?"

Is this what I want? It doesn't even matter anymore, because I'm not capable of walking away.

"That's my way of saying that I know you're temporary, making secret plans to be far away from here in the near future, and that I'm setting myself up for…well, for *that*." I exhale and close my eyes again. "And yes, you can ask me out. And yes, I'll say yes."

Eddie is silent behind me. Eventually, he tightens his arms

around me and then presses a kiss to my temple. "I'm not going anywhere right now, okay?"

"Okay," I agree.

"Eddie!" a guy calls from several feet away. "You made it!"

I look over my shoulder and see Toby Rhinehart—Hollywood's hottest actor, the face of Alexander Wang's new fragrance, the star of many movie nights with Elana—walking this way.

CHAPTER 29

Eddie

Finley turns to stone in my arms before I even fist-bump Toby. She does offer him a genuine smile when I introduce her. I don't know why she's so intimidated by this party. She's by far the hottest girl here. But whatever. As long as I can get her to be real with me.

"This is quite a party they threw you," I say to Toby after introductions are done. "Nice outfit, man."

He's wearing jeans and a hooded sweatshirt, not exactly party clothes, but they're designed by Wang. I only know this because I wore the same outfit in the catalog shoot. Toby spreads his arms wide and looks down at his clothes. "I know, right? Model off duty is what made Wang who he is. Why fight it?"

As if on cue, two of Wang's female models walk by us, hair gelled back, wearing dresses that have collars made of something stiff and covered in jewels.

Toby whistles under his breath and tugs at his own shirt collar. "Yikes. Hate to be them." He glances at Finley. "So how do you know Eddie?"

I'm about to open my mouth and answer for her—the standard "we met at a party or a photo shoot" response she fed dozens of people at her brothers' party—but Finley gives me this sideways glance that is all mischievous.

"We hooked up at a party," Fin says. "I decided I wanted to be a bit more rebellious—trying to get rid of the too-sweet typecast. But Eddie forgot to leave the next morning, and then he showed up at my shoot for Marc Jacobs—"

"Wait," I interrupt. "To be clear, I was *in* the Marc Jacobs shoot."

Finley tilts her head and looks at me. "Were you?"

Toby laughs and lifts his hands. "No judgment, man. Stalking can be hot. With permission, of course. My wife loves it when I pretend to follow her around town."

He's married? I forget that famous actors can do that. Get married. I glance around for someone who looks like she could be his wife. "Is she with you?"

"She's over at the bar pretending some strange dude is watching her right now," Toby says, and when both Fin and I turn our heads to look at the bar, he laughs. "Kidding. She's at home with the kids. Sleeping, I'm sure. It's late as hell. Think they serve coffee here?"

He's got a wife *and* kids? I'm about to ask him this when both Toby and I notice Finley trying to gesture about something.

"What—" Toby starts to say and then looks over his shoulder. A small crowd has formed behind him, all people waiting for something from the guy. "Shit, I forgot to be on," he mutters, then plasters on a big grin and raises his voice. "Well, it was great networking with you two. I hope we can do business in the future. Lots of business-type things. Yada, yada, et cetera, et cetera."

He lowers his voice and says to Finley, "Consider it a positive that you haven't been asked to lay across a public bathroom sink, wearing designer clothes, and looking like a drug addict in withdrawal." He offers me another fist bump, while I'm still scratching my head over the bathroom sink reference. "Talk to you later, man. I'll text you about watching the game next week."

Toby walks away from us and immediately drapes an arm around two guys hovering nearby who are probably some of his "people." "Sorry about that. Work. It just never ends. But you should hear some of the stuff those two are doing. I'm thinking about endorsing their book. Writing a foreword for it. Compelling shit."

We wait for that whole crew to be out of sight, and then both of us start laughing. Finley rests her forehead against my shoulder. "Sorry. About the stalking thing. I was just trying to be cool."

"You are cool." I rub the back of her neck, since casual touching seems to be a thing for us tonight. Not that I'm complaining. "And he's got kids? How old is he?"

"Twenty-nine," Finley says right away, surprising me. "According to iMDB. And he's got four kids. Two are twins. Assuming the Internet doesn't lie."

"Jesus," I say. "He could establish an unclaimed country with that kind of fame and reproductive capabilities."

Finley laughs. "Okay, let's go meet some more people. I've already tackled the biggest man at the party."

"That's the attitude to have." I glance around the room. "Too bad we already met the only people I know here."

Finley looks up and steps out of my arms just as Summer is brushing past us. "There's someone who knows all the big names. Hey, Summer!"

Summer spins around to face us, one hand on her hip and an expression that says *you better make this quick*. "Oh, look who it is? The famous authors to be. What is it you're writing about?" She eyes Finley. "Does it involve knitting needles or how to care for stray animals?" She glances at me when she says that last part.

"My beautiful bitchy roommate," Finley muses, hooking an arm through Summer's. "Let me count the ways I could eliminate you. Except, wait...you *are* surprisingly helpful when I need you. Like now."

"She wants to meet some important people," I explain.

To my surprise, Summer does actually walk around with us and introduce Finley to a big Gucci designer—who has already heard great things about the book—and a Prada designer who recognizes Finley. The guy claps his hands together when he sees her and says, "The ballerina! I've been trying to find you! Do you have a business card or website for your services?"

"My services?" Finley asks, looking confused. Summer slides behind the guy and shakes her head, directing her to go with it. Finley gives a slow nod. "Right. My services. Well, it's more of a word-of-mouth system."

The designer leans on one elbow against a small drink table. "All the best ones are, honey."

"I can give you my personal email. Promise not to give it out?" Finley asks, dead serious.

The guy comes to life, punching the information into his phone and then explaining a bit about a tutu line he's developing for men. I can barely hold in my reaction to that, but luckily, we're interrupted by a middle-aged woman seated one table over. "Did I hear that right? Prada is using real dancers as consultants?"

"Well, of course!" the designer guy interjects, putting on his best networking face. "Wouldn't have it any other way."

Summer, who Finley says is still scarred from her day in pointe shoes, snorts back a laugh.

"I'd love to run that story in a *Cosmo* issue," the woman says. "Maybe February. I think we've got a slot open."

She and the guy go back and forth with too much fake conversation for my taste. I reach for Finley again, shift her hair over to one side, and bring my mouth close to her ear. "One party and you're all kinds of famous. Novel-writing, pointe shoe consultant, friend of Toby Rhinehart..."

"I think Toby and I really hit it off," she says. "I'd definitely consider us BFFs."

"Soon, you'll ditch me for someone with a bigger name." I touch my nose to her neck, wishing we were alone. Maybe lying in her backyard again. Or swimming naked in the pool. What happened to that plan?

"I just realized," the *Cosmo* lady says to me. "You're the billboard guy."

I'm about to ask what the hell she's talking about when Finley elbows me in the side and points to a set of three giant posters. The middle one is the biggest, and it features Toby—with very little clothing. The poster on the right is of a guy I did the shoot with, modeling a suit. The one on the left is me. Wearing the exact same clothes Toby's got on tonight.

"Holy shit..." I mumble. I lean in to whisper to Finley again. "You don't think that'll end up—"

"In Times Square?" she teases and then turns serious when she sees my face. "It's blown up from the catalog. I'm sure it won't make any billboards. Just the website, and that's only seen by people shopping for clothes by Alexander Wang."

I release a sigh of relief. Me on a billboard is the last thing I need right now. Toby sends me a text that says #twinning, and when I look up from my phone, he's taking a selfie beside the poster of me. Is he planning to post that online?

Finley turns her head to whisper, "Are you okay?"

I nod, forcing down the bubbling anxiety. It is what it is. Eventually, I'm not planning on hiding anything from anyone. "Have you two ever shot together as a couple?" the *Cosmo* editor asks.

Since I'm not sure exactly what she means, my response is vague. "What did you have in mind?"

"Not a specific piece at the moment, but sometimes, I get inspired to work in reverse," she explains. "We take some shots and let the article emerge from that. I've got a Columbia student shadowing me this month, and she's itching for her own project. I'd love to turn her loose with a camera on you guys." The woman stands, turns around to talk to someone at the table beside us, and then returns with the Ivy-League girl from Dima's party. "This is—"

"Eve," Finley says, grinning. "*Cosmo* now, huh?"

"I take it you know each other," the woman says. Then she catches Eve up on our Prada ballet shoe discussion.

I almost don't recognize Eve. She looks very different than she had at Dima's party. Instead of casual jeans attire, she's wearing a business suit, her hair up in a bun.

"Eddie, right?" she says to me, and I nod. She and Finley seem to share some silent conversation, but eventually, Eve turns back to the *Cosmo* lady and says, "Did you have any concept in mind for the photos?"

The woman studies us in a way that's too intrusive for my taste. "Might be fun to turn you loose with them. Especially going with the ballerina theme. We haven't done that in years."

Eve lifts an eyebrow at the ballerina mention. "So something couple related, coupled with dance...sexy, yet artsy..."

The *Cosmo* woman beams at Eve. "Are you sure I can only have you for a month?"

Eve turns a bit pink but doesn't respond to that comment.

"Let's get them into a studio soon," the woman says. "Just take it and run, see where you end up. You know my rules: give me something good, and whatever else you get for yourself is fine by me." She flashes us a diplomatic smile. "I always support educational pursuits. How do you feel about this project?"

Finley is sharing some inside joke with Eve and trying not to smile. "I would be up for that if Eddie agreed to it."

JULIE CROSS AND MARK PERINI

Cosmo. That's pretty much as safe as it gets for me. "Yeah, sure."

"What about pointe shoes and sex for a concept," the Prada guy suggests, butting in.

I scratch my head, trying to get a visual for that. Yeah, nothing. But then I remember being alone with Finley in her parents' studio. "Private lessons?" I suggest.

"Oh, that's good," *Cosmo* lady says.

Eve doesn't respond, but she seems to be deep in creative thought. The *Cosmo* lady wants to introduce her to someone, so she mouths something to Finley that I can't decipher before taking off.

"*Cosmo* usually uses couples in their shoots, so I've never even been to a casting for them," Finley explains once we're alone again.

I turn her around to face me. "Are you as distracted by you as I am?"

She closes her eyes and groans. "Worst line ever."

"I'm sorry. I kind of wish I was joking. Especially with all the networking potential."

"So unprofessional," she says before pushing her hands into my hair and bringing my mouth so close to her that I can barely hear above the rush of blood to my ears. "Want to leave?"

"Yes, so much," I say, earning more blushing from Finley.

I wait by the bar while she leaves to retrieve her purse and goodie bag. While I'm standing there, Toby appears beside me.

"Here I thought I was being nice, scoring you an invite to the hottest party, and you're the fucking poster boy."

I laugh, but when I look at the giant picture again, my stomach turns. "Yeah, I wasn't expecting that."

"So not a good surprise?"

I tug at my shirt collar, not sure how much I want to divulge. "Not so much. It's complicated. Family shit."

"Right. I get it." He nods like maybe he does get it. "And modeling…isn't it usually a bridge to somewhere else? What do you do in real life, Eddie Wells? Besides stalking pretty blonds who are obviously too good for you."

I laugh at that. "You have no idea. And what do I do? Not sure, but so far, I've ruled out being a Princeton grad. I considered subway musician, but I only play piano, so that gets tricky, hauling that instrument around."

"You'll figure it out," he says. "There are literally a hundred ways to do everything. No one ever talks about that—it's always about finding the one best way—but there are hundreds of ways to do shit."

Finley returns to my line of sight, still a distance away from us. Toby adds, "Even falling in love. One day, you're trying to hook up with a stranger, and the next…"

Finley appears in front of us, and Toby changes topics, pointing to an older man several feet away. "Scored you guys a spot on *Good Morning America* when the book releases."

"Great," I say. "What exactly are we writing about?"

He holds a hand to his chest. "Meeting me, of course. How I've changed your lives already."

"Totally," Finley agrees. "We've already booked a gig with *Cosmo*."

He lifts an eyebrow. "*Cosmo?* I've got a stack of those in my bedroom. I'll be looking for you two." He gives me another nod. "Dude, give me a call, and we'll hang out sometime. I've got a decoy house uptown."

"A decoy house?" Finley and I ask together.

"Yeah, you know? Where I 'live.'" He uses air quotes on *live* and then turns around, heading out of sight.

That made no sense, but whatever. I know nothing about movie stars.

I take Finley's hand and steer her out of there before we get caught up in any more conversations. It's warm and clear outside, the sky lit up by all that is New York City. "If we weren't wearing the wrong shoes, I think I'd opt for walking back."

Beside me, Finley tilts her head to look up at the sky. "Me too."

Instead, we get a cab, and the ride back to our building goes way too fast. I'm not sure why I wanted to leave so urgently, considering there isn't really anywhere to be alone. But when we approach Finley's apartment door, she looks at me and says, "You're coming in, right?"

CHAPTER 30

Finley

Is it a bad sign that Eddie is hesitating? Isn't that what he meant when he said he wanted to leave?

"I didn't mean—I just..." he starts and then stops. "Do you want me to come in?"

Some of the worry falls away. "I wouldn't have asked if I didn't."

Once I've got the door unlocked, he touches his fingers to my wrist, stopping me again. "What about Elana? And her mom."

I touch a finger to my lips. "Walk quietly."

This time, I don't wait for his response. And he follows me, his feet not giving even the smallest creak against the floors. Once we're in my room, I turn on music, not loud, just enough to keep our voices from projecting outside of the room.

Eddie glances at my dresser top then picks up a little plaster creature Connor made me in school a couple months ago. "It's weird being here now. Not strangers."

"Sober," I add. I watch Eddie move around the room, studying objects, keeping far too much space between us. It's surprising, considering how cool and confident he'd been during the party. Not to mention all the touching. Which I quite enjoyed. "We can just hang out. I don't want you to think I'm taking advantage of you."

"Now that's a thought…" Eddie turns around to face me. He's wearing an amused expression—exactly what I'd hoped for—and he takes a couple steps in my direction. "You've gone all wild rebel, haven't you?"

My foot catches on the basket where I keep all my knitting supplies. "Yep. Totally."

Eddie reaches a hand to steady me and then slides his fingers in mine. He looks so far away inside his head, I have to ask him what's on his mind.

"I was just thinking…" He pulls our hands to his chest.

"Yeah?"

The smallest brush of his mouth against my knuckles sends my heart racing again. But still, Eddie doesn't make a move. "About the first time we did this and how much I remember and how little you remember…"

"And?" We both step closer, and the little bit of space between us vanishes. My heart beats fast against my chest.

Eddie dips his head, his lips touching my hair. "That seems important, you know? And then I was thinking about something Toby said to me right before we left." He releases one of my hands, freeing it to slide down my back. "He said there's a hundred different ways to do everything, and I was thinking about how true that is."

I'm starting to wonder if Eddie ever had a single shallow bone in his entire body. I wanted him to be that way. It might be the only reason I saw him like that in the beginning. I don't think he actually did anything to prove this theory.

I rest a hand on his cheek, moving my thumb over his jawline. "And how do you want it to be different this time?"

I'm half expecting some humorous if not dirty comment with specifically what should be added to the big event. But instead, Eddie says, "I want you to tell me something I don't know about you."

"Like what?" I ask, but when I see how serious he is, how intensely his gaze locks with mine, I know he doesn't want a fluffy story; he wants to know me. Even the ugly stuff I keep on lockdown. "After my mom died, when my dad was still in the hospital…"

Eddie takes my hand from his face and holds onto it. "Yeah?"

"My grandma had to run to the store, and I promised her I'd watch the boys really closely. She'd been at my house, taking care of us twenty-four seven, and she just needed to get a prescription filled." I pull in a breath, surprised by how shaky it is. "The boys were in their pack 'n' play on the back porch sleeping, and I must have dozed off while laying out in the sun. I woke up when I heard the splash. Braden had climbed out of the playpen and walked right into the pool.

"For a second, I froze up. I couldn't move. My mom was the one who anticipated these things—she was the one who kept everyone alive. I mean, I knew how to feed the boys and change diapers, but I was too busy with my friends and with dance classes. I think that's why I froze. If she had been alive, I would have yelled for her. She would have gotten to the pool before me. Hell, she would have gotten there before Braden even fell in. But she wasn't there."

Even though Eddie looks about as haunted by that memory as I am, he still says, "It was an accident."

"Yeah, it was," I agree. "And it wasn't the first time either of the boys had gotten close to the pool like that. But this time, *I* was the one jumping in to get Braden. It was so real. She was gone. And I had to be her now. I haven't been able to stop worrying about them since. My dad teases me all the time about being paranoid and overprotective, but he doesn't get it. That I have to be. He wasn't there. I don't think he'd believe me if I told him it was a sign. From my mom. Or God. Or the universe. I don't know."

I stop talking and look Eddie over carefully. I'm already regretting the sharing session. That's not a story I tell people. Like ever. "Not what you were hoping to hear, was it?"

He hesitates long enough to make me nervous and for me to notice how blue his eyes are, even in the dim light of my room. Then his hands are touching my face, and his mouth is on mine. I fall into him, in every sense of the words. And every movement that follows, every touch, is fueled with depth that is so much more than…than before. How much different would it be if I told him something else? Another secret I keep close to me? And something else after that?

I'm breathless, my hands working the buttons on Eddie's shirt, his fingers toying with the zipper on my dress, when I think to say, "What about you? Aren't you going to tell me something I don't know about you?"

He stops messing with my zipper and nods. "That night at the party? When we came up here… I've never done that before. Not like that anyway. Not with someone I didn't know."

"Never?" I was right about Eddie lacking the shallow player guy persona I pinned him with in the beginning. When he shakes his head in response, I ask, "Why did you do it?"

I mean, I know why I did it. But him? I don't know. And hearing that it's a singular event for him, the why seems important.

"At first I wasn't going to," he admits. "It seemed like a bad idea for me because of—since all that shit happened last winter. But then you just seemed so...different. More. I just really liked you." He smiles. "Like you. I really like you. Present tense."

My fingers slide back to the untouched buttons on his shirt, and I try to imagine being inside Eddie's head several weeks ago, meeting me, being led into my room...but it's hard not to add what I know now about him to that memory. It really does change everything.

"Plus, there was your beer pong skills," he adds. "That was hot. Big selling point."

I laugh. "Told you I only did it to seduce you."

"It worked."

After I've gotten his shirt off, Eddie is still working the zipper of my borrowed dress. "I think...I think it's stuck."

"Huh." I'm too distracted by forthcoming activities to grasp what he's saying at first, and then my face is hot for completely different reasons. "I had to squeeze into it."

Eddie tugs me toward the bed and sits on the edge. "Turn around."

The only light is a dim lamp over my dresser. I'm hoping Eddie doesn't get a glimpse of any marks on my skin from the constricting clothing. "I can't believe she's a size double zero. Then again, she eats, like, nothing and is super tall. I should have worn something else. But shoving everything in *did* give me cleavage."

"I noticed." I can feel Eddie smiling behind me. His fingertips brush my skin. "Hang on. I'm gonna try to do this carefully."

I'd been fine all night in this dress, but now that I want it off and that's not happening, the material feels even more tight and restricting. I shift from one foot to the other. "Any luck?"

"Got some tweezers handy?"

"Tweezers?" I tug at the top and then attempt to lift the bottom and allow some air to flow underneath. "Is it hot in here?"

"Or I can just use scissors."

"What? No!"

"Kidding." Eddie plants a kiss on the back of my neck and then rifles through items strewn across my dresser top until he locates a pair of tweezers.

I continue to wiggle around uncontrollably. Beads of sweat form on my forehead, chest, and back.

"I think I've"—Eddie hands the tweezers forward for me to hold, and then finally, the material gives, and my lungs expand with fresh oxygen—"got it."

I sigh with relief while the zipper glides all the way to my lower back. I step out of the dress and rub my sore ribs while Eddie drapes the dress over a chair in the corner of my room. "You're my savior."

He laughs and ditches his shirt, which I left hanging open. He takes a seat on the edge of the bed and turns me to face him. "Completely selfless act."

My heart is thudding again, watching him examine the crease lines along my sides. He traces a finger over my skin and says, "Jesus, that really was tight."

I give his shoulder a shove. "Thanks!"

Eddie laughs again, his hands firmly grasping my hips. "I didn't mean it like that."

When I don't instantly forgive him, he hooks an arm around my waist, stands, and lifts me up in the process. "Look how light you are. I can lift you with one arm."

Before I can protest, he tosses me gently onto the bed, then slides in beside me. "Nice move."

Eddie leans in and kisses me. He pulls back and grins. "You're beautiful. And perfect. Obviously, that dress is fucked up."

"Obviously," I agree. It's more fun to get on this train than the one where I stuff myself into my thinner roommate's designer dress. Yeah, let's not do that again.

"I probably haven't told you that enough," Eddie says, and then he disappears from view, his head dipped low enough for him to kiss me right below the tiny bow on my bra. "I haven't really been descriptive either."

"Descrip—" My breath catches the second Eddie's mouth is on the outside of my bra, and I can't complete the word.

"Yeah," he says. "Like telling you how much I love this little patch of skin..." He pulls back a couple inches and strokes a finger over the top of my bra. "It's at least ten or twenty percent softer than the rest of your skin. Have you noticed?"

"Ten or twenty percent, huh? I haven't noticed."

"Not touching yourself enough, apparently."

I laugh, probably a little too loud.

"Shh." Eddie slides upward and covers my mouth with his. "Don't wake the crazy French lady."

"Sorry." I swallow back more laughter and force a straight face. "Continue."

He takes his time, covering nearly every inch of me, voicing observations about various parts of my body until I can't think or breathe or hold still any longer.

I nudge Eddie onto his back and lean over him. "Let me look at you…"

A grin spreads across his face, and he lays still, watching my hands roam over his chest.

Maybe this is the definition of summer fling? Finding someone you can be with like this, uninhibited. Not bogged down with thoughts of the future. Not bogged down with thoughts of much else outside of this moment and us.

A bit later, I've inspected Eddie as thoroughly as he'd done with me, tossing his pants beside the discarded shirt. I place my lips over his heart, feeling the rapid beat increase in speed.

"Come here," he says, reaching for me.

I move quicker than he expected, causing our noses to bump together. I start to laugh, but it's cut off by Eddie's mouth crashing into mine. An involuntary sigh escapes—he really is a great kisser. I'm so caught up in it, I don't notice being turned over until I open my eyes and see my ceiling fan over his shoulder. A thumb hooks into the waistband of my panties, and I immediately shift around, trying to help him remove them faster.

"Okay?" Eddie asks, a question in his eyes.

He waits for me to nod, even though I pretty much flung the panties off myself. My bra is unfastened shortly after, but he takes an agonizingly long time sliding the straps down my shoulders and pulling the whole thing off. The kiss that follows, with almost no clothing between us now, is so intense, I can hardly stand it.

I walk my fingers sideways, feeling for the small drawer in my nightstand. I nearly tip the whole thing over, and Eddie has to reach over and open it for me.

He glances inside and removes something, holding it out in front of me. "Nice. SweeTARTS. Is this what you wanted?"

He pops one in my mouth—a purple one—and then takes the pink one that follows. I'm about to protest, but he quickly ditches the candy and reaches in again, holding up a condom. I pat him on the head. "Well done."

"Need anything else?" he asks, giving the drawer another glance. "Nail polish, lotion, takeout Chinese menu?"

"Stalling?" My fingers tap gently against the waistband of his boxer briefs.

In response, Eddie removes his final article of clothing and is ready in seconds. He pauses for a moment to ask again if I'm okay. I reach up and tangle my hands in his hair, bringing our mouths together and kissing him until he's sure that I'm sure.

··◆··

"Let me get this straight," I say to Eddie, who looks about as good as he ever will, stretched out at the end of my bed in his underwear. "You had friends in high school who've been in boarding school since they were eight?"

One of my SweeTARTS is poised between his fingertips,

preparing to land in the cup I'm holding. I invented this twenty questions, beer pong game with candy instead, but Eddie's gotten super into it. I'm almost out of candy.

"You're from Connecticut, Fin. Boarding school is a huge thing there. How come you don't know all this already?"

I shrug. "It's a high school thing where I'm from." I can only think of a handful of my middle school friends who ended up at boarding school. Many applied though—teachers and counselors talked about it frequently, I guess.

"My grandfather went to boarding school in London when he was eight," Eddie says. He aims his green SweeTART and tosses it. It lands on my hand, the one wrapped around the cup.

"Close enough. That counts." I pop the candy in my mouth. "Would that be Edward James Wellington the first?"

"Second," Eddie corrects. "And boarding school's not as weird as you're making it sound. It's kinda normal. That's what I thought when I first started at Andover, all the people around all the time. I kept thinking this must be what normal family life resembles. My place—my parents' place—is so big with all our rooms at different ends. We could go days without seeing each other. Sometimes, not having alone time bugged me at school."

I try not to look heartbroken by that idea of his family home, but it's hard not to. "What did you want to do with all this alone time, Eddie Wells?"

"This," he says, reaching for me and pulling me under him. "And it's my turn to ask you a question. I know you want to open the studio, but have you ever thought about dancing professionally, like your mom?"

Yes. The answer to that question is yes. For years, it's all I thought about. Daydreamed. Sometimes, my fantasies took me onstage with the New York City Ballet. Other times, I was a backup dancer for Lady Gaga, though hip-hop is not my strength. I even toyed with voice lessons for a while, because I wanted to be on Broadway. But never in my almost adult life have I had those dreams. So it doesn't feel true, saying yes.

"Not really," I tell Eddie.

He lifts an eyebrow, his face hovering above mine. "Never? Come on, you lived with a professional ballerina. I find that hard to believe."

"Maybe when I was really young, like little girl fantasies," I concede. He's getting way too good at reading me. I decide an escape might be best. "I need a Diet Coke. You want one?"

He studies me for a beat and then says, "Yeah, sure."

I slide out from under him and head for the door. I point a finger at him. "Not a sound from you, okay?"

I'm still stuck on Eddie's question while walking to the kitchen. I think I even know the last time I thought about dancing professionally. My mom and I danced a duet for the studio's annual recital once. We had talked about doing it for years, since I got my first pair of pointe shoes when I turned eleven. But the year before, she had been über pregnant, ready to give birth. The year before that, she had just had a miscarriage, wasn't in a good place, and was trying to get pregnant again.

But eventually, nearly a year after she gave birth to the twins, we danced together. A piece from *Coppelia* that my mom had done onstage with the New York City Ballet when she was nineteen. She claimed to be still in a postbaby, out-of-shape state, but I thought she looked amazing. And so did everyone else. My mom even invited her old director from back in the day. He came backstage after and gushed about my mom and then about me. That had been nice to hear. I mean, he was a real-life ballet director. But what made me want something big was my mom telling me I had danced the piece perfectly and with heart.

Three weeks later, she died. And my dad nearly died too. He needed five different surgeries, and he couldn't walk. It's not that I was afraid to try or that I was too sad because dance made me think of her; it's just that it didn't seem important anymore. How could it? So much had changed that I figured dance was bound to change for me too.

But dancing *Don Quixote* in my parents' studio a few weeks ago… It had felt like the duet with my mom all over again. Since then, I haven't gone a day without doing something in those pointe shoes.

I reach for two cans of Diet Coke and then nearly hit my head on the fridge when I hear Elana's mom speaking in whispered French. I look up and see that they're awake, pulling items out of the small stacking washer/dryer in our kitchen.

"I forgot, you guys are heading to New Jersey, right? The shampoo commercial?"

"Lipstick," Elana corrects with a yawn. She heads back into her room for something.

I hang around for a minute so I can say good-bye, and while I do, French Mama appears in front of me, saying something I don't understand, but she's got that sympathetic motherly look on her face again. Already, my gut twists.

She opens the fridge and begins pointing out containers of food. At first, I think she's showing me what's theirs so we don't eat it. Then I quickly realize that it's meals she's prepared. For us. I clear my throat and try to stop my cheeks from burning. I'm not used to people taking care of me.

French Mama rushes over to the dryer and returns with my sweater. I must have left it on the couch last night while I tried on dresses in Summer's room. She sets it in my arms, and the scent of soap and dryer sheets wafts up toward my nose. It's folded in that special way that stores do, with the arms tucked inside, making a perfect rectangular shape.

My mom folded sweaters like this too. I'd come home from school and find the sweater I left lying around the house folded neatly, like a gift, at the end of my bed. It always made me smile, no matter what. I swallow the lump in my throat and mumble a thank-you, then I mumble a good-bye to Elana. I close and lock the door to my room, but I'm still staring at the sweater when Eddie stands and takes the Diet Cokes from my hand.

"You okay?" he asks.

I lift my head, force a smile, and nod. I carefully place the sweater on my dresser top. Eddie tugs me toward the bed, probably sensing that something is off with me, and makes a joke. "So should I head upstairs to my apartment? I don't want to mess up again and have my pants thrown in my face in the morning."

I laugh, breaking out of my trip down memory lane. "You can stay. If you want."

"Good," he says with a grin. "Because we still have three SweeTARTS left." He pulls me under the covers with him.

I don't feel like being on opposite ends of the bed anymore. And I'm tired all of a sudden. I curl up to Eddie and yawn. "What time did Eve say she wanted us at the studio tomorrow?"

"Eleven," Eddie says. "We should sleep."

"For real this time." We've had several failed attempts to sleep thus far. Eddie's quite a distraction in my room. Even now, I'm completely spent but caught up in my lips brushing the skin on his neck, his hand sliding under the extra-large T-shirt I like to sleep in.

I finally do begin to drift off to sleep, but even half-conscious, I can't help thinking how different tonight was from the last time. How much more I know about Eddie and how that changes the way we both sleep in this bed. It changes so much.

And I'm really beginning to like this new way. Maybe it doesn't have to end?

CHAPTER 31

Eddie

"No makeup?" Finley repeats.

Eve Nowakowski is busy adjusting lights for the shoot but manages to answer with, "Uh-huh."

"Me too?" I ask hopefully. I still don't know exactly what we're doing for this shoot.

"Yep," she says in response.

Finley looks at me and shrugs. It's strange to be at a shoot without the crowd of people around. Not that I'm an expert yet, but just Eve and Finley here is definitely not the norm. We're on the eighteenth floor of this building in Brooklyn. It's basically wide-open space, just wood floors, white walls, and support beams placed here and there. The crew left some lights and camera equipment but no makeup and hair area.

"Hair?" Finley asks, tugging at the wet locks around her face. She came here fresh out of the shower. So did I, but my hair is mostly dry now.

Eve crawls over to a big bag on the floor, the camera lens still clutched in one hand, and pulls out a blow-dryer. "Flip your head upside down and dry it."

I figure I have a few minutes, so I plop down on the floor. "So you're working for *Cosmo?* Or just interning?"

"Neither," Eve says, raising her voice over the sound of the blow-dryer. "Just a short-term project for my independent study. I wanted to gain some experience coming up with photo concepts to go with articles. My mentor, Janessa Fields, gets a kick out of pairing me up with industry people who I would never seek out otherwise."

"Why?" Seems like a mentor would want to help her find someone doing what she hopes to do in the future.

Eve shrugs. "According to Janessa, the worst thing for my career right now is being too sure of what I want to do."

Huh. "That's something the college counselors never told me."

"I know, right?" Eve goes over to her giant bag again and pulls out what looks like a T-shirt and then a black tank top. "I don't think these shots will be right for *Cosmo*, but I have something else in mind..." She looks up at me, concern on her face. "I hope that's okay? Finley said you guys didn't have anything scheduled this morning."

"So this is unpaid work?"

"I like to call it volunteer." She's waiting for my response, looking more worried now.

"In that case..." I start to stand up, but then stop and flash her a grin so she knows I'm kidding. "I don't have any jobs all day, so it's fine." I scratch my head. "Well, I mean, I don't know if it's fine, because I'm not sure what I'm getting into, but fine for now."

"I don't know exactly what I'm getting into yet either," Eve admits, seeming relieved by my response. "And there might be a picture right for *Cosmo*—I'll let them take a peek. Then you'll get a couple hundred for your time. And your"—she waves a hand in front of me—"you know, *body*."

I stifle a laugh. "Right."

"I couldn't resist the opportunity to use their lights and equipment, plus this space is insanely expensive. After that private lesson concept was dropped into my lap at the party, I was up nearly all night spinning ideas." She looks a little embarrassed about this but shrugs again. "We'll make it quick, and if it turns out to be nothing, then whatever."

Finley shuts off the blow-dryer and turns herself upright again. I'm staring at her now, caught up in the memory of last night. I barely hear when Eve says to me, "Mind ditching your shirt?"

"Huh?" I touch the material on my chest. "My shirt?"

"No?" Eve asks, then she looks at Finley. "Probably less weird if you ask."

I roll my eyes but pull the T-shirt over my head. "Happy? Anything else?"

"Not yet." Finley stands in front of me and loops her thumbs through the belt loops of my jeans. She tugs until I'm right up against her.

I use my fingers to comb through her hair, straightening it out after the blow-drying session. I don't think anyone else could have convinced me to "volunteer" to have more pictures taken. I've pretty much sworn off all voluntary photos.

Standing here so close, I'm engulfed in the same feeling that hit me last night—a weight pressing against my heart, a weight that will no doubt be replaced with emptiness if or when it's gone.

I think I might be in love with her. Or on my way there. A little more time and—

But time isn't really part of this thing we're doing.

"Put this on." Eve waves some black clothing in the air, and Finley moves away from me to grab them. "And your ballet shoes."

Soon, she's wearing a black tank top and tiny black shorts. Nothing fancy. Her ballet shoes are tan and blend with her skin. It takes her a few minutes to get them on. Eve sits on the floor, snapping pictures of her going through the process of covering her toes and tying the ribbons. Finley is much less distracted by the camera than I am.

I must have looked uncomfortable, because Eve glances up at me. "This will be painless, I promise."

"No problem." I shrug and fold my arms over my chest.

"Do some warm-up-type things," Eve suggests to Fin. "And Eddie, just stand there and watch."

She flashes me a grin, and I nod. That I can do.

Even though I've seen ballerina Finley a few times, I'm still caught off guard by how fluid her movements are. How there's this other person inside her who comes alive when the shoes are on. But really, if you look close enough—something I made sure to do last night—you can see evidence of the dancer. Her feet, for one—high arches, old healed blisters, a few new ones too. The way she stands with her feet turned out, the calf muscles that flex when she raises on her toes to reach for a coffee mug in a high kitchen cabinet.

Eve is busy snapping pictures, but she pauses when Finley does a series of complicated turns. "Wow..."

Fin stops her turn, sharp and precise, and her blond hair whips around to hit her in the face. "Enough?"

Eve nods, and then her gaze drifts between the two of us until she's guiding Finley backward, toward me. "What if..." She takes one of Fin's arms and hooks it around the back of my neck. "And then..." She places my right hand on Finley's stomach. "Now do that on your toes," she tells Fin, and then to me, she says, "Less grip on her. More supportive and less 'I'm dominating you.'"

Finley busts out laughing. "Sorry." She glances at me over her shoulder and starts up again.

"So unprofessional." I shake my head and have to tighten my grip on her, because she's laughing too hard to balance on her toes. I tickle her sides, earning more laughter. I slide a finger down her leg, and I'm about to lift it up and see how high it goes when my phone vibrates in my pocket.

"Sexy," Finley jokes, then she reaches down and pulls it out for me. Even though it's obvious she's not trying to spy on my phone, the name flashes clear enough for both of us to see: Caroline.

My heart drops to my stomach. I take the phone from Finley, whose cheeks are bright red now. The phone continues to vibrate and flash Caroline over and over again. I suck in a breath—why is she calling? She always texts. And I hit ignore before stuffing it back in my pocket.

Maybe something's wrong? Something must be wrong. But what the hell am I supposed to do about it? I'm not even allowed to—

Finley gives me a tiny glance from over her shoulder again, and I know how this must look, with my face probably tense and revealing a problem. I'm supposed to say something, anything, to explain who this girl is, calling my phone. She's my cousin. She's my friend from school. She's someone from the agency.

But I can't lie to her. Not anymore. So instead, I say nothing.

CHAPTER 32

Finley

I wish I could unsee Eddie's phone coming up with the name Caroline. I shouldn't have looked. But I can't help but be curious. Who's Caroline? An ex? A current fling? We hadn't talked about being exclusive, and we've barely decided to be any kind of "us." Obviously, he's keeping secrets from me, but I should trust that he's not keeping a secret that would hurt me personally, that would make me regret ever meeting him. But I can't help worrying. Just a little bit.

"Ready?" Eve prompts.

Both of us must have forgotten she was standing there, because Eddie jolts to life. He hesitates before returning his hand to my stomach. For a moment, I want to make him nervous. About us. But it's not that easy. I really am pretty sure that he's not here to hurt me, and that makes it more difficult to ask questions about things like girls who call him and seem to instill the fear of God in him.

I put myself into the position Eve asked for, and Eddie leans in to whisper, "Hey…"

I shake my head, cutting him off. "It's fine—I mean, do you need to—"

"No, it's okay." He sighs and closes his eyes.

It's not fine or okay. Obviously. But we're fine. Right now at least.

"That looks great," Eve says. She pauses, getting that glassy-eyed, person-with-an-idea look. "Maybe something a little more tangled up now?"

Eve gives me a look that clearly asks, *Is this okay?* I check on Eddie, who seems to catch our exchange.

"What?" he asks.

"Eve wants you to take your pants off," I tell him, completely straight-faced.

He goes all deer in headlights, and Eve ruins my fun. "Don't take your pants off."

"She just wants to know if we can get a little more touchy-feely," I explain.

"Not what I was asking at all," Eve says. "I just didn't want it to be awkward if it's, like, your second date, okay?"

Eve showed me sketches she'd made while Eddie had run to the bathroom a little while ago, so I'm more informed on the shots she's hoping to get than Eddie. I suggest she show him the sketches, so she does. Eddie looks them over carefully and then seems to relax. Eve picks one to try next, a pose where Eddie is carrying me, his head dipped like we're about to kiss. He must get really into it, because he ends up actually kissing me, realizes this, and stops abruptly before giving a nervous laugh. He looks up at Eve, who still has her camera up, snapping away.

Eve looks at the photos and laughs. "That last one, your face, Eddie… *Cosmo* might want it for their 'caught in the act' article."

Eddie sets me down again, and his neck turns a little pink.

"How about you do some more spinning, and I'll stand back and watch again?"

Luckily, between Eve and myself, we're able to coax him back into the set for several more shots.

"Whoa, what's going on in here?" a voice asks after a while longer.

I'd been lying on my back across Eddie's legs while he tied my shoes together. I lift my head and spot Alex walking across the room toward Eve. He's all sweaty, probably from the gym.

"Eddie is getting a lesson in couples photo shoots," Eve explains.

We hang out while Eve shows Alex some of the shots she's gotten so far. I'm expecting to see some typical Alex—cracking jokes and pretending he's not very smart—but he makes comments on several of the photos and then flips back to stop on a previous one. "This. I like this."

I roll off Eddie and move over to look at the camera. It's a picture of me doing a pirouette. My hair is flying loose all around me. And two feet behind me, Eddie is standing there watching, his hands stuffed in his pockets and his eyes full of...well...I'm not really sure what.

"Hey, I thought I wasn't in that shot." Eddie slides right behind me, looking over my shoulder. His warm breath on my skin is enough to cause goose bumps.

Eve looks at Alex. "It's my favorite too."

She hands me the camera. "Here, look all you want. Alex can help me pack up."

Eddie reaches around me and takes over the controls. He brings me closer, curled against him, before he flips slowly through one picture after another, the tension between us melting more with each image.

"You look so pretty," he says when we're back to the beginning again. "And…striking."

"And you look…" *In love*. But I can't say it, because I'm afraid it'll show. That maybe I'm feeling it too. "…hot."

He pretends to be offended and makes a big show out of retrieving his shirt and putting it back on. By the time we're heading down the elevator with Alex and Eve and the remaining equipment, things seem to be back to the light and fun we ended on last night.

"Lunch on me?" Eve offers.

"I'm in," I say, and Eddie agrees.

Eve leans in to sniff Alex's shirt. "Outside somewhere is probably best. Did you actually run from the gym to Brooklyn? Because it smells like you did."

Alex makes a big show of giving her a sweaty hug, and then Eddie and I try to con Eve out of details about where she's planning to use our photos while we walk toward the lobby of the building.

"You'll know before. I swear, I'd never use anything without your permission," she assures us. "It's really nothing yet, and I don't want to jinx it."

I look at Alex, my eyes narrowed. "You know, don't you?"

He avoids eye contact while holding the door open. I'm about to pester him more, but Eddie takes my hand and pulls me outside into the warm summer air.

"Which way do you want to—" Eve starts to ask.

"What the hell do you think you're doing?" someone shouts, someone female.

Eddie clutches my fingers and comes to a dead stop. I do the same, and Alex and Eve both crash into me from behind.

A petite brunette stands in front of us, her glare fixed on Eddie, her hair and flowery sundress blowing in the wind. My gaze drifts downward, focusing on her big, swollen belly. Like a basketball's been shoved beneath her dress.

"What the hell are you doing?" she shouts again at Eddie.

I feel him stop breathing, his gaze, like mine, fixated on her stomach. He drops my hand and swallows hard. "Caroline…"

Caroline. The phone call earlier.

Nobody moves a muscle. But the girl gets right in front of Eddie. "Look at me and tell me you didn't refuse to sign those papers? Tell me it's all a sick joke someone is playing on me!"

Alex sets a hand on my shoulder, giving it a squeeze like he's debating pulling me back, away from any potential threats. Eddie's mouth falls open, but he doesn't speak a single word. This seems to say enough for the girl. Her face twists with anger, and tears fall at too fast a rate for her to wipe them away.

"Fuck you, Eddie!" She turns her back to us and heads quickly across the street, barely noticing the cars drifting by.

My stomach is in all kinds of knots, my head a jumbled mess, but I notice Eddie still frozen in place. I tug his sleeve, and when he doesn't respond, I say, "Eddie!"

He turns to look at us, completely shell shocked. "I…I'm—" He shoots a glance at the retreating pregnant girl and then back at us. "I have to—"

"Yeah, go ahead, man," Alex says when no one else speaks up.

Eddie's gaze lingers on me for a moment, and I spit out the one last possible bit of hope I have. "That's not your, um, sister, is it?"

I already knew that. His sister's name isn't Caroline.

"No." He scrubs a hand over his face. "I'm sorry, I—" His eyes stay on me for a beat longer, and then he takes off after the crying pregnant girl.

I'm completely numb when I turn and look at Alex and Eve. Eve tries out a few words before settling on, "Do you—I mean, do you know what that's—"

"No." I start walking. Somewhere. I don't know where. And they both follow. "I don't know anything."

Except maybe I do. If I rewind my life and play back everything Eddie has said to me since we first met, I think I know.

"Are you okay?" Alex asks me.

"I don't know." I shake my head. "Probably not."

They don't say anything for a little while. Not until we're getting off the subway near my apartment. Eve clears her throat a few times before she says, "You don't think they're, like…together?"

"I don't know," I say yet again. "But I don't think so."

"So maybe it's just the…" Alex starts to mime a pregnant belly, and Eve grabs his hand, stopping him.

She turns around in front of me. "I'm gonna come inside with you. Hang out for a while."

"Yeah, okay." I don't know what else to do except wait for Eddie to fill in the many missing pieces.

CHAPTER 33

Eddie

I dart across the street, not bothering with the crosswalk. "Caroline!"

She attempts to speed up her walk but isn't able to. My head is pounding from emotional overload. From seeing her. I haven't seen her in nearly two months. And God, her stomach—I mean, I knew what was in there, but...

"Caroline!" I finally reach her and jump in front of her, blocking the way. "Please just listen to me."

Tears streak down her face. She shakes her head. "You lied to me! How could you?"

An ache spreads across my chest. "I just—I can't do it. I can't sign my kid away."

The words come out so fast and easy but carry an unbearable weight. It's the first time I've said it out loud. *My kid.*

"What the hell are you going to do, Eddie?" she snaps. "Raise a kid by yourself?"

She tries to step around me, but I rest my hands on her shoulders, stopping her. My gaze drifts down again—I can't get over that stomach—and I quickly avert my eyes. "Listen…I've got a plan. I've been working—"

She groans. "You are such a fucking idiot."

A couple walks by, pushing a stroller. The woman glares at us.

"You're not even at Princeton, are you?" Caroline asks but doesn't wait for an answer. "Where are you going to live? Who's going to take care of a baby while you work? Your parents will never speak to you again."

"I know." I close my eyes briefly and exhale, all my built-up anxieties hitting me at once. "I get it. It'll be hard, but I'm—"

"And what about me?" she shouts, a fresh batch of tears rolling down her face. "I signed those papers. I had a plan—"

"They're just preliminary agreements." My heart pounds, my mind racing. "You could—"

"No, I can't!" Some of the venom drops from her voice, and she's that vulnerable girl again. The one who sat outside the clinic and cried until I finally convinced her to leave. "I don't want to be a parent. Not yet. I'm—I'm going to London. With RJ."

RJ. Jesus. He must know already. He's going to fucking kill me.

Caroline starts to say something, and then she winces and wraps an arm over her stomach. "Jesus Christ."

"What? What's wrong?" I'm already looking around in case I need to shout for help. She exhales and shakes her head as if to say *it's fine*. But I steer her to a bench anyway, and luckily, she sits. For a minute, I can't think of anything to say. I'm too distracted, watching this girl who I've known my whole life, lower herself to the bench, sitting with her shoulders pressed back, belly popping out. She tilts her head back and rubs a hand over her stomach, making big circles.

She catches me staring. "What?"

"Nothing." I plop down beside her and try to focus on her face. That lasts a good two seconds. "It's just...you're so different."

"You mean fat." She rolls her eyes. "I've been told it's normal to expand a little when a human is growing inside you, but I'm thinking of getting a second opinion."

"Not fat," I argue. "Well, a little bit. But just the way you sit, the way you move around. It's different."

"How did this happen?" she asks, despite the fact that we've long ago exhausted this argument. "What's wrong with us? Why are we so fucked up that we can't see how wrong it is to get high and sleep with your friend?"

Well, I can definitely see the wrong in it now. But I keep that to myself. It won't help.

Tentatively, I place an arm around her shoulders. She leans against me, her body slumped over from exhaustion.

"And why can't I stop saying fuck?" she asks. "This kid's going to come out swearing like a truck driver."

Now that she's a tad bit calmed, I can ask, "How did you find me here?"

"Find My Friends."

Damn. I should have known better. I need to do something about that. Although I already blocked that from my old phone, the one I only use to contact my family now.

"I called first," she says when I don't respond. "And I was in the neighborhood."

I lift an eyebrow. "You were in the neighborhood?"

"My parents went to the Hamptons, and the maid had a family emergency, so I snuck out to see RJ."

RJ and Caroline got together right after our...night together. He's the type of guy her family would never want her to date— poor, immigrant parents from India, on a full scholarship to Groton, her school. He's also a decent guy. More decent than me. More than most people.

"How is RJ?" I ask.

She laughs, but there's no humor in it. "Pissed as hell at you."

I swallow hard. Shit. "How are you? I mean, like..." I wave a hand in front of her stomach.

"Good. Considering I'm ginormous. Everything is normal." She chokes back tears. "But it sucks. Not seeing RJ. Not seeing you. It's just me and this...baby. And it's—"

"He," I correct.

Her jaw tenses. "He's not supposed to be anything to me. You can't do this, Eddie. Please just—" She sighs and squeezes her eyes shut, tilting her face toward the sun. "You don't know what this is like for me. You don't have to carry this kid around. You don't have to wonder what he's thinking, if he knows my voice by heart. You think you can just decide to be a parent and do it. It's not that fucking easy! And what about me? How do you think I feel, being the one who gave him up? I have to live with that forever, and knowing you aren't—"

She stops, too close to full-on sobbing to talk.

Guilt eats through me, but it's nothing new. I've thought about this long and hard already. Since that day at the clinic six months ago, when she couldn't go through with it. I hadn't felt guilty then, but I knew I would be in the same position when it came time to sign those papers.

I pull my arm from around her shoulders and scoot back a couple inches so I can see her face. "I'm sorry. I never wanted to hurt you."

She covers her face with both hands, crying now. "Just go, Eddie."

"Let me help you get back home," I say. "We can—"

"No!" She drops her hands and looks at me in a way that says *do not mess with me now.* "I can get myself home. Please go away."

I do as I'm told, but instead of going home, I text RJ, telling him I'm coming over. He might throw a punch or say something smart and logical that will completely change my mind, but despite those risks, I have to talk to him face-to-face. I owe him that much. He's never looked down on me. Never treated me like the guy who got his girlfriend pregnant. And he's been there for Caroline when I couldn't be. When I should have. Ignoring him this summer hasn't been easy.

He doesn't live far from here. I walk the seven or eight blocks to his neighborhood, and he's waiting outside, sitting on the steps in front of his family's apartment. He stands when he sees me, and I slow my walk. RJ isn't exactly bigger than me, only an inch or two taller, but he's fierce when he needs to be. Considering the distress I've put his girlfriend in, I'd say this might be one of those need-to-be situations.

"I'm not gonna side with you," he says right away, the tension clear in his tone.

"I know that." I lift my hands up, hoping the surrender will save me a black eye. "But I still had to come here. Say it to your face."

RJ's hands clutch into fists but he keeps them down at his sides. "You didn't see her when she found out, man. She's wrecked. What if she can't snap out of this? What if she changes her mind just because of you? Is that what you want?"

I shake my head. "Of course not. But if I sign those papers, the real ones next month, that's what I would be doing...changing my mind because of Caroline. Because it will make her feel worse if I don't choose the same as she does."

Several different emotions seem to cross his face. And then he looks down at the ground, strings half a dozen swearwords together, making the last one, "Fuuuck," nice and clear.

I hold perfectly still, not sure what's about to happen. Finally, RJ looks up at the sky in that *God help me* way and then says, "You want a drink or something?"

I force out a short laugh. "Yeah, sure."

RJ charges up the steps, but I hesitate before following him inside. "Anybody home?"

He's got three younger siblings plus his grandmother and parents crammed in a three-bedroom apartment. Before today, they knew me as the rich kid who got into Princeton, friend of RJ's girlfriend, not the guy who got her pregnant, but I'm not sure if that's changed, and if it has changed...

"Nah," he says, and I follow him. "They went to my aunt and uncle's anniversary party. If they come back early and ask, I've been studying organic chemistry all day."

The scent of curry and clean laundry wafts through the hall

and continues into RJ's apartment. He opens the fridge and lists off the beverage options.

"Water," I say before taking a stroll around the kitchen, glancing at the awards and photos of science projects pinned to the walls. I catch the bottle of water he tosses me.

He lifts the lid on a slow cooker sitting on the counter. I move closer and take a peek. Some kind of chicken in yellow curry sauce that smells amazing. "Want some?" RJ asks.

"Definitely." I glance over at the eight pairs of shoes lined up near the front door. "Unless that's supposed to be dinner? I don't want to get you in trouble."

RJ rolls his eyes. "My mom made it all for me. Study fuel."

"And you were here with your girlfriend instead," I joke. "You asshole."

He gives me a look that's half guilty, half pissed off. They must have had some fun before she got the bad news.

He dishes out food for both of us, and when we're sitting at the table, he dives in with all the logic I was worried about. "So where are you going to live?"

I shrug. "Not sure yet. Somewhere outside of New York." I think of Finley's warm comfortable home. "Maybe Connecticut."

"Expensive as hell. Have you even started looking for a place?" he asks with his mouth full. When I don't react, he sets his fork down and looks right at me. "What are you hiding, Eddie? It's like you're not worried about money at all. Your parents aren't gonna do shit. They must have paid a fortune to keep all this quiet, plus the private agency? When they find out—"

"Swear you won't tell anyone?" I ask, my stomach knotting

at the thought of letting this secret out. "Probably not even Caroline."

He thinks on this for a minute and then nods.

"My grandmother set up a trust for me. One I never in a million years thought I'd get access to. But I will. Because of...you know, the kid."

RJ raises an eyebrow. "She left money for your kid, and you're using it to take care of him?"

"It's for me. If I ever become a father. I used to tell her all the time that I'd never have kids, mostly because I hated my parents so much."

"Your dad's financial people will find a way to get access to that money or at least keep you from it," RJ says. He actually looks a little disappointed, like I should have thought of these things myself. And I have.

"My parents don't even know about the trust, let alone the terms. They don't have any access to it and haven't ever, even before I turned eighteen. She made sure of that. And her lawyer confirmed it last month. The only person who could receive that money besides me is any potential child of mine, like if I died or went to prison."

Now I've impressed him.

"How much are we talking about?" RJ asks, shoveling chicken and rice into his mouth.

I take a huge bite before I answer him—the food is delicious, and I'm starving. "A couple million, I think."

He tries to look cool, but the shock is there on his face. "This isn't why you're not signing—"

"No!" I say right away. "Are you kidding me? If I wanted money, all I have to do is show up for my Princeton classes. Sometimes. Keep my dad happy and let him give me a company title. Plus my trust fund from my parents is way more than a couple million."

"God," RJ says, shaking his head. "You rich kids and your complicated as fuck lives. Jesus. Should I go this way and get two million, or this way and get twenty million? Oh no, I can't decide. It's so complicated."

I launch my water bottle at him, but he catches it easily, but both of us are laughing now. "Let me put things into perspective for you." I scarf down another bite, trying not to burn my tongue. "Neither of my parents have ever cooked a meal for me. I have no memory of being hugged by them. Ever. They've never taken me to the zoo or the park or came to 'eat lunch with your kid at school' day. Once every few months, I'll get a call or a text actually from them. But almost always, they talk to me through their assistants or the—"

"Okay, okay, I get it," he concedes. "But it's hard to sympathize. I mean, the problems we could solve in my family with a little more money. But you will have that. Money."

I nod. He's right. "Not for a few months. And I don't want to use it, not all of it. Just enough to live on modestly. Decent neighborhood, two-bedroom apartment, cheap car, public school..." I look up to make sure he's still with me. "And I haven't touched a penny from my parents all summer. Haven't swiped the family credit card in weeks. I've been living on practically nothing, out of my backpack. I've got some money saved now from working—"

"Really? What are you doing for work?"

"Um…" I glance at the microwave behind him and scratch the back of my head. "Modeling."

RJ chokes on the sip of water he just took, spraying it everywhere. "No shit? Like what?"

"Mark Jacobs, American Eagle, Levis, Hollister, Alexander Wang," I rattle off.

He's laughing too hard to hear all of it. "Never in a million years would I have believed that if I didn't hear it coming from you. Does it pay decent?"

"Depends," I say. "The Alexander Wang job paid really big. Several thousand."

"To do what?" he demands. "Stand around in clothes and get your picture taken?"

I debate explaining hair and makeup, outfit changes, and castings, and then decide it's not worth it. "Yeah, pretty much."

"Don't ever tell my family that you gave up Princeton for that." He shakes his head. "But it's cool that you're working. Caroline will hate that you're doing anything to prove responsibility." He looks conflicted all over again, like I'm asking him to choose a side—I'm not. "This sucks."

I put my fork down. "I'm not trying to take her away from you, you know that, right? I don't want to be with her like that. I never have. And neither has she—"

"Yeah, I know." He looks away from me. "But we had it all figured out. And now she might change her mind, which is fine.

I mean, fuck, I couldn't—I'd understand if she did. Want to keep it. And as much as I want to be with her, I'm not the right person if she's going to—" He shifts his gaze to me again. "I'm gonna be a doctor. I've got a long road ahead."

"Basically, your love life is fucked up, and you're not allowed to complain about it, because her decision holds more weight than your feelings," I say.

A grin spreads across his face. "That's a fucking brilliant summary. Did you think that up on your way over?"

"Nope," I admit. "Completely created. On the spot." But still true.

"You're not an idiot," RJ says, which is his form of a compliment. "We both know you're not smart enough to get into Princeton without Dad's name, but you're not a dumbass. And you're a kick-ass piano player. Ever think about doing something with that?"

I look at him like he's nuts. RJ plays three instruments, all at an advanced level.

"Caroline's always talking about it. Plus, I've heard you play a couple times. Your execution isn't perfect, but you're instinctive or intuitive or whatever the hell it is," he explains. "It's different from guys like me, learning so we have more to add to our applications, more awards..." He waves a hand at the walls in the kitchen. "Remember when you jumped onstage and played at the jazz club? That one dude who's super famous let you jam with him."

"Pretty sure I was high that night," I say dryly.

No better way to make a comfortable situation turn awkward than dropping this kind of shit into the mix.

"Right," he says, probably remembering me hitting rock bottom later that night and needing his help to get home. It wasn't the only time that happened.

RJ picks at the chipped paint on the table. "I've known all along that you both would need to be there, to see it…before you could really decide. I haven't said that to Caroline, because I don't like to think about it, but I knew. If it were me, I couldn't decide until after."

I let that sink in for several seconds before saying, "I take it you don't want me to mention that to your girlfriend?"

"Um, no." RJ releases a breath and laughs. "But if you need something…you can, you know, ask me."

"Thanks."

I hang out at his place a little longer, and then I take off before his family comes home. I'm still shaken up from all the drama, from finally facing the reality of my choices out loud. I can't pick a place to go or to be, so I end up walking miles. Riding too many subways. Sitting at half a dozen parks, watching people with kids and trying to figure out what they're doing and why. I even debate sneaking into Caroline's room to try and fix things with her. But eventually, I figure out exactly who I need to talk to. Finley.

My heart speeds, remembering the way I left things.

God knows what she's thinking.

CHAPTER 34

Finley

Elana's mom dumps more food onto my and Eve's plates, despite the fact that we haven't made a dent in the first serving. Elana has barely touched her food. She's picking at something stuck to the table—probably left from my brothers' visit—not willing to make eye contact with anyone. Especially Eve and Alex, who are eating on the couch, because this apartment table only has three chairs.

I knew it was weird between them, but I didn't realize Elana held this big of a grudge. So yeah, we've definitely reached a whole new level of awkward this evening.

Eve is conversing easily in French with Elana's mom, but she keeps glancing at Elana, hoping to get her to chime in. She and Alex tried to leave the second Elana and her mom returned, because it was obvious Elana was uncomfortable. But French Mama pulled out her frying pan—which makes no sense, considering all the prepared meals she stowed in the fridge—and everyone was sentenced to a country tour of French cuisine.

Normally, I would put more effort into keeping the peace—my dinner guest skills are excellent—but tonight, my mind is elsewhere.

I space out for a few minutes, my fork making circles through the buttery pasta on its own, and when I refocus on my surroundings, Eve is showing French Mama pictures on her laptop. I glance over at the couch. Alex's face is all scrunched up, like thinking really hard will make him suddenly understand French.

Eve has a moment of panic and flips past a photo in her database. A glimpse of that picture is enough to get Elana looking up from the table.

"What was that?" Elana asks.

Eve tosses me an apologetic look. "Just some photos we took this morning for a school project. I took advantage of my *Cosmo* resources and Finley."

"And Eddie," I add, glancing at Eve, sending a silent message that I'm not bothered by the mention of the pictures. Honestly, I don't know if I'm upset. I don't even know what I'm feeling right now. Mostly, it's just confusion.

French Mama says something to Eve, gesturing a hand at me. Eve translates. "She wants to know how long you've been dancing."

"My whole life," I say, leaving out my nearly three-year vacation. "My mom was a dancer and a dance teacher."

Eve translates this, and then Elana chimes in, adding to it. I think Elana must have said something about my mom not being alive, because French Mama gives me that look of sympathy I'm all too familiar with. I grip my cell phone—it's been in my hand for a few minutes now. Maybe I should text him?

Elana slides her chair over to get a closer look. "Wow, this is—" She stops, seeming to remember she'd made a vow of silence, due to present company. Then she looks right at me. "You're so cool in these pictures."

I manage a laugh. "As opposed to real life?"

"Not what I meant," Elana explains. "It's the whole hair down, all black clothes concept—you look edgy."

Edgy. Huh. Who knew all I had to do was put on ballet shoes to achieve this look?

All three of them laugh at the next picture, so of course, I get up to look. It's one where Eddie is sitting down and I'm standing over him, pressing a pointe shoe to his chest, forcing him back.

"Definitely edgy here," Eve says.

The more they flip through photos from this morning, the more I want to grab those shoes and put them on again, move the furniture, and dance that *Don Quixote* solo over and over again. It's so full of feeling and aggression—exactly what I need to release right now.

French Mama is the only relaxed one here. She doesn't seem to be aware of the fact that Elana hasn't exactly been on good terms with Eve and Alex. I'm guessing it's that logical thing again. She shouldn't be angry with them—they helped her. Even though Elana might not think she needed the parental supervision, obviously, her mom did. But to Elana, if not Alex and Eve, who is left to point the blame at? If she tells her mom, then her mom's going to tell her she's wrong.

Eve closes the file for this morning's shoot and opens another one, explaining something in French. Elana sinks back in her chair, unsure how to react when a picture of her pops up.

Eve has some amazing photos of Elana from last year. Her mom is just eating it all up, and even Elana seems impressed. Especially a series of shots of her hands while she was doing homework on set. After Eve promises to send the photos to her, French Mama steps away to clean up the dishes. Eve continues to show images to Elana. Alex watches them for a couple minutes, then steps away, and we both exchange a look. This is definitely progress for them.

Outside, dark clouds rush toward the building. I walk over to the window and look out at the sky. It's gonna storm soon.

"Doing okay?" Alex asks.

I pull my gaze from the window and shrug. "I guess."

"What do you think he was supposed to sign but didn't?" Alex asks.

We've danced around the topic for hours now. Guess it's time to discuss it. I shake my head. "I don't know…paternity papers? Child support agreement? What else could it be?"

"That's what I was thinking too." Alex looks down at his hands. "Or maybe he's stalling on even claiming rights. Like he's waiting for a test to confirm or something."

"This is so Jerry Springer," I joke. "But maybe…"

Except that theory doesn't match up with what I know about Eddie. Unless he's told everyone he'd own up to his fatherhood, and instead, he wants to run away. But he told me he was doing a good thing, not running away.

God, I don't know.

I catch Elana's eye, and she mouths, *Are you okay?* I nod. She doesn't need to worry about me. But later, I do need to tell her about meeting Toby Rhinehart. She's going to flip out. We should have gotten a picture.

We should have enjoyed the lack of drama last night a little bit more. I would have if I had known *this* was coming.

Outside, the rain comes down in sheets, hitting the pavement. People shift to stand under awnings and pull out umbrellas. Some just speed up their walk.

"I didn't know about the dancing stuff," Alex says. "You doing anything with that?"

"A little training on my own, whenever an aerobics room is free at the gym." I don't want to get into business plans and all that. Plus, it's obvious he's just trying to keep me occupied and talk about something other than Eddie Wells.

"There's a studio three blocks from here," Alex explains. "Iris's Toes. Kind of a funky place. My roommate's girlfriend teaches there. She would definitely get you into a couple of Iris's adult classes for free. She's offered me the same thing several times. Eve too. Something about models helping the business…"

I hadn't thought about taking a class myself. Might be fun. Might be tangible proof how out of shape I am and how much my technique has suffered during the time off. My mom was a technique Nazi, so I've had the "bad technique will get you nowhere" mentality in my head practically since birth.

There's a knock on the door that seems to startle everyone— including me.

"Summer probably forgot her key again," Elana says.

I walk over and look through the peephole. My stomach flips at the sight of Eddie's dark hair. I turn the dead bolt and open the door. He's soaking wet, his jeans clinging to him, his T-shirt now semitransparent. I exhale and finally let my gaze travel to his face. The lines on his forehead indicate stress or nerves. He turns those blue eyes on me before breathing out the word, "Hey."

"Hey." I work hard to keep my tone neutral. I don't know if I want him to see inside my head just yet.

"Do you think—" He glances over my shoulder, probably taking in the company. "Maybe we can...talk?"

Behind me, Eve is already packing up her laptop. She passes a silent question my way: *Should we go?* I nod. Not that I need her to leave, but just so she knows I'm okay with talking to him. I pull the door open all the way, and Eddie steps inside, giving an awkward wave to everyone. French Mama is the only one who doesn't wave back. Instead, she narrows her eyes at Eddie and tosses me a look of concern.

I lead him into my room right away, saving him from French Mama or attempting small talk while dripping wet. After handing him the towel from the back of my door, I'm perched at the edge of my bed, waiting for him to talk.

He starts to remove his T-shirt and then seems to think twice about it. Instead, he rubs the towel over his hair and makes a poor attempt to dry his shirt. Then he glances around for a safe place to sit and settles on leaning against the wall across from me. He looks so anxious, I almost say something to make him feel better but decide it's safer to wait for his answers.

"So..." I prompt, staying neutral. "The girl this morning? She's your...ex? Another one-night stand?" I'm hoping the last one isn't true, because Eddie told me he hadn't done that before, and if he lied about one thing, what else has he lied about?

"Caroline is my..." He exhales and twists the towel into a ball. "She's—I've known her my whole life. Our families are—*were*—friends."

That still doesn't exactly answer the question, but I don't want to sound jealous, so I wait for him to offer more.

"Remember that party I told you about?" he asks. As if I could forget that revealing bit of information. "That was the same night that we—I mean, that she—"

"I get it."

"Right." He swallows. "We were both messed up. Really messed up. She just got dumped by an asshole, and I was fresh off one of my dad's famous 'don't screw up your life or we'll be ashamed of you forever' dinners. I don't know why we decided *that* would help things. Especially considering we never went there before."

It's hard to have this conversation under such polite and ambiguous conditions. "So you never had sex with her before that night. And you aren't together now, and you weren't after either?"

"No," he says. "I mean yes. Yes, that's correct. Neither of us remember a whole lot about any of it. Obviously, we weren't—"

"Safe?" I supply.

"Yeah, and it was awful the next morning, not to mention the whole getting busted part." He leans more weight on the wall, almost sagging against it. "And then my parents decided to buy my way out of the rumor mill by tossing Caroline's name out there. Our dads have been good friends since college, and we vacationed together, but it was that easy for him to just write them off."

Jesus. These are the worst kind of people. But I need the rest of this story before we discuss Eddie's family. "And then she got some news?" I prompt.

He nods, his face haunted. "I told my parents right away, and they responded by suing the Davenports—Caroline's family. For slander. Assuming they were planning to tell people what happened. It turned into this big, complicated business thing. Neither of us knew our families were even communicating at all. Our schools were forty minutes away from each other, so we were together all the time—" He must have caught my reaction, because he clarifies, "Not *together*. Just being together. Talking. Trying to figure out what the fuck to do. And then we went to that clinic. Three different times. She couldn't go through with it, and then—"

He slides down the wall until he's seated on my floor, and when he looks up at me, I'm hit hard with the main reason he's here. In my room. With me. And it's not to offer me this explanation. Not to make sure I don't call him a cheater. It's because he literally has no one else.

"Do you think—" Eddie starts and then pauses, forcing his voice to come out even. "Do you think it matters that I wanted her to go through with it? Does that make me unqualified? Am I going to have to explain that to him when he gets older?"

He stares at me, waiting for my answer like it means something. And then my carefully placed wall crumbles, and I'm up, crossing the room and sitting in front of him.

CHAPTER 35

Eddie

Finley slides in front of me, her hands resting on my knees. She's dropped all the apprehensive walls she'd put up since I got here. "You were being supportive. It wasn't about the kid at that point."

No, it wasn't. Not for me. But for Caroline, it was about the baby. She was the better person. Maybe still is. Except I had my moments of doubt too, similar to her not being able to step foot inside that abortion clinic. It was last March when we were home for spring break.

We sat in Caroline's dining room, with our parents and a big-name lawyer for each of us, while they all pretended to get along, pretended they hadn't been trying to sue each other and ruin each other's businesses for months. She'd told them she couldn't terminate her pregnancy, and now we were letting them figure out how she could have this baby and make sure no one ever knew about it. That last part was the one thing all our parents agreed on—no one should know about it. Because despite our families being of similar status, a welcome match for procreation, to quote my mother, "People like us do not have babies while in high school." Or college, my father had added. I didn't bother telling them their opinions on teen pregnancy weren't exclusive to the top one percent of the economic food chain.

Caroline bit her nails the whole time our lawyers rambled on about adoption laws and confidentiality, her gaze bouncing between both lawyers like she was hyperfocused. I, on the other hand, couldn't hold onto a single sentence spoken, probably due to my father's relentless glare, along with both Caroline's parents shooting me the evil eye, all while my mother sat there emotionless, high on whatever painkiller she'd been able to get her hands on that month.

Needless to say, I was jittery and anxious, understanding very little. Until my father's lawyer said, "My client would like to sign a waiver of right to notice, should you choose to go through with the adoption—"

"I am," Caroline stated firmly, shooting a glance at her parents, who nodded their encouragement.

"When you go through with the adoption," our lawyer corrected. "This will ensure my client's name will remain off the birth certificate—"

"Wait," I interrupted. "I'm not going to be on the birth certificate?"

My father's glare shifted to a "shut up now" plea, but I couldn't not ask.

"That's correct," the lawyer stated.

"And what notice am I not getting?" God, I'd felt like an idiot asking these questions. And sure enough, both lawyers looked at me like seriously? This kid got into Andover? He's going to Princeton? But since I'd first found out Caroline was pregnant, I'd been too scared to learn much, too concerned about her, too guilty for what happened and how it happened.

"Notice of the adoption," the Davenports' lawyer answered.

"Why wouldn't I know about it?" I asked. "It's not like I won't be around to help or whatever..."

I glanced around, waiting for someone to explain. My father cleared his throat and tossed a pointed look at his lawyer. Caroline's dad did the same—something else they must have agreed on despite the current war happening between our families.

"Your families have signed an agreement," Dad's lawyer said, lifting a sheet of paper from the table and reading aloud. "You will return to school tomorrow, as planned..." He looked at Caroline, showing the first sign of sympathy thus far. "And Ms. Davenport will remain here—due to serious illness—and complete her senior year remotely. All communication between Edward Wellington and Caroline Davenport shall be severed at the conclusion of this meeting—"

"What?" I asked at the same time as Caroline asked, "I'm not going back to school? I can't graduate?"

"Your school has agreed to issue you a diploma, assuming you complete required work from home," the lawyer said.

Caroline pushed away from the table and looked right at my dad. "What did you do? Did you bribe them?"

"I'm not signing that agreement." I pushed my chair back and stood beside Caroline. "You can't keep us from talking or seeing each other."

Our lawyer lifted an eyebrow. "I didn't realize you were seeing each other." He glanced at my dad. "Would you like to revert to the marriage clause?"

My mouth fell open. "What the fuck?"

"No!" Caroline shouted. She turned to face both her parents. "You know I'm with RJ!"

"Oh God," her mother groaned. "Not the gold-digging Indian boy again."

Caroline's face went pale. I recognized the signs, having been around the past few weeks. She fled the dining room, heading up the steps for her bedroom. I followed behind her but waited outside the bathroom door until I heard the sound of water running in the sink.

She was slumped over, her cheek pressed against the tile floor of her giant bathroom, sobbing. I stepped over her and sat beside the bathtub. I used my fingers to slide the sweaty hair off her cheek. "I haven't been in your bathroom for a long time. When did you get rid of the LEGO net above the tub?"

Through her tears, she snorted out a laugh. "At least ten years ago."

"Got tired of me stripping down during every playdate, huh?" I said, earning another laugh from her. "If you had just gotten over your 'no, Eddie, those are bath toys, and bath toys stay in the bathtub' rule, I would have kept my pants on."

"God, I was a bossy little bitch," she said, laughing some more. "How did you stand me back then?"

"You had toys. I wasn't allowed anything colorful."

"Or noisy or messy," she recited. "Or too childish."

"See? These are the stories great marriages are made from," I teased. "You should probably marry me."

This broke her out of her funk. She rolled on her back, looking up at me and laughing until fresh tears were falling down her face.

"So no, then?"

She sat up quickly, a big grin on her face. "Can we please go back down there and tell them we're getting married and raising a kid together? Please, please, please…it will be the last joke we ever get to play on them."

"Yeah, because they'll murder us," I point out, shuddering at the thought of my father's response to that.

"Hey, they made a clause for it," she reminded me. Then she looked at me for several seconds, her expression turning wary. "You're not—I mean, you don't, like…you don't want me like that, right?"

I glanced away from her, not sure how to answer without hurting her feelings. "I don't know. I'm not even sure what that feels like. I care about you. I'd pick you over my family any day. I'm comfortable around you."

"I'm not fishing for compliments, Eddie. I just wanted to make sure we're on the same page," she said. "And trust me, when you have that with someone, you'll know."

"Like you and RJ?" I wiggled my eyebrows at her. "Think he's still gonna love you when you're all fat and pregnant? Won't be long if you keep eating entire boxes of Little Debbie Zebra Cakes in one sitting."

She smacked me on the chest. "Then quit buying them for me!"

It felt good to banter like that—familiar and so us. Both of us sank back against the wall, sitting in comfortable silence for a minute or two.

"You know they're going to take everything from us if we don't agree to their plan," Caroline said. "No college, no trust funds, no anything. And your dad might screw my family over."

"Yeah, he's good at that," I said bitterly. "But screw them. I don't care about Princeton. I never have. I don't even want my trust fund. Not if it means selling my soul to the family business. If you aren't allowed to go back to school tomorrow, then I'm not going either."

I kept my eyes on the spot above the tub where the LEGO net used to hang, but when Caroline didn't jump onto my eff them train, I turned to look at her. My heart sank. "You're gonna do it, aren't you? God, you can't let them keep you from finishing your senior year."

"I'm still getting my diploma," she argued. "I worked my ass off to get into George Washington, and if I don't go, RJ will be all the way in London."

There was no doubt she had more on the line than I did. I mean, I had to keep my grades up and score decent on the SAT to get into Princeton, but my stats were probably similar to hundreds of applicants who got rejected. Applicants who couldn't list Edward Wellington III as their legacy.

"It doesn't feel right," I said. "Erasing myself from everything. Not having to participate in finding a family for..." I couldn't say it. Couldn't say my kid then, but suddenly, that was what he'd become.

Caroline turned to me, resting her hands on my shoulders. "I'm going to tackle this adoption thing just like everything else in my life—with perfection."

"Everything?" I pressed, reminding her of our night together and her occasional need to escape behind the fog of alcohol or recreational drugs.

"I was going through a phase," she argued. "And getting out of a relationship that sucked completely. You know I can do this on my own, and you know that I know you don't want me to."

I shook my head. "I don't."

"Then trust me," she pleaded. "Trust that I will make sure this baby is with the best family ever—much better than either of ours. And trust that I'm being completely honest right now when I tell you how much I respect that you're here, in my bathroom, ready to give up everything."

I almost made a crack about my emotional connection to her bathroom, but I didn't have it in me. I nodded, agreeing to trust her, to let our families dictate our every move for the next six months, but the weight of this decision started eating at me, bit by bit. We returned to the meeting, gave our blessing, but agreed that I wouldn't officially sign the waiver of right to notification, just in case something leaked to the public. It was a worst-case scenario precaution. Instead, I signed a preliminary agreement to sign the waiver, which held no value at all, because our lawyers made it up to scare me.

When I went back to school the next day, I couldn't get it out of my head—my name would have virtually no connection to this kid. It was worse than my father's negligence, than the cold home my parents created for me and my sister. It was worse, because it was nothing. It would mean that I gave him nothing. Couldn't even be bothered to name myself his father...

"Hey," Finley says, touching the front of my wet T-shirt and breaking me out of that memory. "You're freezing."

"I'm fine." I shake my head and attempt to stand. "I shouldn't have come here. It's not fair to dump all this shit on you—"

Finley responds by sliding closer, touching my face, and then bringing her mouth to mine. For a moment, I get caught up in kissing her, she's so warm—I really am freezing. The air is cranked up in this apartment to North Pole setting, and soon, she's peeling the wet T-shirt over my head, tossing it on the floor beside the towel she loaned me. I grasp her hips and tug until she's all the way on my lap, pressed up against me.

When I finally bring myself to pull away from her, I ask, "Do you think I'm crazy? You must think that."

"I think"—she leans back, her gaze roaming over my face—"that you have a very big heart."

Something breaks inside me. I don't think anyone has ever said that about me—definitely not as a positive attribute. I bring her mouth back to mine, kissing her in a way that seems to say more than any words we've spoken to each other. And I'm wondering if this is what Caroline meant. When she told me I'd know when it was like that with someone.

··◆··

I lean over Finley's bed, scooping my now only slightly damp boxer briefs from the floor so I can put something on. "Pass me another diet cracker."

"They're not diet crackers," Finley argues, hugging the box to her chest.

I pry one of her arms loose and point to the big letters on the front. "Low fat. That's diet crap."

She rolls her eyes but offers me the box. "We could order pizza?"

"Nah." I'm starving, but I know she already ate dinner.

Besides, I'd rather not put my wet clothes back on to retrieve a pizza from the front door.

Finley looks completely sexy, wearing nothing but pink panties and a tiny tank top, her hair all messy and wild from rolling around on the bed with me. "You're going to have to find someplace to live. Probably soon."

I nod. We've been hashing out details for over an hour. The more missing pieces I fill in for her, the more relaxed she seems to get. "I've been looking online."

I grab my phone from the nightstand and pull up a list of links I've saved. She looks them over while I dive into the box of low-fat crackers, eating two or three at a time.

"Connecticut, huh?" She lifts an eyebrow. "Those swim team parents must have really done a good job welcoming you."

"I think I marked that one before."

Fin puts the phone down. "So how does it work? She's already doing the adoption stuff even without your permission?"

"That's allowed." I exhale. "But the rest, I'm not completely sure about. It isn't very straightforward. I need to talk to the lady at the agency... I'm not supposed to know which agency Caroline is working with, but the secretary from the lawyer's office slipped up. And basically, there's one lady in charge of the agency—Dina Jackson. I've got her office address and phone number."

"And you haven't called her yet?" She seems shocked by this. "You could have put a hold to her family search."

My neck heats up. "I didn't want her to tell Caroline before I got a chance. Plus, I was waiting to find out for sure about the trust fund stuff."

Finley shakes her head. I think she's still in shock over that piece of information. "Now that the cat's out of the bag, I'd say talking to this Dina lady should make the top of your to-do list. At least so she knows that you want your right of notice or whatever it's called."

"Definitely," I agree, and then, because I'm still in shock myself, I look her over, waiting for signs of regret. "I can't believe I haven't scared you off."

"Where would I go? You're in my bed." She reaches across the bed and steals a cracker. "But now that I think about it, you're probably right... I'd much rather hook up with a shallow guy who's got no future plans."

"What happened to boring and predictable?" I hook an arm around her waist and pull her under me. I wait for her to smile up at me, and then I lean down to kiss her. "Thank you. For being here. I needed that."

She rests her hands on my face. "I owed you. For watching my brothers. Picking a fight with the asshole guy at the swim meet."

"So is this how it's gonna be?" I touch my forehead to hers. "I do something for you, and then you do something for me?"

"Pretty sure that's how it works," she says with a nod.

Just from that tiny offhand comment, a weight lifts off me. I'm not completely alone.

"You know who knows a lot about all the best neighborhoods in Connecticut?" Finley asks, and I shake my head. "My dad."

The idea of Finley telling her dad all my secrets is, to say the least, really scary, but I don't exactly see another way for this to play out.

"And you really need to come clean with your parents very soon," she adds. "At least tell them you're not at Princeton."

I roll onto my back and groan. "Now I regret telling you anything. Too much logic for me."

She props up on one elbow, her fingers drifting over my chest. "You're not asking them for anything. There's really nothing to be worried about." When I don't respond, her hand pauses its movement right over my heart. "Come on, they can't be that bad."

I scoff at that. There are no words to explain.

"Then let me go with you when you tell them."

"No way," I protest. "Not a chance in hell."

"Fine," she says, all defiant. "I'm never going to believe they're as bad as you say without seeing it for myself. And what if you need backup?"

I narrow my eyes at her. "If I need backup, I'll bring RJ. He's six three."

"It's my breeding, isn't it?" She fake sighs. "You're ashamed of me."

I hold her face in my hands. "I'm in awe of you."

"Does that mean I can go?"

"Uh-uh."

But my protest gets weaker by the second. I really could use a little support. And someone to be a buffer. Hard to murder me with an innocent bystander in the room.

CHAPTER 36

Finley

"I'm this close to convincing him to let me tag along to his big family showdown," I tell Eve while we're walking down the block. "I know it's horrible to say while he's so stressed and all, but I'm a little bit fascinated by the idea of meeting these backstabbing, rich, Manhattan people. Is that terrible?"

She laughs. "I don't know what it is, but it's nice that you're willing to be there."

Eve asked me to do another shoot with her this afternoon, and I gladly agreed, knowing I needed a distraction. Yesterday, I officially submitted my business loan application, and I'm half expecting my dad to show up, Caroline-style, to tell me I'm ruining my life and I just need to go to college or join a circus. So far, he doesn't seem to know.

No reason to tell him until I know something for sure.

I attempt to stretch out my lower back while we're waiting to cross the street. Eve looks down at me, bent over beside her. "What are you doing?"

"I'm sore all over, thanks to you and your demanding ways." I stand upright in time to see her cheeks turn pink.

"Sorry. I just get into finding the perfect shot, and I forget—"

"That my head doesn't actually spin three hundred and sixty degrees?" I suggest, thinking of the shot we pulled off in Central Park today, where it looks like I'm sitting on an invisible chair, suspended several feet off the ground. I surprised myself with the height of my jumps. She just kept saying, "Think you can get any higher?" and I kept doing it. It was exhilarating. But now, I'm feeling the aftereffects.

Eve laughs, and then she glances at me twice in a couple seconds, biting her lip. "So, I was wondering if you'd be willing to do one more shoot."

"Really?" I gape at her. "You don't have any better, more quali-fied ballerinas to use? And when are you going to tell me what it's for?"

"I can't tell you yet." When I roll my eyes, she says, "I know, I know, I'm sorry! But Janessa said—"

"So it's for Janessa Fields," I say, thinking hard. What would Janessa be into that might require odd ballerina photos, some with a hot nondancer guy? Janessa has recently moved into the high-fashion photographer realm, but her background is more *National Geographic* than Prada. She has a *New York Times*–bestselling book of her photos of malnourished children in Africa.

"She's my mentor, and she advises me on everything," Eve says, probably to derail me from whatever path I'm considering.

"Uh-huh," I say.

"Anyway," she says, being evasive again. "I have this concept that's a little more…edgy."

That catches my attention. "Go on."

"It would involve"—she looks away from me and forces the word out—"nudity."

I try to look not freaked out, but Eve doesn't seem to expect me to be cool about it. "Please tell me this isn't for any kind of magazine, because that's where my head is going right now."

"No magazines. It's an artistic statement," she explains, and the way her face lights up, the passion coming from her, I can't help but want to be involved somehow. But no clothes at all—yikes. "I have some sketches..." She whips out her notebook and hands it to me.

While we walk, I flip through the pages, taking in the penciled outline of a nude female dancer. It's definitely not trashy. And it doesn't seem like the parts I'd like to cover up would actually show that much. "I'm assuming this would be an indoor shoot?"

"Of course."

"No team of twenty extra people?"

"Just me." She flashes me a grin. "Unless you want to bring Eddie along."

Yeah, that seems like a distraction waiting to happen. I hand the sketch pad back to her. My dad is always telling me the importance of taking artistic risks. I'd say this is an opportunity for me. "Okay, I'll do it. Awkwardly, I'm sure, but I'll give it a try."

"Really?" Eve practically squeals. I nod again. "I'm gonna try and get a studio booked this week."

We're in front of the dance studio where Alex and Eve's friend works. I stop at the door, feeling overwhelmed by the idea of taking a class. Eve gives me a nudge. "Go on. I'll introduce you to Iris. She's cool."

I take a deep breath and walk inside. The place is kind of dumpy looking but funky at the same time. I learn from Iris, the forty-something studio owner, that most of the students are adults, and most people take drop-in classes, meaning they come when they can and pay per class. I hand over twenty bucks for the six o'clock class—advanced lyrical dance. Not a ballet class, but not a terrible thing, considering my toes are a bit beaten up from all the pointe work lately. I used to take every dance type the studio offered—tap, jazz, acrobatics, hip-hop, lyrical, Irish, musical theater, ballet. But as I got older, I had to drop a few of those to fit in four to five ballet classes a week.

Eve has a night class to get to at Columbia, so I walk into the studio alone. Well, not alone, because there are at least twenty people on the floor stretching. The idea of being under all their scrutiny nearly sends me out the door again. But then I'd have to tell Eve I chickened out. Damn, why did I let her walk here with me? Now I have someone holding me accountable.

"You won't need those," Iris says, eyeing the pointe shoes in my hand.

I shake my head and toss them onto my bag. "Right. I knew that."

The four minutes it takes for class to start are agonizing. I can't stop fidgeting with my tank top, pulling my spandex shorts down, tying my hair up again. But then the music starts, and following along with these warmups that more than half the class seems familiar with occupies all of my brain space.

Later, when we're deep into learning the combination, Iris walks past me and taps her toe against my knee. "Looser. Take that perfect technique and let it go."

I smile down at my feet. Perfect technique. My mom would definitely be proud to hear that.

··◆··

"Did you enjoy that?" Iris asks me after class when the studio is nearly emptied out.

The front of my tank top is soaked in sweat, my hair too. But I'm not tired. I'm high on energy. "Yeah, a lot," I admit.

She grins at me and nods for me to follow her down the hall toward the front desk. "Where are you studying dance? Or are you already with a company?"

"Um…no." I haul my bag up to my shoulder. "I'm modeling right now. But I'm planning to reopen my parents' studio."

She asks me a few questions about this, not shying away from the subject when I bring up my mom. "How old are you?"

"Eighteen."

"That's what I thought." She shakes her head. "Teaching in a studio is great, don't get me wrong, but you don't do it when you're dancing like you are—at your prime. You do it after your knees and back betray you."

I shift uncomfortably from one foot to the other. "I wouldn't say I'm at my prime. I mean, I just started up again. I'm a little out of shape."

"Is that right?" She lifts an eyebrow. "In that case…" She leans over the desk, opens a drawer, and pulls out a business card. "Have you heard of this group?"

I glance at the name of the dance company on the card and shake my head.

"They're newer, lots of young talent, fresh choreography, less ballet, more contemporary," she says. "Pay's not great, but doable. I think you'd be a perfect fit."

I take the card from her, just to be polite, but hold it tentatively between my fingers.

"Go." She waves me off. "Look them up on the Google like all you young ones do. They have auditions next month. I've got dozens in my classes here preparing to audition for them. You might be one of the few I'd bet on making it in."

"Thanks."

I don't know what else to say. I can't believe she thinks I'm good enough for a professional company after one hour-and-a-half class, but then again, auditions often aren't even half that long. My dad used to tell me the first fifteen seconds could make or break an audition. Maybe that's more of a theater saying, because I sure as hell didn't win any awards looking nervous and clueless at the beginning of class tonight.

"Tomorrow, six o'clock," Iris says. "Street jazz and hip-hop. I'll save you a spot."

I mumble thanks again and head for the door, glancing back her way a couple times. What did I just get myself into? First nude photos, then dance company auditions. Talk about rebellious.

But really, I can't let myself be swayed by generous compliments and enticing new dance companies if I want to get that studio open in the next year.

It's too late for those daydreams.

I'm deep in thought the entire three-block walk home, so when I enter my apartment and find Eddie here, seated at the kitchen table, I'm already startled. But then I realize he's talking to French Mama, in French—am I the only one who learned Spanish in school?—and no one is yelling. Or running from spatulas. In fact, French Mama is serving him a plate of food, what looks like half a chicken covered in brown sauce with fancy carrots decoratively placed.

Across from Eddie, Elana is seated, leaning on one elbow, completely absorbed in whatever Eddie is telling them. He does seem to stumble more with his French than Eve, and her accent is better too, I think. But regardless, have I landed in an alternate reality version of my apartment?

Summer, who'd been slumped down on the couch so I could barely see her, grabs the strap of my bag, preventing me from going anywhere.

"Don't go in there," she hisses. "She made coq au vin."

"What's that?" I whisper, though I don't know why I'm whispering.

"It's heaven," Summer says, all dreamy, her gaze roaming toward the kitchen. "A heaven only fat people can go to."

I roll my eyes. "You really need to improve your communication skills. Have you done that 'How Mean Am I Really?' quiz I gave you a while back? I think it's time for another self-assessment."

"I can't live in this apartment," she snaps. "I'm gonna lose all my jobs. All of them!"

I clap a hand over her mouth and grin at the French-speaking table, since they're all three staring at us now. "How's it going? Having a nice chat?"

I look right at Eddie, dying to know how he got into French Mama's circle of trust.

"How could you not tell me that you met Toby Rhinehart?" Elana demands. "Eddie did a whole shoot with him!"

French Mama speaks quickly in French to Elana, her excitement too much to control. Elana translates. "Eddie asked Toby for some autographed pictures, and he said yes! He actually said yes. Eddie's going to his house or something to pick them up. Can you believe it?"

I smile. "It's about as crazy as him endorsing our book."

"What book?" Elana asks, then she moves without waiting for my answer. "My mom is making a batch of croissants and some cookies for him and his kids. You think he'll like that?"

"Jesus Christ!" Summer gets up from the couch, stomps all the way to her room, and slams the door.

Elana's mom shakes her head like Summer is the misbehaving child she can't control. Then she ushers me over to the table. Soon, I've got my own half a chicken, drowned in a brown sauce that has a hint of a wine scent to it. My stomach rumbles in response. I'm expecting them to sit down with us, but soon Elana and her mom are gathering purses and walking toward the door.

"Need anything from the store?" Elana asks me. When I shake my head, she adds, "We have to walk nine blocks just to get European butter."

As an afterthought, French Mama rushes back to the table, sets a red candle in the center, and lights it with a match from her purse. She gives me and Eddie this goofy smile like we're on a blind date, like we haven't already slept together.

When they're finally out the door, Eddie releases a huge sigh and then laughs. "Where have you been?" he asks.

"Dance class," I say, staring at the mouth-watering food in front of me.

"Really?" Eddie sets his fork down and looks at me. "How'd it go?"

"Okay." I shrug, not wanting to get into the business card Iris gave me. "Did you really ask Toby Rhinehart for autographed pictures?"

"I had to. It was kill or be killed. Or charm or be killed." He points to his food. "You know this dish takes two days to make? Is she a chef back in France?"

"Elana's family owns a bakery, but maybe they make this chicken stuff too." I pick up my fork and then set it down again. Summer's right. This is probably deadly. Skin on the chicken, butter all over the veggies. I lift the chicken thigh with my fork and sigh. Mashed potatoes underneath. Summer's right. We're gonna have to move out. We can't eat this stuff every day, and it will be so tempting.

Eddie watches me put my fork down yet again. "You're not eating?"

"Trying not to." I stare at the carrots. Maybe just those…

"Doesn't dance class earn you a treat?"

"Sure," I concede. "Usually a big bowl of fruit."

Eddie takes several bites while I contemplate one bite. He seems to read my mind. "You have to at least try it. It's authentic."

"You're right." I nod. "One bite."

Eddie grins. "I'm a bad influence, aren't I?"

"Definitely." Though I'm not sure that's entirely true. "I still can't believe you got French Mama to turn around like that. She was dead set on keeping you away."

"I have that effect on people," he jokes. "But what she doesn't know is that Toby is a fan of Elana's, or one of his kids is, I think. So I'm taking more credit than I deserve."

"How about I eat a few extra bites and we go for a run later?" I suggest.

"Deal." Eddie's mouth is full, but he holds a hand out to shake on it.

I bite into the chicken and sigh. It's amazing. We eat in silence for several minutes, and then I finally get up the courage to say, "Thanks."

"For what?"

I swirl my fork around. "For making an effort to get on my roommates' good sides—and their mothers'. You didn't have to do that, but it makes life easier."

"Yeah?" he says, looking pleased. "Glad I can help you for a change."

While Eddie tells me about the job he did today in Times Square, I sit there wondering how often he gets compliments, real ones, for things that make him him. Does anyone tell him what he's good at? Or has his whole life been about expectations? All related to his name and the similar names that came before him? I definitely don't envy that part of his life. Yeah, my mom was a dancer, and I gravitated toward that as well, but I never felt like it wasn't mine. Like I hadn't earned my skills. No matter how much people compare me to her, no one can take away the work I put into dance. But how does someone put effort into being Edward James Wellington IV? There is no room left to make any of that your own.

Summer's door opens, and I can feel her behind us, taking in the dinner table and the lit candle. Luckily, Eddie's phone rings, and he jumps out of his seat when he sees the number and heads straight outside for the balcony.

I spin around in my chair and face Summer, waiting.

"I feel like I'm back in preschool," she says. "Watching kids play house. All we need is food made of plastic."

"We could use the ones you stick in your bra?" I suggest.

She glares at me, but it's a look of admiration. Sometimes, I impress her. "God, you've got that knife ready when you need it, don't you?"

I'm about to remind her about that "How Mean Am I Quiz?" again, but Eddie returns. He stares at me, wide-eyed. "That was the agency…"

I lift an eyebrow, knowing he means the adoption agency, not the modeling one. "And?"

"I have a meeting with Dina Jackson. I can't believe she returned my call." He looks more nervous than excited, but I think this is a pretty big deal, considering he's not even supposed to know who Caroline is working with.

Summer brushes past me and says in her low voice, "Fun. Stray cat and now a baby stray. This is a dream come true for you, right?"

I ignore her and turn back to Eddie. That mixed-up, nervous stomach feeling hits me again. I don't know how to be sure about any of this. But maybe this is normal.

CHAPTER 37

Eddie

Dina Jackson from Bundles of Love adoption agency is taking my news better than I expected. Especially given the fact that this is a private agency and she profits from people like me handing over my baby.

"I was told the father wanted no involvement with the child and would be waiving rights." She hands me the cup of coffee I requested after practically being forced to accept something. "I'm surprised you knew how to find me."

"It took some work." And someone had to screw up. "But it seemed like the right thing to do, especially if things have gone forward already."

"I'm not at liberty to give you specifics without the permission of the child's mother," she says, "but I'm happy to help answer your more general questions."

An older dude appears in the doorway of her office. She waves him in when she sees him.

"Eddie, this is my good friend, Henry Brown." Dina points to an open chair in the corner of her office, and the guy sits. "I've asked him to be here because Henry works in the family court system, and he can help you better understand your...rights."

Not a fan of the way she said the word *rights*. I glance at Henry and then back at Dina. "Okay, so I never signed the waiver of right to notice."

"Obviously," she says, her lips forming a thin line.

"What is my next step?"

Henry clears his throat. "Is the child's mother willing to recognize you as the father?"

I almost blurt out, *Yes, why wouldn't she?* But then I remember the lawyers' plan. "You mean officially? Like on paper?"

"Yes," he says. "No one disputes parent names on birth certificates if both parties agree and are unmarried. We don't do paternity tests on every child born in this country."

My stomach sinks. "She probably won't go along with it." More like her wardens won't let her.

"Then you need to file a petition to establish paternity now," he explains. "When the child is born, a family court judge will order the mother to allow the test to be done."

"And then I can—"

"Assuming you're proven the father," Dina interjects.

I restrain myself from glaring at her on Caroline's behalf. She wouldn't have said that if she were in the room. "Assuming I'm the father, then I can object to the adoption?"

Dina and Henry converse silently, and then Henry speaks up. "Establishing paternity and the right to object to adoption are two separate things."

"But if it's my kid, she can't just let him get adopted," I argue.

"In most states, New York included," Henry says, "a biological connection with the child doesn't necessarily give you the right to be named the father."

I lift my hands in the air. "Well, then what the hell does? Because I'm ready to do it."

"Unfortunately, it might be too late," Dina says.

My whole body is frozen in fear. How could it be too late? The kid isn't even born yet. I can't respond, and both of them must realize this, because Henry explains further.

"For example, to establish paternity in an unborn child, the court might ask if you lived with the mother for at least six months prior to birth. If you showed support during the pregnancy—financially and emotionally."

Both of them wait for me to answer these questions. I've turned to stone. Whether from defeat or deciding that these two are not my friends. "We aren't allowed to see each other. Our parents decided that. And my family paid for all expenses, including the PI they hired to follow Caroline and make sure she didn't bring her pregnant self anywhere near me." I toss Dina a pointed look. "And I imagine they're paying a hefty sum to your agency, through the Davenports, to make extra sure those records get sealed as tightly as possible."

"That's not necessary," Dina says. "As of right now, no father will be listed anywhere in the records."

"Is that what you're really seeking?" Henry asks me. "The right to be placed on the birth certificate? Or are you seeking custody of the child?"

I hesitate, probably for too long. "Both."

Dina Jackson opens her mouth, but Henry shakes his head. "If that's your goal, file the paternity petition in conjunction with a custody petition."

I nod, listening carefully now that he's gone back to factual mode. "And then what?"

"You will be notified of the adoption hearing," he says. "You'll have the right to be heard by a judge in the family court system. But I will warn you, New York rules in the best interest of the child. If the judge decides placement with the adoptive family is best for the child, then there is no further action you can take."

"Why would they do that?" I ask. "I mean, assuming I'm not a convict or a serial killer, I'm still the father. Plenty of dads are horrible, and those kids aren't put up for adoption." God, what would a family court judge say about my father?

"They could be if the child's mother pursued it," Henry explains.

"Look at it from a judge's perspective," Dina says, her voice syrupy sweet. "You're how old, Eddie? Eighteen?" I nod. "It sounds like your family isn't willing to provide you support in raising this child. Where will you live? Are you employed? Do you have health care? Do you have a plan for your child's education and religious beliefs? Having you taken parenting classes? Infant CPR?"

One of my nannies taught me infant CPR when I was really young. I wanted to play with my sister's dolls, and the nanny thought my parents would hate the idea, so she made it an educational activity.

"You think I'll lose," I say, my voice flat.

"Winning custody is almost always unlikely in these situations," Henry says. "Additionally, it will take at least thirty days to get to trial. During that waiting time, the child will be placed in the temporary custody of the adoptive family, assuming they don't back out as many do when fathers get involved in this manner. If there is no adoptive family and the mother isn't able or willing to care for the child until the trial, he or she will be placed in state custody until a ruling happens."

"You mean foster care?" I say.

Henry nods. "Correct."

Several minutes later, I'm walking outside, just a few blocks from my apartment. I don't remember much of what was said at the end of the meeting, just me promising that I would indeed be seeking a paternity suit very soon. After the foster care thing was dropped into the conversation, I couldn't process much else. One tiny baby. Two very wealthy families who have the resources to raise a baby with the best care possible. And somehow, he might end up as a ward of the state for the first month of his life.

Because of me.

That's the worst part of it. I could sign that waiver, and that would never happen. He would have a family and a home from the moment he's born.

But he could with me too.

I'm so busy freaking out, I forget that I'm supposed to meet Finley for dinner. She sends me a text, and I must sound messed up in my reply, because she tells me to stay where I am. I walk a couple blocks to a nearby park and plop down on a bench.

"What happened?" Finley is standing over me now, her hair partially blocking her face, but I can see lines of worry.

A few weeks ago, I would have played it cool, tucked the stress and drama away. But it's become easier every day, being honest with her. "I think I need a lawyer."

Her forehead wrinkles. "That bad, huh?"

"And a house," I add. "Definitely need a house. Plus an educational plan. And probably infant CPR again. I can't remember if it's two breaths and five compressions or one breath..."

"Okay, enough of this," she says with a nod, and then she takes my hand and pulls me to my feet. "It's after six, so no lawyer shopping tonight. Schools are closed, real estate agents are off duty... Let's go do something normal."

I sigh. "All this shit of mine is lacking in fun, isn't it? Not what you signed up for when you joined my beer pong team."

"If I'm being honest," Finley says, dead serious, "I would have picked a more skilled partner if I had the choice."

"So what you're saying is"—I pull her against me so fast, she sucks in a breath—"you're expecting me to be good at other things?"

She opens her mouth to reply, but I cut her off, kissing her in a way that I hope shows how much I'm with her on this "let's take a break and be crazy for the night" plan.

There are too many people around. I have to put a stop to the kissing way too early. "Come on." I step back and take her hand so we can start walking somewhere. Anywhere. "Let's go do normal."

Normal for me must mean giving her a good once-over.

She's wearing a short blue dress tonight. I lean closer, examining a white strap beneath her dress. "Is that a leotard? Have you been to dance class again?"

She laughs and lifts my chin to draw my eyes up. "Yes, I have. You caught me."

"Five nights in a row?" I lift an eyebrow. "If I didn't know better, I'd think you were training for something."

"It's research," she says, but her cheeks turn pink, and her gaze drifts away from mine.

I decide to put those questions on hold for a while, right beside the lawyer and the CPR ones. I give Finley a little shove from behind, pushing her a few steps in front of me. "Walk ahead of me, and I'll pretend to follow you. I know how you're into that stuff."

Two dudes in front of us turn around and give us this look like *what the hell?* Finley turns bright red, but she's laughing. I sling an arm around her shoulder and steer us in a different direction. It doesn't take more than a couple minutes, walking beside Fin, for my panic to subside, for me to feel better, a little less burdened. Complete distraction.

This stuff with Fin, it's all new for me. I mean, I've kissed my fair share of girls, but I haven't done any of this. Walking around aimlessly together, taking turns giving each other that sideways glance that says *Is this real? Are you really with me?* And then no matter how much you try to hide your feelings or play it cool, it's not possible.

For the tiniest, briefest moment, I regret opening the custody battle can of worms, because I would love to text

Caroline right now and explain this weird moment to her. I think she would get it. I think she would like Finley a lot.

We end up eating dinner from a taco stand and shopping for something called foot thongs—yeah, I know, right?—that Fin needed for a dance class.

Neither of us brings up my meeting at the agency until we're walking back to our building, when I finally give her the brief summary of what was said.

"Does that mean you changed your mind?" she asks tentatively.

I wait for my brain to form a new answer, but it doesn't, because I didn't. "No."

CHAPTER 38

Finley

I lean over and watch Eddie working on my laptop, rewording my words. He definitely took my mission statement to a whole new level. "You're really good at this."

"Groomed from birth, remember." He keeps his gaze on the screen, forehead scrunched like he's thinking hard. "And my school really stressed writing."

He is terrible at accepting compliments. Maybe he resents the way he acquired skills like good writing so much that he can't be proud of anything he's learned. I sit up on my bed and rub my sore calf muscles. "Was it all bad?"

"What?" He looks at me. "My school? Or my grooming from birth?"

"Both. Either."

I wait for him to make a few tiny adjustments to paragraph five of my business plan, and then he answers. "When it comes down to it, I'm a privileged kid. So no, it wasn't *all* bad."

I know there's much more to it than that, but I decide to leave the subject alone for now. Especially with all the stress he's been under. He met this morning with a lawyer who is going to represent him in his paternity case. We're going to my house this weekend so Eddie can look at apartments and "demonstrate his independence."

"So the lawyer doesn't mind waiting to get paid?" I ask.

He shrugs. "Not sure. I kind of withheld those details. I figure by the time he bills me, I'll have money." He sighs. "Basically, paying the lawyer is the least of my worries."

I lean back against my chair, watching Eddie type. After several seconds, his hands freeze on the keys, and I figure he's about to call me out for staring at him, but then I see the chat box pop up on my laptop.

EVE NOWAKOWSKI: Your nude photos look great!

Heat rushes to my face. Eddie turns to me, his eyebrow lifted, a grin on his face. Then, before I can stop him, he types: **Send one!**

I slam the computer shut and pull it off his lap. I have his full attention now.

"Nude photos?"

"Shh." I hope Summer isn't outside my door, eavesdropping. She'd love this—for tormenting me. "It wasn't like *nude* nude, just…you know, artistically nude."

"You're really not going to let me look?" Eddie asks. "I've already seen all of you."

"Totally not the same."

The shoot with Eve had been much easier than I expected. Really not a big deal at all. It's hard to explain why it felt different than taking "nude" photos, but it did. I wasn't posing for anyone in a metaphorical sense. It was more about being stripped down, being alone with yourself. It was raw, real, showing every single aspect of a dancer's moving muscles.

Eddie tugs me down beside him, causing my sweatpants to shift upward and reveal a bruise below my knee. He brushes his fingertips over it. "What happened here?"

"Street jazz." I glance down, surprised by how big and purple it's turned. "We did a lot of chair work last night. I didn't get along with my chair."

"Obviously." Eddie slides down and touches his lips to my knee. Then his gaze travels to my feet. "Jesus. Is this the chair's fault too?"

My feet are pretty blistered and unattractive at the moment. "That would be the pointe shoes' fault. And Eve's, because she keeps asking me to do more shoots."

"Guess I failed to meet her expectations," Eddie says, faking disappointment. "She hasn't called me with more work."

I'm about to reply with a smart-ass comment about all the work he *is* getting, but then Eddie picks up one of my feet and rubs it. I lean my head back and groan. "That feels amazing."

He's quiet for a while, working on my feet and then moving on to the calf muscle I'd been rubbing earlier. I can tell he's retreated back inside his head where everything is complicated and heavy. I'm feeling a little bit of that weight myself, knowing I've put something in motion my dad won't approve of. If I get the green light from the bank, then I'll have to tell him.

"I have to talk to my parents," Eddie blurts out.

I lift my head so I can see him. "We knew that already." And he still hasn't done it.

"I mean, I really need to. The lawyer…he said I need to make sure I've expressed my desire to be a parent to enough people. And my petition for paternity and custody will go to a judge tomorrow, and it won't take long to get back to my dad's lawyer."

I sit up again. "Great. Let's go now. I'm ready."

He smiles, working hard to hide his nerves. "I already scheduled dinner with them tomorrow night. My sister is in town."

I avoid asking him why he has to schedule dinner with his own family. "Does your sister know any—"

"I don't think so." He shakes his head.

"What do you think she'll think of everything? Will she side with your parents?" I ask. I'm really curious about this sister of Eddie's.

"Hard to say." He thinks for a minute, running a hand through his hair and making it stick up in all directions. "She wouldn't agree with all my dad's bribery and blackmailing but with letting Caroline do things her way, letting it be her decision—I think that will probably be Ruby's opinion. My parents' plan allowed for that."

I wait for him to say more, but all he does is flash this fake grin and say, "We'll find out, I guess." Then he nudges me onto my back again. "So when do you think you'd open the studio? Assuming everything goes through."

"Not until next fall." I exhale and stare at the ceiling. It's hard to wait that long. "Maybe summer as a trial program."

"Remember," Eddie says, planting a kiss on my collarbone, "I'm up for playing piano."

"Guess that means I need to add a studio day care to my business plan." I'm only joking, but he tenses.

"I didn't think about that," he says, concern in his voice. "I have to start thinking about those things, planning for all of them." He scrubs a hand over his face. "Clearly, I suck at this."

"Hey, that's not what I meant." I tug his hand away from his face and kiss him. "You'll figure it all out."

"Hopefully." He distracts himself by kissing me again.

My stomach flutters every time he's within my vicinity. I'm waiting for that feeling to stop—I mean, I see him all the time— but it doesn't seem to be going away any time soon. I don't remember ever being this hot for Jason. We were friends first, hanging out with our mutual friends, and then we went to a dance together and decided to experiment with making out. It didn't go terribly, so yeah. I loved calling him my boyfriend. I loved having someone to hold hands with. I loved seeing other girls envy us. Then last fall…that was all gone. And all I could think about was how to get it back.

With Eddie, I just feel hooked on him. Him talking, smiling at me. Him stretched out across my bed. Watching him play the piano—something he obviously enjoys when he allows himself to. Seeing him make plans to be a father to his kid. Making room for him in my life. I'm hooked on that more than anything else. I love making decisions for me and then watching him mold himself into those plans, like he was part of them all along. Which is the opposite of what my relationship with Eddie was supposed to be that first night I met him.

But some of the essence of that night still lingers, I think that's why he does fit in with my life. Neither of us want to change the other. We've taken each other at face value and ran with it. Which is interesting, because it's kind of the opposite of what Summer claimed I was trying to do with Eddie—change him, save him from himself. He doesn't need any of that. Neither do I.

"I feel like I'm always taking off your clothes," Eddie whispers in my ear between kisses. "It doesn't have to be like that. We can…we can just hang out too."

I slide his shirt off and toss it on the floor. "You don't like taking my clothes off?"

"No," he says, then lifts his head. "I mean yes. I love it. But I'm capable of *not* doing this. Just so you know."

He's pretty cute when he tries to be gentlemanly. Fortunately for both of us, we are on the same page when it comes to preferred free time activities.

"Noted," I say. "I can take my own bra off."

Eddie laughs and unhooks the clasp himself. "You're pretty cool, you know that, right?"

"Cool enough to come to your scheduled dinner? I'm an excellent dinner guest."

His face darkens. "Look, I really think I should go alone—"

"You might think that, but it's not happening." I press both my hands to his shoulders, forcing him onto his back. "You're just gonna have to take a leap of faith and trust me. I'm not gonna change my mind about you because of how your family acts."

Eddie reaches up and rests a hand on my cheek. He doesn't argue further with me, which is a good sign. "Do you think—I mean…" He releases a breath and turns the full force of his very intense eyes on me. My stomach flips over. He strokes a hand over my hair. "You would know better than me, since you've done this before…"

"Done what?" I ask.

"Relationships. The longer kind. The kind that are actually a relationship." He slides my bra strap carefully down my shoulder. "Do think we're doing okay?"

I look down at him, waiting for him to make a joke or tell me he was only kidding. But he doesn't. "I—well, yeah. I think we're doing okay."

"Good." He nods, relieved. "That's really good to know."

And right then, in those seconds after seeing him so relieved by this response, I almost say, *I know we're doing okay because I'm in love with you.*

But it feels too soon, too new.

CHAPTER 39

Eddie

Finley releases a low whistle after being led out of the entry-way and down the hall of our apartment. I glance beside me at her. She's wide-eyed, taking in the extravagance of our family home.

My stomach twists the second we step into the dining room. I don't think I've been this nervous in my entire life. My parents enter the room from the opposite end, followed by my sister walking through a third entrance—typical for us, coming to dinner from separate locations of the apartment.

My mom forces some energy into her typical stoned expression and kisses me on both cheeks before moving on to Finley. "And who is this lovely young lady?" She seems abnormally pleased that I've brought a date to dinner.

My hand shakes as I lift it to gesture beside me. "This is Finley Belton."

Fin does a great job plastering on a smile for them. She glances at my dad and then Ruby, waiting for some kind of acknowledgment.

My father only gives me a tiny nod and says, "Edward."

Ruby's dismissive nod is similar, but she at least offers up an introduction. "Ruby. Edward's sister."

I can feel Finley looking her over, probably trying to see some of me in Ruby. But really, other than her being tall and thin—like both my parents—she doesn't look anything like me. She's pretty in a conventional way, her hair is much lighter than mine, and she wears designer clothes but all simple styles in plain, neutral colors. She's hard to read in every way, including through her clothing.

When we sit down, Fin gets startled by the maid shoving her chair in further after she's seated, but other than that, she seems comfortable and at ease. In fact, I quickly understand how she became a model, besides being beautiful. She has a talent for engaging the entire table in conversation. Watching her is like a lesson in professionalism. But she isn't here to work. She's here for me.

I let that sink in for a moment, enjoying, for once in my life, the feeling of not being alone. I slide my hand from my lap to her thigh and give it a squeeze. She flashes me a tiny smile and then turns back to answer a question my mother just asked her.

"So you're not a Princeton student?" my mom repeats. "That's right. You said you have an apartment on the Upper West Side. Are you at Columbia then? Or NYU?"

She says NYU with a certain amount of disdain. My parents are not fond of any university that is art focused.

"Neither." Finley eyes the maid, who is pouring us each a glass of wine, then shoots a glance at my dad. Maybe that seems off to her, serving alcohol to the underaged? But she doesn't mention the wine and instead goes for a sip of water. "I'm not in school. I live in an agency apartment."

"Oh," my mom says, surprised. "You're an actress?"

"She's a model," Ruby says, her voice flat. We all look at her, surprised. She takes a sip from the glass of red wine in front of her and then stares at Fin. "Marc Jacobs ad, right? You were on that giant cake."

My mouth immediately goes dry. I hold my breath, waiting for Ruby to keep going. To mention me.

Finley's shock echoes mine but only lasts a moment, then she pulls it together and smiles. "Yes, that would be me. I nearly broke my leg climbing on the cardboard hell."

Ruby tosses me a pointed look, confirming that she knows what I've been up to. I sit there, frozen solid, but she doesn't mention seeing me in any ads. And really, it's all going to come out before this dinner is over anyway.

Beneath the table, Finley covers my hand with hers. I relax about five percent.

"A model," my mother says. "That's so interesting."

Dad gives a noncommittal, "Hmmmph."

"Finley's a dancer," I add. "Her mother danced with the New York City Ballet."

Fin looks at me like *Why are you trying to impress these people?* Good question. She clears her throat. "It's more of a hobby now. I'm hoping to get into teaching dance soon." She turns to Ruby. "What is it you're studying at Brown? Eddie mentioned it once, and I've forgotten."

Finley is so calm when she lifts the slice of bread on her plate and then expertly spreads butter over it. Someone has taught her how to fit in here—her mother maybe.

Ruby lifts an eyebrow, probably surprised that I would talk about her with Finley. I doubt she ever mentions me to her friends or boyfriends. "Russian literature and theology."

"Wow, that sounds…"

"Useless," my father says at the same as I say, "Boring."

Only the word is cut off the second I realize I've joined my father's camp. I don't want to spend even five seconds on the same side of the fence as him.

"I was going to say complicated," Finley says, attempting to recover this. "Do you actually read literature written in Russian or is it simply literature with Russian roots?"

My father snorts back a laugh, but Ruby glares at him, then turns to Finley. "Language proficiency is a requirement of the course of study."

Finley opens her mouth to ask another question, but my dad blurts out his favorite question. "What does your family do?"

"My dad," Finley says, setting down her half-eaten slice of bread, "is a high school drama teacher. My mom died a few years ago."

My dad's forehead scrunches up, like he's not sure what to do with this information. He resorts to another dismissive nod and then asks me to help get some "real drinks," which is code for "we should speak in private."

Finley's cheerful voice carries all the way into the parlor where my father keeps his supply of very expensive liquor.

He pours a glass of scotch and takes a long drink before

saying, "You're done ignoring my efforts to set up business meetings for you. I want you at an alumni dinner I'm attending in Princeton this week."

I eye the bottle of vodka. It takes everything in me to not unscrew the cap and start chugging. "I can't this week." *Because you're going to get some interesting news from your lawyer, and you won't want me there.* Among other reasons.

"You can and you will," he says firmly. "I've given you enough time to run amok at Princeton. Do you think I don't know that you're barely making it to your classes?" *Um…barely? Try never.* His detectives are slacking. "Of course I know. I took care of your grade already, but you will make every meeting I set up for you, and you'll put on that charming act everyone seems so fond of, understand?"

"Yes, sir." The words come out with venom I didn't know I had in me. A sense of resolve washes over me. I'm done with this. All of this. With my head down, I pour my mother's usual drink—vodka on the rocks with a twist of lime—and carry it into the dining room.

We've only made it to the appetizer course, but I can't put this off any longer. I wait for my dad to return to his seat, his smug expression plastered on, and then I glance at Finley. She must be able to read my mind or at least enough to guess what I'm about to do, because she straightens up in her chair, game face on.

I shove the appetizer plate toward the center of the table and out of my way. Both my parents look up, surprised. "So…I didn't actually come here tonight for dinner."

Ruby picks up her fork and stabs a shrimp, not even bothering to look my way.

"I came here to tell you that I dropped out of Princeton. Permanently. " My heart beats so loud, I can't even hear my own voice over the blood pumping in my ears. I clasp my hands together in front of me to silence the shaking. "And I've decided not to sign the waiver of right to notice form."

Silence. Dead silence. Both my parents stare at me, openmouthed. Ruby's forehead wrinkles; she's confused. She doesn't know anything. I'm sure everyone else can hear how loud my heart beats. "I've also decided to pursue establishing paternity—"

Ruby coughs, choking on her last bite.

"Like hell you are," my father says in a tone that scares the shit out of me.

I glance at Fin, making sure she's okay. I debate telling her to leave now while she still can, but she lays a hand on my elbow, connecting us.

My mother keeps looking at Finley like her biggest concern is what to do with the innocent bystander now holding our family's darkest secrets. I toss my napkin onto the table, knowing I won't be here much longer. "I've already petitioned family court for a paternity test once the baby is born. Caroline is likely to refuse cooperating with me, so this route is the only way, unfortunately."

The second I say the name Caroline, Ruby chokes on the drink that was meant to help her previous choking. My gaze flicks in her direction for a moment and then back to my parents. My dad's hard expression is on full force, only he's beginning to turn a deep shade of red. "I've also filed a petition for custody."

My mother gasps, but my father seems to have reached some level of control over his anger, because he's nearly calm when he responds. "I'll have that petition overturned in less than twenty-four hours. There's not a judge in Manhattan I can't bribe." He pauses, tilting his head to the side. "I won't even need bribery." He glances at Ruby. "You would know this—what is that motto in family court? They have to rule—"

"In the best interest of the child," Ruby finishes, her voice cold and mechanical, revealing nothing to me about her real thoughts on any of this.

"Placing an infant in the hands of an eighteen-year-old drug addict doesn't seem like a child-centered decision, does it?"

It takes everything in me not to pelt my glass of wine across the table at him simply to wipe that sneer from his face. But then I hear his voice inside my head: *Add streaks of violence to being a drug addict.* Instead, I lean back in my chair, arms folded over my chest. "I'm sure the papers would love to tell that story. The *Wall Street Journal* would eat it up. 'Wellington family hides violent addict son from public eye and fails at their attempts to conceal the existence of his illegitimate child.' I could probably get several months' rent selling that."

My father's face reddens again. My mother looks like she's about to vomit. Beside me, Finley tosses her napkin on top of mine and pushes away from the table. I take her cue and stand up as well.

My dad is on his feet, shoving his chair back with such force it topples over. The maid reaches to pick it up but seems to think twice about it and scurries from the room. I back away from the table, bringing Fin with me.

Dad charges forward but stops before reaching me. "You will not step foot out of this house without my permission. You won't speak a word of this to anyone, and you will sign those papers, understood?"

"No." I shake my head. "I'm not giving up my kid."

"That child will not be a part of this family!" he barks, raising a finger to point it at me.

I lift my hands. "Even better. I wouldn't want to subject a child to this family."

"You unappreciative smart-ass." His voice has lowered, and it's more scary at this volume. "You do anything that attaches that child to our name, and I swear to God, you will never see another penny from us again."

"Fine." I start to turn around, glad Finley is coming with me.

"Consider yourself cut off, Edward!" he says. "Your trust account, your credit cards, everything will be gone."

This hits a nerve with me. I snap back around and pull out my wallet. "You really think that's going to stop me?" I yank out an American Express card that I haven't touched since before graduation and toss it at him. It lands at his feet. "Here you go. It's all yours." I remove another card and throw it his way. "Bank card too."

"You are nothing without this family. You own nothing," he snaps. "I pay for everything. Your housing, school, clothing, phone—"

I remove a Blackberry from my right pocket. "You mean this phone? The one I've only used to contact you for the last six or so weeks? Here you go." I add that to the pile at his feet. "What else? Oh right…my clothes." I reach behind me, and in one swift motion, my T-shirt is off and at his feet.

My mother gasps again and looks like she might pass out at any moment.

"You have no right to that child, no right to list yourself as a father," he shoots at me.

I'm about to explode all over the place, but then I hear, "Yes, he does."

Everyone turns to look at Ruby again. My dad shifts his pointer finger to her. "You stay out of this."

"I'm completely out of this," she snaps. "But it's a fact. He has a right to claim himself as a father if that's what he is. It's a constitutional right."

I give her a nod, surprised but grateful for that tiny ounce of support. One I'm sure my dad doesn't care about in the least. Finley slides her hand in mine and tugs me close enough for her to whisper, "Let's go."

"If it helps you, I'll give him a different name," I offer with as much sarcasm as I can muster. Although, that's exactly what I want for him. Not to be a Wellington. "I might even give myself a new name."

Finally, I turn to leave, my dad shouting to the maid to get his lawyer on the phone. It's not until I'm outside in the sun that I realize (1) my entire body is shaking, and (2) I have no shirt on.

Lucky for me, it's summer, and plenty of people are out and about, jogging without a shirt, so I don't look that out of place. We cross two streets and walk three blocks before Finley forces me to stop and sit down at a picnic table in the courtyard of our apartment building.

I rest my head in my hands, take in a few deep, slow breaths. My heart still beats out of control, and my hands are still shaking. But several more deep breaths later, I'm getting some control back. When I lift my head, Fin is leaning on one elbow, watching me.

"It's not true, you know," she says.

"What's not true?"

"You being nothing without your family name." She continues to study me so intensely, I start to get uncomfortable. "You know that, right?"

"Yeah," I say automatically. "That's what I'm working on. Being something without them."

She shakes her head. "I mean right now. Like this very second. You as this person across from me. You're something."

"Okay." I smile and reach for her hand, tangling it with mine. "Whatever you say."

She jerks her hand back, not returning the smile. "I'm not kidding. You are good at lots of things. And you always have this look, like you're thinking about everything. Turning it around in your mind. I noticed that just minutes after I first met you. And it has nothing to do with your upbringing or your family.

Privileged kids often have a narrowed perspective. You're different. Not because of them, but despite them."

I stare down at my hands. I don't know if that's true or not. I don't really know if I'm that different from other kids like me. I just know that I want to be different. It's kind of the only thing I know about myself at the moment. Despite doubting Finley's theories about me, I lift my head and look at her again before saying, "Thanks. For this. For all of it."

I pull her closer until she's sitting between my legs. When her cheek touches my chest, she says, "Can we please end every dinner with you stripping off your shirt?"

I laugh and then rest my chin on the top of her head. "I should probably call the lawyer now. Update him on my dinner with the fam."

Her lips touch my neck. "Five more minutes."

I close my eyes and sigh. "Yeah, okay."

My heart hasn't returned to normal pace yet. Maybe it won't until all of this is over and dealt with. I glance at the time on my cell and groan. Finley lifts her head. "What's wrong?"

"I have that parenting class in an hour." I pull myself together and sit up straight. I'm so not in the right mind for lessons on lifesaving or diaper changing, but I guess that's sort of the idea. When you have a kid, you don't get to pick and choose when to take care of them. You have to do it, even on your worst days.

CHAPTER 40

Finley

The first thing Ron Miller, family law attorney, says when Eddie and I sit down in his office is, "So, your father offered me fifty grand to not represent your paternity case. He also informed me that you're a drug addict and a compulsive liar. And that the mother of your child feels threatened by you and wants nothing to do with you."

Eddie nods slowly, pulling in a deep breath. "Huh. That's…well, that's interesting."

"It's bullshit," I blurt out, but Eddie lifts a hand to stop me. I bite down hard on the inside of my cheek just to keep from arguing further. He didn't go through the stress of standing up to his family to have this happen.

"Anything you need to tell me?" Ron Miller asks.

"I think my father summed it all up well," Eddie says, his voice tense.

Ron's eyebrows shoot up. "So it's all true?"

"There is a tiny sliver of truth in each of my father's claims." Eddie maintains direct eye contact with the lawyer and taps a finger on the desktop. "I definitely have to give him credit for that."

"Then tell me those slivers of truth," Ron says.

I'm surprised by how calm this lawyer is after hearing all this. But maybe he's seen a lot worse, dealing with family court all the time.

"I have used recreational drugs before. I lied to my parents about being at Princeton for the summer program. I haven't shown up for anything. I've been working in New York and living in an apartment with twenty other guys," Eddie rattles off. "And the mother of my child is very threatened by the fact that I won't sign away my rights, and both our parents forbid us to see each other, but even without that, I'd say there's a good chance she'd rather not be around me. I'm making her decision more difficult. I hate that it's like that, but there is no other way."

Ron folds his hands on top of the desk and looks right at Eddie. "When was the last time you used drugs?"

I open my mouth to protest him answering that question, but I don't get a chance.

"Last winter," he says right away. "In January."

"Alcohol use?"

Eddie glances at me and then back at Ron. "Six or so weeks ago."

The night we met. Great. I'm a contributing factor to that. But he wasn't drunk. Does that matter? It's amazing how terrible our lives can seem when presented in this manner.

"You've been attending the parenting classes I recommended?" Ron asks.

"Yes."

He hasn't missed a single one. Not even the class right after the dinner debacle. I've caught him reading the material they hand out on his free time as well as tons of online articles on parenting. After looking over some of the material myself, I've concluded that both my dad and I suck at parenting by this course's standards.

"I assume you've been taught the course motto?" Ron prompts. "What is said to be the most important rule about parenting?"

"Emotional and physical safety of the child is always the number one priority, and parents must put the child's needs above their own," Eddie recites.

I applaud him silently. That was pretty impressive memorization. Maybe he should go to Princeton.

"Exactly," Ron says with a nod. "And do you think your father's efforts to sabotage your paternity and custody case were done with those guidelines in mind?"

Eddie stifles a laugh. "Uh, no."

"Do you want to know what I think?" Ron asks, and both Eddie and I nod. "I think your father is terrified of this child being legally deemed his grandson because"—he hesitates—"correct me if I'm wrong, but your family is bound by old money, which means he probably can't undo any trust accounts or—"

Eddie sinks back in his chair, his eyes wide. "Inheritance. Jesus. Why didn't I think of that? That's why he's been so against my name being attached to this kid. Even with an adoption."

"And the thing is," Ron says, "adoption, for the most part, removes any trace of surname from any records for the child. And also removes any right to inheritance from the birth family once it's finalized. But there are a few very rare and very unlikely scenarios where that could be overridden. He must really want to cover all his bases."

"Does this mean you're still willing to represent me?" Eddie asks tentatively. "I can find another lawyer, but I don't think it's going to look very good, honestly."

Ron shifts some papers on his desk and then glances at Eddie. "I'm still willing. This is the first time I've ever been bribed by a client's parent, and I can't help it—I get fired up for a win with bribery on the table."

"So you think he can win?" I ask.

"I think it's possible. But unlikely," Ron admits. Eddie deflates a little beside me. "I also firmly believe he has a right to try and should indeed do just that. I wouldn't be here helping you if I thought you had an agenda other than doing what you feel is right for your kid. If this was a selfish, 'I want control over the girl I got pregnant' situation, I'd have told you no thanks."

"But do you think it's best?" Eddie asks so quietly it's almost a whisper. "For the kid, I mean. For *my* kid."

"Hard to say. You or a loving, established family, desperate for a child to parent, hand-selected by the best adoption agency in the country…"

Eddie deflates even more.

"On the other hand," Ron continues, "I was raised by eighteen-year-old parents, and my childhood not only lacked traumatic events, but was also full of healthy and happy memories. And being young and hip, they raised me in a way that welcomed collaborative decision making, and they were too sharp and in-the-know for me to get away with anything rebellious. Who's to say you won't create a home like that? I hope you do."

"Me too," Eddie mumbles quietly.

I reach for his hand, giving it a squeeze. Eddie could be that type of parent. I believe that wholeheartedly. Seeing him with my brothers, watching him watch them, listen to them when they voice their opinions, the way he shut off the TV and found other things for them to do. I mean, he was just watching them for a couple hours. It wasn't his job to be concerned with their long-term health. And he treats them like real people, like adults in the making.

But it won't be easy. None of it will be easy, and he still has so much to learn. The real test, the 'are you ready be a parent?' test, happens after you realize that your kid will always be your kid. Forever. My dad told me that years ago, and I've never forgotten it.

Ron grins like he's satisfied with Eddie's response. "The good news is that the second you become a potential parent, your own parents lose any control over you whatsoever. Family court isn't traditional trial court. None of the judges will give a flying fuck who your father is or what he might do for them. Or to them. They are there to rule on behalf of the child. That's it. I don't agree with every ruling a family court judge has made on behalf of my clients, but I trust the system. I trust that the pros and cons are weighed carefully and that the judge believes they've made the best choice for the child."

Eddie releases a breath. "Okay, that helps."

"Now," Ron says, "try and forget about your father. Work on you and your child—home, support system, list of items an infant needs that you plan to purchase, expected income for the next year, a pediatrician, plans for health care, and that includes yourself." He tosses a sheet of paper Eddie's way that lists everything he's listing off. "It would be wise to assume your father will pull all the rugs out from under you, including medical insurance. And if you haven't made your own health a priority, then a judge is likely to assume that you will do the same for your child."

He gives Eddie a minute to look over the paper, then says, "Now, do you have anyone we could list as support for you? An aunt or grandparent within a reasonable distance of where you plan to live, to help check on you and the baby?"

Eddie looks at me, and I give him a small nod. You can say me. I'll do it. Of course I'll be there.

Ron catches on without Eddie saying anything. "Another teenager. That might not be enough." Still, he writes my name down in his notebook.

"Finley has experience raising her brothers." Eddie quickly explains about my family situation.

Ron lifts an eyebrow. "A father of three, certified guidance counselor, and public school teacher nearby to offer help is definitely something worth bringing up to a judge."

"I don't know if we can—" Eddie starts.

"I'm sure my dad would be happy to offer support," I say.

Eddie looks over at me, a question in his eyes. It's fine. We'll talk to him soon. He likes Eddie. He really likes him. Especially after hearing about the swim meet drama. I know he'll want to help out.

"Okay then." Rod gives a nod. "Things are looking up for you, Eddie Wellington. Keep up the good work."

We both thank him, and Ron adds, "Make me proud. I turned down fifty grand for you."

When we exit the lawyer's office and head outside, Eddie says,

"You think your dad will be okay with this? I don't want to put him in a position he's not comfortable with."

"Relax," I assure him. "It'll be fine."

CHAPTER 41

Eddie

I barely say a word the whole time Finley is going on about the apartments nearby that we looked at earlier today. I'm hanging in midair—not literally—watching Sam to get an idea of what he thinks about everything. Based on the fact that she jumped right into apartments and baby gear, Fin must have given him the basics before we arrived this morning.

"Don't we still have tons of baby stuff in storage?" Finley asks her dad.

Sam takes a bite of the pork chops he grilled for dinner and nods. "Two of everything."

"My dad is a hoarder," Finley explains.

Sam interrupts. "Recovering hoarder."

"Right. Forgot. You went to all those meetings." Fin rolls her eyes. "Anyway, a couple years ago, my grandma rented him a storage unit to pile all his old albums, baby stuff, thousands of pages of sheet music…we should go check it out before you buy anything."

Beside me, Braden sighs. "Babies are gross."

"Yeah?" I smile at him. "You used to be one, you know? Me too."

He shrugs. "I don't remember."

"I don't remember either," I tell him. "But I heard it's true."

On my other side, Connor tugs on my sleeve and waits for me to lean down so he can whisper to me. "What are you gonna call your baby?"

"That's a good question."

Fin and Sam look at me, but I ask Connor if it's okay before I say anything. When he nods, I tell them.

"Is it a boy or a girl?" Braden asks, then he glances at Finley, his forehead wrinkled. "You don't look like you have a baby in your tummy. Are you adoptioning it?"

"Adopting," Finley corrects. "And I'm not having a baby. Eddie is...wait—" She turns bright red.

Sam laughs and then leans on one elbow. "Go on, Fin. I am so going to enjoy hearing you explain this one."

Finley is desperately grappling for words, so I decide to rescue her. "Only girls can have babies, older girls. But all babies have a mom and a dad. No matter what. And the mom of my baby is someone I've known for a long time, way before I met your sister. But we don't really get along anymore."

Maybe that was too frank for their ears. I watch closely for any reaction.

Braden is busy drowning his pork chop in ketchup, but he manages to nod and say, "Cool. Is it a boy or a girl baby?"

"Boy," I say. "But I don't know what to call him."

"Darth Vader," Braden says. "Or Luke."

"Or Spider-Man," Connor offers, barely audible.

I hadn't really thought about the fact that naming this kid

something other than Edward will be ruining a four-generation tradition in my family. Will that piss my father off more than naming him Edward? Doesn't matter. I'm not having a kid with V tacked onto his name.

I offer to help Fin with the dishes at the same time as Connor asks me to check out the puzzle he's been working on. Finley and Sam shove me out of the kitchen. I follow Connor into the living room to see the massive five-thousand-piece puzzle of the Sydney harbor and opera house in Australia.

I sit down on the floor and study the sections he's completed. "Wow...you must have worked really hard on this."

Connor nods, and Braden charges into the room and adds, "He did almost the whole thing at day camp, and then Riley stomped on it. So the counselors let him take it home."

Connor looks down at the pieces, sliding two around on the rubber mats covering the floor.

"Riley, huh?" I say. I glance at Braden.

He immediately says, "I didn't see it, 'cause I'm in a different group since the camp people can't tell us apart. But Riley even tolded me he did it."

"On purpose," Connor adds, whispering the words.

I already want to beat this Riley kid's ass. "He sounds like a bully."

Connor shrugs, but Braden says, "Duh."

"I had bullies at my school too." I dig through the box for a piece to connect. "I tried ignoring them, but that never really works. You know what does work sometimes?"

"What?" Braden says.

"Next time Riley does something that you don't like, just ask, 'why'd you do that?'" I tell them. "It makes them so uncomfortable. Well, not everyone. Some kids will probably be, like, because I can, or because I wanted to. But every once in a while, you'll get to them."

"I already know why Riley did it," Braden says. "'Cause he's mean and 'cause Connor doesn't tell him to stop."

Connor glares at his brother but doesn't object. I put a hand on his back. "It's okay. Riley probably isn't easy to stop."

Bored with the puzzle, Braden heads over to the piano and attempts to play the song from the sheet music in front of him. I help Connor with the puzzle for a few minutes, until he can't seem to handle Braden tripping over the keys. He sits beside his brother at the piano.

"You're doing it wrong," he tells Braden. "Like this."

I watch Connor play through the music perfectly. He's really impressive for his age. Beside him, Braden is fuming. Eventually, he shoves Connor's hands off the keys. "I know how to do it."

But he continues to mess up with Connor trying to correct him. When Braden looks close to tears, I pick up Connor off the bench and send him back to the puzzle pieces.

"I know how it goes," Braden says, stubborn as ever. "And besides, I can do it different if I want."

"Definitely," I tell him. I play through the right-hand portion of the song and ask Braden to do the left for me. It's the part that's giving him the most trouble. He does much better with just the left hand, but when he messes up toward the end, he bangs hard on the keys. Enough to get Sam wheeling into the room from the kitchen.

"Hey, take it easy. That piano's older than me," he jokes.

I still Braden's hand. "Try saying the notes out loud. That helps me when I'm learning a new song."

He releases a frustrated breath and then concedes to trying again, mumbling the notes out loud. When he gets through it without a mistake—left hand only—he has a huge grin on his face. I look over at Connor and see that he's also pleased with this.

I clap him on the back. "Nice job."

"Okay," Sam says. "You guys better stop practicing before the neighbors accuse me of forcing you into music. Ask Fin if she'll take you to the park."

Both of them quickly abandon their activities and head to the doorway where Finley is now standing.

"I can take them," I offer.

Sam shakes his head. "Let Fin do it."

She looks as surprised as me by this. I sit up straighter and swallow. Okay, I think this is the part where he tells me what he really thinks of my current situation. While she's helping the boys find their shoes, Finley gives me a couple glances, a question in her eyes. All I can do is sit there waiting for them to go and listening to my heart race.

When the front door finally closes behind them, I turn to Sam and lean on one elbow. The piano keys respond loudly and obviously, offended by my misuse. I jump a mile, my neck heating up. Then I carefully close the lid and resume my position.

"So..." Sam says, pivoting his chair to face me. It's incredible how much he and his kids match—the blue eyes, light-blond hair, tanned skin from hours by the pool. "Fin told me that you might need to use me as a reference or support for your case."

"Yeah, but I totally get it if you don't want to be involved." I run a hand through my hair. This is going great so far. Not. "I mean, it's a train wreck. Or it will be—"

He lifts a hand to stop me. "First of all, I think what you're doing is admirable. Of course I'm going to help you if you call me up and ask for parenting advice or anything really. So offering myself as your 'support system' is an easy decision for me."

My mouth falls open. I don't know what to say. I didn't expect such a positive response from him. "Really? You mean it? I don't want to need help, but I guess it's important. For the case." I hesitate and then add, "Plus, I probably will need help."

"You shouldn't hesitate to ask *me*," he says with a tone that is both warm and free of judgment. However, I catch the emphasis on "me."

I clear my throat. "I'm guessing there's a but in here somewhere."

"Not exactly," he says, his gaze flitting to the front door and then back to me. "But I have to be honest—my daughter...this is not what I want for her. I'm not saying I won't accept her choices. She's free to do whatever she likes, and I will always support her. But this isn't her child. She's not a pregnant teen—no offense to you and your situation—but it doesn't seem fair she might have to be tied down like you are."

"I never asked her to do anything—" I protest.

"I know that, Eddie. Of course I know that. But this is Fin we're talking about. Do you think she would ever walk away from you, now that you're planning on raising a child on your own? She doesn't know how not to be selfless." He lifts his eyebrow. "My guess is you already know that about her."

I almost tell him that I'm not taking advantage of her because of this, but I don't think he meant it like that. I lean further on my elbow, the weight of this hitting me hard. "What do you want me to do?"

"I don't know." He shakes his head, looking as stressed as I feel. "Maybe nothing. It's just hard for me to see her doing this again… I mean, she helped raise her brothers when she was still a kid herself. That's not your fault, and it's not completely mine either, but that doesn't make it any easier to see her in the same position all over again. God, she's not even twenty."

"I won't make her responsible for my kid," I tell him, hoping he'll believe me.

"No, you probably won't," he agrees. "But she will. Just watch, she'll give up things she wants so she can play house with you. A good-looking guy who loves her brothers and wants to raise a baby on his own—might as well be crack to Fin. And this business plan—"

I straighten up again, alarmed. "What business plan?"

Sam rolls his eyes. "Did she really think I wouldn't find out she's trying to buy a studio in the neighborhood? The real estate agent is one of my best friends."

"You told her you know about it, then?" I ask. This could be a good thing. He doesn't seem angry. She's been worried he'd be angry.

"Nah." He waves a hand. "I'll let her take it as far as she wants first. She definitely surprised me though. I really thought getting her to move to New York would help..." He hesitates before adding, "I thought she'd go back to dancing. She's so talented."

I scratch the back of my head, not sure if it's my place to tell him that she's been dancing. A lot. She's takes a class nearly every night at Iris's studio. And I can see her changing physically from all the training. She's always stretching now too. Every time she's sitting down or hanging out, I look over, and she's got her legs out to the side, stomach flat on the floor. Sometimes, I can't even watch her when she's like that. It looks too painful.

I decide to tell Sam a small portion of Fin's secrets.

"She showed me the studio," I say. "I saw her dancing. She asked me to play a piece from *Don Quixote* for her. She's amazing."

"Yes, she's incredible." He scoops up a red ball in the way of one of his wheels and tosses it in the air. "But I've known since the day she refused to continue dance anywhere else but her family's studio that loyalty would be her biggest curse."

"I kind of like that about her. Loyalty is pretty much obsolete in my family." I take a breath, hoping it will clear my head. It doesn't. "That's not all I like about her. There are so many things. I think..." Sam looks up at me, waiting. "I think I'm in love with her."

He stares at me—not with disappointment, luckily. "I figured."

"So yeah." My neck heats up even more. I hadn't planned on saying that out loud. Especially not to Finley's dad. Before telling her. "That makes it a little difficult to…you know, tell her to get lost."

"Yeah." Now he looks disappointed. "I know that too."

"But I'll try…" I drop my gaze to the piano, tracing a finger over the cracked wood. "I owe you that much."

He gives me this look that clearly says *bullshit*, then he grips my shoulder, giving it a squeeze. "Well, at least you're a millionaire. She can marry rich. That was my other dream for her."

I release a short laugh. He definitely passed on some of his odd, honest sense of humor to Finley. "Glad I could help out with that."

Sam seems to have some resolve about his concerns. Me, on the other hand… I'm having trouble shaking them.

CHAPTER 42

Finley

"Hips! Move those hips!" Iris shouts, beating her sneaker against the dance floor in time to the music.

Hip-hop has never been a strength for me, but I'm definitely getting better.

Iris watches me for a few seconds and then quirks an eyebrow. "Is that an unpointed foot? And loose knees? Look who's learning how to ruin her ballet technique." She addresses the class of twenty or so dancers. "Everyone applaud Miss Finley Belton for pulling that ballerina stick out of her ass."

I start laughing and lose my place, getting behind the music by a few counts. Iris resumes banging her sneaker on the floor while a giant bag of ice rests over her left knee. I refocus and get back into the number we've learned today. But over the course of this class—forty-five minutes so far—the middle-aged woman beside me keeps glancing my way. I can see her gaze roaming to the left through mirrors. She did this during the contemporary dance class before hip-hop as well. I did a good job ignoring her during the last class, but now it's getting to me.

I swiftly swap spots with the dude behind me and then another woman behind him until I'm nearly in the back of the room. I push myself to go full out for the remainder of the class, even though I'm exhausted after a long catalog shoot this morning, standing the whole time and a million outfit changes, plus I took three classes last night. I think I'm addicted. Today, I finally broke down and bought the punch card Iris's been pushing for weeks now. It seemed like too big a commitment, buying fifty classes. Like holding that punch card meant officially declaring my return to dance. But now, instead of twenty dollars per class, I'm paying ten. Money is money, and the last thing I want to do is drain my savings.

We finish class with the usual cooldown stretches. I head straight for my bag in the lobby, grabbing my towel and attempting to dry off my sweat-soaked tank top. I've got the towel over my face, blocking my view, but I can feel someone behind me, standing and waiting. I drop the towel and spin to face the middle-aged woman who had been eyeing me all evening.

She sticks out a hand. "I'm Lenore Jacobs. Founder of a modern dance company in Manhattan."

Uh…

I stand there, holding the towel to my chest and not moving.

Lenore laughs and withdraws her hand. "Iris said you would be a tough sell."

"Tough sell for what?" I crumple the sweaty towel and drop it on top of my bag.

"Auditioning. For my company," she says. "You're an incredible dancer. Lots of heart, but no guts. Yet. Which is something I love. I want credit for helping my dancers grow and find that emotional connection to their dancing."

"Auditioning," I repeat. "For a company."

"For my company," she corrects. "That means I'm in charge. And you've already impressed me…"

When I don't respond—my tongue is literally tied, my brain pulling in multiple directions—she goes on to explain details about the company studio in midtown that they share with a reputable ballet school, the pay, the other dancers, the housing they have if I need it. My head is spinning, but I do catch the part where she says they spend about half the year traveling around the world, performing.

"Touring will be the easiest part. I work my dancers to the ground when we're not on tour. We rehearse four to six hours a day and spend another hour or two collaborating on choreography and concepts. We're world famous because of our artistic visions and how we use dance to show aspects of humanity that reach a very wide audience."

"Don't let her scare you off with that artistic mumbo jumbo," Iris says, walking up beside me. "She wants well-trained dancers with the right body type just as much as any company."

"True," Lenore says. "But my definition of right body type is a bit broader than the New York City Ballet's. We want healthy dancers, so we don't have the same strict rules other companies have. It's very much a collaborative environment built on trust. If you tell me you need a break, I won't ever tell you no."

I can't quite explain the feeling of both dread and excitement building in me. It's something unfamiliar, wanting this big thing all for myself. "It sounds amazing," I finally say to Lenore. "But I'm working on reopening my parents' studio, and my boyfriend needs help with…"

My voice trails off when Lenore starts shaking her head. "Don't answer me now." She hands me a card—the same one Iris gave me after my first class here—and says, "All I'm asking is for you to come and meet my dancers, talk with them, rehearse with them. One day. That's it."

Lenore turns to leave before I can tell her no thanks—on purpose, I'm sure. Iris is still standing there looking at me, along with a couple dancers still straggling behind after class. My face heats up.

"What will it hurt to meet her crew?" Iris asks. "Are you afraid you'll like it too much?"

She leaves me too, abruptly like Lenore. My head is such a jumbled mess when I turn around to exit the building that, at first, I don't even notice Eddie standing right in front of me. I jump after seeing him. Had he been standing behind me the whole time?

"Hey…" I fumble with the strap of my bag, not looking him in the eye. I called him my boyfriend out loud, didn't I? Is that okay? I said he needed me. Maybe that was too much. Maybe he didn't hear me. "What are you doing here?"

"Figured we could walk home together." He takes the bag from my shoulder and puts it on his. He sounds like his normal self. "Are you hungry? Want to pick up some dinner?"

"I was planning to eat leftover casserole. There's probably enough for both of us." I look at him. "But it's super healthy. Just a warning. Green stuff, lentils, the works."

Eddie smiles at me. "Free dinner is free dinner."

By the time we get to my apartment, I'm nearly convinced that he didn't catch any of that conversation. He seems way too cool and relaxed.

I should be relieved. I can tuck it all away as something cool that happened to me once. But I can't seem to shake Iris's accusations that maybe I'm afraid I'll like it too much. I have daydreamed about performing on a live stage again. But I've also fantasized about a studio full of little dancers lined up in front of the mirrors at Belton Academy, bellies sticking out, Care Bear underwear poking out of some of their leotards. Little girls who can't wait to put on a tutu so Grandma and Grandpa can see them dance in the recital. My parents used to put on the best recitals. We sold tickets to people who didn't know any dancers in the show.

I shove those thoughts aside and attempt to not look so conflicted.

Summer is sprawled out on the couch, going through the mail, when we walk inside. She's wearing her bathrobe, her nose is red, and her hair is…well, it's not perfectly in place.

"Are you sick?" I ask her.

"Allergies," she answers, topping it off with a sneeze all over the mail. "Eve dropped these off for you and Elana." She holds out two gold cards with silver cursive writing on the front. "How come I didn't get an invite to the Guggenheim?"

I glance over the invitation. It's for a show displaying Janessa Fields's work and launching her newest book, titled *Limbs*.

I glance down at the bottom of the invite and see: *And featuring work by newcomer Eve Nowakowski from her series titled Hands and Feet.*

Before I can figure out why I got invited to this show, my phone rings. Eve.

"Did you get the invitation?" she asks before I even say hello.

"Looking at it now."

"I was afraid Summer would shred them," she says. "Okay, so I know it's all been super secretive, but I want to hang a couple of your photos in the show, and I want you there to see it. What do you think?"

"First of all, aren't they your photos? And second, that's amazing! Of course it's okay—" I freeze, remembering something. "Wait…which photos? The ones with…with—"

"No clothes?" Eve supplies.

I glance around to see if Eddie or Summer heard her through the phone. Summer is now in the kitchen attempting to make tea with the kettle—a disaster waiting to happen. "Yeah. Those."

"I was hoping to include one," Eve says. "Or maybe two…"

I can hear the concern in her voice. She's dying to put her best shots in it, and those might involve me with no clothes. I sigh. "Okay, you have my permission. Guess I won't be the first nude body to enter the Guggenheim."

Eddie lifts his eyebrow but stays quiet. Eve squeals on the other end of the line. We end the conversation quickly after I promise to be there Friday night.

"I knew a girl who got desperate and did the nude modeling thing," Summer says from the kitchen. "She ended up with pics of her and the Brazilian wax she was wearing all over the Internet. She OD'd on heroin three months later."

"Thanks, Summer. I'll keep that in mind." I head into the kitchen and snatch the tea kettle from her. "Sit. Stop trying to cook things, or you'll start another fire. We haven't replaced the fire extinguisher from last time."

She flashes me her sweetest smile and plops down in a kitchen chair. She looks over at Eddie. "Do you have your own drawer yet?"

I turn around long enough to glare at her. I make Summer her tea and then a grilled cheese sandwich to go with it after she begs me and claims she's too sick to make her usual protein shake. I'm impressed she's actually going to consume solid foods. Finally, I heat up the container of leftover casserole and bring it to the couch along with a couple forks.

Eddie nods in the direction of Summer's bedroom and says, "And I thought I was spoiled."

"No kidding." I stab a vegetable and blow on it. "She knows all this already though. She's too far gone to see the error of her ways."

"What's the green stuff?" Eddie asks, already chewing his bite.

"I love that you eat it and then ask. Testament to your upbringing. Lots of strange green food. It's dinosaur kale."

Eddie leaves his fork in the container and leans his head back against the couch. "You should call that lady, Fin."

"What lady?"

"The one with the dance company." He turns his head to look at me, waiting for my reaction.

I stop midchew. So he did hear that conversation. "Why would I call her? I'm opening the studio. Probably in nine months. I won't have time to join a dance company. Besides, they go all over the world. I would hardly—"

"Be home," he says with a nod. "You could try it out and hold off on the studio opening for another year?"

I set the container on the coffee table. "I don't want to hold off.

Why would I? I mean, you're signing a lease for the two-bedroom near my house, right? You'll be moving in by the end of August."

"It's just an option," he says. "One you should at least consider."

"I want to move back home soon." I pull my knees to my chest, hugging them. "I was hoping…I thought maybe we could split the rent or something?"

God, did I just ask to move in with him? But he stays in my apartment more often than he doesn't. It's not that outrageous. It's just logic.

His forehead wrinkles. "You want to move in with me? And my kid?"

I shrug. "It was just an idea."

"What if you wanted to move out eventually? And then I have this kid and he's gotten to know you. That's not gonna work." Eddie scrubs a hand over his face. "I have to start thinking like that, you know?"

"Yeah, I know." I swallow a lump in my throat. Why does it feel like he doesn't want me around anymore? I hop up from my spot and busy myself getting a glass of water. "Forget I mentioned it."

Not that it doesn't hurt to get that kind of rejection from Eddie, but he's sort of right. If he gets custody of this baby and they're living together, it's forever. And if I jump into their world and it's not forever, it's so much messier now.

When I sit back down, Eddie says, "You might regret it. If you don't try out professional dancing."

"I know what I'll regret." I try not to sound snippy, but it's hard. "Just like you know you want custody of your child instead of a fully qualified adoptive family. Have I tried to talk you out of that?"

His jaw tenses, and he blows out a breath. "Right. Okay. I won't bring it up again."

We both stare at the casserole container for way too long until eventually Eddie stands. "I'm…I'm gonna go. Out. To run some errands."

"Yeah, fine." I close my eyes, not wanting to watch him leave. He hadn't said he was staying here tonight, but I guess I've gotten used to him being around.

But still…what right does he have to tell me what I'll regret? I've done nothing but support him and his choices. And not doing that audition, it isn't only about Eddie. It's about being closer to my family. Being home again.

At least I think that's what it's about.

CHAPTER 43

Eddie

I screwed that up. Big-time. I have too many voices in my head right now. There's Sam, who wants a lot more for his daughter than being some pseudo teen mom to my kid. Then there's the side of me that wants nothing more than to see Finley every single day. And of course, that side of me that feels guilty as hell for wanting that, because it's about me and not her. It has to be about her. I had it right at the beginning, when we were first together. I knew she was better off if we just made this a temporary thing, a summer fling, like she said. But somewhere along the way, I forgot all of that. I got caught up in her.

Who am I kidding? I'm still caught up in her.

Except I'm staring down the front door of another girl's home. I think hurting Fin tonight pushed me over the edge. I need to make things right with at least one person I've screwed over.

I wonder if the doorman would let me up to Caroline's place. I don't want to run into her parents, but I probably should. I should explain why I changed my mind. That's the manly thing to do, isn't it?

I take a deep breath and pull the heavy door open. The doorman looks up the second he sees me. I recognize him, which means he most likely recognizes—

"I'm sorry, Mr. Wellington, but I can't let you go up," he says. And he actually does sound a little bit sorry.

For a moment, I debate making a run for it, but there's no point. Another doorman is up on the penthouse floor, waiting to stop me. Instead, I go outside and stare up at her window like I had done weeks ago. A shadow moves around the room. A rush of adrenaline surges through me. I need to see her. I need to make things right. I glance around to see if anyone is watching, jump and pull down the ladder, then begin the climb up the fire escape. Eighteen floors worth of fire escape.

By the time I reach her window, I'm sweaty and out of breath. I press myself against the building, trying to stay hidden. The last thing I need is trespassing charges on my record. I knock lightly on the window. When I hear the sound of someone opening it, I reveal myself and come face-to-face with RJ.

"Shit," I say. "I didn't know you were—"

"Think you're the only one who knows this trick?" he asks, pushing the window open farther for me to come in.

"Can I come in?" I ask, looking around for Caroline.

"Tell him to jump off the fire escape," Caroline says from somewhere inside the room.

RJ gives me a grim look. "I think that means enter at your own risk."

I decide to take my chances and climb in the window. I look around the room, remembering the last time I was here. The day Caroline and I had to sign our eighteen-year friendship away along with the kid we accidentally conceived. It hasn't changed much, except it's messier, more lived in. Probably because she's not allowed out much. Her parents don't want anyone knowing she's pregnant. I bet they pull a car up in a dark alley and shove her inside when no one is looking.

Caroline is lying on the bed, on her side—the giant stomach trips me up again—a pillow between her legs. Her face is red, and her hair is sweaty.

"What's wrong?" I ask, moving closer without being invited. "Are you okay?"

She closes her eyes and nods.

"Heartburn," RJ says. "And Braxton Hicks. Those are false contrac—"

"I know what they are." Pretentious premeds. I look at Caroline again. "So it's probably a bad time to talk?"

She exhales, her nostrils flaring. "Go away, Eddie."

Her tone isn't firm enough for me to believe she really wants me gone. Some part of her has to know that we need to talk. It can't just be between lawyers. That's what got us into this mess in the first place.

"Jesus," she mutters under her breath. "Why did I eat that pepperoni pizza?"

"Aren't you a vegetarian?" I ask. She's been one at least since middle school.

"Yeah, well, this baby isn't." She opens her eyes and pulls herself up to a sitting position. "Did you really throw your credit cards at your dad and threaten to change your name?" Caroline rubs her chest. "I think five slices was one too many."

"Who told you that?" I ask, but I come up with the answer on my own. The maids. Apparently, our feuding families haven't put a dent in their relationships. "That's mostly what happened." I look around the room again and settle on sitting in the window seat across from the bed. "My dad called my lawyer and told him I was a mentally unstable drug addict who caused you to feel physically threatened by me."

Her eyes widen, and she shakes her head. "I didn't say anything like that..."

"I figured." I glance down at my hands. "I'm just...I'm wondering if you're going to. You know, if someone, like, asks you?"

She clenches her jaw, anger wrinkling her forehead. "God, I hate you for doing this. I can't believe—but no, Eddie, I'm not going to make up lies about you."

I blow out a breath, too relieved to be able to conceal it.

"But I'm not changing my mind either. I still believe the family I picked is the best option for this baby, and that's what I'm going to say when I'm asked."

So yeah, that's a kick to the gut, but I get it. It's her right.

RJ makes a big show of clearing his throat, and eventually, Caroline rolls her eyes and says, "Fine. Show him."

He goes over to Caroline's desk, opens a folder, and pulls out what looks like printed photos. I don't know what I expected to see, but it wasn't the face of my kid. My heart pounds. My finger drifts over the image. He's got his mouth open like he's yawning. The clarity is incredible.

"It's a 3D ultrasound," RJ explains. "The technology is unreal."

I flip to the next photo and immediately lean away from it. "Whoa, is that his—"

"Penis?" RJ says. "Yep. Definitely a boy."

"Jesus, is this legal?" I'm not sure I want images of my kid's private parts floating around everywhere. I flip to the next photo. It's a clear image of his spine.

RJ moves closer and points to the center of the picture. "They're checking for spinal abnormalities. It's so clear you can count each vertebrae and see if they're fused properly. Everything was perfect."

I hang on the word *perfect*. It's kind of a miracle that this kid is perfect, given the conditions he was conceived under. It makes me want him even more. He's already got an attitude, enough to say, *Screw you people who made me. I'm gonna function properly, even without your help.*

Caroline seems super uncomfortable about all this, but somehow, RJ must have convinced her that I at least deserved to see photos of my kid. While I'm poring over the twenty or so pics, she rattles on about anything but this baby.

"Tell me more about this modeling gig. I can't believe you're giving up Princeton to pose in your underwear."

"I only did one underwear shoot," I say while studying a photo of the baby's full body, curled up and asleep. "I did a shoot with Toby Rhinehart."

"No!" Caroline pulls herself up further. "Seriously?"

"Yep. Nice guy." I finish up with the pictures and hand them back to RJ—reluctantly, because I'd really love to keep one.

"What about your model girlfriend?" Caroline asks. "Is she prepared to be your baby mama?"

"You mean Finley?" I turn to face her. "She's definitely prepared and capable, but I don't think that's what she should do." The fight with Finley comes back to me, and I still don't know what to do about it. "Her family is great though."

"Right. Of course. She's perfect." Caroline releases a frustrated breath. "That's just like you, Eddie, finding someone else to do the hard work for you."

"I'm not letting her do anything for me." I stand up. It might be time to go. Before I say something I'll regret or something that can be used against me later. "I'm going to have my own place. A car. Baby gear. Safety covers over all the outlets. Infant CPR card."

"What are you going to do?" she asks me. "Like, with yourself? With your life? I know you don't need money, but seriously, you need something for you."

This sounds like a manipulative tactic, so I don't respond.

"Eddie, you are setting yourself up for insanity," she presses. "Maybe Princeton isn't for you. God knows you couldn't have gotten in on your own merits..."

"Thanks," I say dryly.

"Are you planning to keep modeling?"

I shake my head. Not if I can help it. Maybe if there's a delay in custody or if it takes a while to get access to my grandmother's trust. "I'll probably get another job. My girlfriend wants to reopen a dance studio. I might be their piano player."

This seems to surprise her. She sinks back against the

headboard, looking slightly amused. "You have a girlfriend. That's so…I don't know, not you. But it is though."

I don't know what to say to that.

"I'm happy for you." Caroline manages a smile and then it fades. She opens the bedside drawer and removes a folder. "Just look at this, Eddie. Take thirty seconds to look at it."

I lean closer and read the label printed across the front: The Kingsley Family. I lift my hands and back away. "Uh-uh."

"Why not?" she demands. "Afraid you'll change your mind? Is your choice that fragile?"

"I don't need to look, because my decision isn't fragile. I'm not changing my mind. Why should I feel guilty for you misleading this family?"

"I'm not misleading anyone!" She glares at me. "I'm doing what's best for my kid!"

I'm about to remind her that it's my kid too, but I don't, because (1) technically he's not mine until declared so by the family court, and (2) the bedroom door opens, and Caroline's mom, the maid, and the doorman stare us down.

RJ and I look at each other, both of us beginning to panic. But Caroline's mom does nothing more than look at RJ and point down the hallway. "Harry will see you out."

He nods and gives Caroline a long look before leaving. I attempt to follow behind him, but Mrs. Davenport stops me. She closes the bedroom door, leaving the two of us alone in the hall.

"Name your price," she says right away, surprising the shit out of me.

I lift an eyebrow. "My price?" Did she forget my family is richer than hers? Not that I'm connected with them anymore, but I could be if I did exactly what she's about to ask me to do.

"To drop the custody suit." She eyes me like I'm different than the last time we saw each other. Like I'm more of a threat. I consider this a small victory. "Whatever you want, name it. A giant dance studio for your girlfriend, full private school tuition for her little brothers, a brand-new accessible home for her disabled father…"

My heart thuds with fury, and my fists clench at my sides. "Stay the hell away from her. You have no right to—"

"No right?" she snaps. "To learn more about the girl who is claiming to be a support system for my grandson? And her family who are listed as your references?"

"So he's your grandson now?" I challenge. "Since when?"

She narrows her eyes. "You have no case. No chance at winning. All you're going to do is put my daughter through hell and keep her from getting to school on time."

"If I don't stand a chance, then why are you fucking bribing me?" I don't wait for her to answer. I show myself out, taking the stairs and heading out the back entrance.

CHAPTER 44

Finley

"You'll definitely make sure Eddie gets the cookies and croissants?" Elana asks for the hundredth time today.

"I promise," I say for the ninety-ninth time. It took a while for the baked goods production, coupled with Eddie actually meeting up with Toby Rhinehart, to come together, so I can't bear to tell Elana that Eddie and I have been on the outs for a few days.

Or maybe he's been busy. I don't know. Regardless, I told Summer to hand over the stuff when Eddie stops by so that I would have some more time to deal with everything. I know those cookies are safe with Summer.

"If you ask Eddie," I tell Elana, "he'd probably let you go with him to meet up with Toby."

Elana slows her treadmill down to walking speed—we're at the gym—and then stares at me like I'm nuts. "I couldn't. I would freak out. He's just so…"

"Famous?" I suggest. Though I kind of freaked out too, he really did seem pretty normal. But whatever. I won't force her.

We have to stop the conversation, because my phone rings. It's a number I don't recognize, but it's a state office. I have a feeling I know what this is for. I stop my elliptical and answer it.

A woman on the other end quickly explains that she's setting up interviews for a case and asks if I'm aware of the circumstances and willing to speak with a judge about a client of Ron Miller's in mid-September. That's well over a month away.

"Um…yes, of course. I'll do whatever you need me to." Despite our recent snag, I'd never let that stop me from helping him with this trial.

We set up an appointment, and I quickly add it to my calendar. When I finish, Elana is staring at me. "What's going on?"

I give her the briefest summary of Eddie's life story, and then I wait for her reaction. Her eyes widen. "Oh man… Do not tell my mother any of this!"

Seriously? How exactly would I do that?

"She'd flip out." Elana says something in French, perfectly mimicking her mother's tone. "This is what happens when you talk to boys!"

We go back to working out again, but when we finish, Elana says, "You guys are fighting, aren't you? Or did you break up?"

I wipe my face with a towel, hiding it from her. "Why would you think that?"

"I can just tell," she says. "Something is off."

"We aren't fighting." That's mostly true. We're disagreeing. We're keeping our distance. Not speaking. But fighting…not so much.

Elana looks panicked all of a sudden. "He's still going to give the cookies to Toby, right?"

I laugh. "Of course. He's not that kind of guy."

"Good," Elana reasons. "Because my mother would kill him."
Somehow, I don't doubt that.

CHAPTER 45

Eddie

By the time I arrive at Toby's "decoy house," my fingers are about to fall off from lugging the grocery sack of baked goods from my parenting class. I've still got my fake baby—perfectly burrito wrapped—in one arm when the door to the apartment opens.

A big dude with a long beard glares down at me from his nearly seven-foot height. He looks like he's about to stomp on me, but then I hear a voice behind him.

"Rocko, relax. Don't kill anyone." Toby pushes past the big dude and stands in front of me, grinning. "Don't worry. He only inflicts pain if you've got mud on your shoes—" He spots the fake baby and stops. "Oh, look at that little—"

I wait for him to lean in and then laugh at his reaction. "Plastic doll?"

I remove the doll from the blanket and hold it up by one arm. For just a brief moment, I panic and look around. If Roberta, my infant care instructor, saw me holding a baby like this, even a fake one, she'd flunk me in a heartbeat.

"Dude..." Toby says, laughing. "Totally got me with that. But seriously, what the fuck?"

The big guy is still staring, but Toby nods for me to walk

into this elaborately decorated apartment. It's filled with bright whites and contemporary blues. Off in the corner of the main room, there's a miniset for a photo shoot. A man in a suit is over there talking to a woman.

Toby turns to me and lowers his voice. "Give me that baby. I'm gonna freak out my manager…tell him a woman dropped it off on the doorstep."

He takes the baby, rewraps the blanket decently, and then decides against it. "Actually, I think I already used this prank last year with Bessy's doll." He drops the doll back in my arms and nods toward the hall. "Let me show you around."

I follow behind him, poking my head into a room fixed up in pink and white lace and another one in blue with baseballs stenciled onto the walls.

"Hilarious, isn't it?" he says. "Give my kids three minutes in this place—maybe one minute—and you wouldn't even recognize it. Somehow, people believe the 'interior' photos *People* magazine loves to publish."

I refrain from telling him that my own home—my parents' place—is in similar perfect order.

"So this is just for your marketing or whatever?" I ask.

"And so the paparazzi don't follow me home for real." He opens the door to an office and leads me inside. He's already got the signed pictures ready on the desk.

I offer up the ten-ton bag of baked goods. "I had to sit beside this and smell it for two hours."

Toby pulls out a bag of croissants. He looks them over wearily. "I'm not supposed to eat this shit."

"What, carbs?" I ask. Dating Finley has made me pretty familiar with the anti–white bread movement. I suppress the ache in my chest, thinking about her again. I need to figure out how to fix this thing with us.

"Well, yeah, that too. But I cheat all the time," Toby admits. "I just mean shit people bring that got baked in their house. Security makes me swear not to eat anything someone hands me that isn't sealed." He gives me this look like I'm supposed to come up with a reason I know for sure it's safe to eat. "Think they'd poison me?"

"Hell if I know. But if you're not eating them…" I reach for the bag and grab some cookies, stuffing one in my month. I've developed a motto this summer: never turn down free food. Yeah, French Mama is definitely a baker. "These are unreal." I swallow my last bite and add, "Don't worry. I'll tell them you ate fifty cookies and raved about them. If you want, I can dispose of the evidence…"

I scoop up the pictures from the desk and carefully slide them into my backpack. I figure he's got celebrity stuff to do and doesn't need me hanging around. But apparently, I'm wrong. He drops into a comfy desk chair, tosses his feet up on the desk, and points to an identical chair in the corner.

"Have a seat." He's still eyeing the baked goodies, but after I sit, he turns his attention back to the fake baby that I've dropped onto the floor by my bag. "So what's the story with the doll?"

I glance at the well-diapered doll—I'm getting much better at this—and then back at Toby, deliberating what to tell him.

Why the hell didn't I stuff it in my bag? Probably because I felt Roberta watching me from all angles, sending her detailed report on my infant caregiving skills to a family court judge.

"You really want to know?" I ask Toby.

·· ◆ ··

Toby sits there, silent, his thumbs wrestling each other. It's the most serious I've ever seen the guy. Finally, he says something. "Your family fucking sucks. I don't even know them, and I wanna send Rocko to kick their asses."

Toby reaches under his desk and opens the door to a minifridge. He takes out a beer for himself and offers me a soda. I take a long drink and then panic for a second. "You're not, like...gonna tell anyone about this, right?"

He makes a big show of punching buttons in his cell. "Just a sec. I got the *Enquirer* on speed dial. Hello? Anonymous caller here. I've got a story for you... It involves some Manhattan elitists and one very rich baby daddy." He tosses the phone on to the desk and rolls his eyes. "You're in my fucking decoy house. You know how many people step foot in this place? Less than ten or twenty...I don't know exact numbers, but it's not many."

I lean back in my chair, not sure what to say about that.

"I'm not saying I'm naive enough to assume you're trustworthy—I barely know you. But I did know, from when we first met, that you were a guy who knew how to keep his fucking mouth shut. And I was right." He tosses a guilty look at the doll by my feet. "Sorry, I shouldn't swear in front of the little one. It's just that I keep it in check at home, so it's, like, all bottled up and shit whenever I leave the house."

"You ever take infant care classes?" I ask him. In my class, I'm usually seated between two middle-aged pregnant women whose husbands aren't in the class, but all the other dads are there. Though not alone like me.

"Yeah..." Toby says slowly. "No. None of that. We just dropped the first one a lot and then figured it out. That's not gonna fly for you though. Plus, it's always better if you don't drop them. So I hear." He eyes me again, thinking. "You're good with this lawyer you've got? Because I could make some calls..."

I nod. "He seems good. And he hasn't made me pay him yet, so that's another plus."

"You'll be rich again soon enough." Toby starts to say something else and seems to stop himself.

"What?" I ask.

He blows out a breath. "What if you lose and the kid gets adopted? Are you gonna stay cut off from your family?"

I sink back into my chair and look up at the ceiling. I mean, I guess I hadn't thought about it like that. Not exactly. But how could I just go back home and be in that world again? Even before Caroline got pregnant—before I got her pregnant, 'cause I'm all about owning—I fantasized about running away, moving somewhere in South America, living in a little hut on the beach. Doubt I would have ever gone through with it. My guess is I would have gone to Princeton, taken a job with the family company, basically been completely miserable.

I shake my head. "I don't know."

"I'm not saying you should go back to being their kid," Toby reasons. "But just keep in mind that's it near impossible to get by. I had a friend in high school, kinda like your situation. His family's not as rich as yours, but his dad beat him. It was fucked up. He just decided to say the hell with it, I don't want anything from them. He went to college and, of course, didn't have money to pay for it. And he couldn't get loans or anything, because his parents made too much money. Then he wrecked his car, broke a bunch of bones, and had a hundred-thousand-dollar hospital bill. Turns out he'd missed payments on his car insurance too, and they'd canceled his policy the day before the accident. He was twenty years old and filing for bankruptcy." He stops to think again and then adds, "I guess if you keep booking Wang jobs, you'll be fine. But you don't want to do that, right?"

"I will if I have too," I tell him. "Beats a lot of other jobs. And Finley wants—" I almost say she wants to split rent, but then I remember that was the source of our tension the other night.

"Finley? The blond from the party?"

"Yeah." I explain a little about her family and then how we're sort of on the outs.

Toby finally gives in and grabs one of the cookies from the bag. "YOLO!" He holds it up in a salute before taking a bite. "You should fix that. The girlfriend stuff. Let her do what the hell she wants. She seemed smart to me. Plus, you two have probably blown past the point of no return a long time ago."

He's right. Even Sam pretty much said the same thing. It's

too late to tell Fin she can't be a part of my life. She's right too. It's not my choice. It's not my place to tell her what she may or may not regret.

And somehow, I have to make things right. Not just because I need her, but because maybe she needs me. And if she does, I'm for damn sure not going to miss a chance to help her out for a change.

Then I remember something. It's Friday. I bend over, unzip my bag, and remove the invite Eve had sent me earlier this week. I glance at my cell to check the time. "Oh shit."

"What?" Toby says. "You gotta go?"

The words *formal attire* near the bottom of the invitation catch my eye.

I look up at Toby, a sheepish look on my face, I'm sure. "You don't, by any chance, keep a suit lying around in your decoy house? Or a tux?"

He quirks an eyebrow. "As a matter of fact, I do."

CHAPTER 46

Finley

I've never been to an art show before or even a gallery where you meet the artist. Definitely not at the Guggenheim. The first person here that I recognize is Alex. He's dressed in a jacket and tie, and I'm relieved I remembered to put on something dressy. Since my sort of fight with Eddie a couple days ago, I'm really not in the mood for this type of event, but I couldn't not go.

Alex waves when he sees me. "Hey, nice feet."

"Nice feet?" I look down at my open-toed sandals. I did take the time to polish my toenails. Then I remember the theme of Eve's work—Hands and Feet. "Oh right, thanks."

My dad is supposed to be here in about fifteen minutes. He went through a lot of trouble to arrange transportation and parking. I decide to wander through the exhibits while I'm waiting. Might be best to scope out my nude photos before my dad sees them. Eve is busy talking to an older couple along with Janessa Fields.

I didn't realize she would have an entire room devoted to her photos. They're hung at different levels with various explanations below, and each has a title. I start at one end and study each photo. The first few are images Eve took of Elana's hands. I glance around the room and, sure enough, spot Elana and her mother roaming through Janessa's even larger gallery. I turn back to Elana's hands. Eve has titled one of the photos "Finer Motor Skills." I'm proud of myself for actually getting the pun. I don't possess the intellectual abilities to even begin to comprehend most art. But this one is more obvious. Elana has such a precise, particular way of holding her pencil that seems to defy the mundaneness of the activity.

When I finally arrive at the first unclothed photo of me, I'm surprised by how not weird it is. It helps that you can't really see any of the parts that, you know, aren't ones I'd normally flash to a photographer. I'm bent over in the photo, touching my toes, the lens zoomed in on my spine and the back of my neck. Just looking at it gives me goose bumps; it's revealing and yet not. I glance down at the title: "Spineless."

The next photo is from the first shoot we did together, the one with Eddie, except it's just me midjump, the floor not even visible. Eve named it "Underwater."

The third photo is by far my favorite, but it hurts to look at. Eddie is in this one. He's standing several steps behind me, watching, definitely in a way that is only done when you think no one can see you. The outline of me turning is barely visible, more like a shadow at the far left side of the photo. Eve called this one "Unconditional."

I rub my hands over my arms, ridding them of the goose bumps. My chest aches, and my stomach is in knots. I didn't even realize until this moment how anxious I've been since he left my apartment. His words had seemed so impactful, so important. And mine had felt the same. But now, staring at the photo of us, I want

JULIE CROSS AND MARK PERINI

to tell him it doesn't matter—where we live and what we're doing doesn't matter. Just keep looking at me like this, and we'll figure the rest out.

I reach in to my purse, digging for my phone. I need to call or text him or something. But I'm stopped by a warm hand that lands on my hip. I look down and recognize his fingers right away. I release a sigh of relief, but I don't turn around. I stand there perfectly still, hoping he'll tell me everything is okay. And if not, I just want to stay here for a minute, believing it is. I continue studying the photo until his arm slips all the way around my waist. I close my eyes and lean into him. There is no doubt now—I'm completely wrapped up in him. No way out. But how do I know if I'm wrapped up for the right reasons? Or is it Jason all over again—I need him because I think I need someone? But Jason was safe and comfortable. Eddie is none of those things. The challenges he's facing are nowhere near easy and comfortable. And since the moment I met him, I've done nothing but break out of my comfort zones.

It's real. Completely and unforgivably real. And if I weren't so wrapped up in it, I'd be wise enough to be scared out of my freakin' mind.

I break the silence by touching the fingers splayed across my stomach.

Warm lips touch my ear. "I'm sorry."

Yeah, me too. I nod, not wanting to speak.

"I'm trying"—his head drops to my shoulder—"not to be selfish."

I nod again.

"I promise never to tell you what to do again, okay?" He kisses my cheek, making it impossible to nod for a third time. "And...I love you."

I swallow a lump in my throat and rest a hand on his face. "Yeah, me too."

Eddie laughs quietly, his voice vibrating against my skin. "That was not supposed to happen."

No kidding. I turn around and let him kiss me—more politely than either of us would like but still too much to not get a few looks from others—and then I just stay there, my cheek brushing against his blue tie, my finger hooked into his belt loop. "Where did you get the jacket and tie? I know it's not yours. Your entire wardrobe fits in a backpack."

"A friend loaned it to me," Eddie says.

"This photo is something else," an older man beside us says to the woman beside him. "The rawness is such a brave creative choice."

"I love her expression," the woman says. "That drive for perfection is captured so well... I've seen this dancer before. I think she did *Coppélia* last year."

"You're right," the man says. "She must be with the New York City Ballet."

"Probably one of those Swedish imports. I can see Northern Europe in her."

I lift my head from Eddie's chest and look up at him. I'm trying not to laugh. Do they really think they've seen me before, or is this one of those "I'm going to out-know you" contests that are so popular in the art world? The latter is most likely.

"Swedish, huh?" Eddie whispers. "Does that mean if I take you furniture shopping at IKEA, you can translate the names of all the desks and shelves?"

Janessa Fields walks behind the couple and rolls her eyes—she must smell their BS from a distance. I step out of Eddie's grasp and take a minute to say hi to her and introduce Eddie. Janessa glances at the picture of us but doesn't mention the fact that Eddie's in it. Instead, she says to me, "I didn't know you were a dancer. I was surprised when Eve showed me the photos."

"Yeah," I say, my face heating up. "It's something I'm just getting back into."

"You know she worked with over two dozen dancers," Janessa says. "Didn't use a single photo of any of them for the show. Every dancer your age was too poised, too perfect. None of their photos revealed anything outside of their dancing ability."

With that final note, she walks away. I'm left scratching my head, trying to catch up. But that woman is too smart and so far ahead of me, it's probably better if I don't try to analyze anything. My dad arrives, providing a good distraction, though it's Eddie who goes over to greet him. They make their way around the gallery while I stay parked in front of a photo of me sitting on the floor, fixing my shoes.

"What do you think?"

Eve is beside me now, waiting, like she really needs to know that I like her work. Of course I like it. It's amazing. But it's me. So that's hard to say. "I think I'm wondering what these pictures of me reveal?"

Eve's forehead wrinkles. "What do you mean?"

"Janessa said you ditched all the other ballerinas' pics for mine because I revealed things." I flash her a grin so she knows I'm not a hundred percent on board with this theory.

Eve seems to take the question seriously. "That's hard to put into words…some photos are easier to explain than others." She points to the picture of me tying my shoes. "I had the School of American Ballet senior dancers pose for me."

I lift an eyebrow, wondering why she failed to mention any of this.

She glances at me and looks away. "Sorry. I didn't want to make it a big thing if it didn't end up being one, you know? Anyway, they all tied their shoes like they did it five times a day, which is probably about right. And your expression is different. You're thinking about the actual process. It stood out."

She slides over to the next photo, of me leaping. "Here, your face is kind of…concerned or maybe just not completely sure of how well you're doing. I don't know much about dance, so I can't find anything wrong, but it seems like you did. And the other dancers were so mechanical. They were working. And you…" Eve pauses, searching for a word. "You weren't working. You were the opposite of someone working."

I stare at the picture, trying to see what Eve saw.

"I guess that's why you were the most interesting to me. I only planned on doing the couples shoot for the sex appeal. You stole my attention. People search their whole lives to find something that produces that kind of passion—the work that doesn't feel like work. People search for it, but no one knows what it looks like. I wanted to take this picture, hold it up, and say, this—this is what it looks like."

Something stirs in the pit of my stomach. It's my photo. I should know what it really represents for me. Anyone can pull something else out of, something of their own. But it was a job for me, wasn't it?

"You know Alex is one of those people wandering around looking," Eve says, keeping her voice low. "He's still trying to figure out what he wants to be when he grows up." She laughs at that. "It's strange to see someone look for something I found so long ago, but it's not always that easy. If you get too logical—totally Alex—or too afraid of failure—my roommate Stephanie—or too emotionally invested in something else…then all these things get in your way. Life gets in the way, you know?"

Life gets in the way.

I look over my shoulder at my dad, maneuvering the room in his wheelchair, Eddie beside him, the two of them deep in conversation.

Life gets in the way.

A middle-aged man interrupts us, pulling Eve away for an interview. I continue to move from photo to photo, searching for some sign that Eve is wrong. That I'm not in my element dancing alone for her. And how do I know I wouldn't be the same, training young dancers, telling them how great it feels to do something you love for a living and what skills will get them there?

And how will I really tell them if I've never been there myself?

I'm lost in thought when someone taps me on the shoulder. I spin around and face Eddie. The color has drained from his face, and his eyes are wide.

"What's wrong?"

"Um…" His eyes dart around the room, then he runs a finger through his hair. "Caroline is…she's…having a baby."

"Now?" She's not due for three weeks.

Eddie nods. His phone is still clutched in his hand. I tug it and glance at the screen, reading a text from RJ along with the name of the hospital.

"Can you…" I start, not sure if I should say it. "Are you allowed to go?"

He nods again. Beads of sweat pop up on his forehead, and he looks even paler than a few seconds ago. He reaches up and loosens his tie.

My dad wheels up beside us. "You should probably be there," he says to Eddie. "At least in the waiting room. And maybe contact your lawyer…make sure he's up to date."

Eddie still looks like he's in shock.

I rest a hand on each of his shoulders. "Hey, are you okay? Want me to go with you?"

"No," he says but nods at the same time.

My dad stifles a laugh. "I think that's a yes."

I look between my dad and Eddie. Dad came all the way out here for this, and I'm leaving ten minutes after he gets here?

He nods toward the exit. "Go. I only came to meet the artists. I already talk to you enough."

I tug Eddie's arm, and he comes to life. Finally. "Cab. We should get a cab."

He moves quickly through the gallery and out the exit. I follow behind him as best I can in heels. We walk half a block before catching a cab. Once we're in the back of the cab, Eddie checks his phone again and inhales a sharp breath. He turns the screen toward me.

Another text from RJ: **Boy. 6 lbs. 4 oz.**

Eddie looks at me, and it's like I can read his thoughts... Shit. It's real.

CHAPTER 47

Eddie

"He looks like a Tommy or a Mason," Finley says.

"I like Mason." I rest my forehead on the glass window and lean more of my weight onto Fin—she and this window are literally holding me up. "Anything but Edward."

She gives my arm a squeeze. "I like Eddie. But I get it."

"Baby Boy Davenport" is written on a card taped inside the clear bassinet. Tommy or Mason or not-Edward is wrapped up like a burrito in a blue-and-yellow blanket, with a matching knitted hat on his head. The burrito wrap is supposed to give infants more security. But he looks confined in there. Tied up. He's also the tiniest of all five babies currently in this nursery. If I touch him, he'll probably break into multiple pieces, and I'll have to get Connor to put him back together.

"I already want to buy him a pony and candy and a million LEGOs," Fin says. "He's just so sweet. I can tell."

I release a breath. He does look sweet. He looks perfect, actually. A brand-new start. A slate that's never been written on. He doesn't have to grow up in a cold home like mine. He doesn't have to go to fancy private schools or be part of a hundred-year legacy of business dictators. I can make sure his life is full of *Star Wars* birthday parties and backyard barbecues and soccer practice or baton twirling or whatever the hell he wants to do.

"Eddie," a voice behind me says.

I look over my shoulder and see Ron Miller, family law attorney. My attorney. "What are you doing here?"

"Got your message," he says. "Figured I'd hand deliver the order from the judge." He holds up a piece of paper. The paternity test order. "Hopefully, they can take care of business tonight and get us our results tomorrow or the next day. Not likely, but I've seen crazier things." He glances at the baby through the window. "Good-looking kid."

I turn my attention back to not-Edward. His face is red, and his mouth is open. He's crying. "What's going to happen to him? I mean, like, right now? Will Caroline take him from the hospital?"

"The baby's mother isn't willing to bring him home with her temporarily. Not at all uncommon in these situations." Ron clasps a hand to my shoulder. "Don't worry about those details right now. You're doing everything you can."

I open my mouth to protest or ask more questions, but RJ appears in the hallway, and immediately, my concern shifts. I release Finley and step closer to RJ. "How is she?"

He looks worse than me—pale, exhausted. He shakes his head. "I don't know—fine, I guess. She's okay."

God, I should have been here sooner. But how could I if no one told me what was going on? Except RJ.

RJ scrubs his face with both hands. "I've decided against procreation."

Ron Miller and Finley both laugh. I wait for RJ to drop his hands before I ask, "Can I see her? Will she let me?"

"She's alone. Probably not in any shape to toss you out, so I'd say now's as good a time as any."

He doesn't have to tell me twice. I get the room number from him, and I'm off, ignoring Ron Miller, probably trying to legally advise me on why I shouldn't visit the opposition without consent.

I stop in the open doorway of Caroline's room. Everything on this floor is decorated with tiny prints of baby feet in pink, blue, yellow, and green. Caroline is hooked up to an IV, wearing a hospital gown. I haven't spent much time in hospitals. Like ever. Not since my grandma died, and that was four years ago. It's hard to tell if Caroline's stomach is flat again with her under the covers, but she looks like she's been through hell. I almost leave, but she turns her head and sees me.

I walk slowly into the room, just a couple steps to get me inside. "Hey, how are you?"

"No baby in here, Eddie." She lifts her hands up as if to prove that she isn't hiding him under the thin sheet and blanket. "Nothing to see."

"I saw him already," I admit. "I came to check on you."

Her face softens just enough to give me the courage to drag a chair beside the bed.

"I'm never ever doing that again," she says, swiping her forehead, which seems to be sweaty still.

I give her a weak smile. "Then you and RJ are perfect for each other."

"You know how many people told me that I'd be in labor for twelve or twenty-four or even forty-eight hours? Hold off as long as you can on the epidural." She shakes her head, obviously frustrated. "But no, that kid came out so fast, I didn't have time for any drugs."

I wince, imagining experiencing childbirth—something I was forced to watch a video of in my parenting class—with no drug intervention at all. I end up saying this out loud.

"Wait, what class? I thought you skipped out on Princeton?"

"The parenting class," I say as if she might know through the grapevine all the tricks I've put on the table for my case, though I was more than happy to have the opportunity to learn how not to kill my kid. "It's something my lawyer recommended. Pretty helpful."

She turns her head, looking up at the ceiling instead of at me. "You're much braver than I am, you know?"

"Um, no. I'm not," I protest. She's nuts. I got a text and took a cab while my kid was being born. While she was giving birth. "Compared to what? The person who just gave birth?"

"But I didn't choose it," she says quietly. "I didn't do anything but sleep with you and then sit around, waiting for my water to break. If I had to be the one to stand up and say 'okay, I'm ready for this labor thing right now,' I would have kept that baby inside me forever." I laugh, but she shakes her head. "I'm serious, Eddie. I've never considered keeping him. Not once. Did you know that?"

Tears fall down her face, too fast to catch. I reach for her hand and give it a squeeze. "Hey, it's okay. Let's not talk about this now."

"I want to talk about it," she demands. "I would never be brave enough to raise my hand and say 'I'll be his mother. I can do it. I will do it.' That's what you're doing, Eddie. That's exactly what you're doing."

Then let me. Just give him to me, I want to say, but I can't. Now isn't the time for that fight.

"Brave people can still be idiots." She gives me a pointed look. "I mean, he's not going to have a mother if you get custody."

Her words are as pointed as the look she gave me moments ago, but I can hear the concession in her voice. She's accepted that I want this. I want him. Footsteps echo from the hall, growing louder. I have a feeling whoever it is, it will be my cue to leave. I glance at the door and then back at Caroline. "If I win...if I get custody, I promise you, I won't do anything to make you regret giving him up. Knowing that, it will make me even more determined to be a great parent."

She pulls herself up to a sitting position and makes a bad attempt to wipe the tears from her face with the bedsheet. "I won't ever see you again. You know that, right? I can't. There's no way—"

I hold her hand between both of mine. "Yeah, I know."

"And I'm not good at making friends," she says. "You know I'm not. If something happens between me and RJ, I won't have anyone to talk to. It used to be you." She sniffles. "And that's what I'm thinking about right now. Not that I have to give up my kid but that I have to give up my friend."

She covers her face with her hands and starts crying harder. I don't know what to tell her, so I don't say anything. I just stand up and put my arms around her. The thing is, I'm not sure what she's saying is completely true. I think some part of her does want this baby. The part of her that couldn't go through with the abortion. But she's not letting herself open that wound.

RJ returns and takes my place beside Caroline. He gives me this look like he's saying to hang in there. And I get it. I've made the same choice RJ would have made if he were in this position—though he never would be, because he's too responsible to screw up like I did—and he's the reason Caroline has been even a little bit compliant with me.

A nurse stops me in the hallway. "Are you the one I'm swabbing?"

I glance around until my gaze lands on Ron Miller, who gives a tiny nod. The nurse glances at the paper he must have handed her and asks for some ID. Seconds later, she's retreating down the hall, carrying a cotton swab that will link my DNA to the baby's.

I'm about to ask Finley if she wants to go grab some dinner, with or without me, but then I notice someone standing beside her, looking at the babies in the window.

Finley looks up at me, concern on her face, and then she says, "I called her."

"Ruby," I say, giving my sister a nod. I don't know why Fin called her and, even more, why she came, but whatever. I don't care anymore.

"He looks like you," she says. "Same dark curly hair."

I roll my eyes. "Me and all the other Edward Wellingtons."

Ron interrupts us to promise me that he'll let me know as soon as the results are official. "Keep our fingers crossed for a twenty-four-hour time frame. That would be a gift from the family court gods."

When Ron leaves, Ruby, being her blunt, somewhat insensitive self, says, "There's no chance it'll come out that you aren't—"

"No," I say, firmly enough to get her onto another topic.

"So who gets to name him?" Ruby asks. "I mean, will Caroline, or will he just not have a name until someone makes a decision?"

"He won't have one until a judge makes a decision," I tell her. "It's not like we're sitting here with our heads up our asses. I have no power until I'm declared genetically related to the kid. And even then, it's not much."

She lifts her hands in surrender. "Okay, I'm sorry. That's isn't what I meant, but okay. So he doesn't have a name. Not a big deal."

Finley, the peacekeeper, jumps in. "My mom took a week to name my brothers. She had Andrew and Henry picked out since the day the test came back positive, and then she saw them and decided they didn't look like Andrew or Henry, so she started over. They went home as Baby A and Baby B Belton."

I almost wish Connor and Braden were here right now. To distract me with their endless and innocently intrusive questions. Plus, I'm way behind on all the day camp gossip. And Sam would for sure make a lot of bad jokes to lighten the tension.

"Guess that's one advantage of being fourth-generation namesake." I step close to Fin and put my arms around her again. I'm so grateful she's here. That I'm not alone with my insensitive sister. But I do appreciate Ruby being here. She looks fucking uncomfortable, but she's still here. Against our parents' wishes, I'm sure.

"What do you think we should call him?" I ask Ruby.

"Something spelled phonetically," she responds without a pause. "Definitely not a name spelled oddly. Too complicated."

"Finley says he looks like a Mason."

Fin's cheeks flush. She's afraid of overstepping, I think.

"I like Mason," Ruby says. "Simple. Classic. Easy to spell. No short nicknames that he'll hate."

I look at the kid again. He's asleep now but still in that clear bassinet. I wonder if anyone is going to pick him up. I already know I won't be allowed any closer until that test comes back positive. "I wish there was a way to ask him what he wants to be called. Seems like he should have a say."

Sometimes, I wish there was a way for me to ask him if wants me to take care of him. What if he doesn't? What if we don't even like each other?

But I look at him one more time before the nurse closes the blinds, indicating the end of visiting hours, and I know that's not possible. It doesn't matter what he does or who he becomes; we're going to be connected forever. Because if he ends up exactly where I am eighteen years from now, though I hope not, I'll be here with him. I won't force him to choose my way or not have a family anymore. I won't be my father. Not ever.

"You ready to go?" Finley asks. She steps out of my grasp and places her hand in mine. When I hesitate, she adds, "We can come back tomorrow."

"Yeah, okay." I thank Ruby for coming, and she mentions something about adding herself to Ron Miller's list, whatever that means. Then I get into another cab with Fin and sink back against the seat, completely beat. Thank God I didn't have to actually be there for the birth. I wouldn't have survived. My head is finally clear enough to take notice of Finley's behavior. She's in her own world, working something out on her own. I reach across the back seat and rest a hand on her knee. "What's on your mind?"

She shakes her head. "Nothing." No surprise there.

"I'm sorry you had to miss the show."

"I think I saw enough."

I'm left to sit there and wonder what the hell that means.

CHAPTER 48

Finley

Eddie hesitates in the hallway of my floor, like he's not sure if we're back to a place where he gets to sleep over. I roll my eyes and nod toward the door. We tiptoe to my room, and once we're behind the closed door, he turns on that "let's talk about it" look on his face.

I'm so tired, I can hardly stand it. I know Eddie must be feeling even worse. Everything tonight—it's draining in a way that physical exertion couldn't ever top.

"It can wait, okay?" I kick off my shoes and crawl up to the pillow on my bed.

Eddie ditches his shoes and ends up beside me. "You sure?"

I press my cheek against the cool pillow and nod. Before I drift off, Eddie's arm slips underneath me, pulling me closer until my face is buried in the crook of his neck. We fall asleep like that, fully dressed in our party clothes, the light still on.

·· ◆ ··

I shoot upright, my breath ragged, my heart pounding. The room is dark but slowly coming into focus. And my mom…she was here. Or maybe I was there. Not that I don't want to see her again—sometimes, I want that more than anything—but knowing that's not possible makes her appearance more than a little freaky.

There's a rustle beside me, and I'm too jumpy not to react. My elbow makes contact with a solid form.

"Ow!"

The lamp beside the bed clicks on, and Eddie is in front of me, holding a hand to his cheek and looking more than a little concerned. I glance around the bedroom, realizing quickly that I'd been dreaming. My face warms. Now I know why Eddie was so embarrassed by his brief flashback/nightmare that one night.

I sink back into my pillows, waiting for my heart to slow down. Then I see Eddie still holding his cheek. "I'm sorry. Did I hit you?"

"It's fine." He smooths a hand over my hair, which is sweaty and tangled. "Bad dream?"

"Yeah, I guess." I swallow the lump in my throat as the fear and emotions rush back. "I thought my mom was here. It was disorienting. I don't really know where I was, but she was there, and she didn't…she didn't recognize me."

Eddie doesn't say anything at first, just kisses my hair and leaves his lips there. "This kind of thing happens to me when I'm really stressed. You can try to analyze it, but most likely, you just need some help. Figuring things out."

The truth of his words cause a few tears to tumble down my cheeks. I don't want to figure things out. I'm afraid to. I had a plan. It's the right plan. Isn't it?

He dips his head enough to look at me. "Just talk to me, please."

I take a breath and then finally nod. "Tonight. Or last night. Whichever. Eve said something that…well, I don't know what it means."

I explain what she said about my pictures and all the theories about finding what you love and doing it. And how it's making me doubt turning down the company audition. "But then there's the studio… If I don't open it—"

Eddie's forehead wrinkles with concern. "Is this my fault? Because of what I said the other night? I shouldn't have tried to make decisions for you."

"I don't think it's that." I brush a finger over his now-bruised cheek and then lift my head to kiss it. "I've never really let myself think about what dancing is for me. But Eve's right—it's never work for me. Even when it is, you know?"

He shakes his head but smiles. "I'm not sure I'm there yet. Too much was decided for me my whole life. I haven't had a chance to think about what my version of dance is."

Hearing him admit that doesn't make things any easier. I know what I'm meant to do, and he doesn't. I'm lucky and maybe throwing all that away. It seems cliché, but I think it's true.

"You know what I think you should do?" Eddie asks, and I shake my head. "Talk to your dad about this. You're keeping a lot from him, and I imagine that's the biggest cause of your nightmare-inducing stress."

I sigh. He's right. I need to talk to Dad. But there's one thing my dad can't help me work out.

"Don't think I'm pathetic," I say, preparing to tell him what else is holding me back. "But I'm not excited about the idea of traveling all over the place with a dance company because I…I like being here. With you." I turn my head, pressing my face into his shoulder. If Summer heard that, she'd give me a dozen different lectures.

"I kind of hate that part too," Eddie says, stroking my hair again. "But I'm not going anywhere. You can dance around the world for five years, and I'll still be here waiting for you to come back. So now who's pathetic?"

I lift my head. "Yeah?" He nods, his hands lifting to touch my face. "Promise?"

"I promise. So give yourself some time to process without deciding yet." He kisses me, long and slow, adding weight to his words.

My eyes flutter and then close. I fall into this trap door of heated kisses and lips on my skin. "Maybe this is your thing…does it feel like work?"

Eddie laughs, his mouth against my neck. "Uh-uh."

"Well, there you go." I turn my thoughts off for a little while while Eddie distracts me, and then I have a whole new thought. I press a hand to his chest and hold him back. "You know, you're really good with my brothers. Maybe you're a kid person? Or a teacher?"

"Hopefully, I'm a kid person," he says, half-joking, half-serious. The anxiety of what's to come returns to his face.

I feel guilty for bringing this back to the surface. I mean, he can't do anything but wait, so for Eddie, there is no point in worrying or obsessing over outcomes tonight. "Okay, it's my turn to distract you."

"I'm in," he says with a smile.

But while I'm working through the buttons of his shirt, I can't help thinking, what will it do to him if he loses? If Mason—I'm calling him Mason, I don't care what anyone else says—ends up with the handpicked, apparently perfect adoptive family?

I don't want to think about that any more than Eddie does, but the reality is that it's a likely outcome. It's likely a judge will not see Eddie as the best option for this baby. For his child.

CHAPTER 49

Eddie

ME: Wtf am I supposed to do with your suit?

TOBY RHINEHART: Keep it. It's my decoy suit. I don't actually wear it.

ME: So…that kid I was planning on having? It happened.

TOBY RHINEHART: Whoa. Congrats man. I was messing with u the other night about dropping babies. I do know my stuff. Let me know if u need any help.

ME: Thanks. And wait…u were messing with me? Shit. I already sold that story…

TOBY RHINEHART: I'm working on my comedy. My agent doesn't think I'm ready yet. Getting a little tired of ripping off my shirt and taking out bad guys.

ME: Yeah I feel so fucking sry for u.

··◆··

I rub my eyes. They're blurry from staring at my laptop for hours. The hospital waiting room changes every time I look up. I'm not sure exactly what I'm waiting for, but I just felt like I needed to be here. I even backed out of a job this morning. Shay Silver chewed me out for ten minutes but ended by mentioning something about canceling going well with my rebel image. Glad I didn't mention the hours I'd planned to spend completing online quizzes for my parenting class. Probably not great for that image.

Finley hung out here for a while this morning, but she had a casting to get to and probably a dance class if I know her well enough. And I think I do. Now, anyway.

I'm working on finding the answer to a question on introducing solid foods when Ron Miller appears in the waiting room. "Back again?"

"Good news," he says, plopping down beside me and holding out an envelope. "You're a father. Congrats."

I roll my eyes and take the envelope. Not that I'm not ecstatic that it came through in lightning-fast time for family court, but I'm not surprised by the results. It was just a formality. Although no one else seemed to believe me when I said I was sure. The thing is, Caroline and I were best friends. I know everything she's ever done with a guy. And she knows everything I've done. There was never any question. Until this summer, when I lied to her about my decision, we've never kept any secrets from each other.

I skim the letter while Ron watches me. I'm a match. And a judge has granted me the right to notification. I sigh with relief.

"Normally, it takes three to six months for a custody or

adoption hearing," Ron says. "But you have a court date thirty days from now. That's a big win, Eddie."

He looks extremely pleased, so I work hard to hide my disappointment. "What happens for the next thirty days?"

I've already hired movers to take the baby gear from the Beltons' storage unit to my new apartment next week when my lease starts. I don't have furniture for adults yet, but whatever. Baby gear takes priority, and I don't have to buy much. Sam seemed to have kept everything. Two of everything. I don't even know what half that crap is—bouncy seats, high chairs, and changing tables. I did look up the crib model to make sure it wasn't made with lead paint per my parenting class instructions. I also checked each item for recalls.

The grin fades from Ron's face. He leans forward and lowers his voice. "The judge will allow the family Caroline chose to take the baby home. Temporarily."

I knew this already, but hearing it now, in context, it's hard to imagine. Do they have an apartment full of baby gear? Have they searched for product recalls? What are they going to call him?

"So…" Ron says, hesitating, giving me time to digest. "If you want to see him, that's also been okayed. In the nursery under the nurse's supervision."

I lift my head, staring at him. "I can see him?"

Ron nods, and I close my laptop and quickly stuff everything in my bag. I watch the nurses carefully, looking for signs of judgment or concern that I'm here. But I don't get much on their end. One nurse fastens a bracelet around my wrist that has some computer chip in it so they don't hand me the wrong baby. They read a long list of procedures and policies before allowing me inside the nursery with all the babies. I'm grateful that Ron takes off during this phase, because I'm feeling way too many things, and I don't know if I'll be cool or...not cool.

I'm instructed to cover my shoes with these plastic things and scrub my hands all the way to my elbows, and then I get covered in plastic as well.

There are five babies in the room right now. I'm pretty proud of myself for being able to pick out my kid without looking at the names on the bassinets. Regardless, my bracelet microchip thing is scanned and matched with the baby's ankle bracelet microchip. He's all wrapped up and sound asleep.

The younger of the two nurses stands on the other side of the bassinet, her hands clutched to the glass like I might make a run for it. But it doesn't bother me. It's good that they're protective with these babies. I take my index finger and brush it along his cheek. His skin is soft.

"How is he doing?" I ask.

The nurse lifts a clipboard from the end of the crib and reads it quickly. "He's early but no trouble breathing. His lungs are in great shape. He's eating well. He's a strong little guy."

I shift the hat up a bit and brush my finger over the exposed hair. Ruby is right. He's got my dark curly hair. His eyes are blue too, like mine. I saw them last night. But they could change. Caroline has brown eyes.

I'm not sure how long I stand there, watching him, doing

nothing but barely touching his face and the bottom of his hair. And his ears. They're oddly pliable, like clay. I notice all the other babies are in and out quickly, getting weighed or checked by a doctor and then taken back to their rooms.

The nurse must have deemed me trustworthy enough, because she's been moving around the room, giving us some space. She looks up from her clipboard when I lean over the bassinet to snap a picture. I text it to Finley, and then I'm hit with a wave of sadness, realizing that I don't have anyone else to send the picture to. I mean, I could send it to my parents, but that would only piss them off. I hesitate for a second and then do exactly that.

Another baby beside me is shuttled away, back to one of the patient rooms. "Has he been here the whole time?" I ask.

The younger nurse glances at the older one before answering. "Mostly."

"It's not uncommon in these situations," the older nurse says. "For the mother to not want to see the baby. We're taking excellent care of him."

I nod, but I can't help feeling guilty that Caroline is so torn she can't even look at him. Guilty that he's all alone. No family fawning over him. Then again, I can't imagine my parents anywhere near a maternity ward. What were they like when I was born? Or Ruby? I can't imagine my father in the waiting room, chugging coffee and eating cafeteria food.

He stirs, his eyes opening, one of his hands coming loose from the burrito wrap. I reach down and touch his hand before tucking it back in, pulling the blankets around him again.

"Nicely done," the nurse says, complimenting my burrito skills. "You've done this before?"

I hear the questions behind that question. Yeah, I'm eighteen, and I've gotten a girl pregnant more than once. "I took a class. The teacher was a drill sergeant about the burrito wraps."

The older nurse lifts an eyebrow. "I know where you went. Loretta's class. That's the best new parent program in the city."

"So I've heard." From Ron Miller. Over and over. Classes are expensive as hell too. Because my family is rich, I didn't qualify for free tuition.

"Well, in that case," the nurse says, "I think you can handle picking him up. If you want?"

"I haven't officially graduated yet," I admit. "I still have to take my final written test online."

She narrows her eyes. "What's your average right now?"

"Ninety-four," I say and then add, "point six."

She gives a satisfied nod and pulls a chair up behind me. Before I can ask if it's okay to wake him up, he's in my arms and even lighter than I expected. And warm. Very warm. I sink back in the chair, getting comfortable. He turns his head back and forth, disturbed by the movement. I hold my breath, trying to keep my body from stiffening. Part of me is afraid he'll start screaming, being in the arms of an unqualified parent. But he quickly settles down and goes back to sleep.

"Is anyone going to name him?" I ask after several minutes.

"You can," the younger nurse says, surprising me. "Unofficially."

"Mason."

"Family name?" she asks.

"Definitely not." I glance up, and she's writing Mason on the light-blue card taped to the bassinet. "How long do you think he'll be here?"

The older nurse looks at Mason's chart again. "I'd say he'll be released in a week or so. The pediatrician is pretty careful with the early ones, but he's doing so well."

Only a week. I don't think there is anything that can be done to push the court date up. It will be thirty days at least before he has a real home. I try not to think about that while I'm hanging out with Mason, long enough to get through one bottle feeding and two diaper changes, during which the nurse tries to ask me about circumcision, and I get light-headed and have to sit down again so I don't drop the baby. I take a few dozen pictures, and while I'm parked in the rocking chair, an older couple comes in to visit one of the babies in a covered bassinet. They look like grandparents. They take as many pictures as I did. The woman cries a lot, and the nurse has to grab several tissues for her.

The whole time I'm watching them, all I want to do is tell Mason that he won't be left alone any more. And that we're going to get to know each other, to be a family, but what if I lose this case? What if the first words he hears are broken promises? I don't want that.

So we don't have a lot to talk about right now. Not yet anyway. And Mason doesn't have any grandparents to cry over him. I'm almost glad he doesn't get to choose who he lives with, because my side isn't looking too attractive—no mom, no grandparents. But there's Fin. And Sam. And Connor and Braden.

Around dinnertime, the nurses practically force me to leave. I grab food at the cafeteria and sit back down in the waiting room, setting up my laptop so I can graduate from that damn class. At least I'll have that certificate to offer as a selling point. I have a dozen texts from Fin, begging for more pictures, asking me if Mason smells like a newborn. I sniff the front of my shirt, and sure enough, it's got that baby scent. She must have forwarded pictures to Sam, because he replied to some text, cracking jokes about his wild hair "in the making."

No response from my parents. Fuck them. Fucking assholes. Maybe I'll blow up a picture of Mason to poster size and have it delivered to my dad's office. I'll write "Grandfather of the Year" on it.

Ron sent me an email detailing the judge assigned to the case and including some stats on his previous custody decisions. He's ruled in favor of single fathers several times. According to Ron, I couldn't have gotten a better judge out of the large NYC pool. I get brave and reply back, asking him about payment. He responds immediately with one line: Pay me when you're a millionaire.

Shit. I forgot. I quickly compose an email to the lawyer in charge of my grandmother's trust, and I include a picture of the paternity results. I'm hitting send when a middle-aged couple enter the waiting room, an older woman trailing behind them. Lots of people have been in and out of this waiting room, and I wouldn't have looked up, except that the woman is sobbing so loudly, I can't possibly not look up.

Everyone in this waiting room thus far has been happy and

celebrating. I imagine not all areas of the hospital are this way. Maybe they've wandered into the wrong place.

I try to go back to my online test, but I start picking up bits of their conversation.

"I can't go in there," the woman sobs. She's being comforted by the guy with her—her husband? She is dressed casually, jeans and a plain purple top. The woman behind them is dressed in a business suit and high heels. She's glued to her phone but occasionally pats the crying woman on the back. "I don't understand how this happened."

"We don't know," the guy says. "We don't have the whole story yet."

"But we were supposed to take him home," the woman says, finally raising her head. Her face is red and splotchy.

"You still can," the business-suit lady says.

I pop my headphones in my ears so I can at least give them the appearance of privacy.

"But then what? We hand him back in thirty days?"

My whole body stiffens, my breath catching in my throat. Shit. They can't be...

The business-suit lady ushers the couple to a couch and pulls a chair in front of them. I should take off, but I can't. I can't move. Because I know who they are.

This is who Caroline picked to raise our kid.

Mason, I think just as the woman says his name out loud.

"He named him. Not that I mind, but it just feels like he's slipping away. He belongs to someone else."

The man seems shaken up but holding together. He looks

at the lawyer, his wife still wrapped in his arms. "What are his chances of winning?"

My hands are literally shaking above the keyboard. I open a blank email just so I can pretend to type.

"Normally, I'd say slim to none," the business-suit lady says. Then she exhales, frustration or defeat in it. "But I know the lawyer involved. He's the best for this type of case. The judge has ruled in favor of fathers in similar cases. He's from a high-profile family, though that's confidential information. His family isn't involved. Quite the opposite."

"Why does he want custody then?" the man asks. "If his family is against it."

The business-suit lady shakes her head. "I don't know."

My heart is literally beating out of my chest. I'm worried they can hear it all the way across the waiting room, but all three are too involved in their own problems to even notice me here.

"If I see him and then I have to..." The woman breaks down again.

"But if we don't take him home," the man tells her, "he'll be turned over to the state. It seems wrong for him to be with strangers the first few weeks of his life, and who knows what those homes will be like?"

I shudder at the thought.

The woman sits up and wipes her face with her hand. "No...you're right. It's not fair to that poor baby. Just because I can't handle it."

"You don't have to move forward," the business-suit lady says. "You have no obligation to care for this baby if a judge might not approve the adoption. Most couples would back out at this point."

The woman nods and then gives her husband a small smile. "Well, we aren't most couples, are we?"

A brick sinks into the pit of my stomach. My heart continues to beat loudly enough to drown out parts of their conversation. But I catch the woman saying, "My parents are flying in from Seattle. I can't even tell them anything, because they're in the air right now. They'll be devastated."

"You've definitely got a piano player on your hands," a familiar voice says. "Either that or a pickpocket."

I jump and turn my head to see Sam rolling into the waiting room. I feel like I've just been caught watching porn or something. My head is still deep in the conversation across the room when I greet Sam. "Hey, what are you doing here?"

"Thought you might need someone to hang out with," he says like it's no big deal when I know it had to be. "Fin said she's stuck at that casting for a few more hours. The boys are at a campout with their cousins."

The couple finally notices me sitting here, and they halt their conversation. The guy stands and holds out a hand. "Let's go see him. He's all alone in there."

He's not alone, I almost say out loud. But he kind of is. I don't know what happens to me—it's like an out-of-body experience—but when they walk out of the room, I tell Sam I'll be right back, and I follow them.

The couple leans against the glass, watching Mason while the business-suit lady hangs back, messing with her phone.

"He's perfect," the woman says.

"That hair is something," the guy says. "My mom will go nuts over it. You know how she is about babies with curly hair."

The woman sighs. "He really does look like a Mason."

The man nods and puts an arm around her shoulders like this means they've lost. I force back the lump in my throat, and before I can stop myself, I open my mouth and say, "I'm sorry."

CHAPTER 50

Eddie

Both of them look over at me, and it doesn't take long for the pieces to click into place. From the corner of my eye, I see the business-suit lady—their lawyer, I assume—tuck her phone away, her eyes wide.

I rest a shaking hand on the wall and repeat the words again. "I'm...I'm sorry. I didn't know about the parents flying from Seattle and...I didn't know. I'm just—" I release a shaky breath and look at Mason. "I'm just trying to do the right thing."

No one says anything. I touch my forehead to the glass and wait for this ache to leave my chest. What am I doing? Why would I take that baby from this family with grandparents and—

The woman takes a step in my direction. "Maybe...maybe we can work out something..."

"Eddie," Sam says from behind me. His voice is sharp and direct. "Let's go back to the waiting room."

"Wait," the woman says, her eyes pleading with me. My own mother would never fight for me like this. "Just give us five minutes—"

"Eddie," Sam says, and I peel my eyes from them and follow

him. When we get to the waiting room, he points to a chair and orders me to sit. "You can't talk to them."

I don't want to fall apart. Not here. Not now. I press my thumbs against my eyelids, ordering them to stay dry. Then I look up at Sam. "What am I doing? I can't do this. I can't give any kid what they can."

Three point two million dollars won't buy Mason that life. One with generations of love.

Sam rolls forward and grips both of my arms. "Look at me."

I do.

"Those people are desperate for a baby. They can't help you make this choice. You have to figure this out yourself."

"I just don't want to be my father." I shake my head. "I have to be better than him. Or else, I've got nothing."

"So be better than him," Sam says.

"But he deserves that family or one like them," I admit though it kills me.

"I don't mean be a better parent than him, Eddie. Be a better person. Do something with your life that says 'Fuck you. I'm not you.' You don't have to raise a kid at eighteen years old to prove you're not him."

I nod, but I'm still not sure I can just… Fuck. I don't know.

"Turn all of it off," Sam tells me. "All those other people you're listening to right now. Screw them. It's just you and what you want. What will make you happy? Knowing that baby is with you, or knowing he's happy?"

I nod again, too afraid my voice will shake if I talk.

"Whatever you decide, you have to make peace with it," Sam

says. "You have to think it and not feel that ache, that feeling of guilt or regret. Choose whatever does that for you, okay? You have your whole life to be a father to someone. And you can be a great one. Now, or it doesn't have to be right now."

"I'll never see him again?"

"You can see him," a woman's voice says. "You can see him whenever you want."

Sam holds up a hand, stopping them from coming closer.

The lawyer tries to get the woman to leave. "Mrs. Kingsley, we should discuss this privately—"

Sam gives them a pointed look. "Good idea."

"But if we can just talk about it together," the woman argues.

The lawyer steps in front of her. "He can't authorize anything. He's not the one who created the adoption terms."

"But he's the father," the man says. "He has a say in this."

I look at them, grateful for their offering me the choice. "She's right. I don't really have a say."

"Maybe on paper you don't," the guy says. "But to us, you do."

"I think adoptive parents manipulating a birth parent is frowned upon in family court," Sam tells them.

Both of them clamp their mouths shut, their eyes wide with fear. I appreciate Sam's help. I do. But they didn't mean to manipulate me. They're honest people. My whole life has been about contracts and policies and how to get around the rules. My parents couldn't even trust Caroline to keep my identity a secret. She knew I was the father, and she still couldn't just say that so we wouldn't need the court-ordered paternity test. I'm so sick of that shit.

"It's okay," I say. "I want to talk to them."

"Eddie," Sam starts at the same time as their lawyer tries to get them out of here.

I look at Sam. "I've got nothing to lose talking to them."

With a sigh, he concedes, and they politely tell their lawyer to get lost. When they sit down across from me, I try to study them enough to see hidden flaws, parts of their lives that are ugly.

"Caroli—" I start to say Caroline and then remember that they don't know who she is and they aren't supposed to. "Mason's mother isn't going to change the terms. She's…she's just not."

They look at each other, and then the man speaks up. "We don't need a contract to tell you that you can see your son. Anytime you want."

"You have our word," the woman adds.

Tears prickle in the corners of my eyes. I fight them off again. I can already see Mason with them. I can see them hanging pictures of him on the wall, taking him to swim meets. I want to hate these thoughts, to banish them, but I don't. It feels right. I think this is what Sam meant when he said I need to be at peace with it.

Call me the most crazy naive businessperson ever, but I believe them. I believe they mean it. I can see him. I don't have to say good-bye forever. Caroline might need it to be all or nothing—she has plans, and she knows who she is. I don't know any of that yet. I just know that I created someone, and I want to see how he turns out. I want that more than almost anything else.

I wipe my face with the bottom of my T-shirt. "Okay."

"Okay?" they both say, confused.

"Okay, I'll take your word."

Sam opens his mouth to say something, but I shake my head. I stand up. I have to get out of here. "You don't have to call him Mason if you don't want to."

That's the last thing I say before tearing out of there in search of someplace where there aren't any people.

CHAPTER 51

Finley

"Can you pull your hair up above your ears," the casting director says. "Face right…"

I do as I'm told, moving without thinking. My mind is still back at the hospital with Eddie. I can't believe he got to see and hold Mason. I wish I could have seen that.

Maybe I can see it soon. My agent said this was for a pretty big job, so that's why I didn't skip it and stick by Eddie's side all day. But it also means they're likely to be done with me in the next thirty seconds.

"And face forward again," the man with my card directs. "You can put your hair down and relax."

I drop my arms and stand there, waiting to be told they've seen enough. On impulse, I glance at the exit and then quickly back to the director's face. Finally, I just decide, *screw it*. I'm over worrying about my every little move, scripting my answers if I'm questioned at a casting. I haven't knitted in almost two months.

"Anything else?" I prompt.

The casting lady had had her head down, flipping through a fold on her clipboard. But she lifts her head and smiles at me.

"Sorry, I was just admiring these photos an agent sent over today. We have stacks of portfolios of models who list dance as one of their hobbies or talents…" She looks over at the three or four other people in the room, and all of them laugh, in on some joke, I guess.

They take one more full-body picture of me, and I'm about to take off, but then a woman wheels a chair over to me. The director waves a hand at it. "Have a seat, Finley."

I almost tell them I have to be somewhere soon, but I'm too curious to take off. Dad is at the hospital with Eddie now. I'm sure they're both having a blast, teaching Mason show tunes. It's never too early to start, my dad always says.

After I sit down, the director does the same, setting her clipboard on the glass table between us. "As I was saying before…lots of dancing models that turn out to be…well, not dancers."

Maybe Summer has ballet listed as one of her talents? That would explain the pointe shoes in the Prada shoot.

"Well, I actually have some dance experience," I admit, figuring I'll cut to the chase.

"Oh yes, we know," she says. And then she lifts a photo from its envelope, and my mouth falls open the second I see it. It's one from Eve's exhibit at the Guggenheim. One of my nude ones, though I'm folded in half and sideways. All you can see is the side of my leg and my spine.

"How did you get that?" I ask. "I don't even have a copy."

She flips over the envelope and reads some slanted print scribbled on the back. "It's from *Vogue*'s offices. Someone named Summer had it sent to your agent, who sent it to us today—"

Summer had this sent over for me from her mom's office? How did she know about the casting? Why would she help me? Did Summer just do something nice? I can't help but smile.

The casting director looks up at me and matches my expression. "Well, it's stunning, as are you and your dancing. Is this something you're passionate about or simply well trained?"

That's a tough question to answer. "I'm well trained, but…" I think for a second, wanting to explain it properly. "I'm kind of falling in love with it all over again." My face heats up, and I clear my throat. "So to speak."

I replay all the hours I've danced over the last month or so, trying to figure out if that's an exaggeration, but I think it's true. That's what's happening to me and dance right now. What had Lenore Jacobs said when she invited me to audition for her company? I danced with heart but not guts. Not yet.

I can't just give up on opening the studio, but shouldn't I be able to say the same thing to the dancers I teach that Lenore said to me? Shouldn't I know firsthand what it's like to dance with guts and emotion that you can only have by taking a big risk? I can guarantee Lenore knows—she's done it. She had enough love for dance to start a nonprofit company in NYC. That's no small feat.

But how long will the studio sit there waiting for me?

"So…are you interested in working for us?"

"Uh…" I pull my head out of my ass and pay attention to the woman talking to me. "You want to hire me?"

Usually, offers come after I leave the room. Plus, did she say who this job was for?

"We aren't going to negotiate here, but I'm just curious if you are intrigued by the idea of representing Chanel in a new ballet-inspired line."

I blink. Once. Twice. "Wait…did you say Chanel?"

Everyone in the room laughs, but warmly, not like when someone made the joke about Grandma's knitting needles. The director pats my hand. "How about we let you see some of our dresses? You can try on anything you like."

Never in my entire modeling career, not even at sixteen when I'd barely hit puberty, did I have the right measurements for Chanel.

She must be able to read my mind, because she says, "Misty Copeland will be part of this project. It's an ongoing series inspired by lovers of dance, whether dancers or not."

Misty Copeland is one of my all-time favorite ballet dancers, and like me, she won't have Chanel model measurements. She's got an athletic build.

"So this really is a new direction," I say, and then I'm on my feet, heading over to look at these designs. I brush my fingers over a long, pink tulle dress. "I think this is love at first sight." Eddie is going to have some competition, because I'm about to steal this dress and sleep with it.

"You like?" the director asks.

I look at her, staring at the dress, and put two and two together. "Wait a second. You're the designer?"

"Yes."

Holy shit.

I turn to face her. This just seems too good to be true. "And you want me to wear these? And Misty Copeland? Even though I'm not going to fit into a Chanel sample size?" Definitely don't need another repeat of the Valentino dress fiasco.

She grins. "But it is your size."

"Really?" Yeah, I'm a little skeptical still. "You're sure you want me?"

"No," she says, and I sink back partially behind the clothing rack of dresses. She reaches for the photo again. "I want this girl. Do you think she's available?"

I glance at my photo again, and I'm back at the Guggenheim, trying to see whatever Eve saw when she picked me over dozens and dozens of trained ballerinas. Maybe it isn't about what I see in the picture but what I'm feeling when I'm there. It's up to everyone else to see inside me. And in the picture, I'm more me than anywhere else.

I turn back to the dress and touch it again. "I think she might be available, but you should probably speak to her agent first."

She gives me a nod. "Of course."

When I finally walk out of that casting, having tried on four different dresses and proposed to each of them on the spot, there's a bounce in my step that I haven't had in a long time.

I quickly dial my dad's number. He picks up before the first ring even completes.

"Fin, good—"

"You won't believe what just happened to me," I say.

"You should get over here soon, Fin."

··◆··

It doesn't take me long to find Eddie. My heart is already breaking for him. I don't know all the details—I took off before my dad
could finish explaining what happened—but I know enough to
know he needs someone.

He tries to discreetly wipe his face with his shirt when he sees
me. I plop down on the floor beside him in this dark hallway and
wrap my arms him. I don't say anything for a while, and when I do,
I keep it simple. "Are you sure?"

He lifts his head and nods. I study him, trying to figure out
what happened between him texting pictures and being ready to
sign his rights away.

"I don't understand what changed."

Eddie takes a breath and rests his head against the wall. "I
just thought… I wanted him because he's my family. Maybe my
only family."

I shake my head and turn his cheek until he faces me. "That's
not true. You have me. You have my dad and Connor and Braden."

His eyes close, and he leans in to kiss me. "I love you."

My heart swells to double the size. "I love you too. And I'm
here for you."

"I know, but I don't know what I'm supposed to do now," he
says. "I mean, I don't want to go to Princeton. It's not me."

"No, it's not you," I agree.

"I've been planning on this…on taking care of Mason or whatever they end up calling him for months. I don't know what to do."

I kiss him again. "Anything you want. That's what you can do."

"I just don't know how to pick up all the pieces." He looks at me like he wants to say something else but stops. He glances over his shoulder and then back at me. "My grandmother's trust…I'm not going to get it."

"Oh, well, that changes everything." I roll my eyes. Is he serious? "Oh wait…does that mean you're not taking the apartment in Connecticut? My brothers will be devastated."

"It's cheaper than anything in the city. I can still afford it," he says. "I think it'll be nice to try living somewhere besides New York City. At least for a while."

I'm completely content to sit in this dark hallway all night, but Eddie decides that it's time to come out of hiding. "I'm gonna go check on Caroline."

"Are you gonna tell her? What you worked out with—"

He shakes his head. "No. She doesn't need to know. She's made peace with her decision. I don't want to mess that up for her, you know?"

I don't know. I've never had to make a choice like he has to right now.

I end up back in the waiting room with my dad. He looks stressed, probably from having to play lawyer for Eddie when he's, well, not a lawyer.

"He's okay," I promise him for, like, the tenth time. Once we move on from worrying about Eddie, I remember what I'm supposed to talk to him about.

I spill everything in a matter of minutes from the business plan to the company auditions. And my dad doesn't look all that surprised to hear about the studio stuff. "Did you know?"

"Yeah," he says. "I wanted to give you a chance to, you know, figure it out."

"Or fail," I accuse, but I'm not really mad. I'm relieved that he isn't.

"What if I told you that I found someone?" he says, and at first, I'm thinking he *found someone*, like, yeah, but then he adds, "To run the studio. For a while."

"Who?"

"Do you remember Sophie Lucas?" he asks.

She was one of the studio's best dancers. In high school when I was really little, so of course, I worshiped her. "Yes…"

"Well, she's done with her ballet career, and if you're still dead set on dumping your money into the studio—"

"I am," I say right away. Because that's really all I want. For it to be there again. Open and running with my mother's way of making every dancer the best they can be—Sophie would know all of that. Maybe more than me, because like my mother, she's danced professionally.

"Then you can be the owner, and Sophie can be acting director." He looks at me, showing the first signs of emotion all evening. "And I'll…I'll figure out how to get back in there and, well, do whatever else needs to be done."

"That's what you want?" I ask. "It's not just for me, right?"

He shakes his head. "For me. It's time."

I nod, fighting a flood of tears. "Yeah, it's time."

My dad rolls his eyes and tugs me out of my seat. "Enough of this. Let's go get ice cream. I've had enough feelings for a month."

I laugh and follow him out into the hall. We bump into Eddie. "Hey, are you up for ice cream?"

"Yeah, I think that sounds perfect." He tosses an arm around my shoulder and leads us toward the elevator.

When we're inside the elevator, I go back and forth about bringing up my casting, and then finally, I can't keep it in any longer. "So…I sort of booked a big job today. With Chanel. And Misty Copeland. And dresses I want to marry."

My dad is not one to ever look shocked. I think he makes a point to not be shocked. But his mouth falls open, and he can't think of any words to say.

Eddie scratches the back of his head and looks bewildered. "Did I miss anything else big today?"

Dad and I exchange a look and then laugh. "Um, yeah, one other thing."

I fill him in on the studio news and my plan to audition for Lenore Jacobs's company, then my dad says, "Want to help me build a ramp into that studio?"

"Yeah, sure," Eddie says. "I think I picked up a hammer once. Seemed pretty simple. Plus, I'm looking for a job."

"Well, I wasn't planning on paying you," Dad says.

Eddie laughs. "Okay, sure. I'm up for it. I'll find a manual or something."

"This sounds promising," I say with a groan.

Eddie gives me one of his looks—the intense, heated kind that I haven't been able to resist since the day I met him. And I know he'll figure it out. He'll build a ramp for my dad, and even if I can't be there all the time, he'll help get that studio open.

Knowing my dad, he'll probably put Eddie through some *Karate Kid* "young grasshopper, find yourself" program with a hammer, nails, and discount plywood.

And that's probably exactly what he needs.

Eddie

"Let me get this straight," Jason says, leaning forward in his lawn chair to pick up the toy Mason just dropped. "This kid—this baby—is worth a few million?"

"You can't put a price on a child." I grip Mason's fingers from his seat on my stomach. He shakes the hair off his forehead. It's even more unruly than mine. "Besides, he won't get any of that money until he's twenty-one."

The world is an incredibly weird place. Because over the past few weeks, since he came back from college, Jason, my girlfriend's ex-boyfriend, and I have become pretty good friends. He's been a huge help with all the last-minute prep for the studio opening.

"But seriously, his parents are, like, average, middle-class people from Hartford. And they're gonna have a kid richer than them."

"He's richer than me too." Especially considering I'm broke as hell. But my name on Mason's birth certificate along with that paternity test earned him my grandmother's prize. "And they're from New York. Upstate. They just moved to Hartford six months ago."

The Kingsleys won't admit it, but I think a big factor in them moving was to make my commute to visit Mason a lot shorter. And right now, they're on a three-day tour of our nation's capital. It's the first time they've ever left me with Mason for the weekend. First time they've ever left him overnight period. With anyone. It's a big step for them.

Mason grabs my nose and pinches it. "Bab."

"Think he's saying Babe?" Jason asks.

"Maybe." I lift him and walk over to the pool. "Are you saying Babe, Mason?"

"Bab."

We sit on the edge, and I splash some water onto his legs. He squirms a little. It's too cold still. Barely June. Though the temperature won't stop Connor and Braden.

"Okay, no swimming for you."

Mason has brown eyes like Caroline. They changed a few months ago. Sometimes, I see so much of her in him. At first, right after I signed the papers and before Caroline left for school, it was hard for me to talk to her, knowing I was lying about seeing our kid. But Fin told me that most likely, Caroline really wouldn't want to know—it's the type of lie that helps someone. And deep down, she would want me to see him if that's what I needed.

So I made peace with this big lie between us, I basically put it behind us, and now I have my friend back. Well, via Skype and phone anyway. She's still in London. With RJ. Becoming doctors or whatever.

And Finley…she's been even farther than London. For an entire month. It hasn't been easy.

I glance at my cell, checking the time. She's supposed to be home anytime now.

"Fin's going to be home soon, right?" Jason asks. "Think I should go?"

"She knows you're here. She'll want to see you." I walk Mason around in the sunny part of the yard to warm up his legs. He gets that drunk, sleepy look, and soon, his head is resting on my chest.

The sliding doors on the back patio open, and I glance up, hoping its Fin. But Braden and Connor come running out, full speed, preparing to jump in the pool.

"Walk, guys," I say but too softly to stop them. They plunge into the pool seconds later. Cold water. No problem. Connor and Braden see too much of me now to listen to everything I say. Sam got me a job at their afterschool program last fall; they run the camp the boys attend for the summer too. Soon, I'll be fighting off bullies for Connor as a camp counselor.

I cross over the spot in the yard where Fin and I made out last summer.

"How's she liking the dance company thing?" Jason asks me.

"It's a lot of work, but she loves it. You saw a show, right?"

"Yeah, in Austin." He looks up from his book. "Great show. Fin was... I mean, she was...well, not Fin, but still her—" I laugh. I can't help it. He's weird about talking about her around me. "The last time I saw her dancing was with her mom."

He must have been at the recital. There's now a huge photo of the two of them dancing that duet in the lobby of the studio.

I turn to face him, resting my hand on the baby's back to get him steady and sleeping. "What was that like? After..."

"Awful." He sets his book down and releases a breath. "I was fifteen, so I didn't really know how to talk to Fin about it—not like I'd be much better now. There's nothing you can say. But the absolute hardest part for me was seeing Sam like...well, like he is now. You know he used to run marathons?"

"I didn't know that." But he's a dictator in the gym. That I know. I've been thinking I need a replacement workout buddy for weeks.

"Fin's mom was a bit of a control freak." Jason laughs and then seems to feel guilty about it, because he turns serious again. "She did everything, wouldn't let anyone even fold laundry because it wasn't the way she did, so you can imagine how things fell apart after she..."

He stops, unable to say the word out loud.

It occurs to me right then that Jason and I are on polar opposite sides of Fin's life. I don't know the version of Sam who ran marathons and carried his kids when they fell asleep somewhere that wasn't their bed or had a wife cooking and cleaning for him. And I definitely don't know the version of Fin who wasn't completely independent, taking care of herself and other people in the process. If she were still that Fin, if her mom were still alive, even if we had met somehow, I don't think our connection would have been the same.

I wonder if the things Jason loved most about Finley faded away after her mom died. And what I love most about her came to life after. It's weird how these things happen.

Sam wheels out to the backyard and heads straight for me and Mason. "Nothing more adorable than a sleeping baby. How are the Kingsleys handling their separation anxiety?"

I laugh. "Okay, I think. Only three texts in three hours."

He gives a nod of approval. "Not bad at all. They trust you. That's why."

They do trust me. Not just because I'm biologically Mason's father, but because I've worked hard to earn that trust. Everything I do with Mason is a hundred percent effort. If he were mine full-time, I don't think that kind of attention to detail would be possible.

Fin made fun of me a few weeks ago because I was making organic baby food while we Skyped. Considering the conditions Mason was conceived under, I have no desire to contribute to any more toxins being put into his body.

Inside the house, the front door opens. Sam sees it at the same time as me, because he immediately holds out his arms to take the baby. I hand over Mason, and I'm inside, across the living room, before Fin even has her suitcase in the door.

I stop several feet away from her. She's been in Copenhagen for the past week, so we haven't Skyped for that long due to Internet connection issues. Her hair is short now, shoulder length with purple streaks in it. I take in a breath. She's hot. Like rock star hot.

"Who are you?" I ask, leaning against the wall. "I'm waiting for my girlfriend. She should be home any minute."

Finley drops the handle of her suitcase. It lands on the tile entryway with a clank. She turns to face me and stays rooted to her spot, giving me the same once-over I gave her. "And who is the guy with much bigger muscles? What are you doing in my house?"

Sam the gym Nazi. I've added nearly ten pounds of muscle in a month.

"That would be your dad's fault. He's been dropping hints about making me do those bar exercises—*Arrow*-style." I reach for her hands and bring her closer until our noses are less than an inch apart. I run my fingers over her hair. "I missed this. A lot."

"We added a new number to the show. It required purple hair," Fin explains, and my heart is already picking up just having her in my personal space. "It'll wash out in a couple weeks. I think?"

I plant a kiss on her forehead, her cheek, her neck. Fin closes her eyes and sighs. "God, I missed you," she says.

Me too. I do think it's even more difficult being the one still here, not out having adventures. Time moves a little bit more slowly for me than it does for her.

I trace a finger over her lips before kissing them. I'm about to pull away—reluctantly—to avoid an audience performance. But then Fin sets her hands on my face and doesn't let me move away. My tongue slips in her mouth, my hands wandering everywhere. My gaze flits in the direction of her room—my room, at the moment—and then back to her face.

I pry myself out of her hold and kiss her forehead. "Later."

She glances out back for a split second, spots Mason, and squeals. Soon, I'm left standing on my own in the foyer. I take my time heading back to the patio and watch Finley steal Mason from her dad and cover him with kisses—Connor and Braden have decided they're too old for kisses from their sister, so Fin has moved on to my kid.

My kid.

It's still weird to think about. And it took me a while to let myself think of him that way again. A couple months after I'd been visiting Mason regularly, I sat down with the Kingsleys and made sure to tell them that I was okay with whatever role they wanted to pin on me when Mason got old enough to ask questions. They just looked at me, confused, and I had to say straight up, "He doesn't have to know I'm his dad. I won't ever tell him if that's what best for you. I think it probably is best."

Jody just patted my hand and said, "Why wouldn't we tell him who you are?"

"Because I gave him up. I don't want him to think he wasn't important to me," I'd said to them.

"He'll never think that," Keith had said. "What other sacrifices could you have made for that child? You gave up everything to have your name listed on his birth certificate as his father."

It's still so incredible knowing that Caroline picked this family. The most perfect family possible for Mason. She did exactly what she'd promised that awful day in the bathroom when we were both so lost.

After the onslaught of kisses, Mason wakes up, lifts his head, and looks around until he spots me stepping outside. His little arms stick out in my direction.

That's the thing…I don't feel like I lost. All I've done is gain some very important things.

Finley

I'm so glad that Eddie planned this "before" tour of the newly remodeled studio, because if I had to go through this with the crowd waiting in anticipation for the ribbon-cutting in an hour, I would have been humiliated. And without mascara.

I can't even see the rest, because I'm too caught up in the photo of me and Mom dancing the piece from *Coppélia*. It's so beautiful. Everything about this place is beautiful. It's like they changed it but without removing all the traces of what it was. We've got a ramp outside now and a wheelchair elevator to go down to the lower level. It's everything I could have hoped for and more.

Eddie hooks an arm around my waist and kisses my cheek. "Come on, let's see the studios downstairs. I wrote you a love song, and I'm gonna perform it for you."

I laugh and wipe away the remaining tears from my face. "No love songs. I won't be able to take it."

"So marriage proposals are out too?"

I groan. "You've been spending way too much time with my dad."

Sophie, who was my mom's top student for years, brushes past me, and she looks almost as wrecked as I am. I give her a pat on the shoulder and a tissue from my pocket. I'd been around for a lot of the construction, but so much came together over the last month that it's really a transformation to me.

After I've seen the entire studio—and become dehydrated from all the tears shed—I clean off my face in the bathroom and then head outside where we've already got a big crowd gathered for the ribbon-cutting. As much as I'd love to believe they're all here to be the first to sign up for lessons or welcome an old business to the neighborhood again, I know the truth. Many of them are here to meet a movie star.

When an SUV with tinted windows pulls up in front of the building, I nearly cover my ears from the screams that erupt. Eddie and I are some of the few people who know where Toby Rhinehart's real house is, and it turns out he only lives about an hour away from us in Greenwich.

He's behind the wheel, and I about have a heart attack, thinking he might be stupid enough to drive here alone, but then Rocko, the bearded giant, steps out of the backseat first. Eddie's got Mason in his baby carrier, and they disappear into the crowd. Eddie's very worried about Mason ending up in photos, especially one of them together. He doesn't have any contact with his family, except Ruby on occasion, and he's happy with that. I imagine it's Caroline seeing him with Mason that worries him most.

Two more tinted SUVs pull up behind Toby's, and a whole team of security swarms the place. I can't believe he's doing this ribbon-cutting. He's insane. Not that I'm complaining, but still…

News cameras are everywhere, paparazzi, reporters shouting out questions. I smile when I see Gretchen and Bessy, Toby's daughters, who are eight and ten. Both are sporting ballerina buns and little girl versions of the tutu dresses Chanel designed that I'm wearing on a billboard in Soho. They look precious. Toby insists that he's enrolling them in Belton Academy. Even though I know our instruction will be better than other dance schools, it might not be enough to make an hour-long drive just for ballet class.

I give my dad's hand a squeeze, and then I greet Toby's girls before ushering them over to my grandma, who's keeping an eye on them for a little while. Toby also prefers they not end up in any photos. His people have the media pretty well trained on who to include and who not to include. That is if they ever want an exclusive again.

Dad, Sophie, and I all say a few words to the crowd, and then Toby gets up there and gives an amazing speech about how he met me and how supportive he is of the arts and my efforts to promote healthy body image through the Chanel ballet line that shows models and dancers who are a healthy weight and taking good care of themselves, etc... He's good. Very good.

Finally, he cuts the ribbon—ballet pink with pointe shoes attached to each end—and I back away as the crowd rushes over to Toby's autograph table inside. He's signing Belton Academy gear. As in you buy gear, he signs it. His idea, not mine. I search the crowd for Eddie, and my gaze locks with his. I tear up again but get it under control quickly and instead mouth, "thank you."

··◆··

"So, kiddo," my dad says, waving a hand to the dance studio in front of us, full of a select group of people invited to a post-ribbon-cutting party. "Is it everything you wanted?"

I smile at him. "Yeah and more, I think. Definitely more."

Eddie's entertaining the room with some jazz piano improv. My dad bought him a top hat, and he's created this new identity under its spell. That's not entirely true. He works at a local piano bar a few nights a week and on weekends. He serves food and drinks and sometimes entertains the audience when the regular players are on break or call in sick.

On the other side of the room, my grandma is hovering over one of Toby's daughters while she holds Mason in her lap.

"Finley?"

I turn around and try not to look surprised by the presence of Eddie's sister. "Ruby, hi… I didn't realize you were coming tonight."

"Last-minute decision." She gives me a tight smile. "I hardly recognized you…the hair is…"

My face flushes. "Eddie's over there, at the piano."

"Right." She doesn't move. "How's he doing? I mean school and whatever?"

Eddie started classes at the local community college this past January. He finished up the semester a few weeks ago and did great. All As, I think. My dad talked him into getting a teaching degree. He always says it's the best fallback. When he couldn't get his wheelchair into his place of business, he was still able to get a job and pay the bills because of that teaching degree. Truth is, Eddie would make a fantastic teacher. He loves kids. I doubt it will be his plan B.

"He's doing well." I glance at her. She looks nervous. "You should go say hi."

Eddie's playing a high-energy tune, and my dad has joined him with a saxophone. I walk past Connor and Braden and say, "Did they talk you into playing tambourine or something?"

Ruby instead heads over to see Mason.

I take a seat beside Eddie on the piano bench. "I'm ready for that love song now."

"Oh yeah?" He grins at me and immediately shifts to something slow and romantic. I watch as Toby's girls try to get Connor and Braden to waltz with them. Connor dives under the refreshment table, and Braden steps on one of their toes and then starts practicing karate moves, complete with cartwheels in the center of the room. Several of my dance company friends are here, and I love them to death—don't get me wrong—but they are incapable of leaving a dance floor empty.

"Did you see Ruby?" I ask, and Eddie gives me a smile. His smile says that he's glad she's here.

He ends his song and lets my dad take over with a saxophone solo. I lean against him and enjoy the view. "I'm looking forward to the future."

"Me too," Eddie says, whispering in my ear. "Later."

I laugh. "I mean the future future. Like when I'm too old and injured to dance, and I get to come here and see this every day. Maybe have my own kids running around. My hot thirtysomething husband, playing the piano and doing important things with power drills."

He tosses a leg over the bench and pulls me between his legs so we can both watch everything happening. "A thirtysomething husband? Anyone I know?"

I smile to myself. "Maybe." Eddie rests his chin on my shoulder, and I look up at him. "Would you do that? Have more kids someday? Even with Mason—"

"No more than six," he says immediately. God, my dad really has been a terrible influence. He turns serious again. "I think so. Of course, we're gonna have to deal with the trust fund from Grandma issue yet again."

"You can raise kids to not be ruined by money," I say. "Mason won't be affected by it. I know it. Not with you and the Kingsleys around."

He kisses my shoulder. "Not with you around."

My dad takes a break from saxophone, but Eddie doesn't return to playing piano, and everyone still continues dancing, even with no music. We sit there for a long time, watching.

My mind drifts to the fact that I'm only nineteen. And Eddie's only nineteen. And we've already risen above so much. Lord knows what else is in store for us. But I let that fleeting thought pass me by, because sometimes all there is left to do is savor these perfect moments.

Acknowledgments

We would both like to thank our brilliant editor, Annette Pollert, who saw potential in Fin and Eddie long before their story was polished and complete. Thank you for your guidance, and for allowing us the space and freedom to bring these two characters to life. To the Sourcebooks team, who is putting some amazing feet forward to get this book into all the hands possible. Thanks to Nicole Resciniti, our agent, for her continued support and encouragement. To Eve and Alex, our main characters from *Halfway Perfect*, for continuing to provide inspiration for another story in this world we've created and grown to love so much. And thanks to readers who have followed us from *Halfway Perfect* and those who are just finding this series.

Eddie's story is fictional and by no means reflects our opinions on teen pregnancy or parental/paternity rights as a whole. For those of you facing decisions related to parenthood at a young age, we encourage you to seek out a strong support system who will help you make the best decisions for you. We believe each situation, *each person*, is unique and should be treated as such. *You Before Anyone Else* is both a title and a message to those who need reminder that their voice deserves to be heard.

FROM JULIE:

I'd like to thank my husband, Nick, and family for believing in me. My kids Charles, Ella, and Maddie for providing me all the baby care experience needed to help Eddie along the way. To Mark Perini, who continues to be an amazing partner in crime as well as a great friend. To my aunt Dawn and cousin Alex for helping me understand Sam's disability. To my mother for paying for and driving me to all those ballet classes even though, unlike Finley, I didn't have the feet or turnout for advanced ballet. The moves are all in my head and heart and provided amazing inspiration for this book. To fans of my other books, thank you for following me here. To Appel Farm Arts Camp, where I "lived" while much of this book was written, thank you for providing me a place to grow and become an even better writer.

FROM MARK:

I'm splitting this acknowledgment into fourths. For my sun and stars, Rebecca, for your love, support, and for always sharing in my loony daydreams. For my parents and my family, for all of your love and support and for always encouraging me to let my imagination run wild. For Julie, whose passion and talent is infectious. Thank you for being my mentor and my writing partner through this epic journey. And finally, for Eddie and Finley who were utterly mixed up in this crazy world but ultimately found their way together.

About the Authors

Julie Cross is a *New York Times* and *USA Today* bestselling author of new adult and young adult fiction. Julie lives in central Illinois with her husband and three children. Her knowledge of the modeling and fashion world comes from viewings of the movies *The Devil Wears Prada* and *Zoolander* and her unwavering devotion to the first three seasons of *Ugly Betty*. On a recent trip to NYC, she also took the time to walk past both the Gucci and Prada stores, spending at least fifteen seconds viewing items through the windows.

Mark Perini began his career as an international fashion model eleven years ago, while simultaneously obtaining a business degree from Seton Hall University. Turns out fashion's hurry-up-and-wait mentality lends itself quite well to writing. Mark is now a New York City–based author, and *You Before Anyone Else* is his second young adult novel. He is also a featured author in the new adult anthology, *Fifty First Times*. When he's not working, Mark's traveling the world. He's made a blood pact with friends to see all seven ancient wonders of the world before he's thirty. Five down, two to go.